A FAMILY IN WAR

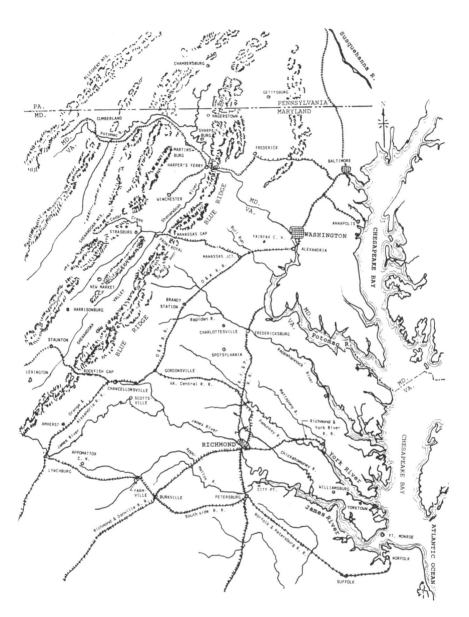

A BATTLEGROUND: THE ARMY OF NORTHERN VIRGINIA

A FAMILY IN WAR

Robert Spurney

VANTAGE PRESS
New York

Published by Vantage Press, Inc.
516 West 34th Street, New York, New York 10001

Manufactured in the United States of America
ISBN: 0-533-11268-0

Library of Congress Catalog Card No.: 94-90529

0 9 8 7 6 5 4 3 2 1

To my wife, Florence, for her help and patience

Contents

Historical Note

The American Civil War caused much pain. Its essence can be sensed in the personal narratives of those who lived through it. Perhaps its meaning in the course of human history can also be found in such tales. The novel that follows is, of course, fictitious, but it is a story of a family living through this cataclysmic struggle. The members of the Lynn family, *A Family in War*, are a product of the author's imagination, but they act within a framework of actual events and among historic personages. They are intelligent and caring. In the morass created by conflict, anguish follows success, and disappointment leavens pride as lives change.

The author has attempted to portray accurately real events as they are experienced. Care has been used to show each individual in the correct place, time, and ambiance that existed when the event occurred.

Literary license has been used in specific situations to simplify the story. For instance, a member of the Lynn family, James Lynn, a young lawyer and soldier, is stationed in Richmond at a site designated in the novel as the "War Department" or "War Office." The Confederate War Department activities in the city were not housed in a single building, as the story suggests, but were maintained in a series of buildings mostly south of but in close proximity to the Virginia state capital. The War Department Building, often referred to as "Mechanics Hall" or "Mechanics Institute Building," was where the Army and Navy had their headquarters. Other functions such as the Ordnance Office, the Patent Office, the Office of Medicine and Surgery, etc., were also housed in this building. It was located on the west side of Ninth Street in Richmond at the intersection of Bank Street.

Other government offices were clustered close by. The Treasury Building, the principal office building of the Confederacy, was on the north side of Main Street between Ninth and Tenth Streets. The Quartermaster Department was in the Quartermaster Building at the southwest corner of Ninth and Main Streets. The Assistant Quartermaster General's office, which is where James Lynn would probably have been stationed, was at Tenth and Bank Streets.

Commissary functions, the Bureau of Exchange of Prisoners, the Army Intelligence Office, the Railway Bureau, and many other government activities were in nearby structures. The exact locations of offices were not thought vital to the story and were not included in the text.

A fact possibly not adequately emphasized in the manuscript is the large number of hospitals in wartime Richmond. The renowned Chimborazo Hospital, a complex of 150 unpainted frame buildings with herds of cattle in nearby fields for food, is briefly mentioned. It was located just east of the city. Over 76,000 men were treated there. Several state hospitals (Kentucky, Missouri, Tennessee, and Virginia) were within this complex of buildings.

Twenty-eight general hospitals, other state hospitals, church and private institutions were also maintained within the city, and a number of treatment encampments were in close proximity to Richmond. These many treatment centers emphasize the frightful number of casualties caused by the war.

Prologue

It was an epic. It was also a tragedy. It was a time of selflessness and bravery, dimmed by greed and brutality. It drew bitterness from hidden depths. It wrought hate and terrible violence. It pressed upon a nation an awareness of a great wrong. Within this abyss, there was a will to survive. On trial were the character, traditions, and ideals of a people. It consumed thousands, yet dignity remained; a nation became whole, a government of the people lived, and a race in bondage began the long trek toward freedom.

Violence began slowly, insidiously, like a plague. The general mood was almost festive. There were no early great battles, and most folks didn't think much about the consequences. The flags and marching lines of men were new and exciting, and fears were covered over by enthusiastic faces and the beat of drums. Such were the forces that altered a nation's future.

The events that led to war were vague. Yet events change lives, and as the weeks passed, more and more persons were drawn into the storm. When the first year of the fighting ended, the bitter conflict had pervaded much of the land. One home saddened and marked by those years was that of James and Ann Katherine Lynn. They were good people. They became *A Family in War*.

Though the early encounters and skirmishes were light and brief, fighting men soon learned their trade. Tragedy came. It lasted four long years. Tattered veils of smoke quickly disappeared, and the blood on the fields was soon covered by brambles and clumps of grass. The anguish from the losses of fine men lingered on. The struggle did end, and like the dawn, there would be a new beginning.

Katherine Lynn had been watching when the fighting stopped. Now she came back to the place of that last battle. She returned to Appomattox Courthouse, just east of the Blue Ridge Mountains of Virginia. It was a dark day, and a fine rain was falling. There was a sense of deep sadness in the air. As she waited, the silence was occasionally interrupted by the chirping of birds, soft coughing, and the murmur of voices. Faces were moist, mostly from the rain, but some from tears.

A few days earlier, she had stood near this spot in sunlight amid the smoke and falling shells. She had seen that final effort by men of the South to break through the ranks of blue soldiers who stood firmly astride the old Lynchburg stagecoach highway. They could not be broken. A strange and foreboding stillness had then crept over the valley, as white flags crossed the space between the two armies. The War between the States, the American Civil War, had ended.

She now watched patiently . . . and listened. Her clothing was wet, and water from the rain dripped onto her face and into her eyes.

"There they are," said a woman nearby. "Their last march. Oh, God! It's so sad!"

"They fought so hard," another woman answered.

A man farther off spoke hesitatingly. His voice was soft and strained. "God, it shouldn't end this way. We need something to remember. Not silence! They fought the war for us, and so many are dead. Where are the shouts and the cheers?"

Katherine saw the marching column of gray soldiers. There was no band or even a drum to lead the way and give a proper cadence to this last march. Tired feet scuffed the ground, and weapons and canteens made a soft clinking sound. Beyond the marching soldiers, through the mist, she could see the blue-gray hills of Virginia.

She looked again at the approaching regiments. Rifles and other weapons were to be stacked in front of federal divisions standing at rigid attention. This was the formal surrender of the Confederate army, the Army of Northern Virginia. Many of the troops had been injured. Arms were in slings, and hands and other parts of the body were wrapped with torn strips of cloth and bandages.

The whole long column was decked with the red and blue of stained and ragged battle flags packed very close together now because few men were left. Thousands and thousands had been cut down. The flags were the symbols that had led troops into battle. They were the essence of pride. They, also, would be surrendered. Brigades had been reduced to regiments and regiments to companies, but these ragged pieces of cloth remained the embodiment of manhood.

She thought about the words the man behind her had spoken. "There should be something more for us to remember," she said. "Not just silence!"

As she stood and watched, she began to think of the time when the first shadows of the storm had become real to her. She thought about the happiness and the sunshine and the fields and streams around her home.

She suddenly remembered that she was but a little child of eleven when the mysterious word, war, had become a frequent topic of conversation by her family. "Such a long time ago," she said to herself. "We all sat near the hearth. That was the center of life for me then.

"And war didn't worry us in those days. Maybe it was because Henry played with soldiers. We were used to the lines of toy soldiers and guns. 'Bang, bang!' we would hear." She shook her head as she thought about her brother and her oldest sister, Emmie, who played with him. Katherine smiled wanly, and a soft laugh crossed her lips. "Emmie was a great nurse, but a bad general. 'No, no!' Henry would shout. 'You do it this way, dummy!' Those soldiers would fall and die, but they were always well and ready for battle again a few hours later.

"Maybe that's why we children didn't think war would be really bad. It would be different and kind of fun. We wanted to get away from the dullness of ordinary days. Then we did. Too far away. And now it's over. But the memory is there!"

A FAMILY IN WAR

CHAPTER I
Shadows of a Storm

"Katherine can't catch us. Look, Kath, Dee and I can run faster than you. Come on, Dee. I'll race you to that apple tree." Off they scooted like two little rabbits.

"You go on, Mary. I'll walk with Papa," Kath shouted. "He's telling me about that big oak tree he planted when he was a boy." She turned to her father and smiled. "You did, didn't you, Papa?"

"That was when your Grandpa Lynn owned this farm, Kath. I was about your age when we walked out here with a shovel and dug that hole. It grew, didn't it?"

Kath just smiled and nodded her head. Her blue eyes were wide and bright as she looked toward the top of the tree. "It's still growing," she finally said. "See, I can hardly put my arms around it now. But I could last year." Her father looked compassionately at his daughter. His eyes were deep, and, though slightly drawn, they were wise and caring. She, too, he reflected, still had a little growing to do.

Katherine lived with her family just east of the Blue Ridge Mountains of Virginia, near the little town of Amherst. This had been her home since she was born. It was a beautiful place in which to grow. She loved to roam the streams and fields and kneel down to see the detail of plants and insects. She grew up loving nature and the peacefulness and brightness of the countryside.

Papa continued to smile at his daughter. She was a wee farm girl with freckles and straight, straw-colored hair. He knew that she was in a hurry to get bigger, now that she had reached that "ancient" age of eleven. They were a big family. Kath had two older sisters, two younger sisters, and two strapping brothers. Her Uncle Wen and Aunt Suellen lived with them and helped her Papa and Momma, James and Ann Katherine Lynn, run their farm.

Folks often told Katherine that she was "thin as a broomstick." They

1

didn't seem to suggest, though, that she was pretty like her older sister, Annie, who was the vivacious one of the family. This didn't bother Kath much. She loved her older sister. Annie had long dark tresses and a smooth, pink complexion. She gathered men around her like flies to honey. It wasn't just her looks. She was lively and bright, and she had a teasing smile that boys loved.

Kath's oldest sister, Emmie, in contrast, looked a little like her. She was tall and slender with high cheeks and deep eyes. Her smile was warm, and she was kind and considerate, except when her little sisters, Dee and Mary and Kath, were acting like rascals. It should be emphasized that they did this often.

Their parents were older than most mothers and fathers with young children at that time. Papa had taught school in the Shenandoah Valley for many years. He had married late. He was of moderate stature, and his hair was graying and his face lined. Momma was several years younger, but she looked much his junior in age. She was gracious but frail in appearance. Her soft gray eyes shone when she smiled, which she did often. Her voice was kind and soft, but when needed, it became resonant and firm like the growl of a bear. She was strong-willed but patient, as she directed the work of a large family and ministered to the workers in the yards and fields.

James, Kath's brother, was the oldest of the children and nearly full-grown. He looked tall to her, but actually he was only a medium height. He was muscular, with straight dark hair and a broad, enthusiastic smile. He seemed so polished and worldly. Henry was two years younger. He, in contrast, was more introspective, with a fair complexion and curly flaxen hair. He was tall and gangly, with long arms and a serious face. It was a friendly face, though, especially when he played with his younger sisters. He would laugh loudly and tease them. They loved it. They were happy children.

The children grew up on a farm surrounded by woods and underbrush. It had been cleared for cultivation by past generations of the family. They had a large home with stone walls topped by hand-hewn beams. These supported the second floor, which was covered with weathered siding and a split-shingled roof. To the west were the mountains, and to the east were rolling hills. The farm was called Doria after an ancient people of Greece who had terraced the mountain slopes of the Cyclades Islands in the Aegean Sea.

Shallow streams and creeks crossed the meadows and fields then wandered irregularly through the woods. The water drained to the James

River, which here flowed northeast from Lynchburg to Scottsville, then east some eighty miles to Richmond and on to the sea.

In the spring, the green pastures of red soil stretched out like a large patchwork quilt that had been laid over the land and pressed onto the tops of the hills and into the angular valleys. The gray-green trunks of sycamores and the dark trunks of the black willow trees bordered the streams and brooks.

It was now autumn of the year 1860, and Katherine and her sisters were walking the fields with Papa. The orange sun was creeping toward the distant mountaintops, and the two younger girls, Mary and Dee, were far ahead. They were laughing and talking, and had found a small mouse scurrying for safety. Kath had continued to ask about the trees and flowers in the fields. She also wondered where birds went in the wintertime.

Papa suddenly looked serious. In the dimming light, his face was deeply lined. "Katherine, this soil is good; it's meant to be worked. You children must carry on someday. You're my practical one and you remember. You also love the land. I need a promise. When you're older, tell your sisters and brothers about our farm. Remind them. Maybe one of you'll come back. It's nice to know family will continue what we've started."

"We'll come back, Papa. I'm sure." They did, those who lived, but only to visit. None of them returned to farm. Katherine, however, always remembered his wish. She was later in business and in the fringes of politics. She always loved the feel of the soil, though. It became part of her. She and Papa then walked for some time without talking, but as the sun set that evening, he pointed far out across the meadows. "Look carefully, Kath; from this distance the red soil has a fine lacy pattern. It's beautiful. Those are the stumps of the corn and cane. We'll plow them under soon. They'll return to the land and give it strength. Good soil means life."

A few days later, they stood in that same field and watched the black "V" pattern of the turkey vultures gliding back and forth against a pale sky, searching for food. "They have a purpose, too," he said, smiling.

"They're terrible!" said Kath. She squinched up her face at the thought. "They eat dead things."

"Hmm," he uttered and laughed. "That's true." He was grinning, but his voice was earnest. "You're right, Kath, but the dead then live again. We've talked about that. We live in a wonderful world. I hope we can protect it. Tobacco was the main crop in Virginia for many years. It almost wore out the soil. It wasn't the land that was wrong, but the way it was treated. We're sensible now. We've learned, I hope. We rotate crops and let

3

some fields lie fallow. They regain their strength, and things grow." Kath had begun to see nature better with Papa's teaching, and she saw a twinkle in his eyes as he spoke. He was proud of his work with the farm. She smiled shyly, but glowed inside. What he said made her feel proud. This was her home.

That evening, Kath heard the sounds of wheels grating on the entrance roadway just below her bedroom window. The wind was picking up, and silvery moonlight filtered into the room from below the shade. She could see clouds and stars in the sky. The curtains at the windows bent and twisted with the breeze, and trees in the distance moved to-and-fro like great giants.

She had crept from bed and was gazing at the open space below. Shrubs and flowers were in deep purple shadows. A surrey was parked near the barns, and a man stood close by with a finger to his lips. She saw Annie's slim, graceful figure move silently toward him. "Mary," Kath called to her younger sister who was still asleep. "Mary, come here. Annie has a visitor. Wake up, Mary. Wake up!"

"What do you want, Kath? I'm tired." She stretched her arms and yawned. "I gave you back that dolly. The one with the blue dress and black hair. Go back to bed."

"Oh, pooh. I'm not interested in dollies now. Let's go out and see what's happening. Annie has a man down there. They're walking toward the lake and the little woods beyond. She has her arm through his. Now he's hugging her. I think he just kissed her. Mary! Get up, you lazy thing. Let's go listen." She suddenly realized Mary was beside her, staring off toward the little lake that Papa and Uncle Wen had made by extending a beaver dam across the small creek.

"Let's go," said Mary. "We'll leave our shoes off." Her face was red with excitement, and she had a crafty smile on her lips. They went quickly down the backstairs, out across the yard, and into a big field that extended beyond the woods. They were bent low and looked like two cats getting ready to pounce on an unsuspecting mouse.

"Quiet," said Katherine, as Mary stepped on a dry twig. Kath's eyes were glowing like white-hot coals, as she looked for the best spot from which to listen.

They could hear Annie's soft voice in the woods nearby. She was laughing gaily as she always did. "Georgie Morgan, you love all the girls. What about that painted, pale thing with golden hair? You spent half the evening with her the other night, while I sat with your little brother, Jamie."

"You mean Miss Mary Sue. But she's just family, Annie. We aren't in love."

"And at the Lewises' in July. Why, you just had a wicked, big smile for that little Miss Jane Carter. You never looked once at little ol' me." There was a trace of petulance in her voice, which Kath knew was entirely contrived. She could see Annie's eyes in the silvery light. They were narrow and teasing like those of a tiger playing with its expected dinner.

"But you were with Alvin Ripon, Miss Annie. He was the one who brought you that night. I did wave and smile when Miss Jane went inside to help her ma. But you just looked the other way. I'm sorry if I displeased you.

"Miss Annie, I've saved a little money from my job with my pa. Ever since I got back from school in Lexington, I've been doing the books and records for him at the store. It's not much, but we could have a right good start in Amherst." He put his arm around her, and his face moved very close to hers.

"He's kissing her," whispered Kath. "Well, Mary, what do you think of that? Annie's got herself a second proposal. I think it was John Redman last month. The moon wasn't up that night; I couldn't see him well."

"How do you suppose she does it, Kath?" Mary's face was serious and mostly hidden in the shadows. Then she started to giggle. "Annie sure knows about men."

"I hear you two back there," blurted Annie. "Now don't you go telling Momma about my friend Georgie. He's a nice boy. He'll be my beau one of these days. Won't you, Georgie?" She gently rubbed the back of his neck with her fingers and smiled pertly. Kath thought she looked like a cat that had just swallowed the canary.

"I'd be delighted, Miss Annie." His cheeks were scarlet in the silvery moonlight.

"Now you little girls just scat, or I'll tell Momma how you sneaked out tonight. Shoo! Georgie's going home. He has work to do tomorrow. Don't you, Georgie?"

He looked crestfallen, but he started toward the buggy. "May I call again, Miss Annie?"

"You may, but not 'til next week. Good night, Georgie." She waved and smiled as he drove away.

Kath and Mary crept softly up the stairs to their room. "May I call

5

again, Miss Annie?" asked Kath, snickering as she climbed into bed. They both just smiled, then laughed. Then they went quickly to sleep.

In November of 1860, the loveliness of the countryside was gone. The sun was replaced by cold, murky weather. Uncle Wen kept saying, "It certainly stays dark. Usually there's sun, even when it's cold. This goes along with our country's problems, I suppose." Her uncle was tall and lanky and a little younger than her father.

Papa chuckled as her uncle spoke. "It's not the weather, Wen; it's our politicians. The clouds will go away; the politicians won't. They're puppets to powerful people with money. Most are interested in the next election, not what's good for this land. Our children might do a better job. The problems of this country have been a long time coming, though. We compete with the North for dollars. It comes down to economics—the way we create things and how we sell them. We're also criticized for what we think about slaves and for the way we live. We're called arrogant and feudal by their papers.

"We did own slaves. My father freed most. I guess he sold a few to big planters farther south. Many stayed here with the farm, though. They're good people."

"You pay them fair, James. You also give some schooling."

"We both do, Wen. It's not legal, but, like a number of folks in the South, we're trying to teach love and humility and impart some knowledge of Jesus and of the Christian faith.

"However, Virginia's problem is not slavery, but what to do about it. In both the North and South, the slave trade began for the same reason: profits. The land and climate in Virginia were right, and it continued and grew. Our Constitution was written recognizing the existence of slavery. If legislated out of being, all should be responsible for the big problems we'd face. There would be four million Negroes and six million Whites. Even Abe Lincoln said we'd have a greater evil. I'm afraid the fanatics up North don't think about that," said James.

"I don't believe the fanatics talk much about the problems we'd face if slaves were free—much less about what to do about them," said Wen. "A few have suggested we form a colony outside of America or send the Negroes back to Africa. It wouldn't be easy to do."

"It wouldn't! It might not be fair either. They've lived here too long." Papa shook his head slowly as if that idea were wrong. "Geography and climate have shaped us. The upper Atlantic region is hilly and rocky with deep forests. It kept farms small along the coast. Mills and factories were

6

built using water power. Fishermen went to sea and ship-building flourished. Our land, in contrast, had navigable rivers, wide plains, and a long growing season. We've gone along separate paths. We're two different people now. The North has many factories. They also have more rails and trains. We're still farmers. We use men, not machines."

Papa thought a moment. "McCormick's reaper is making a wheat empire in the Midwest, Wen. It was invented just west of here, near Lexington. We need modern machines like that. Maybe we'll change. Perhaps we'll have to. We have to think carefully about where we're heading. We have the schools. Possibly we should be teaching engineering and mathematics rather than the humanities and philosophy. We're capable, but we don't always fathom what's important."

"We still need that philosophy," replied Wen. "Besides, we're not competing with the North. They're ahead of us. They take what we grow, change it, and sell it—mostly to us. We need what they make, but with the high tariffs, we pay dearly for what we get. We're wretched colonials, I'm afraid. Also, they think differently from us. We love the land and the time to enjoy it. They love dollars and what they buy."

"You're being the philosopher. I'm not sure about the dollars, but you're right that we do love the land. That's held us back. We want to be outdoors—not in factories. We're craftsmen, though. All kinds of goods. Our problem is getting what we make to our own markets. We send things north, not east. We tried to develop waterways like the Kanawha-James Canal. It was never finished. We forgot about a railroad to Norfolk. Sad. It's hard to change old ways," said James.

"That's true, but we'd better solve our farm problems first if we want to eat." Wen pointed toward the fields. He laughed, but he looked serious, then rubbed his eyes as if tired. "I guess you know our harrow's broken. Where will we get that crossbar fixed? Old man Jordan in town is ill."

"His son is a fair blacksmith, too. He'll fix it. Maybe."

Kath never knew if the harrow was fixed that day. She did remember those weeks as a period of isolation. Spring and summer were past. The hills and mountains were hidden by rain. Her elders sat by the fire and told stories about farming, schools where Papa had taught, family, and many things. They often sang songs, accompanied by Aunt Sue on a poorly tuned piano. Momma rarely sang with them. "I'm tone-deaf," she said to Uncle Wen with a smile. "You asked about our musical skills. In my family, we had a great-aunt who once sang for a famous director. 'Who would you suggest should accompany me?' she asked. 'A body guard,' he

7

answered." Momma then laughed and laughed, but she looked a little embarrassed. They all laughed with her. Momma loved listening to music, but she had trouble singing a tune.

Wen was still chuckling as he turned to Papa. "James, you once told me how many students you had at college in Lexington. Tell us again. It's a lesson for the children."

"That's an old story, Wen. But it's true. I think I said, 'About one in ten.' Unfortunately most of the boys aren't there to study. We treasure the ones who do." Papa grinned. "Enough talking. How about a game of checkers, Wen? You won the last three times. I'll beat you tonight."

Uncle Wen had the board ready across the room as Aunt Suellen spoke to Momma, "That's not many students, is it?"

"That's always worried James. It's natural, though. Most students of college age want excitement and to see the world. They're just spreading their wings. You can see it in our children, too."

"And they're thinking about love. Just look at Annie's eyes."

Momma smiled as she looked over at Annie, who was slouched over a big pillow. "And she loves to read," their mother said softly. "You're right, Sue. She's been reading book after book about romance and the struggles of girls in love."

The family also did much whispering. Katherine later realized it was about the possibility of secession. Until the eve of this separation, though, most Virginians didn't believe it would happen. They were for the Union.

Kath's parents warned that fighting might come. She and her sisters weren't too worried. Their brother, Henry, played with toy soldiers. It was kind of a game, they thought. They also read stories about knights and pretty ladies. War and fighting would be exciting. Maybe they would be carried off by a handsome prince. They often laughed and talked about that. Momma heard their giggling one evening.

"Hi, Momma." Annie smiled.

"Girls, listen. I love your laughs, but we should talk about what's happening. Our world is changing, and it's good to laugh at ourselves once in a while. Besides, we've caused the problems. They're our fault, but I'm afraid the results might be bad. We could lose friends and even family if we have a war.

"You girls are young, but you should know about these problems." She continued telling them about cotton and tobacco and the large plantations, and also about the smaller farms like theirs. "The latter," she said, "are owned and run by farmers like Papa and Uncle Wen. They're yeomen.

They do much hard work." She then told how the small farmers had gradually been pushed farther west by the bigger planters. She talked about iron and factories and big cities in the North. "We're like two nations. We disagree on how the country should be run. Many people in the South believe they won't ever get justice from our government. They think we should secede—or separate."

"Where would we go, Momma?"

"Nowhere, Emmie. We'd be two countries."

"That's bad, isn't it?"

"I think it's bad." She suddenly turned her head toward her daughter. "Katherine, wake up! I'm talking to you. And sit straight in that chair. That's the way, and keep those eyes open."

"She sneaked out early," said Mary. Kath's sister then turned toward her. "See. Momma knows now. You'll get it, I bet."

"Stop it, you two," ordered their mother. "Or you'll both get it. And that room of yours is a mess. You're to clean it up first thing in the morning, and none of that play and running about before chores. Do you hear me?" She didn't wait for their answer. "Where were we, Emmie?"

"It's not good if we leave our country. Secede, you said."

"That's right. We're proud of the United States, but those in the North talk badly about us. Most of the talk is by extremists and Abolitionists—but the anger they cause! Papa taught literature in college at Lexington. Now he's reading that literary giants like Emerson in Boston are saying dreadful things. They tell us we're 'vile,' that we 'own human beings.' We don't. We have no slaves. Most people in the South don't own slaves. All our field and yard people are free, and we pay them well. They like it here. They also like Papa's teaching—his Sunday school."

"We know about that," said Emmie.

"Their children learn. He does it like Professor Jackson does in Lexington—the Negro Sunday school he started. It's in the Presbyterian church there."

"Jackson?"

"Yes, Prof. Thomas Jackson. He teaches about cannons and things at the military school. He's also a very religious man. And he organized that church school. He's Papa's good friend. They still write often."

"Do his pupils also sing 'Amazing Grace' so they can be saved?" asked Annie, smiling, "That's what Papa has us sing."

"You need saving," Kath said softly.

Annie gave her a sharp punch in the arm. "Quiet, little girl!" she whispered. Her eyes were narrowed like a cat's, but she continued talking pleasantly to her mother, who was looking very sternly at Katherine.

"Now, now, you two," said Momma. "And yes, Annie, they do sing that in Lexington." She then paused as if wondering if she should say more. "Some folks think teaching Negro folks is dangerous, but Papa believes it's good. Professor Jackson wondered about that, too. Actually it's not legal in Virginia, but as Mr. Jackson said, 'It's Christian.' No one's tried to stop the teaching."

Annie looked very serious. "Will we separate, Momma?"

"I hope not, but we've lost many of our great elder statesmen. Calhoun, Clay, Webster, and others. They compromised. They would have found better solutions for battlegrounds like Kansas. They gave their lives to keep this country whole."

"Papa told Emmie and me about Kansas," said Annie. "He told us about the killing, and that murderer, John Brown. Papa said he killed nice people. They were farmers and didn't own slaves. I guess 'Bloody Kansas' is a good name. But what happened to the Missouri line? It changed, Papa said."

"The line didn't change, dummy. It was that compromise about Missouri," said Emmie. Annie gave Emmie a stern look, but didn't speak.

"The Missouri Compromise," said Momma, smiling. "And Emmie, Annie's not a dummy."

"I'm sorry, Annie. I didn't mean it that way," said Emmie.

Annie didn't hear her. She was deep in thought. "Papa said the North hates that law the Congress passed to make Kansas a state. I wonder why? He gave us a reason, but I don't remember."

"Papa better answer that, Annie, but for now, we worry about the future. Words like 'irrepressible conflict' and a 'house divided' scare us." Momma's eyes were soft and thoughtful. There was no spite. She looked straight and steadily at Annie—a curious expression with a feeling of hope. "Can we ignore those words, and will our government find peaceful ways? We hope so! But with men like John Brown—that bad man in Kansas and at Harper's Ferry—we aren't sure. He wrote a note just before he was—well, just before he was executed. He was hanged. It's painful, girls, but I guess necessary. Sad that such things happen. He said, ' . . . the crimes of this guilty land will never be purged but with blood!' He didn't act alone. There's much hate in our country. We wonder what will come of it. God help us!"

"He will," said Mary.

"How would you know, small one?" asked Annie laughing.

"I know," Mary growled. She was angry.

"Now. Now. None of that," said Momma. "Off to bed with you. James will be here tomorrow."

"Yea!" they all shouted.

"He's always fun," smiled Momma. "He's becoming a lawyer now. I'll be up soon. Emmie. Annie. You're older. You can stay up for a while. I'll be with Will's family in the morning. They're ill, I'm afraid." Old Will was the yardhand and getting older. "Take care of James if he's here before I'm back, and you should ask Papa those questions. We all need to know."

CHAPTER II

A Convention in Charleston—
Soft Breezes and the Scent of Flowers

Papa did tell Emmie and Annie about Kansas the next day. The fighting in that state began after passage of the popular sovereignty bill sponsored by Sen. Stephen Douglas of Illinois in 1854. This law cancelled the historic demarcation line set by the Missouri Compromise of 1820. Previously, all states formed in the Louisiana Purchase territory north of latitude 36° 30' were to be free. Douglas's bill changed all that. Now the people of the territory would decide. Oh, the trouble that caused!

The bill passed only after fierce debate, and almost immediately proslavers and Free Staters rushed to the territory. There was a call to arms by Free State men. One of those responding was the terrorist, John Brown. "Bleeding Kansas" became a grim reality. These results were a hassle for Douglas—a thorn that wouldn't go away. He wanted to be president, but, though the Kansas issue bled dry, his chances were finished. The issue became a foil for Lincoln during the Lincoln-Douglas debates. If Douglas changed his stand, he would lose the South. If not, he would antagonize the Midwest, which likened slavery to sin. These were also practical people who opposed the possible blocking of free land by big estates and the contamination of hard, honest labor by slavery.

These tough Swedes, Germans, migrant Easterners, and some native-born Southerners dreamed of a working democracy in the Midwest without the "loose morals" portrayed in the Abolitionist literature. The Abolitionists were wrong about "loose morals," but the beliefs were there and the hate intensified.

The lives of the Lynn children went on, and these events were past history when James returned home in November of 1860. "There he is!" Kath and Mary shouted as they saw their brother through the window. It was raining, and he looked like a wet bird with limp feathers.

Uncle Wen laughed when James arrived at the door. He had ridden from Amherst on a scraggly nag of a horse. "Where did you get that animal?" Wen asked. "He looks like he was run down by a wagon."

"Old Mr. Ames loaned him to me, Uncle Wen. I took what I could get," James answered, smiling. Papa had been telling Emmie and Annie about Kansas when James arrived. Mary and Kath were by a window playing with dolls made from old scraps of cloth and a little string. They all had names and each lived in a box. They were their extended family.

Some two years earlier, James had completed studies of the humanities at the university. In late autumn, he had looked for employment in Richmond and in large communities to the north.

"There must be something I can do," he had said to Papa and Uncle Wen. "I hate banking. Printing and publishing are boring. I could never sell for those awful merchants, and I'd probably never be nice to their demanding customers. I hate bookkeeping. As for wholesale tobacco—ugh!" He felt some enthusiasm for the railroads. They were a path to the future, the mysterious West.

His parents had tempered these worries with alternatives. "You've a fine mind, James. You also like to talk and reason." He shook his head quizzically. "Yes, you do. Since you first spoke, you often took the other side—right or wrong. What about a training in law? You can live by talk and reason. It's a natural."

Kath's brother had taken this advice. During the early winter of 1858, he began reading law with an attorney, Benjamin Jason, near Charlottesville. Mr. Jason was Papa's friend.

"James," Katherine said a few years later, "you still love to argue."

"It's not just arguing, Kath, it's rational debate. We provide sensible reasons for and against something." He thought for a moment, then continued, "Well, I guess in a way it is arguing."

"I'm glad you admit it," she laughed.

James grinned, then became serious. "Katherine, my little sister, you frustrate me at times. What we do is different from what you do. You act according to your own intuition. We act according to the laws and their interpretation by the courts. I believe that's an important difference."

Kath always had deep respect for James. When she was eleven, though, it was different. It was more than just respect. He was carefree and jovial then, and it was special and exciting to be with him. She even dreamed about him at night. He was a man on a great white horse. He was dashing, like a cavalier of earlier times.

During the tired, dark days of November of 1860, James stayed with his family for several weeks. Narrow roads progressed through rivulets of mud and pools of water, then twisted under big trees into dark woods. His presence brought sparkle to their lives. Perhaps it was more than just sparkle. They had been indoors much of the time, creating havoc for Momma and Aunt Sue. What a delight to have him home! He would sit by the fire and tell stories for hours about his studies at the university and his new profession, law.

James often traveled to large cities on business. "Parts of them are dirty," he said. "We should live as we do on the farm, where the air is clean. Ah, but the ladies, they're lovely." He was beginning to savor the cordiality of Southern families. He was also beginning to enjoy the handsome women of the South.

He spoke about the excitement in Richmond. "Trains roar into the city, and some factories are lighted all night. The air around them is filled with that awful noise of hammers and machines. And then there's the soot. It comes from the furnaces. The buildings around are black like a glass chimney over a candle." He hesitated a moment—thinking. "I watch many of the men who work there. They push into the mills like puppets. It's sad. Our lives are different now. We're becoming modern."

James described other wonders. "The streets in big cities are lighted by gas now. And then there are the new oil lamps with flat wicks. They're much better than our candles. We're old-fashioned, girls. Tell Momma that. And you should see all the beautiful carriages, and the lovely ladies who ride in them. It's wonderful, especially the ladies when they smile. I've met several. They like me, I believe." He sat dreamy-eyed for a while, looking off in space.

Annie interrupted, "What about the nice boys? We want to know about the good-looking men. You weren't the only man there."

To Annie's exasperation, he ignored her. He went on chuckling and talking. "Bands play in the parks on Sundays; the dances and the balls are fun. And oh, the pretty girls! I wanted to put my fingers about them." He made a circle with his hands stretched wide.

"You'd better not," smirked Annie. "That's not allowed!"

James continued to talk. He didn't even look at Annie. "Some were in yellow silk, dotted with little flowers. Others wore light blue dresses. And, oh, the scrumptious lace. Yummy. I can't wait till you girls grow up."

Annie was furious. "I'm almost grown. Momma said so." She stopped him several more times, but he ignored talking about men as if they had been invisible.

It was some years before Katherine realized that James was a real ladies' man. He admired the fairer sex. His eyes glowed when he spoke about soft flesh peeking out above beautiful gowns with billowy ruffles and edged with black velvet or small red ribbons. He was handsome, and he seemed so old and worldly.

It was still raining that November when Papa rode to Amherst on business. James was with him. That lovely town south and west of their farm had big trees and fine homes. It stood close to the Orange & Alexandria Railroad. They returned home at dusk. "Abraham Lincoln is elected," Papa said. His face was tense. "We'll be fighting. It means war!"

"Why war?" Kath wondered. "Who is this Mr. Lincoln?" Her family had talked about him. Their father had even agreed with him at times, but if his election meant war, she thought he must be bad. Kath didn't really understand about war, and she was frightened that night while she listened to her family talk.

"This is for young men, Wen. You're too old," said Aunt Suellen.

"It hurts young men. It hurts many others, too," Uncle Wen said. "Everyone, if it lasts. We old people deserve it; we've started it. God save our children, though. James," he said, nodding to his brother, "I remember your description of war. It's not nice."

"War has no sentiment or charity, Wen." Papa's face was serious. "Cannons, rifles, illness—they all destroy. Why it's starting, I don't truly understand. We've talked about reasons these last few months. I'm not sure we're right. It's funny though. Most of our people are against war, yet here we are speaking as if it's about to start. We'll fight, I suppose. Perhaps it's pride. I think we misjudge each other. We believe they'll let us go. I'm sure they're just as determined. Lincoln has talked about disunion in his speeches. He cautioned, 'We won't dissolve the Union, and you shan't.' He means it. He believes the nation will become all one thing or all the other—no longer a house divided. I believe he's right. It won't be just a skirmish. He'll fight." Papa paused and looked hard at each face around the room. "We should listen to him—especially now that he's elected."

"I hope you're wrong, James," said Wen. "If we get at it, it may be a bigger fight than any of us expect." He hesitated as if wondering if he should say more. "They're strong. I wish I could say we're stronger." He turned slowly toward their brother and smiled. "James, you'll be in this before it's over. As Aunt Sue said, it's for young men. You're the ones who'll do the fighting. I just hope that somehow we avoid it altogether."

"Why?" Kath wondered. "Why would James fight? He doesn't even play soldier. Why would he to go to war?" In contrast, her brother Henry had many toy soldiers. He lined them up in long rows. "Bang, bang, bang," they would hear. The girls knew about playing soldier. War didn't worry them much. Emmie often helped Henry. She was a great nurse, but she failed as an officer.

"Emmie, you do it this way," Henry would shout. "You'll never be a general or even an officer."

His face would become red, as she looked sternly at him. "I don't want to be an officer," she would say. Then she'd laugh and smile.

"Girls!" he would reply and walk off. The next day, they were at it again.

It wasn't the idea of war that worried Kath that night. It was the grim faces of her family. It was cold out-of-doors just then. The chill pushed back the warmth of the fire, and eerie shadows clothed the walls like bad spirits. Kath cried a little that evening, but James laughed and sat proudly, pink cheeks bright in the glow, as he softly whistled "Dixie," then sang a few of the words, "I wish I was in the land of cotton. . . . "

"What is it like being shot?" Henry asked Papa.

"Like being kicked by a horse. And don't you be a hero, son. It hurts!"

"Hear. Hear!" said Aunt Sue.

Kath's brothers were strong, vigorous, lusty, and unashamed. How could disaster come to such fine young men? They dreamed of glory. They dreamed of release from cluttered desks, chores, and the humdrum of dull days. War would be a welcome change.

The talk of war should not have been a surprise. When the silver-tongued William L. Yancey stormed into the Democratic National Convention at Charleston, South Carolina, in sultry April of 1860, he came for a day of triumph. Soft breezes mingled with the scent of flowers. "It's Mr. Yancey who's led us on this sorry path," said Momma.

"Someone should tell us about Yancey," said Emmie. "He was a senator once, I believe, from the State of Alabama, and he was a lawyer. He was, also, always talking about having a country just for growing cotton, separate from the United States. Uncle Wen has spoken about him. I can't remember all that he said." Their uncle was out of the room just then. He had left in a hurry—probably to go to the outdoor privy house.

"It'll be cold out there," said Aunt Sue, smiling. "However, Wen may be out there for a time. You'd better answer those questions, James."

Annie interrupted. "Wasn't Yancey that leader for the Southern

Democrats who walked out on the convention in Charleston? He could talk real smooth, I guess, and he was against Senator Douglas. I wonder what he said that changed the minds of all those politicians."

"Ann, Emmie, Annie, you're all right," answered Papa. "Yancey is a leader. He speaks words that can almost turn iron to gold. What a disciplined man. With a steady gaze and a firm handshake, you'd think he was a man of peace. But there's fire inside him. For decades, he's been using that to inflame minds all over the South. Give him a few drinks and there's magic in his voice. He can talk for hours. Several of my friends have heard him speak."

Papa hesitated. "Henry, go see if your uncle's all right. He left very quickly." Their father looked over at Aunt Sue. "He's not ill, I hope?"

"It was all that pudding," smiled Aunt Sue. "I think he's all right."

"He had three helpings," said Momma. "And he loaded it with those cherries soaked in brandy." She looked sternly at their father. "You men," she said, chuckling.

Henry returned smiling. "He's fine. Go on, Papa."

"Strong pudding'll do that," Papa laughed. Then he continued his story. "In Charleston, Yancey had but one purpose, to defeat Douglas. He did, and he broke into pieces the one party that has protected our Southern interests in Congress. This was not an accident. It was done with a purpose. He and his associates are not imprudent men. Their motives were well beyond the defeat of Stephen Douglas, a Northerner. They're warriors. They're fighting for a Cotton Kingdom. They want to be free of the North. They want a land of cotton. Now they've almost got their wish."

Papa ridged his brows as if his thoughts made him uncomfortable. "For decades Yancey has fought for separation. His words last April put fire into politicians' hearts. It was emotion not logic. He's driven a wedge between the people of this country. He's awakened a revolution, I'm afraid. Now men will die to set things right."

Papa's words were true. Yancey and his followers came with terms the national party could never accept. In forcing those issues, the Democratic Party became torn and fragmented. Stephen Douglas was defeated. The Northern Republicans triumphed. The stage was lighted. Secession was in the wings. A "house divided" and "irrepressible conflict" became grim realities.

As a child, Kath didn't understand much about politics. Over the years, she would learn. It would come mainly from reading, but, also, she would later be a secretary for a representative in the Virginia legislature.

He would serve two terms. She would come to know some of the fears people face. War is one of them. In November of 1860, however, the word "war" didn't seem particularly ominous. She did cry, but only for a short time. She soon forgot. Life went on quietly in her sheltered world.

"Can I go out now, Emmie? We're almost done."

"You finish one more pair, Kath. Honestly, I don't know how you and Mary get such big holes in your stockings. Look at this! I can almost put my fist right through. Well, it can't be fixed."

"You did fine mending on Dee's dress, Emmie. See. You hardly can tell where it was torn," said Kath.

"How did she ever rip it so bad? It's her best dress."

"Down near the creek, after Sunday services. Mary was chasing her." Kath laughed.

"That's why Momma spanked them both, I guess. I wasn't sure why."

"Look, Emmie. Someone's riding up fast. He just jumped over that stone fence. Now he's riding over part of Uncle Wen's potato patch. It looks like Henry," Kath said.

"That's Alvin Ripon. He's probably here to see Annie. Or Henry. He and your brother often ride together," said Emmie, smiling. "He's nice-looking too!"

"Mmmm! He sure is," said Kath. They both hurried to the door, then walked sedately out, trying to give the impression of only casual interest. The horseman was moist with sweat from the hard ride, but there was excitement in his eyes as he jumped from his horse. "Is Annie here?" he smiled. "I've got big news."

"Now, Alvin. She can't always be here waiting for you. You know that. And no, she isn't here, and she won't be back till near dark. Papa and Annie took seed over to Uncle Elmer. They may stay there for dinner."

"Would she mind if I rode over? I'll be leaving for Charleston in the morning to visit my uncle. Pa wants me to get some experience with selling. My uncle's in the leather business there. You know, tanning and things. I'm not sure I care about leather. I'm a farmer deep inside. My cousin, though, is in a militia group there. He's asked me to join 'em. I think I will, and I'm lookin' forward to being in it. They do marching and things. We may be needed soon.

"Hello, Kath." He then smiled. He had suddenly noticed her. He reached over and shook her fingers firmly with his big hand. It was rough and red from work in the fields.

"Hello, Alvin." She nodded as she smiled back. It was nice to be noticed.

"Will you have some lemonade, Mr. Ripon?" asked Emmie. Her eyes were warm and enticing. "We have some good raisin cookies too. Unless Kath and Mary have eaten them all." Kath looked a little grim as her sister laughed softly about this.

"Annie'll want to see you, I'm sure, Alvin, but maybe you should rest a little after that ride." Emmie stopped talking and looked steadily at their friend. "You sure did look fine when you jumped that high fence. You seemed to fly in the air." She put her hand gently on his arm. She could feel the strength and tautness of the muscles. The skin was still perspiring from the ride.

"Thank you, Miss Emmie, but I have to go. Perhaps I can take several of those cookies, though. They're always special. You're a fine cook. My brother, Donald, says you're the best. He'll be over tonight, I think."

Emmie beamed as Alvin rode off. He had a fist full of cookies, which he seemed to be enjoying immensely. "Say hello to Henry for me," he shouted back. "Tell him I'm joining the militia in Charleston."

"Things are changing," said Emmie. Her face was serious. "Men are thinking about marching and guns. I hope he'll be back sometime. Charleston is a long ways off, and time is spilling away like sand in an hourglass, Kath. What will happen next?"

Kath looked at her sister. This was a rhetorical question, and she had no answers. She was fascinated with these thoughts, however. She, too, had a disturbing sense that things were changing.

The winter of that year was a time of great turmoil. Robert Rhett, the editor of the Charleston *Mercury*, grandiloquently proclaimed, "The Union is dissolved." Oh, the passions of those mad days, in December 1860, with the formal ordinance of secession by South Carolina. The family then heard that Mississippi had also rushed to secede, followed by Florida, Alabama, Georgia, Louisiana, then Texas. Jefferson Davis, soon to be president of the Confederate States, feared that hate and distrust, driven to the extremes of disunion, could not be resolved by peaceable separation.

Davis's prophecy proved to be true. The land, both North and South, mobilized for battle. Even in '59 when John Brown, the mass murderer of Kansas, seized the U.S. Arsenal at Harper's Ferry, young men rushed to form militia units in Virginia. In their capital, Richmond, seven companies of artillery, sixteen of infantry, and a mounted guard unit were formed. Davis, on leaving Washington for the South, said a prayer, "May God have us in His holy keeping, and grant that before it is too late peaceful councils may prevail."

The majority of politicians at Montgomery, Alabama, believed, as they gathered to create a constitution for their kingdom, that the seceded states would be allowed to leave the Union peacefully. Most people of the South knew differently. It would not be peaceful.

"We have thousands of new soldiers," Momma said one evening. "They're like children. They play at war and marching. Perhaps we never grow up completely. The difference is these soldiers have real guns. They want a chance to fight the enemy." She shook her head slowly while she thought a moment. "I wish it weren't true, but Papa's right; Mr. Lincoln's election means war. I hope your brother keeps working at law." She then turned to Henry. Her eyes were soft, but her voice was firm. "You're not grown yet; we need you. Stay home!"

Their mother froze as Henry answered, "I'd make a good soldier, Momma."

CHAPTER III
The War Begins

"Thank you for riding to town with me, Katherine. It's nice to have a pretty young lady along."

"You took Annie last month, Uncle Elmer. She had a wonderful time. So have I today." Her uncle was rotund and red-faced. He was a little older than her father. "Amherst is fun," she continued. "I don't get here very often. I like to see the people."

"Well, we'll start back after I talk to those men by the store. You get in the buggy. There's a sack of candies there. You better take one. Take two if you want. They're for you children. And move that bacon and wedge of cheese over so you have room to sit."

"Mmm! It is good," she said as she tried the candy. Her uncle didn't hear her. She took a second piece as he had offered, then surreptitiously a third and a fourth. Feeling a little guilty, she looked over to see if he was watching. He wasn't. As she moved the other packages, she found a large bottle of Stonebreakers Blood and Liver Bitters. The label said it cured everything from gout to debility due to imprudence. Her Uncle Wen later told her that it had a high content of alcohol, which cured things the bitters didn't.

Uncle Elmer stood near the store entrance beside a worn wooden Indian with a fist full of cigars. The paint was chipped, but the feathers were a vivid red, white, and blue. One of the men broke off a piece of tobacco from a long coil called a "pigtail." He handed it to her uncle. Elmer stuffed it into his mouth and started to chew. "I'll be there in a minute." He smiled toward Katherine.

Elmer had shaken hands with the men by the store. They were laughing and joking at first; now they started talking more seriously. "It's coming," said one of them. "They'll be fighting soon. I just had a letter from my son in Charleston. He's with the militia there. He said they have can-

21

nons aimed at three sides of the fort. Sumter, that is. They're loaded and ready to fire if Lincoln tries to reinforce it."

"Sons or no sons, they won't let us go," said a second man. "They talk about reprisals, and they've asked for arms to put down the insurrection. We're just fighting for our rights. If we don't fight there, it'll be somewhere else."

"We passed the point of no return when the delegates from our seceded states met in Charleston. They parade through the streets and raise Cain. Fuzz-cheeked boys mostly. They're ready for a fight, I'm sure. Also, I hear Jeff Davis has Lincoln's letter about reinforcement. War'll begin if he tries. Back in January, the *Star of the West* sailed to Charleston to bring back men and guns. Our friends fired then. That was months ago. The ship quickly came about and sailed north. That's when Washington really started talking about insurrection. We've had a kind of truce ever since. It won't continue."

"They'll fire again, I'm afraid," said Elmer. "The seceded states already have captured a number of federal forts and arsenals." He looked serious; then he smiled. "Well, I'll have to go. I see Kath's chomping at the bit. I'll be back tomorrow. Good-bye for now." He raised a hand as if saluting, then he turned toward the buggy. "Let's start home, Kath."

Elmer stayed with Kath's family until late that night. He seemed to need to talk. Her red-faced uncle was married to Momma's sister. His farm was near theirs but a little closer to Amherst.

Kath suddenly saw that Henry had hurt his hand. "It was with a hammer," he said, smiling as he saw her looking toward him. The fingers were swollen and blue.

Kath's sister, Mary, snuggled close to him. She looked compassionately at the discolored fingers. "I'm sorry, Henry," she said softly. She patted him on the shoulder.

Momma smiled. "It'll get well, Mary. Nothing's broken." Henry looked pleased with his sister's interest. Momma turned to their uncle. "How was your trip, Elmer? Kath said she had a fine time. She thanks you." Kath smiled and nodded happily that she had.

"We both had a fine time," he said. There was a twinkle in his eye.

"And Kath," Momma continued, "thank you for the soap and the bolt of cloth. It's from Miller's, isn't it? We owe money, I assume."

Kath nodded agreement. "I said you'd pay them, Momma."

Momma turned again toward their uncle. "How are things in town, Elmer? You'd better take me next time—and Sue. We have a number of things to get. Now tell us what people are saying. I suppose they're worried like we are. What's happening?"

"Everyone's talking about war," he said. "It's coming. A few folks seem happy. Almost cheering. Most worry about their farms and shops, however. Especially about their sons." He looked at Aunt Sue. "They should worry, I guess. If we get at it, God knows where it'll end. In a way, it's exciting, though. Most of us want a change. Something new."

"We don't," said Aunt Sue. "Not that kind of something."

"Sorry, Sue!" He smiled meekly. "But that's the way people are talking. Bill Ripon said his son's in Charleston. They have cannons aimed at three sides of Fort Sumter. They're ready to fire. That's all it'll take."

"I know his son, Alvin," said Annie. "Uncle Elmer, you remember he came to visit that evening before he left for Charleston. I had a letter from him, too. He's in charge of a group of cannons there, or something."

"That's an artillery company, Annie," said Papa, smiling. "He's always been a leader. We've seen him in town at fairs and gatherings. He seems to have good ideas about how to do things, and then he gets people to run them and make them work. I just hope his men don't start shooting."

"He's nice-looking, too, and sensible," said Emmie. "I bet he's a good soldier. And he's in love with Annie."

"Oh, pooh," said Annie. "He is not. And how about you and his brother, Donald? Ha, ha!" She laughed.

"We're just friends," Emmie said. She glared at her sister.

"I'll bet you're just friends," Annie continued. "What about that walk in the gardens the other night? I saw you two."

"Hush, Annie." Momma's voice was soft but firm. She then looked apprehensively at their uncle. "And, Elmer, as Sue said, we don't want that kind of something. Not if it means fighting."

Elmer thought for a moment, then turned to Papa. "James, how about a little brandy? Let's forget these fool politicians. They've done it. The Yankees hate us. They'll fight. We may lose a lot of people before it's done." Uncle Elmer poured a liberal helping in a tall glass. He was smiling, which surprised Kath, and he looked relaxed.

"I hope you're wrong about a lot of people being killed, Elmer. You're right about war. It's funny, though. The sounds of drums should make us miserable. Yet, here we sit pleasantly, and, strangely enough, as you said, we're excited. It's like seeing a tragedy on a stage. With the play, you're safe. You see what's happening, but you know you aren't part of it. We are. It's real. A war is beginning."

23

Uncle Elmer just smiled. The brandy was good.

"I met a young professor in Lexington when I taught there," Papa continued. "We were at different schools—but friends. Jackson's his name." He turned to Momma. "Ann, you remember his lovely wife, Anna Jackson? Her maiden name was Morrison. You met her last year at the graduation in Lexington."

"She's a capable woman," said Momma. "I liked her."

"He's a little stiff and formal, but nice when you get to know him. He teaches artillery. He knows about war. He was with our old army in Mexico in the forties. It's not fun. The dead lie around like limp rags. It was ghastly! Elmer, I pray you're wrong about a lot of killing. I have faith most of us will survive, but we may get to know about death. Maybe we'll learn too much. Still, we are cheered by new things like soldiers marching and flags flying. Some folks in town seem happy. They probably feel that way because life can be dreary. As you said, Elmer, we all want a change. Something exciting."

Papa hesitated a moment. "A friend of mine was in Alabama in early March, Elmer. His name's Orion Jones. He lives near Lynchburg. Perhaps you've heard me talk about him. He sells ladies' things."

"They're necessary," said Aunt Sue.

"I guess they are, Sue," Papa said, chuckling, but he blushed a little.

"Sorry I interrupted, James. Go on with the story. Was he in Montgomery?"

"Montgomery. Yes. The capital. He did say that. It's crowded with people now. Young bucks while away the evenings with their ladies. They're waiting to be called to arms. All kinds of folks. Good and bad. Adventurers, pickpockets, sightseers, office-seekers, ladies-of-the-night. Thousands. Orion said they push into the bars like ants into a hole. Bands are playing. Men drink. Slave auctions. It's like a county fair but a bad omen. So many of them are looking for a fight."

"It sounds more like a cage of wild animals," said Momma. "Why was he there?"

"Selling, I guess. I'm not sure. He wasn't just visiting friends. He said that young men on the streets shook his hand. 'We're ready, sir!' they would shout. 'Ready for what?' Orion asked. The answer was firm: 'To fight, sir. To fight!'" Papa smiled. "We all talk too lightly about war. It's as if we're planning a picnic or a day in town. We forget the bad part."

Uncle Wen then spoke seriously. Kath would always remember the patient look on his face. "They build big machines up North. They can make more guns than we can. I hope we're not overwhelmed. We're brave, but it won't be one hero against another. It'll be what the *Richmond Examiner* wrote: '. . . men against iron and steel.'"

"We need guns, Wen, but we have factories," said Papa. "Not as many, but we'll make them—or buy them, I suppose. We're resourceful, but I agree, we should worry about the many factories up there. Elmer's right, too. A lot of folks may be hurt. Perhaps after a battle or two, we'll have enough sense to stop. What worries me is pride. It takes brave men to stop fighting. I almost wish we couldn't get those guns."

The war began on April 12, 1861. Fort Sumter, the harbor fort near Charleston, South Carolina, was bombarded by Southern batteries. As the flag came down, there was dancing and singing in the streets. A fifty-gun salute was fired in celebration, and the garrison of Union soldiers disembarked. Little thought was given that this first battle portended a modern war.

People of the North were determined to fight. Abraham Lincoln issued a call for seventy-five thousand volunteers "to cause the laws to be duly executed." He did not declare war. He considered the seven states as acting illegally, but still within the Union.

While in Virginia volunteers were drilling, she had not seceded. The state convention was under the control of a conservative majority. A point of agreement between conservatives and secessionists was that Virginia would not be a party to "coercion" of any Southern state. Most representatives were for forbearance to the last.

With the call for volunteers, Virginia's Governor John Letcher spoke for Border states, which until now had argued to save the Union. He replied to Mr. Lincoln, "You have chosen to inaugurate Civil War." Four more states, Virginia, Tennessee, North Carolina, and Arkansas, joined the movement to secede.

The Cotton States' power to wage war was vastly increased. The total manpower was doubled. They gained an industrial capacity, a buffer of Border states, and the materials for war. The Norfolk Navy Yard became "the chief store" of the Confederacy. The U.S. Arsenal at Harper's Ferry was seized. It was the only arsenal maintained in the South with machinery for manufacturing those desperately needed rifles.

The Lynn children's lives did change as armies mobilized, but it was only a gradual change. Dee, Mary, and Kath were up at the crack of dawn, much to Momma's disgust. "Stay quiet if you're up, and none of that loud

25

laughing while Papa's sleeping. And don't forget, you're to be on time for breakfast."

As spring came, they forgot Momma's warning, and Papa's usual school lessons were not until later in the day. They were out of doors as the birds began to sing. The sun was golden and pink as it lit up the clouds in the still dim sky. Down into the valley they would run.

"I can beat you," Mary would shout.

"No, you can't," Kath answered.

"Yes, I can."

They raced for a swing on a heavy knotted rope hanging over a little creek. There was a barrier across the stream a little to the east—a beaver dam that created a small inviting pond where they could wade on hot summer days and catch toads and things.

Papa and Uncle Wen had also fashioned a rope with a loop at the bottom for kids to swing on, out over the pond. "That will give them some excitement," Wen had said, grinning. "Just be careful." This was too risky for smaller children, but it was used constantly by their brothers.

The girls and their friend, Josh, preferred the thrill of using the shorter knotted rope over the brook. They ran down the slope, leaped from the rather steep bank, and caught the knot at the rope's end. They were high above the water—at least to them it seemed high up. Across the stream they would swing to and fro, then drop to the ground on the other side. They landed on the soft soil of a large flood plain. Needless to say, they were often dirty before breakfast.

Dew covered the ground. The freshness of the new green leaves under the early morning sun would for years bring delightful warmth to Kath's mind. Droplets of water on all the foliage sparkled in the warm rays. The bluish hepatica with hairy stems was just blooming. Back up the long hill they would run when the breakfast bell rang. There was always time for one more swing across the stream, however. "Uhh, aahh," they would gasp when they reached the top. They sounded more like chugging engines than happy children.

Josh was their best friend. He was the kitchen boy. He was always with them for those early morning romps. "We'll help with that bucket, Josh," the girls would say, laughing. Then all of them grabbed the handle to help him carry the spring water to the kitchen—hobbling more like a three-legged fly than enthusiastic children. The water was for cooking that day.

Besides fetching the spring water, Josh's job was to keep flies away from the delicious baking done by Momma and Mary, the cook. He would sit on a high, wooden stool in the center of the kitchen, flourishing a long, feathered flybrush across the table and over the stove. He often dozed in the midst of the warmth, the feathers of the flybrush draped on the floor.

Mary, Josh's mother, would trip on the end of this unwieldy instrument and then turn sternly toward him. "Wake up, you lazy thing. Look at all those flies." Kath was sure it was a boring job.

The girls would giggle. "Can we help?" Kath imagined they were more in the way than they were help.

"Go, all of you!" Mary would order, perspiration covering her brow and lips. Her eyes were kind, but her patience frazzled. Out they would scamper to pick up nuts and apples and other things.

"They sound like chirping birds," said Momma, smiling to Aunt Suellen one evening. These days were delightful, but those early morning romps in the spring were special fun. The woods were lovely.

After these morning adventures, the younger girls were scolded for being late for the breakfast blessing. Thankfully, their near-grown brother usually arrived somewhat later, much to the consternation of Papa. There he would sit, dignified, but stern. Solemnly, he would reprimand: "Look at you; where did you find all that mud? At least your hands are washed." When older, they would remember that he always had a twinkle of understanding in his eyes as they slid into their places.

"We're sorry, Papa," they replied, grinning. They then dug into griddle cakes covered with apples and homemade syrup. "Mmm. Good?" They would smile. Finally, Momma would also smile, and soft voices and laughter would follow. Their sins were forgotten, they hoped.

Henry, their brother, was also contrite. "I'll be on time tomorrow, Papa." Generally, he had overslept. He always looked as if he had been hastily put together, with his shirt and trousers only partly buttoned.

After breakfast, Kath and her younger sisters would rush to the door to go out and play. They didn't always make it, though. Momma usually had chores for them. Indoors, they could hear the cardinals sing, "Cheer-deer cheer-deer-deer." The work came first, though. They had to wait to see the crocuses along the edge of the walk, and the mayflower buds and daffodils which were just peeping up from the hillsides. Their hearts were filled with the wonders of spring, until Momma said, "Children, I have big news." It would change their lives.

Momma shocked them that evening. They were sitting before the hearth in the glow of a big fire. There was a chill in the air. "Children, we're going to be moving." Surprised voices filled the room.

"Leave Doria? It's our home."

"Move? Move where?"

"We've always lived here."

"Why?"

Papa sighed, then gave a patient smile. "Don't fret, children. You should see more of the world. This is an opportunity. We're not moving far. It's only to Staunton in the Shenandoah. It's over the mountains and north of here. If the mountains weren't in the way, you could almost see Staunton on a clear day."

His face was kind. "I taught school in the Valley for many years. Now our country is at war. Young Mr. Green, who teaches day school, has resigned." Their father hesitated a moment, then went on. "He joined the militia. We need soldiers. The children need a teacher. It's as simple as that."

Momma explained, "Papa's fine at teaching. You all know that. Also, we have many friends in Staunton, and they know his ability. With so many young men volunteering for military duty, teachers have become scarce." She moved her hands gently to emphasize what she was saying. "Papa thought it was his duty!"

Mr. Green had joined the militia in Lexington. It would soon become part of the provisional army of Virginia. The Rockbridge (County) Artillery was made up of students mainly from Washington College (now Washington and Lee University) and the University of Virginia. This unit was under the command of the Episcopal minister of Lexington. Mr. Green had been educated in Lexington and returned there to become an officer in that unit.

Papa didn't know Mr. Green, but the townsfolk knew Papa. A formal delegation had visited the farm. "We implore you!" Kath had heard. She thought they were from Amherst, close by. She didn't know what they were imploring.

Emmie, her oldest sister, startled her. "It has something to do with Annie."

"With Annie?" Kath cried. "What's wrong with Annie?"

"Annie the cow, silly. Honestly, Kath, you're so dumb at times."

Her face burned. "You're not always so smart either," she squeaked, clenching her fists. She now thought Emmie was talking about the time their cow was loose in Mr. Hall's garden.

Mr. Hall was a neighbor. The kids didn't like him very much. "I wonder what he ever did with Gretel?" Kath once said to Momma. She was answered with a hard swat on her backside.

Annie, the cow, was a drifter. This was her undoing some months later. This will be part of the story. For the present, the children were asking about their new home.

"Where will we live? We need a big house."

"When do we move?"

"Will you ask boys to our home?"

"Who will take care of our farm?"

"Annie's friend, Georgie, asked her a big question, Momma. What will happen to that?" asked Emmie laughingly.

"I know about that question, Emmie. There's nothing planned, though, so you just be quiet. That's her secret. She'll find lots of beaus. All of you will, wherever you go, so don't you fret."

"Georgie's joining up anyway," said Annie. "I just hate these silly men and their ideas. Why would anyone want to be a soldier? Guns and things. And sleeping in tents. They're like children."

Momma and Papa looked frazzled. Momma answered the questions as best she could. "Uncle Elmer will manage Doria. He's gruff, but he does a good job. He's thinking of enlarging his lands."

Uncle Elmer Post, Momma's brother-in-law, visited often. His face was big and red, and he squinted a little as he tried to read. Most children will experience this someday. It's called old age.

"Elmer isn't trying to buy our land," Momma cautioned.

Their father had grunted, "Your brother-in-law can't have our farm. He can work it and share the profits, but we'll be back."

This last sentence calmed their worries. They knew they'd return.

Momma again smiled. She had retreated from talking about Uncle Elmer. "We'll have neighbors close. You'll make lots of friends. Also, we'll buy more from the stores now. You girls can help, and I bet you'll love what you find."

Momma was wrong with this last thought. Much would be missing from the stores; the war changed things.

Papa had been a teacher for many years. As a young man, he had been the schoolmaster in many towns in the valley. His family had lived in the Shenandoah for almost one hundred years. "The Lynns were Scotch-Irish from Ulster," he had told the children. "They were humble persons.

Like most folks, they wanted a better life. This was a new land, and it should be easy, they thought. It wasn't! There were no streets paved with gold. To survive, they worked hard."

The Lynns had expected abundance and fertile lands. However, others had claimed the better lands in Maryland and eastern Pennsylvania. Their ancestors were forced to move inland. With these initial expectations shattered, they struggled on to the great valley to the south. They were poorly prepared for the hard life on the frontier. However, good land was there to be tilled. They survived.

Many other immigrants traveled these rugged trails and settled in the upper valley. This region was later known as Augusta County, named for the consort of the Prince of Wales, son of George II of England. These new settlers were not Tidewater colonists moving westward, but new immigrants of Swiss, German, and Scotch-Irish origin, and religious dissidents, such as Moravians, Mennonites, and Quakers.

Papa and Momma were married while he was still a teacher. They became James and Ann Katherine Lynn. When Papa inherited their fine home, he gave up teaching and began farming. He came to love Doria. While field hands worked the land, Papa loved the feel of the soil and often worked with them. He still loved teaching, though. "You children can learn without schools," he would tell them. They had weekly lessons in reading, writing, and numerals.

Papa often talked about the history of their farm. "It was named by your grandfather for the Dorians. They were grim warriors on mountain islands of ancient Greece. They terraced the rocky slopes to catch the rain they needed to nourish vines and crops. We do the same. It's become our life. And it's a good life."

Papa was an idealist and philosopher. Momma complemented these qualities with a delicate but pervasive firmness administered with kindness and good sense. Though she spoke softly, she guided the lives of many. Their Uncle Elmer used to say, "There is beauty in her face and eyes that immediately tantalizes the beholder, but it takes time to see the iron in her soul." When she made a decision, she displayed this firmness. Time usually proved her judgments correct.

"James, it won't hurt these children to work," she would say to Papa. "They have lessons. They also have jobs. Don't pamper them!" She would look sternly at her children. "Kath, get out there and feed those chickens, then upstairs to sweep the floors. And, Emmie, I have a basket of sewing in the closet; get at it. Now, Mary, tell me what Annie said; I'm sure it's not so bad. Annie, you help in the kitchen. Now get going. I'm angry with you." The children knew she meant business. She was also a patient listener, not only for her family, but for those who worked the fields.

Momma was a person with a hundred jobs. She directed the cooking. She oversaw the gardens around the house. She looked into every nook and cranny for dust and dirt. She helped Papa with the books. "James, there's a mistake here. Add up those columns again." She would then glare at their uncle: "Wen, the vegetables need tending. Look at all those weeds." They thought their brother had it easy. Momma was furious when Henry brought in the table he'd repaired. "Get out there and ask Uncle Wen to help you. This is sloppy. The table legs are crooked. Go!" Things got done around the farm.

For five years in the decade prior to the war, Papa taught rhetoric and composition at Washington College in Lexington. He had been a student in Lexington at the Virginia Military Institute (VMI) in his boyhood. During those years he spent many hours drilling and marching. He became disciplined in the manual of arms and the intricate commands to move bodies of troops.

Their father had the bearing of a soldier, and he loved the drama of marching with bands playing, flags flying, and colorful uniforms. He decided early in his career, though, that he could not shoot at other human beings. He could write about strategy. He could analyze tactics. "If I were in battle," he said, "I would never order my men forward. I'd fail as a soldier. It meant killing. Some must do it. I decided early that I would not. That's why I transferred to Washington College. The college was also in Lexington and next to the campus of VMI. I preferred writing and the using of words." Their father later put these skills to use in the classroom.

When he taught at Washington College just before the Civil War, he spent the week at school, then returned home to manage the farm. He preferred teaching college students, but patriotic fervor led him to accept a position at Staunton so that a capable but much younger man would become available for the cause.

Momma was in charge of the farm during Papa's absences. When he came home, he would ask, "How did things go, Ann?" He called Momma "Ann" in casual conversation.

"Fine," Momma would reply. Then they would sit for a long time, just whispering. The children often saw Papa's hand reach out and gently brush Momma's cheek.

To Kath, it didn't seem possible they would be moving. Yet, her

31

mother and father sat calmly and discussed the move. Emmie, Mary, and Henry were to go with Papa to Staunton in a few weeks and prepare for the rest of them. This would mean finding a new home, big enough for them all.

Papa would also assist with the drilling of a regiment to be formed at Staunton. "Can we drill with the soldiers?" the kids would chime.

"You can watch all you want," Papa would answer.

His student days at VMI would be an asset for Virginia. He would later be called "Colonel" and would be remembered as a fine administrator with enthusiasm and good sense.

Perhaps a strong motive for their father's accepting a day-school position after teaching at college level was the opportunity to return to the drama of marching. He couldn't resist a parade. Also, there were several female academies at Staunton. Later in the war, he lectured in these schools. This work satisfied his talents for teaching mature students.

"James," Momma said, "it's time for bed. I thought you weren't going to do any work tonight."

"Just a while, Ann," he said, smiling. "I'm writing my friend Jackson at the Institute."

"Tom Jackson? In Lexington?"

"Yes. Maybe he can tell us what's happening. We need professional soldiers now. Real fighters. He'll know about the war."

CHAPTER IV
A Virginian Comes Home

Everyone worked on a farm. The lives of the Lynn children were part daily grind and part vigorous play. There weren't many hours left for idleness. Time passed quickly before their move. They were often in the yard under Old Will's direction, helping with many of the general chores. They picked up branches, trash, sticks, and all kinds of things. These they would pile high.

"Can we help burn 'em? Please, Will. Please!"

Old Will tried to look severe. "Children, get away from that fire. Your ma'll flay me alive if you get burned. Go help Master Wen with those flower gardens."

Will stopped, smiled, then pointed to the vegetables. "Want to help, turn that. There's a shovel and rake in the barn." Kath, Mary, and Dee worked hard in the vegetable gardens and then helped Uncle Wen cultivate the soil around the flowers.

They also helped with the churning of butter and the making of candles, and Kath would remember that they were constantly called to shell vast numbers of peas, as well as snap beans, the young and tender pods of which were broken into small pieces and cooked. Biblical quotations were of little help. *Many are called, but few are chosen.* She smiled to herself. She thought a moment. *But we're always chosen.* There was a look of passive acceptance in her blue eyes, and she remembered that frequent complaining to her mother didn't change things much.

"Kath, we're better people if we work. That's how we learn," said Momma. "And now that you bring it up, I have several other things that need doing. Would you please fold that laundry that's out on the line? And don't drop it on the ground like you did last week. Then those books in the parlor need dusting. And straightening too. Then you can go out and play." She smiled at her daughter, who looked a little grim at that moment. "Thanks, Katherine!"

Later in life Katherine decided that never for anything would she go back to those days when much of what they wore and ate was produced by their own hands. Time would soften these thoughts, though, and a fondness for the "old days" finally overcame those less pleasant memories. "Besides," said Katherine, "modern ways now make things much easier on a farm."

After work, Dee, Mary, and Kath would race into the woods, where crawling things abounded. Henry was often with them. "Look, Momma, what Henry found!" Mary and Kath would tramp in with their treasures. Henry and Dee had the sense to stay out. "Here's a green snake. Mary, show Momma. And I've got a nice toad with spots."

These animals on the family's best sofa brought fire to their mother's eyes. "You take those out of here. Wen, where is that slat? Mary, Katherine, look at the mud." The two girls both stood for dinner that evening. They were too sore to sit.

"Momma," said Kath, smiling as best she could the next day, "here are some pretty blossoms."

Momma was strict, but compassionate. "Emmie, put these lovely flowers on the table. Thanks, Katherine, they are pretty."

"Emmie, where's Henry?"

"He's hunting, Momma. Papa's old rifle."

Henry loved the woods, but he didn't shoot much. Kath wasn't sure why. He told her, "I like to walk." He was avoiding work at times, but he also got away from people that way. He enjoyed moments alone.

Henry often played games with his sisters—sometimes under duress. "I Spy" was most fun. He also made whistles from tree branches, which thrilled his sisters. They gave beautiful trills, though each of slightly different pitch. Some gave a deep croaking sound, like a frog.

"Listen to these," the girls would shout to their family.

When all were blown at once, the adults would cover their ears, then send them scampering off, with a loud, "Get out of here."

Papa was conservative and freethinking about religion. He never denied its importance. He would tell his children, "It brings some goodness to the hearts of men. Also, it gives peace to many.

"I've never been strong on denominations, though," he continued. "You can love God from a bare mountaintop. And, children, there is only one true God; the rest is an argument about details." He worried about the myriad of sects and religious groups. He called their varied beliefs "religious camouflage." Some of these ideas came from the writings of Queen

34

Elizabeth of England, a great woman of practical and dynamic temperament.

Church services were held weekly on the farm. The distance to Amherst was too great for regular attendance at a church. Thus Papa held "prayers" at home for family and workers. The children were expected to be on time or experience the wrath of God. However, they were often late.

Papa would sit, shaking his head in disapproval. He then rose and stood with the big, leather-bound Old and New Testaments before him. He said little until they were all seated, then he began, "Lord, please forgive them for their improprieties. They forget this is the time we set aside to give thanks. . . . Bless them and teach them; also care for those who live amongst us here. Help us all to meet the problems of life. We face frightening troubles now. Our world is being torn into pieces. Great troubles, though, build endurance, then character and hope. It is the spirit, your spirit, which gives us strength. Shallow optimism collapses. Endurance and hope through your guidance will enable us to survive. . . . "

He read from Psalms, after which he began the sermon, usually developing an idea from the New Testament. After all of this, the children later decided that they were well bathed in religious ideas. Papa's teaching skills made most of it interesting for the youngsters. However, it was warm in the summer, and it was hard to listen and look attentive.

Mary's and Kath's friend, Josh, would doze off; he sometimes made a grunting sound. As his lids sagged down, he held them apart with his fingers. The girls could hardly keep from laughing. Momma would notice their smiles, though. "Quiet, you two!" she whispered. "Or would you like to take a walk out behind the barn?" They both knew what that meant—a spanking and time in their room. They were suddenly quiet like shadows in the moonlight.

When weather permitted, services were outside amongst the beautiful flowers and shrubs. Papa would stand beneath the roof of a small porch, attached to the back of the house. This contained many shelves that Momma used to rejuvenate indoor plants. The Bible rested on a narrow shelf facing the audience. Papa always looked sage and enthusiastic. Onetime, though, he paled as Momma shouted, "James, the plants!" Several large potted shrubs crashed to the ground.

"We'll pick 'em up, Papa," the girls chimed delightedly. They were happy to be freed from the task of listening.

"Oh, my God," he said. It wasn't often he took the Lord's name in vain. Fortunately, this wasn't heard above the noise. "Let's all sit down.

Please." He waited, his eyes slightly drawn. "Well," he groaned, "we'll continue next week. I hope."

On rainy days, they played on that small, covered porch at the back of the house. It was open on three sides. At other times they were out in the barns. On very bad days, they were indoors.

"Momma, it's too cold."

"Well, you can't play in the parlor, and Mary doesn't want you in the kitchen, do you, Mary?"

Mary shook her head, then looked at her son, "Josh, you stay here. And fetch those potatoes from the cellar, and get water. Now, children, you all go. Git." Her voice trailed off behind them as they rushed up the stairs.

"We'll see you, Josh." They wanted him to come, but he didn't like dolls anyway. "We'll make a doll-baby for you, Josh." He would scowl as they talked about dolls.

Josh didn't like the cellar. It was dank and smelled of fresh earth. Lath racks were filled with pears and apples. Cobwebs abounded—good for bandaging cuts. Kegs of cider were hardening in a dark corner. Sacks of potatoes were below the shelves of preserves and often covered with those sticky cobwebs.

Dee, Mary, and Kath often played in their sleeping rooms, but another favorite spot was a narrow, L-shaped room just below the roof. This was entered from a dark hall that ended in a carefully locked, heavy door. A big storage room was beyond, with all sorts of treasures crammed within.

Papa's secluded study was across the hall, packed with papers and many books. "You children stay out of there," he warned. "Don't go mussing up those papers." The wind mussed them one day.

"Mary was in the study," Dee and Kath chimed.

Papa looked stern. "If she's partially at fault, you two probably helped. Just be careful."

Papa kept money records in a large ledger resting on a bookshelf to the side of his heavy, oak desk. The study was brightened by walls papered in a coarse, striped pattern. Momma had put delicate curtains at the windows that moved as the wind blew, sometimes giving the young ones a fright as the shadows of late day crept upon them. "It's a ghost; let's get out!" Dee shouted.

"Oh, fiddle," Mary answered, but they all ran down the stairs to safety, not waiting to find out for sure.

"Crash, bang, clop, boom," their heavy footsteps echoed down over the stairs.

"What got into you?" Aunt Suellen called.

"We saw a ghost."

"Ghost, my eye. There are no ghosts. Sit down. I'll tell you a story. There once was a beautiful princess, good and sweet like you girls. You are, aren't you?"

"Yes," they said dutifully. Then she went on with the story. They soon forgot about ghosts and the cold weather outside.

The L-shaped playroom was unfinished. The roof beams stood out like sinister arms above them. They were practical, though. Old spreads and blankets could be fastened to the beams and used to perform plays or to hide behind as the children romped and ran about.

There were a number of big boxes at the far end of the room for winter clothing, extra bedding, and old fabrics. Some were open at the top but carefully covered with cloth or paper. It was fun to creep into them to snooze or hide, producing all kinds of disarray.

"You children get off of there," Momma would shout from the door. "I spent hours arranging those boxes. Git. You can play here, but be careful. Do you hear?"

They all nodded, "Yes'um. We're sorry." They weren't, but, though Momma was patient, they knew she meant business. She never gave a second warning when they were creating mischief. Punishment followed swiftly if they continued.

They were not allowed alone in the locked storage room. They did often see the inside, though, usually accompanied by Momma or Aunt Suellen. Winter garments hung from hooks and bars in the corners and by the large dormer windows. Heavy coats looked like staunch knights in the shadows, preparing for battle. The lighter clothing would move to-and-fro as the wind blew, like dancing minstrels, serving their master, the knight.

In that storage room, Momma kept various dried fruits, including cherries, apples, plums, and grapes. The children had helped pick and dry these. She also stored chinquapin nuts, loaf sugar, unused furniture, old toys, boots, winter shoes, a spinning wheel, hinges and locks for doors and cabinets, pots and other cookingware, earthenware jugs, dishes and glassware, square and decorative round panes of window glass, stoneware jugs of homemade wine, candle molds, quilting frames, and any number of interesting things. Boxes of old clothes from past generations were stored there. Bonnets, papers, hammers and augers and other old tools, nails, unused paintings and pictures, and seed for the fields could be found.

"What's wrong with that picture, Aunt Suellen?"

"Kath, your papa doesn't want that downstairs; don't look—it's too scary." Naturally she looked at it every time she got into the room. It was in a dark corner by the sage and other herbs.

She would later remember that old painting, *Wolf Hounds in the Hunt*, showing ferocious, fearsome beasts giving chase to a frightened bleeding doe. Papa thought it too vicious for display, even though the colors were pleasant.

The sage was for sausage. Mary, the cook, also used it in stuffing for chickens and especially turkeys. Coriander seeds and other aromatic herbs were also stored here. This room was a history of the family and a picture of the way folks lived back in the mid-nineteenth century. It is still there in the Lynn family's old house.

Dee, Mary, and Kath had many dolls, not the store variety, but ones they made themselves from old cloth and string. Sure, they owned a few store babies, but these were treasures, more to be looked at than played with. Momma had boxes with fabric ends that the girls could use to make things like doll clothes, rag-doll babies, bonnets, and belts. The boys didn't like these games. But, oh, what fun the girls had till dark, when they scampered down to safety.

In mid-May of 1861, Katherine lay awake in bed. She kept worrying about her family's move to Staunton—a step into the unknown. It was dark outside, but the sky was clear. She could see a few billowy clouds partially covering the golden moon. Her sister, Mary, was sleeping nearby. She occasionally moaned as if she were having a dream.

Kath wondered if she too were dreaming as she saw her sister, Emmie, moving below. Suddenly a man in a uniform grabbed Emmie and held her in his arms. They were standing near the porch in the shadow of a big wisteria bush. It was not a dream, and her sister didn't seem to be struggling.

Donald Ripon was the handsome officer below with Emmie. His arms held her tightly at the waist. She was leaning back and talking softly. He seemed to be trying to pull her closer. She put her arms up and gently pushed him away. Kath could barely hear her words. "You men!" her sister said. "You're always running off. Some new interest or other."

"Emmie, I'll be back. Really I will. You're my girl now, and don't you forget it," said Donald.

"Hmmm!" she said. "Men always say that—even if we women don't really agree." The last words were almost whispered, and deep feelings were partly hidden by a broad smile. She looked carefully at his face and then his uniform. "Donald, you certainly do look handsome. That gold sash and sword just fill a woman's heart. Now you just be very careful of yourself. Like Papa said, see if you can be appointed to a general's staff or something. I don't want you stopping any of those awful bullets. You wouldn't look so pretty then."

"I'll be fine, Emmie. And don't you worry none. My ma cried today, but I think she's a little proud."

"She certainly should be."

"We'll get those Yankees. You'll see." He hesitated as he looked softly into her eyes. "I have that lock of hair you gave me." He patted his broad chest close to the heart to show where it was hidden. "I just hate to leave you though, Emmie."

She knew Kath was above watching. She could almost see her high cheeks and bright eyes peering out through the window as clouds parted and moonlight splashed onto the window-glass like a beam from a giant lantern.

Well, she and Kath were much alike. In a way, one was almost a mirror image of the other, with each changed slightly, as by a magic that could add or take away a few years. They both loved life and wanted to see more of it. Kath especially enjoyed the out-of-doors, while she, Emmie, loved the creative arts of a home with sewing and cooking and bustling about with flowers and plants and a brood of younger sisters.

Donald Ripon was now gently holding her hands. She felt how coarse and rough his skin was. He was a kind man—or should she say boy. He was in uniform now and was to leave for the war in the morning. He had been searching for something new—a change. Now he had found it.

Donald's father had sent him to Lynchburg a few years back. Now, through the help of his proctor there, he had received an appointment as an officer in the burgeoning Virginia military forces. He was on his way to Richmond, and he was very handsome. Dark hair, blue eyes deeply set, and a firm mouth, made him a picture of what an officer should look like.

Emmie also wanted something new—a taste of life. She, in contrast, had had little formal schooling, but over the years, her family had instilled in her a love for words and a desire to learn more. Her father, a teacher, had sat with her often. She had grown up writing and working with numbers. These skills had come easily. Now, perhaps, the move to Staunton would give her the opportunity to learn more of the world and its wonders.

"I'll write you often, Emmie."

"You'd better, Donald. I know you write well." She smiled shyly. "I want you to tell me everything. Lots of words on paper. And you stay away from those high-toned ladies James has been telling us about. 'Ah, but the ladies,' he said, 'they're lovely in those light blue dresses with scrumptious lace.' My brother's eyes almost popped right out of his head. You stay away from that kind if you really want me to be your girl."

Emmie saw that Donald suddenly had that dreamy look she had seen in James's eyes when he spoke of the lovely ladies. She quickly changed the subject. "Will your Ma and Pa be all right? You've done so much of the work at home."

"They'll be fine. We'll only be gone for a few months anyway." Emmie wasn't so sure. She didn't have that male aura of invincibility. He suddenly drew her close to him. His arms held her supple body like strong cords. She could feel his breath on her cheeks, and his sunburned face against hers. "I love you," he said. He kissed her hard, then turned and walked toward the big stallion that was the pride of his family. "Let's go, Roger Boy," he said. As he rode off, he turned and shouted loudly, "I'll be back, Emmie!"

Kath sat enthralled. What a wonderful way to end the day! She saw Emmie look toward her. It was a satisfied look. Was it because of love or a sense of freedom? They would soon be moving. Emmie had often talked about a new chance in a new place. Maybe in Staunton this dream would come true for her sister. Kath wasn't worried anymore. It would also be the place for other dreams and excitement.

The following evening, the family was seated before the hearth in front of a brisk fire. Uncle Elmer was talking with Papa and Uncle Wen about managing the farm after their move.

"Go ahead with the north quarter tomorrow, Elmer. The south fields are finished. You'll still need to harrow and seed. We're doing well with corn. Those fields were exhausted—too much tobacco. We're using deep plowing now and gypsum. Seems to help."

"James, I mentioned those ideas—remember? They're from Edmund Ruffin. He's old now. States' rights man to the ends of his toes. He fired that first shot at Sumter, I believe. And I'm told that that was truly an honor. He also attended the secession congress in Charleston last year. I have some of his writings. He's not writing much now, I guess, but he still lives in Virginia. You, a man of words, should read them."

"I have." Papa hesitated, then grinned, "Thanks to you. His ideas probably saved Virginia some years back. He also suggested manure and crop rotation. Practical ways to save the soil. I've read what he preached. I think I'm a better farmer because of it. He started that journal about these ideas years ago."

Papa stopped and stared at Uncle Elmer. His jaw tightened. "He was a violent man, though. It caused him troubles with people. After that he had money problems and had to stop printing. Too bad. He helped a lot of farmers. Interestingly, he had little formal education, but he found answers. We fortunately listened. Newton in Westmoreland mentioned another chemical—guano from Peru. It's too expensive. We use our own wastes."

Papa laughed. His laugh was high-pitched and almost a giggle. He tried to swallow the next few words, then smiled as if they were funny. "With all the loud politicians around, we have lots of waste in Virginia. I'd use another word if the children weren't here."

"James, hush. Remember what you said about bad language."

"Sorry, Ann Katherine."

Papa used both of Momma's names when he was speaking formally or with great feeling. Also, he used both when she was suggesting his actions might not be quite proper.

Momma's lips quivered, then ended in a knowing smile. She mumbled something to herself. The family didn't understand the words. She thought it best not to emphasize that even Papa needed scolding once in a while. All men do. Her eyes looked laughingly at her husband. He knew what she was thinking as he turned to listen to Uncle Wen.

"There was a riot in Baltimore last month," Wen commented. "Paid regiments from near Boston. The tracks were barricaded, I'm told, and the crowd got angry. Soldiers were killed. Then they fired on the crowd. Young boys. Scared, I suppose. The people mainly had rocks and sticks and were throwing them. Some fool had a gun and started it. The others helped. If I were a boy, maybe I'd fire back, too. I think I would."

"You're too kind, Wen," said Elmer. "Those were troops heading for Washington to kill our men. Our army's also busy. They captured the arsenal at Harper's Ferry. Both sides are getting ready to fight. Harper's Ferry's a hard place to defend, I'm told. You know. John Brown's raid— that devil. Anyway, it was taken easily, and we need those guns. The arsenal also has machinery. I hope is was saved. We'd better move it soon, or the North'll take it back."

"Machinery?" Wen asked.

"Yes, to make guns. Not cannons. Rifles."

"I hope you're right. We need the machinery. We've got the military men, I think. Many professional soldiers are from the South. But as we've discussed, we still need the weapons. We'll have to make them or buy them."

Uncle Elmer turned to Papa. "James, old man O'Brien died. You know, that kind old gentleman who lived fifteen miles north. He was a good man—at least in his old age. I'm not sure what happened. He just collapsed."

Papa looked sad. "Ann," he said to Momma. "Send a note to Mary O'Brien when you have a chance. Remember all the advice he gave when we started. Tell her how sorry we are. He was a nice gentleman."

"James, you should write too. We both should."

"I will," he answered.

While Momma and Papa talked, Kath saw Wen smile at Elmer and turn his eyes up as he pointed upward. Elmer shook his head, then looked down and to the side. It was years before she understood these gestures. She didn't know then that Mr. O'Brien was somewhat of a hellion in his younger days. She hoped his final destination was up, not down. There was a lot of good in that man, as her family said.

Papa sat back and shook his head. "Elmer, O'Brien told me about deep plowing before you did. He's lucky. Our world's going to pieces. He's out of it now—no worries. By the way, Richmond is the Confederate capital now. Probably every soldier in the North will try to shoot at it. Tom Jefferson's capital building will be leveled. So will our sons. Damn! We sure need the other Southern states now. Their boys are just starting to arrive in Virginia." He thought for a moment. "There's sadly been another call for troops both North and South."

Papa turned to Momma. "A great Virginian came home, Ann. Colonel Lee. Remember? Tom Jackson told us about him. He's General Lee now. He once was the commandant at West Point. He's been nice to Tom and has even written letters of recommendation for him." Papa hesitated. "I just got another letter from Jackson. He saw Lee a few weeks ago in Richmond. Tom was there with his cadets—his students. He's a colonel now, and Lee ordered him to Harper's Ferry. Jackson's a good man, and he said glowing things about Lee. They 'think alike,' he told me."

Papa gazed through the window at the planted fields. "Jackson's quiet," he continued. "I'll bet he's a fighter, though. There's intelligence behind that grim face. He won't give up. We're fortunate to find real soldiers. I hope he's right about Lee!"

Lee, about whom Papa spoke, was a noble man. He had a kind face, but serious. Kath would meet him one day. She would remember he was nice to children and to his soldiers, and that he would listen as they talked.

In the spring of 1861, Lee had no beard. That came later. His hair then was dark brown, salted with gray, and bunched at the sides. This made his reddish face seem wider. His mustache was also dark. It curved gently above his mouth. His eyes were brown and deep, and he had prominent brows, which blended into a straight, distinguished nose below a high forehead. He was an excellent horseman. Mounted, he made Kath think of a knight of the Middle Ages. Time never changed these memories.

"He's said to be a great soldier," Papa commented. "At least Jackson believes that. 'There is no one better,' he told me."

"I hope he'll help us," Wen replied. "We've taken on a giant."

The Lees of the country had always been Americans, but they were Virginians first. Robert Edward Lee had come home.

CHAPTER V
History Says They're Soldiers

Early in the war, few people realized the superb talents of the two soldiers Katherine's family spoke of that evening in May of 1861. Lee and Jackson would emerge as great leaders. During the war, she would meet these soldiers. For brief moments, she would hear them speak and sense that they were good men.

Robert Lee was logical and precise. His mind leaned to dealing with numbers and magnitudes. Men and natural things from the earth (for stout fortifications) were the raw materials for these disciplines. From seasoned soldiers, such as General Winfield Scott, he had learned about war. He had fought with Scott in the Mexican conflict.

As war began, Lee was recognized as being adept at drill, planning, observation, and the management of at least small bodies of troops in the field. On paper, however, he had limited knowledge of the handling of regiments in action, of the service of supply, and of the duties of quartermaster and commissary, so important in building an army.

As fine as were his skills, he was still learning his trade when he reached Richmond in April 1861. Some wondered, was there "enough firmness" within him to fight battles? Also, they asked, "When our country cries for leaders, why Lee?"

These were thoughts men spoke as Lee assumed command "of the military and naval forces of Virginia." He was appointed to the rank of major general. Veterans of the old army knew his qualifications; beyond these professionals, few were aware of his ability. He soon demonstrated his resolution and skill.

Lee established an excellent administrative staff. He supervised the formation of militia and volunteers for Virginia's provisional army. He handled vain, pretentious military and political leaders with tact and patience. He directed arms production, procurement of equipment, laying out and construction of river fortifications, and manufacture of gun carriages for light artillery and for heavy ordnance. These guns were captured at Norfolk; when mounted, they provided a vital artillery arm for the emerging armies.

Lee ordered the moving of equipment for the manufacture of rifles from the vulnerable town of Harper's Ferry to the more protected environment of Richmond. He proclaimed a policy of defense while he prepared Virginia for fighting. His most perceptive skill lay in the selection of men to train and command the developing legions. Patriots abounded. They had to be molded into soldiers and adapted to military organization. Passion for striking a blow against the enemy were calmed until trained regiments were created.

Companies were disciplined in close-order drill and organized as regiments, then formed into divisions and brigades. The average brigade was about two thousand men. Cadets from the Virginia Military Institute were directed to Richmond, Harper's Ferry, and other centers. These well-schooled, fine young men were to become the drillmasters to train an army for the field. They were invaluable.

Lee also recognized the futility of mobilizing beyond a certain stage, until equipment and arms could be provided. As arms became available, he adjudged needs, answered the questions of hundreds of officers, advised strategy, and disbursed the military property. This gentle Virginian, whose early efforts are largely unknown, was the imponderable force that trained an army for Virginia and then for the Confederate States. The war would last a long time because of this great soldier.

Jackson was different. Though Lee was the perfect commander, Jackson was the ideal subordinate and lieutenant. In war, he would accept orders and move quickly and responsibly. He was James Lynn's friend, and the family spoke of him often, even before the war. During the war, he was known as the famous Stonewall Jackson.

Thomas Jonathan Jackson was sober-faced, rough-hewn, disciplined, and plain, with light-colored eyes, prominent brows, and a rust-colored beard. This unsmiling man was a young professor from the Virginia Military Institute (VMI). Lee had once recommended him for another college post, but, until the spring of 1861, he had not laid eyes on him since they had fought together in the Mexican war. Jackson was breveted a major in that war for his daring when under the test-of-fire and for his cool brilliance in directing troops.

As a boy, he had grown up on a frontier farm in the Alleghenies in western Virginia. He was orphaned when only age seven. Like his Scotch-

Irish ancestors, he was inspired with a will to succeed and a feeling of self-worth. However, he was very aware of his rude preliminary education, and graduation from West Point necessitated anguish and hard work. In his room, after "lights out," he studied by the dimming coals of the fire; he "burned his lessons in his brain."

Promotion was grievously slow in peacetime, and finally Jackson resigned from the Army. He became a teacher of natural sciences and artillery at VMI in Lexington. Though he hungered for approval, he was regarded as colorless and odd by students and professors alike.

In the decade prior to the war, James Lynn (Papa) had taught rhetoric and composition at Washington College, adjacent to VMI. It was during this period that he came to know Jackson. Papa was an outsider, and he and Jackson became good friends. However, Professor Jackson was always quiet and somewhat distant.

It was in his home, a small red brick house off Main Street, that Jackson revealed a side of his character seen by very few. At home he was gentle and tender, with a thoughtfulness and kindliness of nature never seen in the classroom or when in command.

James knew Jackson's delightful wife, Anna, one of the "four fabulous Morrison sisters." He saw the affection and caring this stern, firm-willed, awkward man expressed toward this lovely woman. When at work, he was demanding and severe. At home with family, he would laugh and tease.

While at VMI, Jackson became a celebrant of the Presbyterian Church; his native piety thrived with this responsibility. Though a disciplinarian, he was devoutly religious. He prayed for strength to carry out what God willed. When Virginia seceded, he said, " . . . all I am and all I have is at the service of my country."

From the day Jackson reached Harper's Ferry, that little town nestled among the hills along the Potomac River, to the day he died, he never passed a single night away from duty and from caring for the men under his command. He was a dedicated soldier. His campaigns would become legendary.

Emmie and Katherine accompanied Papa to Lynchburg in mid-May of 1861. This busy town was a trading and distribution center in a rich agricultural area. It was twenty-five miles south of their home and just east of the Blue Ridge Mountains. Papa went there on business. Kath had seen trains, but this was her first ride on one. It was noisy and smoky but wonderful. There were angry clouds above when they arrived, but it didn't rain.

They left the train at the recently completed Orange & Alexandria station just west of the Kanawha Canal aqueduct. The James River was nearby. They walked over the Blackwater Creek bridge, then east on Water Street. "Emmie and Kath, this is an important place. That's the depot for the Virginia and Tennessee Railroad." Papa pointed east. "The tracks go all the way to Chattanooga. And see! There are soldiers coming in even now."

"They don't look very neat," said Katherine.

"You wouldn't either if you'd ridden all night," said Emmie, smiling.

"Emmie's right, Kath," replied Papa. "And those other tracks farther off are the Southside Railroad from Petersburg. Lynchburg has become a very, very important place, especially with the war." They were now standing on a stone arch that passed over the canal. A wooden bridge spanning the James River was just before them. Papa looked at the water under the arch. "The Kanawha Canal below us, though, I've been told, carries more freight and produce than all these railroads put together. But that's another story. Let's get our work done. Then we can have fun."

Papa rented a small city wagon pulled by a sway-backed old horse called Martha. Emmie wanted a surrey with a more handsome animal. "We're picking up packages and equipment, Emmie," said Papa. "This is business. Martha isn't much to look at, but she's dependable. Is that all right?"

"I guess so," she replied. As he turned away, she gritted her teeth and smirked, then whispered, "If we meet soldiers, what will they think?"

Papa knew the town well. He pointed out mills and offices, churches and homes. As they drove along, they saw hundreds of "pretty new soldiers." That's what their father kept calling them. They were marching in columns and heading for camps on the outskirts of town. Lynchburg was a mobilization center for newly organized companies arriving in Virginia from the deeper South. They would soon be formally mustered into the Provisional Army of the Confederate States of America (CSA). A number of these men waved and gave hoots and cries of welcome as the Lynns passed by.

"We're the Eleventh Mississippi!" one group cried. "Come see us tonight."

Kath saw Emmie smile. "Can we visit that group, Papa?"

"I hope we can. I want to see some of the drills and marching." He turned to his daughter and smiled. "And, Emmie, that's a 'company,' not a 'group.' Each company has about one hundred men. They break into smaller units called squads for drilling. Both you and Katherine better start learning the names. We'll see lots of soldiers from now on. And don't you worry about this old wagon. None of them care. They just like to see pretty girls."

They finally arrived at their destination, an old brick building on a narrow street near the center of town. Emmie and Kath sat in a dark hallway for what seemed an eternity. It smelled bad there of old cigars and oily machines. Finally Papa came out of a dingy office. "I bought it, girls," he smiled. Kath thought one item Papa bought was a new plow. She wasn't sure about the rest. The big pieces would be shipped to them by rail. For the other items, they went to a warehouse near the railroad. Their father had a number of formal-looking papers, which he gave to a man at a window. Workers brought out several big boxes and loaded them into the wagon. "There. That's done," Papa said. "Let's get a lemonade. I'm thirsty."

Emmie nodded her head in agreement. Then she spoke in a most pleasant voice. "Can we see the soldiers, Papa? It's getting late already." There was a pleading look in her eyes. Papa saw this and smiled.

He looked at his watch. "I think we can, Emmie. We have plenty of time. We don't leave till late in the afternoon." He, too, was excited about watching the soldiers, but for a different reason. He loved marching. They stopped for the lemonade. Kath had a sarsparilla instead, which she enjoyed. They ate the lunch Momma and Aunt Suellen had prepared as they drove to the camp. It was at the Fairgrounds, south of the city. This was a recruiting center and camp of instruction during the entire war. Crude sheds were being built to house tentless soldiers. Later they would be used for Yankee prisoners.

Emmie Lynn was delighted as they arrived. "There they are!" she shouted. "Aren't they wonderful?" Kath wasn't so sure. It was a bleak, rutted meadow, and the marching soldiers were surrounded by thick clouds of dust. It gets hot in Virginia during mid-day in May. It hadn't rained, and Emmie coughed and Kath sneezed as they stepped off the wagon.

Besides the sheds to the north, there were hundreds of tents at one side of the parade ground with spits for fires, dirty pans, kettles, stools, small tables, bugles, unwashed dishes, shovels, parts of uniforms, and all kinds of army gear strewn around. It didn't look very organized to Katherine. She saw that Emmie was still smiling. She wondered how her sister, who loved a clean, tidy home, could be happy with such disarray. Her father looked pleased, too.

"Thank goodness they've come. Virginia's not alone anymore," remarked Papa. He stared quizzically at some of the uniforms of the men close by and laughed softly. "They look decorated as if they're going to a parade," he said. "Almost like a bride at a wedding."

"Papa, they're nice," Emmie smiled.

He then looked with a professional eye at some of the knapsacks near the tents. He seemed surprised. "Can you imagine?" He laughed while pointing at them. "They have white vests, linen collars, white gloves, neckties, extra shoes, coffee boilers, kettles, basins, shovels, lamps, dress uniforms and even bottles of wine. Hmm! They can't carry those very far."

Knapsacks were objects of disbelief as regiments were organized. These men would finally travel light. Only the basics—a blanket, rubber ground cloth, tent flap, canteen, cup, haversack, and perhaps a few items like a spoon and knife. A half of a canteen might be used as a dish and for cooking. Of course, they had their fighting gear. This was kept polished and perfect. Shoes would be treasured. The other items were discarded during hot marches on rutted roads.

Papa spoke to several of the officers, then introduced his daughters. Kath blushed a little and shied away, but Emmie glowed inside as Papa talked with them. One handsome man with blond hair and a twisted mustache was very serious as he discussed the war with Papa. His eyes, though, would occasionally flick over and look at Emmie, then he would smile.

The man had gold braid on his sleeves. Kath saw that Emmie's cheeks were gradually becoming pink and bright. They were crimson a moment later as he winked at her, but he went on talking with her father: "We have boys from Alabama, the Carolinas, Mississippi—even from Texas. We're growing. We'll be an army soon. We're learnin' to march now, and we officers are gettin' the hang of it. It's exciting. All we need now are those Yankees. We'll make 'em run."

"Maybe you should train a little longer," Papa smiled. "War's not easy. I knew men from that Mexican fighting. Marching and battle were tough. It wasn't as easy as they thought."

"I know, but we boys from Alabama think we're tougher. I've heard about those soft Yankees. Give us a battle or two. You'll see. We'll be ready for 'em." He turned to Emmie. "We have parades on Sundays. Come see us

49

when we're really polished." He whispered something to Papa about parties on Saturdays. "I'd love to see your daughter again, sir," he said, smiling.

"Can we, Papa? Please. Can we come back? It's not far," said Emmie.

"Talk to Captain Foster over there. He does the planning. Pretty ladies are always welcome."

"We'll see," Papa said softly to Emmie. "You and Annie should start meeting more boys." He turned to the lieutenant. "Son, what about tactics and things? You've gotta get there and be placed right. It's not just marching and being tough. I was at VMI years ago. Some of my classmates became regulars. That's what they talked about. Get 'em to the right place with the most. Hold one part of the line and attack at the other. That's tactics."

"Our colonel worries about that, Mr. Lynn. He'll get us there. That's his job. He stays up nights with books. He also lectures to the captains. We do the visiting, and we'll do the fightin'."

Emmie was pleased with what she heard. Papa didn't seem too happy. He closed his eyes and took a deep breath but didn't speak further, except to smile. "Good-bye, son. I hope we can come back and see you soon."

As they walked on, Papa said softly, "They're not ready yet. If they really get to fighting, it'll probably be worse than either side expects. That's what happened in Mexico. Also in other wars. It's always worse."

Few officers understood what was required to prepare troops for real war. They were nonprofessionals, learning a new craft. They would become good soldiers. However, when they arrived in Virginia, experienced men were in short supply.

Later that day, the Lynns met the men of Company A of the Eleventh Mississippi. These sturdy boys were in uniforms with handsome gray frock coats. Hats of black felt were topped with pompons and looped on three sides. They were a colorful group, like many then assembling.

"Papa, those are the boys we saw in town," Emmie shouted. "They asked us to come see them. Don't you remember? They're handsome."

"They do look handsome, Emmie. We can meet them if you like."

While Papa talked with the captain, Emmie met a nice young soldier called Marc. She talked to him for some time. He would smile, then she would smile. Kath stood at the side and watched. She tried hard to look happy.

As they started toward the wagon, Kath smiled at her sister and laughed. "Emmie's got a boyfriend. My, he's nice. Just wait till I tell Annie—and Alvin. He's home now. He can write Donald all kinds of nice things."

"Stop it, you little monster!" Emmie frowned. "I'll hide those new shoes Momma bought if you don't." She suddenly sneered, "Eeeeh!" and she made a face with her tongue out. She was happy all the way home, though, and sang softly. Marc and Emmie became good friends. They would write often.

The soldiers around them that day would finally be ordered to combat areas. For some, this would be the lower Shenandoah Valley. They would learn. Many had servants, but they still became able soldiers. As they marched hundreds of miles on dusty roads, they became very aware of what war was about. However, there was a carnival quality with early mobilization. There were as many "armies" as Italy had kings. Alas, there was everything except an army. Training consisted of a series of long parades and sumptuous parties. Virginia cordiality was infectious, and ladies' smiles were wonderful.

The trail for the Eleventh Mississippi men, formerly the University Grays from the state university at Oxford, led to Winchester, near the valley town of Harper's Ferry. There they met an array of resplendent companies from all over the South. There were generals and colonels everywhere, but sadly, little organization or discipline. Finally, Lee ordered the newly appointed colonel, Thomas J. Jackson, to take command of this hodgepodge of troops. A capable soldier was placed in a position of authority. The training of men for battle began.

"He's tough," Marc wrote Emmie weeks later. "He doesn't look like much, but we're busy and things get done. We're building defenses on high ground now. I've been digging trenches all day long. Then we drill for hours. This isn't what I expected at all. I don't have time for ladies anymore. Next time I'll join the cavalry; just ride around and scout the country.

"We captured fifty-six locomotives from the Yankees some weeks back—the B&O Railroad. The Yankees were furious, I've heard. Also, several hundred of our boys are across the river (Potomac) on the Maryland heights. They're Kentuckians. That's Yankee land. I wonder what Old Abe is thinking now. No fighting yet—but it'll come soon enough."

The frolic and partying of the militia and volunteers in the Shenandoah Valley were abruptly ended with Jackson's arrival. This plainlooking officer, who, against the array of plumes, pompons, and color, looked outright shabby, began the transformation of this conglomeration of troops into an army.

"Jackson's methods were harsh," Papa would tell his family later. "His main preoccupation in war was duty. In the darkest hours of the Confederacy, he became a hero. His campaigns baffled the Union generals. People soon recited a poem about Jackson, my grim religious friend: 'Silence! Ground arms! Kneel all! Caps off! Old Stonewall's going to pray....'"

Papa, Emmie, and Kath returned to the farm after their day in Lynchburg. Time passed quickly. James would not be with them for the move. He had "joined up."

"Hey, Annie, look at James! He's a soldier," shouted Henry.

Annie came running out of the barn. "You're handsome, James, my dear brother," she said, smiling as she snuggled close to him and blinked her brown eyes in a most charming manner. The dangers of war even eluded Annie.

"James, you're home," Kath shouted. "Wonderful. Wonderful!" She held his arm and looked at his gray jacket and new-grown beard. He was fanning himself with a black felt hat and grinning broadly. Kath reached under his coat and snapped his suspenders.

"Stop that, Kath," he said—then laughed. She noticed there was no gold braid on his sleeves such as she had seen on the gorgeous officers in Lynchburg. "I'm finally a soldier," he told them. His face was radiant.

Henry kept pumping James's hand up and down. "Well I'll be darned. You do look like a soldier," he said. There was a look of envy in his eyes.

Mary and Kath carried James's knapsack into the house while he hugged Momma and Aunt Suellen. "You look good enough to eat," said his aunt. "But where are your books and things? You can't live out of that knapsack."

"I shipped them, Aunt Sue. A week ago. My whole trunk's in Richmond. At least, I hope it is."

James left the next day for the war. He went by train to Charlottesville, then by the Virginia Central to the capital. "Be careful," was all Momma said. She then turned away. She was usually very articulate. "I don't want James to see me cry," she said later to her daughters.

"Say hello to Jeff Davis," said Uncle Wen, smiling.

"Good-bye, Papa, Momma, Uncle Wen, Aunt Sue."

Papa hugged him gently, then firmly, then patted him on the shoulders. "Good luck, son. Be careful."

James left with his knapsack, his mouth covered with kisses and a handful of admonitions on conduct from Papa. Naturally, these admonitions were not followed very frequently.

Good sense had prevailed as James had gone to volunteer for service in the army. He was very enthusiastic about getting involved in the war. He went to join up among back-slapping friends and other fellow citizens. He, their brother, dreamed of resplendent gray with gold braid, jingling spurs, dusty roads, and marching columns. He finally settled, after Mr. Jason's advice and help, for a dusty, small wooden desk in a dark corner of the War Department in Richmond.

James wore gray, but no gold braid. He was later commissioned, but for the present, he suffered menial tasks, which, he thought, were better suited for others. "Ruling lines on paper," he said, "could be done by any young schoolboy."

On the train north to Charlottesville, he found himself smiling. "I still love Richmond. It's nice to be going there. Not as heroic as a battlefield, but maybe what I've learned will help. I have friends who are executives with the railroads. They say that rails will be needed with a war coming. They will be. I've negotiated with several on the lines of rights-of-way. Now, maybe, I can help them with all the problems they have with our government." He looked very smug. Then he became more serious, as he nodded his head slowly. "But I'd sure like to fight those Yankees. Show them how strong we are." He thought for a moment. "But that's silly. As Jason said, bullets don't care how brave you are. I guess he's right."

Benjamin Jason was James's preceptor. He had been a boyhood friend and long-time political colleague of Governor Letcher of Virginia. They both hailed from Rockbridge County in the Shenandoah Valley. They were level-headed, conservative, and irascible gentlemen, short on patience, and firm with ideas.

"There is a good way to do things," Jason had once whispered to James, "and that is our way."

John Letcher knew the mind of the people of Virginia. He was not a soldier, and he sensibly deferred to Lee in military matters, with the result that a sound military organization and defense were developed. This was a lesson that Jeff Davis should have learned early in the war. Jason thought James would benefit from contact with high-ranking officers, such as Lee. It was an opportunity. James finally accepted. His knowledge of law would be an asset.

The move to Staunton in the Shenandoah Valley was planned for late June. Papa, Emmie, Mary, and their near-grown brother, Henry, were already there awaiting them. James was in Richmond. Uncle Wen would stay with the farm for several weeks to help Uncle Elmer with the work and planning.

"Georgie's riding up, Annie. He looks handsome. That uniform has braid on it now," shouted Kath. Annie ran to the door as Georgie arrived in a cloud of dust. His horse seemed to skid up to the porch at the front of the house.

"Won't you come in, Georgie?" said Annie. Her eyes sparkled. "My, you look fine." He did look self-assured and handsome, she thought. He seemed to be older now and much more mature. It almost frightened her. Evidently boys became men when they worked at war.

"We're on the way to Winchester, Annie. I just had to see you." He gave her a dutiful kiss, then held her hand. His mind seemed to be far away; perhaps he was thinking about the war. "Your father's friend, Jackson, is in command there. We'll be fighting soon, I think."

"You silly men," she said. "You just have to show how big and brave you are."

"It's starting, Annie. You and I can't stop it now, and I'm not so sure it will be over in a few weeks. We'll see. I've been in Lynchburg for training. My company's at the station now in Amherst."

He saw Mrs. Lynn approach. "Georgie, it's nice of you to come. I heard that you're on the way north. God bless you, son. We'll miss you. James left several days ago. He's in Richmond now, I hope. All our young men are leaving. Our cheers go with you, though. We'll be going to Staunton soon. Several of the family are already there. Well, you two have things to talk about. Good luck and be careful!"

George and Annie talked for some time. No one heard the conversation. He finally rode off at a full gallop, jumping fences and big stone walls. His black hat was swinging above his head, and he gave a high-pitched shout as he reached the entrance gate. This was the cry that would one day scare the britches off Yankee soldiers when they saw the Southern ranks approaching. It was the famed Rebel yell that both armies would always remember.

"He said he'd write soon," said Annie. "He's grown up, Momma. It's almost frightening to see. We're really not in love, but we give each other strength. Perhaps that's good."

"It is. And Annie, you and your brothers and sisters are all growing up. I'm afraid this will happen much more quickly now to you and your friends. War does that to people. It's the real trials in life that bend us but make us strong. You'll see. We'll have to be strong, too, I'm afraid." She looked at her daughter—that patient caring look. Annie took a deep breath as she peered back. Then she looked thoughtfully and soulfully downward. She understood what her mother meant.

Thomas, the drayman, brought their black-covered carriage to the door. "Get in, children. Now?" With these pleadings by Momma and threats by Aunt Suellen, they were all finally herded aboard to begin the trip to Staunton.

Annie was the last to come out of their home. She had stayed indoors, roaming the rooms for one last look. Kath saw that her eyes were moist. She didn't speak as she stepped into the carriage. Uncle Wen kissed her good-bye. "You'll be back, Annie," he said softly. "And I'll be following soon. It won't be long. I think you'll find that living in a lovely town with lots of people will be a wonderful experience." He looked around at all of those in the carriage. "God bless you all," he continued. He then held Momma's hands and squeezed them gently. His eyes were soft. Finally, he gazed again at his niece.

Suddenly Annie gave a feeble smile. "I know, Uncle Wen," she said. "But it's hard to leave our home. We've lived here so long. I love this old house." Aunt Sue and Momma looked kindly at her.

They were to go first to Amherst, then by train to Charlottesville; from there, they would travel on another train to the Shenandoah Valley. Maggy and Dan, their big chestnut-colored horses, pranced and bucked as if they were anxious to be away.

Kath also found it a sad moment in some ways, but it was fun to be free and traveling farther than ever before. Uncle Elmer was there to see them off. Their fiery, pink-faced, good-bellied old uncle came from his home several miles away. He was to manage the farm in Papa's and Wen's absence.

Elmer had a shock of gray hair. His white shirt was soiled, and his collar askew and torn like fragments of cloth in a bird's nest. He had an utter lack of patience with female caution and logic. "With yor Pa away," he said, "you've certainly become sweet, unworldly women. Hmmm, what should we do about it? I'll have to write yor Pa."

"Now you just quiet yourself, Elmer," scolded Momma. "They're good girls. Now hush."

"You need a little toughening, Anne," he continued. "A firm masculine smell again will be good—a little sleek-oiled hair, tobacco, harsh voices, quarreling, and whiskey. Tell James I said that."

"I will, and Elmer, we need affection, not debauchery, so hush. I'd tan your backside if you were younger. Tell my sister, Joan, I said that. Write us soon—both of you. Now kiss me good-bye. We love you."

"You're a strong woman, Ann," he said. His cheeks were very red. "Good luck and God bless." He kissed them all. "I'll miss you, but things will work out." He waved vigorously as they left. Kath noticed that, for all his joking, he was serious now.

Their home was soft as a bird's nest. Momma and Sue made it that way. They didn't know then, but the toughening was coming. They would learn about war.

"We're off," Annie shouted as they left. "Good-bye, Uncle Elmer. Uncle Wen. Good-bye, Mary. Good-bye, Josh. Good-bye, all." They waved and threw kisses.

The children were glowing with excitement mixed with anxiety at leaving all they knew and loved. They forgot something their parents had told them: "Your home is where your family lives. You'll be surprised, but Staunton will soon be our home."

It would have the same gentleness they had always known. But there would be more. The war would pervade their lives. Not the battles, but the terror of the injured and dying, the ambulances, the tangle of heavy-laden wagons, the rivers of mud, the wagoners toiling and swearing, the anger, and the soot and dirt, would all be with them. This they would come to know.

As they passed the main gate of the farm, Kath turned and saw the big sign at the entrance:

DORIA

The Lynn Family

"Good-bye, old farm," Annie whispered. Again there were tears in her eyes. "Will our new home be nice?" she asked.

"We'll see," Momma answered.

CHAPTER VI
A Beautiful Valley

The roads were dry and dusty as the black carriage wound through seemingly endless woods and fields. Momma, Aunt Sue, Annie, Kath, and Dee sat quietly at first. Dee then broke the silence: "When will we get there? Momma, why aren't we there yet?"

Aunt Sue looked a little stern. "It won't be long now, honey. You'll love the train. And Kath, let Dee hold that other little dolly you made."

Kath resisted at first, but she saw that her aunt was serious. "Here, Dee. But you give it back. You shouldn't have packed all those dollies you made." Annie sat quietly, looking at the rolling countryside and the bright sky. She was aloof from the little squabbles between her two younger sisters. Their mother shook her head resignedly, but didn't speak.

They finally entered Amherst and reached a humming beehive of activity beside the iron railroad tracks. "God's nightshirts?" blurted Annie on seeing crisp uniforms and shiny gold braid. She shivered with delight.

"Look at all those handsome men," she said as she took several short, running steps toward a man with gold braid over his sleeves and flaxen hair. His eyes were deep and blue. "Momma, he looks nice." Her face was pert and fresh. He was fanning his reddish cheeks with a broad-brimmed felt hat.

"Hush, child," Momma ordered. "Act like a lady. You don't chase men that way."

"How am I supposed to chase them?" Annie countered.

Momma swallowed, then gave Annie a sharp whack where children are supposed to be whacked. "I'll spank you right here in front of all those boys, if you don't stop," Momma warned.

"I'm sorry," Annie smirked. "I don't know what gets into me."

"I do!" Momma said. She tried to be stern, but there was a faint look of amusement in her eyes. "Don't you worry, young lady, you'll get along," she continued. Kath heard this, but Annie didn't. "I've got to hold you

57

down a mite, but like bees to nectar, Staunton'll be your chance." Kath took a deep breath and smiled shyly. She understood what her mother meant. Dark hair, bright eyes, pursed lips, her sister, Annie, was lovely.

Annie's cheeks were fiery, and she had tears in her eyes. "Momma would have done it right there," she said softly. "I'd have been mortified. Wasn't she ever young?" Kath wasn't sure where Annie got the word "mortified," but she was sure that Momma never threatened lightly.

Annie's back was toward the handsome officer she had spoken about. Kath, though, saw him chuckle. She then noted that after he had finished giving orders to his men, he turned and looked at her sister. It was a very interested look. He started toward them, but he was interrupted by another officer with much gold braid. She thought it best not to mention this to Annie just then. She would tell her sister later on—perhaps in Charlottesville.

The family viewed hundreds of new soldiers who had "joined up," and who shared the prevailing desire to come to blows with the enemy. Almost all of them thought the war would end after a battle or two. Many would endure a seemingly endless trial of marching and waiting before they would taste the "thrill" of fighting. The Lynns picked their way carefully to the platform edge, and finally they were all aboard the thundering iron monster. Their trunks had been shipped earlier.

The day was very hot, and the surging crowds did not lessen the discomfort. Battle flags rippled, and the companies became aligned, as their officers shouted commands: "Attention. Right face. Forward. Halt. Now into the trains, quickly."

Men were directed to coaches, boxcars, and an occasional flatcar. A few scudding clouds streaked the distant blue sky as they began their trip northward. The men devoured cakes and other goodies received from generous women at each stop. The children also shared in these delights.

"Thank you very much," Dee and Kath said to a big man with stripes on his sleeves. He had huge, strong hands. The little cake he gave each of them looked like a small coin between his fingers. Fatigue finally overwhelmed these boys; they were still boys. They had traveled for days, and many now drifted off into troubled sleep.

They stopped once near a sparkling brook. Hundreds of men crowded out. Many bathed warm feet in the pleasant stream; others close by voraciously lapped up the cool water. Kath started to get up to do the same. "May I go, too?" she shouted.

Aunt Suellen was firm. "Katherine, you sit right there. Don't you dare get up."

Kath started to rise. "I'm going too," she said loudly. Her aunt's big hand came down hard, and her arm stung and was red for some time after that.

"You stay right there," Aunt Sue continued. Kath did. None of them left the train.

Packs of playing cards appeared as the train again lurched forward. Gambling was common throughout the war—card games such as keno, twenty-one, and poker were a frequent diversion. The game this day was poker.

Aunt Suellen, though, pointed out several nice young officers who were playing the old game of whist. "Children, it takes much thought," she said. "Two men play the other two. The best of the four cards played each round wins that trick. That's what each group of cards is called. See how each trick is whisked away by the winner. That's where the name came from. They then count up the number of tricks. Your Papa and Uncle Wen play it once in a while when friends visit. It's fun. And, as I said, it takes thought." Kath and Dee didn't look very interested, but Annie listened to every word.

Crowds outside shouted as the train went by. A few daring souls jumped off when the train slowed, to steal a kiss from pink-cheeked girls in butterfly-light dresses.

"My, you're pretty," a strapping man said to a glowing little thing on the station platform. "Bye-bye. I'll come back," he shouted as he jumped to the steps and caught the brace by the train car door.

"War's not so bad," he said, laughing as he walked down the aisle. "Girls are so much fun," he said to his friends.

"Why are girls fun?" Kath asked Aunt Suellen.

"You'll find out, dear," she confided.

The train ride itself was a novel experience for those aboard, and for the kids, too. Some soldiers riding in boxcars knocked holes in the sides of the cars. Now they could enjoy the adoring people.

"Momma, those are bad men. Look at the holes in those cars," Dee said.

"They're just boys, dear. I'm not happy about it either, but the army will probably fix it. I hope."

Later in life, Dee would realize this was also a practical solution to provide light as well as needed ventilation for the stifling interiors of the cars. At the time she was shocked as well as amused by this destruction. These soldiers rode along cawing and shouting at pretty ladies. Their heads stuck out of the openings like chickens in a cage. She later wondered if strong beverages caused some of this cheerful behavior.

In Charlottesville, they left the dazzling hordes of plumes and sashes. They were good men and would become real soldiers. "Good-bye, good-bye!" the Lynns shouted at the receding train.

With a wave and a cheer, the men had again started north. Heads were out of the train windows, like peaches in a store, as they returned the Lynns' calls. "Good-bye. Good luck," a hundred voices shouted.

"We'll get a Yank for yah," several promised.

"We'll get a hundred Yanks," another replied.

They were headed toward the Manassas Gap Railroad and then through the pass to the lower Shenandoah Valley.

Dee and Kath stirred impatiently while they waited for the train on the Virginia Central Railroad. This would be the final leg of the trip to Staunton. Up and down Main Street they ran. Momma and Sue looked frazzled and tired. Both occasionally spoke sharply to the children, but it didn't do much good. They had too much energy left inside.

This town, the home of the University of Virginia, is nestled among the red clay foothills of the Blue Ridge Mountains. It was named for Queen Charlotte, wife of George III. Roads wander out from the town, then wind among wooded hills, fertile pastures, and tilled land. In the spring, bright blossoms decorated the apple trees in the orchards. This lovely community was only lightly brushed by the war. University buildings were turned into hospitals. Also, other temporary structures were erected to care for the wounded. Sheridan later occupied the town, but little damage was done.

"Kath, Dee, come with me," Annie called. "Aunt Sue and Momma are all tuckered."

When boys weren't about, Annie, bless her soul, was often a picture of domestic responsibility. She sat with Kath and Dee beneath a big tree and read from a small book of stories about women who were threatened by mean men. People shouldn't laugh. These were read by the wagonful. They ended with a pretty young girl outwitting those bad persons.

Annie filled in the mean parts of the story with her own nice words like, "'I've come for the rent, the rent.'

" 'No, you can't have the rent, the rent.' "

She continued to read: " 'I'll tie you to the railroad track if you don't pay it all right now.' His voice was mean.

"He grabbed her by the arms and began to drag her away. Amidst her screams, she turned toward the barn and called for her brother. He was big and strong and angry. He had just arrived, breathlessly, from far away. She had seen his face at the window. He had been jailed unjustly for supporting his sister's claims.

" 'John, save me?' she cried.

" 'I will save you,' he said, as he throttled the bad man who was hurting his sister." These bad persons always suffered.

Kath and Dee later remembered Annie's saying "His face became twisted and blue, and he made terrible breathing sounds."

Both forgot the exact ending. The man was probably not completely throttled. It is likely he was finally taken off to jail after the sister produced papers she had found. They were often in an old trunk in the attic or within the pages of the family Bible or even somewhere in the barn. Needless to say, she "did the bad one in." He usually suffered terribly. If she lost the struggle, she died peacefully, knowing she was right.

These novels and short stories were a portrait of the deep, unspoken longings of women in the decades just before the war. They seem to have been a response to the resentment of strong male influence. Hawthorne wrote about " . . . public taste occupied with . . . trash . . . What is the mystery of these (books)?" Thousands of copies sold, however. In contrast, as war went on, women showed their real strength while their men were away. They weren't weak, consumptive creatures. The thrills of these "fairy tales" were no longer needed.

After a two-hour wait, the family finally boarded the Virginia Central for the final forty miles to Staunton. Their home would be in the green upper Shenandoah Valley. This was the luscious granary of Virginia. A harsh whistle signaled departure; a needle-fine rain began to fall.

"Will we get up the mountain?" Dee cried.

"I think we will," Aunt Suellen answered, "unless we have a flood."

The train continued to chug up the tiring climb to Rockfish Gap. They neared the pass.

"There's a flood out there, Aunt Sue," Dee said with tears in her eyes.

"There, there, everything's all right," Aunt Suellen comforted. "We'll be in Staunton soon."

They finally felt safe as they hurtled through the tunnel and pass and started down to the valley. The rain lasted the best part of their journey, but finally the sun burst through.

"How green and beautiful it is," Annie said to Momma.

"There's a golden mist over everything," her mother replied. "It is beautiful." She thought for a moment. "I can almost forget the drums."

"What drums, Momma? I don't hear any drums."

"Annie, I can hear them. They're very real to me!"

CHAPTER VII
The New Family Homestead

The engine chugged into Staunton. A shrill whistle sounded as the train came to a jerking halt. This is a town set amongst mountains. Round about are fertile fields, grazing lands, and acres of orchards. The streets in the town wind perilously, following the trails once used by Indians, wagon caravans, and stagecoaches. Old mellow brick and clapboard homes stand close to the sidewalks, with gardens tucked behind. Narrow streets climb from the business district toward residential neighborhoods.

Early in the war, the town was designated a remount, mobilization, and training center. With these functions it also became an army depot and commissary post, with warehouses, workshops, and arsenals.

Into a milieu of wagons, buggies, and carriages, the Lynn family was thrust. The sun was vigorously at work, trying to dry wandering rivers of mud from the heavy storm. Puddles of water etched the surface; mud spattered Dee and Kath as they stepped to the wagon brought by a stooped, gray-haired Negro employed by Papa. Uncle Jim was a free man, and they came to treasure his service and caring.

"I'm from your Pa. I'll take you children to your new home. We've had a mighty pour just now. Ol' Sallie'll have to pull hard."

Uncle Jim smiled and turned toward Momma and Aunt Sue. "Hello, Miz Ann Katherine, Miz Suellen. Welcome to Staunton. Master James is waiting."

They made their way slowly through the mudholes and soft churned ground.

Staunton was alive and humming. Wagons, deep in the mud, were moving west. "Look at all those wagons, Sue," said Momma. "There's not much out there, James told us. Just small towns."

"Jim, why? Where are they all going?" asked Sue.

"There're armies out there, Ma'am. All kinds of soldiers."

"Ours?"

63

"More of theirs, I'm afraid. They're coming this way. Ask Master James. He'll know. He said they're headed for our back door. Many soldiers in gray uniforms marched right through here a few days ago. Going out to help, I guess. Looked proud. Pink cheeks and a little fuzz. Most didn't even have beards yet. Just chillen. I hope nobody gets hurt out there." He smiled a broad, friendly smile.

Virginia was a cross-section of America in the mid-nineteenth century. The oldest traditions of the country lay within the boundaries of the Old Dominion. Westward was the rude frontier. The eyes of the people, both North and South, were drawn to this historic area between the Potomac and the James Rivers. Other regions seemed less important.

Gradually, however, people became vaguely aware that the beginning of the war was to the west. These campaigns would be fought by relatively untrained soldiers. The combatants in the early battles, however, fought from the heart. From these blundering actions, men would learn their trade. Such was the struggle in western Virginia, which was the Union's back-door approach to Richmond and a vital railroad connecting Virginia with Tennessee. Things went badly for the South in those Appalachian Mountains, where a great turnpike from the Ohio River ran southeast to Staunton.

The town of Staunton was named for Lady Rebecca Staunton, wife of colonial Governor William Gooch. As the new town grew in importance and population, crude log cabins were enlarged by the addition of a second story. Clapboard siding to cover rough logs improved decor. Native stone and later brick became common building materials.

With the dawn of the nineteenth century, architecture suggestive of the Greek and Roman Classical periods became fashionable in Staunton. These stylish homes and public buildings had stately columns, domes, and decorative pediments. Papa, however, seemed to prefer the Gothic style, with high-pitched gables and pointed arches. Later in the war, he showed his family a quotation from his records by the Victorian critic, John Ruskin. It denounced this Classical style as " . . . base, unnatural, untruthful, . . . and impious . . . in which luxury is gratified, and all insolence fortified . . . "

Aunt Sue, who was interested in sketching and later in painting, never agreed with Papa or with Ruskin. "Both are beautiful," she said to her nieces. "See the two styles, then make up your minds."

Ol' Sallie did have to pull hard. She plunged and strained up the wandering roads pulling the old squeaky wagon. Momma sat calm and satisfied, her pretty face gazing out at the town. She was frail and thin, with a few strands of gray hair curling down over her forehead. Her face was good-natured, but shrewd and commanding, yet having a dainty, impervious air.

The children sat quiet and apprehensive as their trip was about to end. Dee finally broke the silence, "How long, Momma?"

Annie chimed in, "Will it be a nice house?"

"Let's get there soon," Kath groaned. "I hope Papa's there. You said it would only be a little longer, Aunt Sue. Why aren't we there yet?" Her voice was whiny and petulant. She had forgotten that Momma and Aunt Sue were also tired.

Aunt Suellen was tall and somewhat stout; her bodice jutted forward like the prow of a great ship. A border of brown hair curled down at the sides of her face, hiding strands of gray. A fringed shawl covered her broad shoulders. She talked in a distressed whisper. "Be patient, children. We're doing our best. Uncle Jim will get us there."

The carriage strained through puddles amongst army wagons, loading and unloading supplies, and other vehicles with taut drivers cursing at straining mules, spattering mud far to the right and left, and churning the soft ground. Sallie was pulling hard.

"It's pretty up here," Momma smiled, as stores and other structures gradually became farther apart, and lovely oaks, beeches, and elms decorated the sides of the narrow, rolling streets. Stately porticoes, white-paneled fences, neat square hedges, yards lighted with brilliant yellow flowers, green shrubbery, and a sweet evening silence greeted their arrival.

Suddenly, "There they are," shouted Emmie, their oldest sister. She had gone ahead with Papa to prepare for the family.

Momma breathed a sigh of relief. "We're home, children!" She smiled at all of them, then patted Annie on the knee. "Thanks for your help, darling. You are growing up, and you're wonderful with your sisters." Kath and Dee didn't hear this. They were already out of the wagon hugging Emmie and Papa.

For all the sea of sticky mud, which spread around them like a churned animal wallow, their new home had a shiny face. Papa, Emmie, Mary, and Henry were so excited to see them that it sent pins and needles right down to the tips of Katherine's toes. Even Henry kissed his sister, which made her blush a little. She then gave him a big hug. "It's beautiful here," she blurted.

The new residence was a spreading brown-and-white clapboard

structure, with square white pillars bordering a large porch. Above this was a lovely Gothic window centered in a high-pitched gable and surrounded by gingerbread moldings. A white railing stood before the window at the outer edge of the roof that covered the porch. "It's lovely," said Momma. "Just what I imagined."

"Welcome home, Ann," James smiled to his wife. He took several deep breaths while he looked carefully at her. "You're more beautiful than when I left Doria several weeks ago."

"Don't look too closely. You'll see all my wrinkles," she said, laughing.

"We all have them, except the children. They haven't worried enough yet. Besides, your face is soft like the petal of a rose. Anyway, it's what's inside that really counts." His smile broadened. "Come see your new home. You, too, Sue. You're vivacious as ever." He squeezed their hands gently as he led them toward the brick entrance walk to the door.

The house was located a little to the southwest of town, just to the south of the Staunton-Parkersburg Pike. This historic turnpike led from the Shenandoah Valley to Parkersburg on the Ohio. It was the road to great rivers that led west. It traversed the crests of four principal mountain ridges—Rich Mountain, Cheat Mountain, the Greenbrier, and the Allegheny. These imposing ranges of the Appalachian Mountains ran northeast and southwest through all of Virginia. The two armed forces would come together in this forbidding watershed. Here they would fight for control of the mountain passes. Here men would begin to learn about war.

Many of Papa's friends living close by waved and shouted welcome to the family. Mister Robert Raymond, tall and gaunt, with well-trimmed gray whiskers, hurried up the walk. "Hello," he said, smiling to Momma and Aunt Sue. He gave them a little hug as if he had known them for years. "Welcome home," he continued. "Staunton awaits you. It's a friendly town."

Robert asked about their trip: "Was it exhausting? What about the delays? Were there soldiers aboard? Were they nice? Were the children good?" A few well-directed questions told much about their ordeal. His clothes hung on his spare frame like sheets on a line after a wind storm. He was kindly, however; later, they came to know his wisdom and moral strength. What a remarkable new experience! Never had they lived so intimately with others.

They went in a procession through the house that Papa and their sisters and brother had picked out. The dining room was a distance from the kitchen through a dark, rough-floored passageway. Momma shuddered at this, but Kath and her sisters giggled.

"This will be fun play," Dee called.

"Here, Dee, you can't find me," Kath answered, tucking herself behind a small chest.

"Stop it, you two," said Momma, frowning. "Take a look at your new home."

"The parlor's very nice, James," said Sue. "I love that old mahogany."

"It's been used," said Papa, "but it's still in good shape. Emmie helped pick things out. Henry did most of the carrying with Uncle Jim."

"The stripes are pretty loud," Sue continued. "You did a good job, though." Papa just smiled. "Ann, what do you think? Are the stripes too gaudy?"

"It's fairly dark in here, Sue. We need a little color. James, I think it's beautiful. You can decorate any time. Glad you have those little stools for the children, too. The embroidered covers are a little fancy for our brood, though."

"They should have something nice, too," said Papa, laughing.

"You children are to sit on those stools, quietly, and none of that running around in our best room," said Emmie firmly, with a trace of a smile. "And keep your feet off the furniture, too."

"That's the way, Emmie," said Momma. "They need to learn what's right. You can spank 'em a little if they're bad. Not too hard, though."

"She's still a child, too," said Mary sharply. "She better not spank me."

"Quiet, small girl," whispered Annie. "You'll probably need it. Emmie and I are both full grown now, so be careful."

"Now, now, children," said Papa. "Stop quarreling! Let's go upstairs. There's lots of space up there." He turned toward Momma. A smile crossed his lips. "Ann, wait till you see our room. It's bright and sunny as the sun comes up. Yours too, Sue."

They started up the stairs. Kath looked back at the parlor. This would be the place where the family would gather. They would spend many evenings in this lovely room with family and friends.

"What a handsome bedroom!" said Momma in a high, gleeful voice. "It is bright, even late in the day. It's lovely, James. I'm proud of all of you. Where did you find that fine four-poster? That's a treasure."

"Robert had it in the barn behind his home. Terrible shape at first. Henry and I refinished it. I'm proud of you, Henry!" Their brother nodded with pride. He didn't say anything—just looked happy.

"It's so soft and nice," shouted Annie, flopping down on the quilted cover of the bed. "Can I sleep here, Momma? You and Papa can use my room."

"Get off there," growled Aunt Suellen. "You need a good switching, young lady."

"Ha, ha. You'll get it," said Mary, smiling.

At the back of the house was a brick walkway with a covering roof. It was open on one side and had square pillars to support the roof. This was a sunny, warm place to read or play.

Papa had a new kerosene lamp in the front hallway by the stairs with a large, flat wick and glass chimney. This was carried to the dining room or parlor in the evenings. Later, the family had four such lamps. With the dawn of electricity, kerosene lamps would not seem so bright, but in the mid-nineteenth century, these gave off wonderful light—much more so than candles.

Gas lines were installed in Staunton in the 1850s. Though gas was not available to the Lynns on the far side of town, many streets and homes glowed at night with light from gas fixtures. What a thrill to behold, especially for children who had grown up away from these wonders!

It was summer. School was still far off, thankfully! Dee thought differently. "I wish school would start soon," she said. She was a student and loved lessons and reading.

"Oh, darn," said Annie. "I'm glad it doesn't. It's only July. I want to meet our neighbors, and I hope they have lots of sons. Yummee," she said, smiling. "I'll bet they're fun."

Annie was eternally interested in men. Her youngest sister, Dee, in contrast, loved words and ideas. She was the scholar of the family, and she would teach languages and composition in Augusta Academy in Staunton. This school would later be known as Mary Baldwin College. Momma and Aunt Suellen often read to Dee during long summer days.

Informal lessons went on constantly for all the children. The younger girls had McGuffey's Readers as frequent companions. Emmie and Annie worked with them over difficult spots.

A white picket fence surrounded the open yard behind them. A heavy wooden gate opened to a copse of woods beyond, a path that Papa would take on school days. The children would follow a little later. Other houses and neighbors, as well as a white-steepled church, were in that direction. Horses had chewed and gnawed at the paling around the house to which they were often tied when families visited friends or attended church.

That evening Papa spoke about the wagon train they had seen moving west. "Those are supplies to Garnett in the mountains," he said. "General Garnett was Lee's assistant, his adjutant, in Richmond, until a few weeks ago. I guess Lee trusts him. He's with the army near Huttonville now. There's much trouble there, I'm told."

"Where's Huttonville?" asked Sue.

"About thirty-five miles that way." Papa pointed to the west. "Not far. Not far enough, I'm afraid. His men are on Rich Mountain. In the passes. It's cold and wet on those mountains. Our boys aren't used to it, but they're needed. The enemy's getting close. They're just beyond Huttonville, I guess. I hope Garnett can stop them. Lee just sent four more regiments to him. They went through Staunton a few days ago."

"They marched with a gay step," said Emmie proudly. Her eyes were bright. "Mmmm! They looked nice. We were at the streetside waving and cheering, handkerchieves in the air. It was exciting. Officers bowed. Ladies leaned from windows and called to the men. Horses reared up and soldiers saluted and threw kisses."

"Young boys, but proud and tough," said Papa, smiling. "They came in by train. I guess they're ready. Lord, I hope so!"

A large field was just west of the copse of woods behind the Lynns' new home. It provided an open vista down to the Staunton-Parkersburg Pike, where army wagons were moving, even at dusk on the day the family arrived. Mounted soldiers rode close by.

Dee, Mary, and Katherine watched the wagon train for several hours that evening. "What a long line of wagons," Kath finally said. "I guess that's food for our soldiers."

"And gunpowder," said Mary. "For fighting."

There was urgency in the sound of cracking whips, the angry voices of drivers, and the shouted commands by mounted officers. Kath had a vague feeling of uneasiness as she watched them. She looked at her sisters. They, too, looked serious and surprised. "We can hardly see them now," she continued, as the sun was setting and the advanced part of the column disappeared in the shadows of the hills and mountains to the west. An army waited on those distant misty ridges. Men would fight to save their valley. Too many would die.

CHAPTER VIII
The Sight of Blood

Blindman's Bluff, I Spy, and Fox and Geese entertained them for hours. Then they crept quietly into the family parlor.

"That's my chair," Mary whispered.

"I was here first," Kath growled.

"Stop it, you two," Papa ordered. This wasn't whispered; Kath was so startled that she fell right off the stool. As she crawled quickly back onto it, she wondered if Mary had pushed her. It was still hers, though. A wry smile crossed her face, as she got ready for battle to defend it.

Dee, Mary, and Kath always competed for who would sit on the embroidered stools. Usually they then sat quietly. However, this evening Mary glared angrily, "I was here first. See?" Kath ignored her and held her chin disdainfully high. She then gave Mary a short punch with her fist.

"Katherine," Momma said. Her voice was firm. "Stop it!" Kath was instantly quiet. Momma would threaten only once. If trouble continued, she took swift action. The children knew she meant business.

Dee smiled. "You'll get it, Kath." Kath knew it. For quite a while, she was as silent as a worm.

The adults talked about the farm, politics, the expected battle in the mountains to the west, and other boring things. Momma spoke of their new neighbors. Kath sat dreamy-eyed, remembering their trip and soldiers and the excitement of flags and bands.

Feeling she was growing up and believing that what she thought made fair sense, she tried to elaborate a few ideas that had occurred to her during their recent travels. "I think trains should be run better. They're smelly and dirty." Her face was squinched. "And there's so much waiting. The conductor-man said most don't run on time, even without the war. Engines break. They have to stop for water. Logs are gone, to run them."

"Many use coal," Papa corrected.

Kath blushed and laughed inappropriately, not being sure her facts were correct. "It was fun playing," she continued, remembering the streets in Charlottesville. "The soldiers were nice; so were the people." She now divided her world into two groups, people and soldiers. The latter were different. She forgot they were mostly just folks, sons and fathers, who had volunteered for service. Her voice choked from shyness. "Maybe I can run trains when I'm grown up."

Henry glared. "You'll never grow up, Kath. That's for boys anyway. You're a girl. You stay home and clean. We'll do the work."

Kath glared back. Momma saved her, though. "Henry, hush. Kath has plans. Let her dream." She then spoke a warning: "Remember, Henry, we ladies can do more than just clean and cook. Be thankful we're willing."

Mr. Raymond pricked up his ears. "That's right. Ladies are able. Look at what your mother has done. She managed the farming while your father was teaching in Lexington, and she runs this house like a general. Also, she began a local aid group in town—what's the name, Ann?"

Momma didn't answer. She just nodded agreement.

"Careful when you speak, Henry," Mr. Raymond continued. He could scold their brother in a very gentle way. "With terrible war, we're lucky to have these strong ladies to carry on at home. They're the ones with sense. They'd probably stop the war, if they were in charge. Right, James?" Papa just smiled.

Emmie scowled at her brother, however. "There," she agreed. "He told you."

It was humbling and a little frightening for Kath when she realized all these grown folks had listened. Mr. Raymond, their kind neighbor, had listened intently. "You, my lass," he later told her, "for all your silliness, have a grain of good sense. Your mind bespeaks of some judgement and logic. You should delve into these qualities, my sweet young lady. You can go far. We need strong women. Your mother and Aunt Sue are fine examples of the way women should be."

Kath blushed a little, but it was nice to have someone say good things about her. Besides, a mind filled with fun, without thought or direction, was not what she planned. It would be a wasted existence.

After the war and after some years in school, she did go to work. It was not to a farm that she went. It was into the periphery of politics and into business. Many believed that a woman shouldn't be in business. Several childhood friends were violently against it. "Unwomanly work," they told her. "Our place is in the home." She was determined to be different.

Following schooling and a few years as a secretary, she learned a trade in Richmond. Andrew Lake was a businessman there. "Ladies shouldn't be in business," he told her. "However, you can write and add columns. You're hired." Kath accepted and shyly entered the offices of Lake Wood Products on the outskirts of the town.

Katherine later began her own store. Papa helped her with funds; others loaned money. Her business became a profession; ideas, new products, records, reasonable prices, attention to details, honesty, and interest in customers paid off. It was successful. It took time, though. Sticktoitiveness was her answer and the ability to see beyond the setbacks. Possibly the encouragement by their kind neighbor started her on this path. This would all be in the future. Their life in the Shenandoah continued.

The gardens behind the Lynn home were soft with color that July, spattered with marigolds, day lilies, daisies, and a variety of flowering shrubs. Bright green bushes climbed to the beeches and elms of the small woods beyond the paling. Gnarled vines were wrapped around the brick chimney. This was a great place for games.

"Where's Dee?" Kath would shout. Dee was smaller than the rest, and she always lost in their games.

"She's reading," Mary answered.

"Reading. Why? Dee, come on and play. Come on." She didn't. Dee's mind was in castles and beautiful forests. Early July passed quickly, cool nights, warm sunshine, dew glistening in the early morning rays, and Momma patiently organizing a disorganized household.

"They've been beaten; they've been beaten! It's terrible! Please help," their oldest sister, Emmie, rushed into the yard, shouting. Her voice was shrill and frightened, and the last few syllables hardly audible. "Momma, you must come! Please, Momma!" They all ran. Through the copse of trees, over the fields and down toward the pike they headed. It was only a short distance, and they soon saw the soldiers below.

Dee, their six-year-old, fell, then struggled to her feet with Momma's help. Her shin was bleeding, and a big scratch marked the side of her face. "You're not hurt bad, Dee. Wash it quickly, then fetch another bucket from the well. Hurry!" Momma had stopped long enough to see she was more frightened than hurt, then rushed on.

Their mother carried a bucket of water and an old clean sheet. "A full bucket," she shouted back to Dee. "Also towels and sheets—lots of them." This response stemmed from years of responsibility for all those on a working farm. She had cared for many sick and injured people.

"Oh, Jesus!" Momma whispered. "There are hundreds." They hadn't heard the sounds of cannons or the roll of guns, but here were the results of war. These were the walking wounded, straggling to safety. They had tramped for miles, in one's and two's and as disheveled herds, blackened with dust, wounds unbandaged, and the pungent smell of gunpowder from tired bodies. Sweat poured over faces. Clotted blood covered heads, clothing, arms and legs. Flies swarmed like locusts over the perspiring flesh and on the surfaces of wounds. "Oh, Emmie, I never expected this!

"Emmie, Annie, Kath, help those men. They can sit right there. Here, take this cloth." She had torn off strips from the sheet and wetted them. "Well, come on, start cleaning. Get all that dirt off." Kath had never seen blood caked in great gobs over clothing and skin. Her stomach twisted like an engine. "Kath," Momma shouted, "get started. Mary, brush off those flies." She turned to a young soldier close by. "What is your name, son?"

"James, Ma'am."

"I have a son named James. About your age. Now just sit peaceful. We'll help you. Sorry. I know it hurts. Mary, help that man; he can lie right there. Where is he hurt? Emmie, help Mary. For God's sake girl, don't be shy now! Roll him over. That's the way—gently. Annie, get Henry then rush and tell everyone you can find! We need help! Get more sheets—all you can find. Also water. Hurry, girl—please! These men need help terribly."

More and more soldiers arrived. Many staggered and a few fell by the roadside, mumbling, "Help! Please help us." Faces were pale beneath the darkened surface of black powder. Momma and all the children stopped for a moment. They were aghast.

Momma removed her shawl and Mary and Emmie their shoes and placed them beneath the heads of several of the more severely wounded. People came running from nearby houses. Whites and Negroes, both, stood in the hot sunshine cleaning wounds and faces, removing wood fragments and other foreign objects from bleeding arms and legs, ladling water into parched mouths, patting backs as men retched and vomited, brushing away flies, and binding wounds.

Many children ran home for more sheets and towels, and several adults headed toward town to find professional help. More water, much more water was needed. A number of the men were recognized by neighbors who came to help. These friends cried softly as several of these soldiers with little strength left, silently closed their eyes and died. Not many died without the supporting arms of someone who cared.

Most of the children were too fascinated to leave this wild scene.

They loosened clothing, comforted where they could, helped clean and bandage wounds, and even stopped to say a prayer. Momma's fresh, unprinted cotton dress was streaked with clotted blood and soiled with reddish valley mud and dirt.

"Is God punishing us?" Kath heard Momma say. She looked at her daughter. "Don't stop, child. More are coming." Sweat moistened the bodice and back of her dress. Wide, irregular rents angled across the sleeves and skirt. These had been caused by sharp thorns and twigs. The skirt was torn away, up to above the knee, to use as bandages.

The scene around them was not a picture of grandeur, as was the battlefield of Kath's fantasies. It was a distorted, freakish dream, filled with searing pain and terror, accented by the scent of soiled bodies, and the desperate cries for help. There was honor but little glory.

"Momma," Emmie mumbled. "Why? No one ever told us this."

The macabre cast of players seemed unlimited. Now came wagons and some carriages filled with those too hurt to walk. Trickles of blood had exuded to the floors and run out over the edges of the vehicles. This gave a ghastly hue to the already tragic scene. A friend found his son wedged firmly below the other soldiers in one of the carts. "He's dead. Don't remove him." Emmie saw tears in the man's eyes. His son couldn't be taken from the cart without disturbing the injured men around him. The boy's face was dark, and his mouth was distorted into an ugly grimace. The cart moved on.

"I wanted to fight," the man said. "It should have been me. It's terrible. Forgive me, John!" He followed his son into town.

"No one told me this, either," Momma answered Emmie some moments after the cart moved away. "This happens in life. We do what we can." She looked for a moment at what her daughter was doing. "Good job, Emmie. Now help those others. Press the cloth on that cut. That's the way. See the bleeding stop. Kath, don't run away. We're just starting. Help that man there."

They worked for hours. Carriages and wagons were brought. Men were moved from the road to shelter in town. Late that night, the Lynns crept into bed fully dressed and exhausted.

"Look what I have!" Emmie rushed in to tell her family in the morning. Her face was glowing. She proudly held out a red ornamental cord with a tassel. "Maybe I can find the owner. I'll bet he's handsome." She asked hundreds of men in the treatment shelters. She never found the owner, but it was an introduction to the man she finally married; it truly became a treasure.

For days, the children helped clean up the remnants of the scene by the turnpike. Dust and growing weeds and grass finally covered what remained. Cap boxes, toothbrushes, buckles, buttons, haversacks, spoons, and other accoutrements could still be found months later.

This service to others was not finished. It was just beginning. Staunton was filled with painfully injured and ill soldiers. Family, friends, officials, and children, rolled up their sleeves and continued working.

CHAPTER IX
In Service to the Land

In town, shelter was difficult to find for the wounded. Men lay in the hot sun for hours. A few died unattended. Medicines were in short supply with so many casualties arriving at once. Hospitals were very inadequate, and hundreds of the men were finally sent to private homes. Warehouses and barns were used, and doctors from miles around swarmed into Staunton. Pain and the cries for help continued. Many injured failed even after reaching the town.

Three young soldiers stayed with the Lynns. They were housed in a large shed, really a small cottage, which had been used by former owners for their house and yard workers. This was before the Lynn family had arrived in Staunton. Lieutenant Arnold had a severe leg wound that was swollen and raw. Private Snyder had fallen from a high rock. His head was swathed in bandages, and one leg was fractured. He also had small wounds on one cheek and on his left hip from shell fragments. The third man was disoriented from fever. The Lynns were unable to learn details about his regiment and family. His name was Harold. He coughed and moaned constantly. Local doctors thought he had pneumonia.

Momma tended these men night and day with Aunt Suellen's help. Both Emmie and Annie assisted. Emmie became very good with bandages and with encouraging these men to eat and gain strength. Momma taught both of them how to clean wounds with good soap suds and water. She then helped them with dressings and feedings. Kath washed faces and hands and held cool cloths on wounds and bruised parts. The men seemed to be gaining strength.

Working with Harold was difficult. Emmie's patience with feedings of broth, crackers, and cool liquids seemed to be helping his recovery. He talked more sensibly as she spoke kind words and ideas.

Momma heard the lieutenant calling in the early morning hours one day. Harold had suddenly died. It was a sad moment for the Lynns. He was buried in a small cemetery near an old farmhouse just beyond the city. Kath would never forget this moment. Papa said kind words, and Annie had written a poem. The lieutenant and private were taken to the services in the old wagon driven by Uncle Jim. The family and neighbors helped them walk to the graveside.

A few days later, both Lieutenant Arnold and Private Snyder went to one of the local hospitals. It was in an old warehouse. The whole family often visited the two soldiers. Mr. Snyder later came to their home and read stories to Mary, Dee, and Kath. He had been a teacher before the war.

Besides these stories, the Lynn children watched the militia, played games, shelled peas, cleaned carrots, helped with bandage washing, and gazed with wide eyes at the tired, less-seriously-injured troops in the city of tents just west of the town. Canvas shelters, fire spits, straw mattresses, and grim faces met their gaze.

These men limped about, chewed bites from huge tobacco twists, mended with thread and needles, talked, and read crumpled letters from loved ones. Small and later larger groups began drilling and marching. Canvas-covered wagons, tents of various shapes, and spits over smoking fires were set about. A few tired nags stood nearby. A scraggly old tree gave sparse shade in the hot sunshine.

Momma, Aunt Suellen, and the older sisters helped with the nursing in the hospitals. They also made dressings and rolled hundreds of bandages. They told about the demise of many who had passed swiftly and quietly. Others had died amid agony and pain—gangrene, lung infections, blood poisoning, measles, fever, nausea, diarrhea, mangled faces, torn arms, amputated stumps, the pain from limbs no longer there, the fright of losing a leg or an arm. These terrors abounded.

It is hard to realize conditions in the mid–nineteenth century. Medicine was primitive. People didn't have screens on windows, and terrible infections were frequent. Lazy flies swarmed about, rancid smells permeated the air, red streaks marked limbs, bright knives cut into painful flesh, and the kindly but firm doctor would say, "Son, it has to be taken off!"

"No! Please. No. Not my leg!"

"You'll die if we don't."

"I'd rather die. Please, not my leg."

"Your family needs you, son. We have to do it. I'm sorry."

Anesthetics were often in short supply, even in the early days of the war. The pain must have been terrible. There were so many injured and sick. Some died unattended even after those first few trying days. The doctors worked night and day. Amidst this horror, Emmie sneaked away one day. She was sick at heart. "I can't go back, Momma," she struggled to say.

"I don't blame you, Emmie. It's hard. This you'll have to decide for yourself."

"They played the 'Dead March' so often," she said, "it made me almost scream. All those poor men! It hurts, Momma. I can't return. I just can't go back and face the others."

"They need pretty women, Emmie. Especially when they're sick."

Emmie was ashamed. She stayed home for several hours, then returned. Years after, she remembered saying, "I gazed on pale faces through a mist of tears."

Kath's sister, Mary, told them a few evenings later, "There were hundreds of soldiers at the train station. They were all sick and had a funny gray color. Many were on the ground. Others could hardly walk and had bandages all over, with boards on their arms and legs. Eeeh!" She squinched up her face. "It was smelly." She had gone with Momma and Papa to pick up Uncle Wen. He had stayed to help manage the farm, then had come to Staunton by railroad.

"Ghastly faces," Momma elaborated. "Most were so pale and weak, it hurt to see them struggle. It was unpleasant, as Mary said. These boys were being sent to Charlottesville and Richmond for care."

"Uncle Wen and I helped them board the train," said Papa, smiling. "Aunt Sue and Momma stayed out and held hands and encouraged. Real angel work. They're better at that than we are. However, no special train cars were used. Just ordinary passenger cars. They're not very comfortable for sick men. I'm sure the trip was hard."

Emmie and Annie continued their work at the hospital. They washed faces and limbs, helped change dressings, fanned perspiring bodies, brushed away the flies, patted pillows, and wrote letters home. Linens, bloody bandage strips, and dressings, all were saved, washed, ironed, and reused.

"I just hate all this silliness—bandages and things," Annie would complain. To see her in action at the bedside, though, was sheer magic. She could wrap men around her little finger. Emmie and Kath heard Annie's smooth voice one day, "Why, Lieutenant, I just love walking with handsome men."

"I'll bet she does," Emmie mumbled.

"I'll go with you," said Annie, smiling, as she coyly twisted around to help him stand. Her white shawl moved delicately in the sunlight. "Here, lean on me, sir; your leg is still sore. That's better," she continued.

"She looks like a spider," said Emmie, her voice filled with sarcasm.

"You've found nice friends, too," Kath replied. "I've heard you and Momma talk about those friends."

"You're right, Kath." Emmie laughed. "Especially that Billy Kramer." Her eyes became distant and thoughtful, and a trace of a smile crossed her lips.

This hospital work finally became a happy hunting ground for affectionate young ladies. Quickly, bonds of friendship were formed. As the men could walk about, limping and unsteady, a soft round shoulder was a blessing. Gradually the soldiers became dashing figures again. Uniforms were mended, cheeks regained color, and smiles were pervasive. Jokes were heard, and pretty girls bustled about and made much fuss about "their men." Male diffidence melted under this shower of flattering attention.

Walks began beneath stately trees with pretty girls in flowered dresses. Demureness was hidden by glowing faces, colorful bonnets, swishing fans, and delicate scarves of pastel colors covering pale shoulders. "I love you" was not an infrequent promise. The younger Lynn children would sit back and giggle.

"Why, Sergeant, I'm surprised at you. I'm just helping where I can, sir."

"I'll bet she's just helping," Mary would whisper from behind a deep thicket on moonlit nights. "She has claws like a cat. She's been waiting for him for years."

Many of these young people were later married and lived happily. The Lynns saw the beginning of these travels, as the clinking of spurs and the soft voices sprang delightfully from the shadows cast by a bright moon. All this again occurred, as it had before the war. There is love and passion in the human heart, and human beings are resilient. They recover. They go back to their work. These men went back to the fighting.

Although men from the defeated small western Virginia army had straggled back for days, the organized units were intercepted, rested, and ordered to strategic areas in the Allegheny Mountains. The community to the west, the small town of Monterey, had also seen the devastation of war. They had responded just as compassionately.

Other folk in lonely houses along the highway had done the same. Men received assistance and kind words. Women on these farms had stood with pails of water and ladled patiently to tired soldiers. These strong people had dressed wounds and encouraged and cared for those too ill to go on. When death prevailed, remains were placed in family plots, and loving words were spoken. Theirs was an endless day of binding, cooking, feeding, washing, and lifting. Because of these fine people, many sick and injured survived, and they would fight again.

The war was still sacred to most of the people. The rallying cries went on. Orators spoke of noble purpose. One fiery politician from Richmond helped say good-bye to those in Staunton who had died: "Neighbors and friends, good people of Staunton, we are here today to bless the remains of proud young men. They gave their lives to protect this valley, and they paid grievously for their efforts. Many lie within the soil close by. We thank them for their caring."

The speaker's face was florid and his voice resonant. He continued: "These men were sons and fathers of our countrymen. Their proudest moment was in service to our land. This valley provides the fertile soil to feed our people. Railroads close by connect with friends to our south and west. They, this soil and those rails, are vital to our efforts. . . . Great causes give a breath of life. Breathe deeply the air of freedom. Self-denial, discipline, work, and service lie before us. We must gird ourselves for further pain. With patience, though, we will prevail. God bless you all!"

The speech was magnificent to hear. The man was rotund and polished. His black coat and string-tie moved as he strode before the crowd. The real reasons for war—pride, money, and economics—were hidden within the elegant phrases. Appropriately, a band began to play on the far side of the audience as several wooden boxes were carried away for burial.

"That's Handel's 'Dead March' again," murmured Emmie. "I heard it night and day at the hospitals." She was shaking her head slowly. "It's so sad."

"It's beautiful, but, as you said, it is so sad," answered Momma. "If it just didn't mean what it means; if it were just music, we could enjoy it." Momma looked kindly at her daughter. "Emmie, you're a gentle person. You try not to inflict pain. Nothing is so fine as women who show real strength. I'm proud of you. Though we ladies hurt inside, we do our work as you have. Thanks!"

The fighting continued.

CHAPTER X
The Children Meet a General

Papa spent much time training militia units in the fields southwest of Staunton. This work had begun when he reached the town.

"You can watch, children, but keep out of the way."

"It's fun, Papa. Can we march behind? We're practicing, too."

"No," was the answer. "We need these soldiers. You'll disturb them." He hesitated, then continued with a teasing smile, "Especially if you're better than they are."

Each Sunday, a parade was held. Many neighbors attended. The first time Kath and Mary watched, an officer forgot the proper commands, and the boys walked right through a briar hedge. "Halt!" their father shouted. He had fire in his eyes.

In stark contrast to these bright militia uniforms with plumes and sashes were the patched gray uniforms of companies now bivouacking in the open fields just to the west of their home. From their officers the Lynns heard about the trial they had faced.

"It was hard in the mountains," related Lieutenant Gilbert. "Rain, mud, sleet, frozen ground. A number of my boys became sick with fevers. Plain old measles with many. Young men away from their ma. They're like little children. They need you ladies," he said to Aunt Suellen and Momma. There was a pained look in his eyes.

Major Randall also told them about these trials. "When General Garnett reached western Virginia, he found his troops in desperate shape. Poorly armed, equipment and clothing missing, discipline terrible. Even so, as the Yankee regiments approached, our men had to be rushed to the passes on Laurel Hill and Rich Mountain, twenty miles beyond Monterey. A call for volunteers turned up only a few new men. Twenty-three to be exact. Not many patriots farther west, are there?"

"Not many?" answered Uncle Wen, shaking his head. "I'd 'uv thought there'd be more."

Most persons still don't realize that when Virginia left the Union, a majority of her people west of the Alleghenies dissented vigorously. Western counties announced they had nullified the ordinance of secession. Little sympathy was expressed for what they called "Tidewater aristocracy." Now, as real battles were imminent, few of them were disposed to "join up."

Garnett had 4,500 troops in those mountains. Half of these were in fixed places. This reduced his ability to move quickly. Lee, in Richmond, had dispatched the regiments that were available. They had marched proudly through Staunton, as Papa had mentioned before. Lee wrote to Garnett, ". . . . if he (the enemy) can drive you back, (he) will endeavor to penetrate as far as Staunton. Your object will be to prevent him, if possible. . . . "

At this time, brilliant George Brinton McClellan arrived on the scene in command of the Union forces. His divisions of Midwesterners advanced to a position just north of Garnett's troops. Southern intelligence was atrocious in this forbidding, barren country amongst the people of the western counties.

Using a stratagem learned from Lee in Mexico, at Cerro Gordo, McClellan used an undefended, narrow path to the crest of Rich Mountain. He attacked the battery there on July 11; the Confederate troops retreated. The road was open to march rapidly on Beverly on the twelfth. At Shiver's Fork on the Cheat River, in a rear guard action, Garnett was killed. Many under his command were captured. Monterey and the road to Staunton were only a few days' march away from Beverly.

Few organized Confederate forces remained to resist invasion by the Union troops. Twenty miles from Monterey was the railroad that led directly to Staunton. Several days' hard marching would have placed McClellan in the heart of the Shenandoah Valley.

"They'll be on top of us soon, right here," said Major Blake who was in command of troops in the Staunton area. He was tall with smooth red cheeks. "Those boys in the camp by the woods can't help much today, but they will soon. Seein' folks in town has given them some courage. They still need organization, though. Also, they're still exhausted."

"Major, you'll need my companies. They're almost ready," said Papa. There were deep lines in his leathery face from years in the sun.

"That's why I'm here, James. We need your men. And those boys by the woods too. They'll be used. They'll be ordered out in a few days."

James Lynn's militia companies marched off two days later to the sound of several drums. People in town waved and cheered, but a few wept. Many of these men were from Staunton. They stepped jauntily off, shoulder-to-shoulder, for the western mountains. They were handsome in their bright uniforms. Papa had trained them. He did not march with them.

On paper, McClellan's invasion of the Shenandoah Valley was not only possible but likely. However, maps didn't show the atrocious roads and barren land. Fortunately, no army, as James, in Richmond, later told his family, could make such a lengthy advance and still supply itself. The people in the Valley didn't know this. All available soldiers were vital.

Several days before the militia departed from Staunton, word had come of another battle, a great battle, to the east where the Manassas Gap Railroad met the Orange and Alexandria. This was a place called Manassas Junction. Nearby, a little stream known as Bull Run Creek ambled sluggishly between the contending armies of partly trained patriots.

These Southerners had stood to resist the presence of armed foreigners within Virginia; those from the North had advanced "to cause the laws (of the United States) to be duly executed. . . . " The battle in the end had been decided by troops from the non-slaveholding part of the Shenandoah Valley. Many of these men had been trained by the sober-faced ex-mountaineer, General Thomas Jackson.

The newly titled Army of the Shenandoah was not commanded by General Jackson. Lee had ordered General J. E. Johnston to that post. Thomas Jackson's First Brigade, later the immortalized Stonewall Jackson Brigade, had marched eastward out of the Valley with this army. "We marched through woods and brush and over big rocks and loose stones. It was a hard march, especially with a full pack and weapons," wrote Marc, Emmie's friend in the Eleventh Mississippi. "We led the climb to Ashby's Gap in the Blue Ridge. What a struggle. Long after midnight we reached the eastern side. We then fell to the ground and were instantly asleep. At dawn, we continued down. At Piedmont Station, we boarded the train for Manassas to join Beauregard."

General P. G. T. Beauregard, who had ordered South Carolinians to open fire on Fort Sumter, was in command of the Confederate Army at Manassas. To Manassas had come the Army of the Shenandoah. United, these armies were formidable. On Sunday, July 21, 1861, General Irvin McDowell, commander of the Union forces, had ordered Northern regiments to attack. A full-scale battle began.

It was a hot, sultry day. Many men lost heart, but most dug in their heels and fought. Union divisions struck the Confederate left. Here, where it was needed most, had come the Valley army. The First Brigade came up as broken Confederates stumbled back. General Bernard Bee shouted to Jackson, "They're beating us . . . !" Bee and Jackson had been fellow cadets at West Point. "Sir," said Jackson, "we'll give them the bayonet." Bee turned to his defeated men and shouted, "There stands Jackson like a stone wall. Rally round the Virginians. . . ."

Marc wrote, "Old Bory made good preparations while he waited for the Yankees. The captain told me they were near perfect. The General was considering a big attack from behind that little stream (the Bull Run) when the Yankees came at us. Thank goodness we didn't have to attack. We were near exhaustion after being rushed up to our lines. We saw plenty of fighting then. It wasn't fun. There was smoke all over. We couldn't see the enemy. Other Southern regiments were retreating. I'm not sure who they were. Jackson knew. Suddenly we saw the Yankee line coming at us. I think I killed several Yankees. I'm a pretty good shot. I only got a skin cut on the arm. It's small and healing. Not all our boys were so lucky. Our company lost twenty men."

General Bee was mortally wounded in that battle. McDowell's forces, however, were driven back. After great suspense, there was wild rejoicing throughout the South. The people of Staunton had helped many wounded a few weeks before. Now they wondered how badly families farther east were affected by the many injuries from a much larger battle. Still, the South had triumphed; they hoped the war was nearly over. They were wrong. It was just beginning.

"We finally won, thank God," continued Marc. "Old Stonewall made us stand up and fight. He's tough. We're heroes now. I had to tell someone about this. I'll write you again soon. I'm not sure where we're going next . . ."

General Thomas Jackson, now affectionately known as "Stonewall," had stood with his well-trained troops. They helped carry the day. His men finally appreciated his rigorous demands. His brigade was a proud group even after the war. Besides Marc, Kath later knew several other men who were with Jackson at Bull Run. Billie Palmer told her, "He trained us for battle. We quickly learned war is not just parades. Jackson knew when to stand and fight, when to go forward, and where to hit the enemy. He was a good soldier."

Anna Jackson wrote to Ann Lynn: "Word from the front was impatiently awaited by me and many friends here in Lexington. A letter was received by our pastor, the Reverend Dr. White, of the Presbyterian Church. It was in Tom's familiar hand. He didn't mention a word about the battle. He wrote, 'Dear Pastor, In my tent last night, after a fatiguing day's service, I remembered that I failed to send you my contribution to our colored Sunday school. Enclosed you will find my check for this object. . . .'" In God's good time, recognition finally came to this dully earnest professor.

Prior to the war, the husband of Anna's youngest sister, the fourth Morrison "girl," commissioned paintings of all the sisters and their mates—all except Jackson. Perhaps his portrait was not worth the expense involved. Before Manassas, few people recognized ability and greatness in this man and soldier.

The Lynn children had spent days watching the training of militia. They, too, had learned many military commands. With fence pickets for weapons, they could order-arms, shoulder-arms, present-arms, about-face, right-face, rest. They were good at rest—sometimes disappearing for a drink of water or to do other things. "Squad. Attention!" Mark, their fourteen-year-old neighbor, shouted. "Kath, get back here. We're just getting started."

"Oh, all right," she replied, returning reluctantly. It was a hot day.

"Right—dress! Front!" Mark continued. "Squad, right wheel. March! Halt! Squad, right—face! Forward—march!" They all faced right, then the even numbers stepped quickly to the right and forward so two children were marching abreast.

"Keep step!" Mark shouted crisply. "Keep step. That's the way Squad. By file left. March! Now double quick, through the woods. Mary, don't walk into that tree."

"I won't," she replied. "But you directed us there."

"Quiet in the ranks," said Mark.

Into a field he led them. There, they began to display their skills to real men in gray, who had lost their fervor for war, after facing the violence of a real battle. These men were worn and discouraged. Many were still sick. The children, too, looked ludicrously bedraggled. Yet, in late July, a high-ranking officer was with these soldiers. He watched the children march.

"Halt!" Mark shouted. Dee stumbled into Kath, who then gave her a very mean look. Mark's face was immobile. "On the right, by file into line. March!" he commanded. "Right—dress. Front. Attention! Load at will. Load! Squad—ready. Aim. Fire!"

"Bang, bang," they all shouted.

"Reload!" Mark continued. "Now charge!" They ran forward. Halted. "Bang, bang!" they cried again. They then lay stretched out on their backs, loaded, rolled over, fired, and charged again.

"What regiment is that?" the general called.

"The Eighty-fifth Virginia," and officer answered, with a wink of his eye.

"Three cheers for the Eighty-fifth Virginia," the general cried.

A hundred voices gave them a rousing cheer.

Their friend Lieutenant Randall came over a little later and commended them. "You boys and girls have done more for morale here than a thousand politicians. That's General Lee himself. You did yourselves proud." The children were thrilled. Kath would always remember Lee after that. There was something about his bearing and appearance and voice that gave one courage. He was like a guiding light in a rainstorm. She had always expected greatness to look like greatness. Lee certainly did.

Kath noticed another fine quality in Lee that day. He had empathy for his men—the common soldiers. He would talk to them and listen. He heard their worries and troubles. She didn't think much about it at the time, but she could always recall the kindness in his voice. "Boys, you're becoming soldiers. You've been beaten and you're sick. It takes time to get well, but you will."

"General, suh, we were hungry up there—and cold. And many of us had no rifles."

"I know, but the enemy's close by; we must stop him. I'll do my best to get you those guns and powder. You must do the rest. What else do you need?"

Can you imagine the effect this had on morale throughout the war? He worried about his soldiers; they knew he cared.

Lee headed west. These men soon followed. Lee rode to Monterey, a small village just to the east of the main ridge of the Allegheny Mountains. The citizenry of Virginia thought Lee would be in direct command of western troops. This was not true. The *Richmond Examiner* of July 31, 1861, correctly reported the nature of his assignment: ". . . . a tour of the

West. . . . His visit is understood to be one of inspection and consultation of the plan of campaign."

Though much was expected of Lee, his mission was only to advise and create harmony; he was not to direct operations. It was an impossible mission, people later learned. Authority was divided among several pretentious general officers. Regiments were widely scattered. Also, in a letter to his wife, Mary, Lee wrote, "It is difficult to get untrained people to comprehend and promptly execute the measures required. . . . " Even professional soldiers, touchy and envious, were loathe to move quickly.

Needless to say, in these remote mountains and valleys, with only the authority developed through Lee's tact and patience, what happened gave no hint that one of history's consummate soldiers was there "commanding" troops in action. Also, this region, which can be heaven itself for breathtaking mountain beauty, tore the elements apart to find the worst of rain, fog, and hail. Roads became impassable. Typhoid, measles, and other fevers decimated the ranks of young soldiers. Lee's first campaign ended ingloriously.

Papa's militia boys fought with Lee. "They were strong," Papa said. "But that doesn't stop bullets." He found it difficult to tell loved ones about their sons. "I'm sorry, so sorry," he struggled to say to one father in town. Kath heard this. She saw they both had tears in their eyes.

Lee attributed failure to the weather and to the will of Nature. He did not criticize the inexperience of nonprofessional soldiers, the reluctance of professionals to move quickly, or the unmended quarrels and jealousies between powerful political commanders. Also, though it was not then realized by most patriots, he was still learning his trade.

He accepted severe criticism for this campaign by politicians, the newspapers, and private citizens. Though badly stung, he made no public reply. However, "critics began to call him 'Granny Lee.' " Had Providence willed that he disappear after this western campaign, he would probably have been remembered by history as a qualified officer whose potential was never realized.

CHAPTER XI
A Planter's City

The oil lamp on his desk flickered and cast dark shadows over the letter he was writing. James's eyes were tired, almost closed. He struggled to stay awake. It was still noisy outside and dark. The gas street lamps in other areas of the city were not found in this neighborhood. He could hear several drunken voices singing in the distance. Richmond in wartime abounded with rootless people—shady characters, adventurers, spies, thieves, soldiers on leave, and lesser bureaucrats—all kinds of men. They were out searching for the pleasure houses with cheap whiskey and other stimulating pursuits.

This east end of town was rundown in appearance, with warehouses, tobacco factories, liveries, slave markets, marginal businesses, and less prestigious homes. The more prosperous shops and residential sections were farther west. As James looked through the window in that direction, he could see Richmond's churches and the Capitol on Shockoe Hill in the moonlight. They seemed to sparkle like castles in the sun. Broad Street rose up the side of the hill, accompanied by the Richmond, Fredericksburg, and Potomac Railroad tracks.

James had traveled to Richmond by the Virginia Central line, arriving at the depot on the southwest corner of sixteenth and Broad Street. This was not as fine as the Broad Street Depot for the other railroad. It was a modest wooden building. Momentous events took place there, though. It was a strategic line going north, then west. It connected important battlefields in the Shenandoah Valley and the Virginia Piedmont with the heart of the Confederacy, the capital. Around these ribbons of steel, great armies would march and fight. To protect them, many men would die.

James decided early that it was less costly to live in the old section of the city. His boarding house was up high on Church Hill. The room was small but adequate. Even with early autumn, it was still very warm, and the breezes of late day were barely felt.

This was a planter's city, and "baccer" for years had been carried here by canal boats and wagons to be processed and shipped throughout the world. He liked the tangy smell of tobacco in the air, and warehouses were everywhere along the James River. The pleasant smell, though, was dampened by the sour odor of the outdoor privy houses just beyond a fence separating a once-lovely deep-walled garden from an open yard beside James's room.

He loved Richmond though, with its shade trees, brick walks, green front lawns, changing clouds dappling a blue sky, slant-roofed houses, iron grillwork, vines and ivy on mellowed brick walls, and roses and other flowers tucked below double balconies overlooking walled gardens.

The long-time residents sensibly rested during the heat of the day. They stayed in cool wide halls on pallets laid directly on the floor. Many houses, especially in summer, were darkened from early light to dusk. As the breezes came up from the James River late in the day, the ladies again promenaded along the streets and visited the military camps for the big event of the hour—the daily review. Their bright dresses billowed in the soft flowing air. The grim business of war still wasn't felt by all, and the soldiers were like cavaliers and knights to the adoring people.

James shook his head sadly. "I wish I were marching off with those regiments around us." He thought for a moment. "But they're not marching off either. Since we fought that battle at Manassas, not much has happened. Our soldiers are bored with camp life—the guard duty, the picket-rope watch, roll call, outraged lieutenants, punishment. All that foolishness. No wonder people are complaining about inactivity. So are the soldiers and the politicians. They all want to march north and drive the enemy back where he belongs.

"Poor Walker, though. He's taken the blame. But it's the president who sets policy. And right now we're still on the defensive. Davis should leave the war to the generals. But most people think it was because Leroy Walker did nothing. I never envied our recent unhappy secretary of war. He sure wasn't trained for the job. It was a political appointment." James chuckled. "Our office was run so badly, though, that it was almost funny. And that was his fault."

James hesitated a moment, thinking. "But despite all this, Secretary Walker was still able to organize an army with Lee's help and find enough guns for the men to fight with. And he won the big battle at Manassas. He literally started with nothing and did a lot for our people. He deserves some credit. Much more than anyone gives him. Now Benjamin's in charge of the War Office. Things are more efficient, but he's no general either. At least his letters are shorter. Thankfully, we have Josiah Gorgas in ordnance. He's a genius. He's starting to get things going for making rifles, powder, and cannons—what we need to fight with. For a transplanted Yank, he's amazing."

James pulled the desk drawer out fully, almost dropping it on the floor. "Damn! Where's that other pen? This one's broken." He searched through the drawer, which was filled with scraps and papers. His watch was hanging from a hook above the desk, ticking away like a cricket by a stream. "Here it is," he smiled.

James had been writing a letter to his family. He still had a bit to finish, and he was also waiting for word from a lovely friend who he hoped would invite him out to one of the finer places in town. He could hear a train arriving in the distance, probably crossing the Richmond and Danville bridge now. He also heard shouts and swearing by workmen on Rockets Landing, unloading the cargo from seagoing vessels. He could visualize the open-sided sheds nearby filled with wagons and carts and jammed with cargo. "I hope those rifles arrived," he mumbled to himself. Horse-drawn omnibuses rattled along the streets below.

He put his head close to the paper and continued to write: "I've been laboring at the War Office," he told his family. "I copy dispatches, troop orders, assist with correspondence, run errands for senior officers, and answer angry commanders as to why supplies aren't available. All kinds of unpleasant jobs. It's dull and frustrating. So many things are beyond our power to correct. How do you obtain rifles when we only manufacture a limited number of them? And we've worked desperately to alter old flint-locks for percussion caps. We're short of pistols and swords—and so many other things. Even ordinary wagons and harnesses are a problem, and transporting supplies along our dirt roads, especially in the rain, is very slow. We're gradually getting things done, though, but the paperwork and long lists are terribly boring. It's hard to fortify a new country against an invader who has unlimited resources.

"I'd rather be in the field and fighting. Then I'd be a real soldier." He thought about the daily reviews at Camp Lee a mile or so to the west. "Those are the heroes these days," he said to himself.

"I drill with the militia during my few free hours, but this just tantalizes me. I'm reading about tactics and strategy. I want to put these skills to use somehow. How can I? They tell me I'm needed here. I do come in contact with high-ranking officers occasionally. Even with President Davis on rare occasions. Trains and train schedules are becoming my special interest. Captain Jarvis, my boss, says this is very important. Possibly it is."

James continued to pour out his heart to his family:

> I heard about General Lee the other day. There are rumors that he'll be sent to our southeast coastal area to develop defenses. What a distinguished-looking man! Some now wonder about his skills, though, and others call him Granny Lee after his losses in western Virginia. I think he's a statesman, however, as well as a fine soldier. He's on his way to Richmond now, I believe. Not much was accomplished by him in the Allegheny Mountains west of you.
>
> Lee speaks softly, but his ideas are sensible and concise. I saw him often until his tour of the West. Few truly understand his ability. I hope Davis will use him in a military command. Up until now he's only been an advisor to Davis and to other officers in the field. No real authority. Well, back to mundane things. I spent this week again on long lists. Today I'm an expert on shoes, large and small. We have big feet here in the South. Not sure what this means—probably many folks don't wear shoes much.
>
> Soldiers march through Richmond; their officers only complain. This is the "puzzle of logistics," professional soldiers tell me. Where the money comes from to buy big numbers of guns and equipment, I don't know. By some means, foreign or otherwise, money seems to be found. I hope the fighting goes on till I can be in it. It's the real soldiers who are admired by our people!
>
> Rails, which carry our men east and west, baffle the Yankees. This is my one important activity. We have the power to take valuable property from the railroads and use it to supply our men and more regiments. The best strategy for the South may lie in this power. We can move troops quickly from one field to another. We have fewer men. This allows us to use them more effectively, and concentrate our regiments where they're needed most. We did this at Manassas. I hope our generals will use this on other fields. By shorter interior-lines, we can beat the enemy. Woe to us if those Yankees learn to attack everywhere at once. Also, woe to the owners of the railroads. They may lose a great deal.
>
> I enjoy the sights of Richmond. They're ennobled by the Virginia state capital. What a beautiful building, especially when seen at sunset. It's proud and dignified. As a lawyer, perhaps I will someday serve as a delegate in its chambers. This building was conceived by Thomas Jefferson from the Classical style of the Maison Carrée of France. It is as fair a thing as e'er was formed. . . . It's so exciting to see a fine creation by one of our own people!
>
> Late in the day it captures the sunlight like fine marble. The white columns and stately portico become a delicate pink color—so beautiful.

The marble statue of George Washington sculpted by Houdon stands inside. I understand it was made in France from drawings and sketches. How amazing!

Several days ago, I stood on the portico of the Capitol between those great pillars and looked out at the countryside. The James River wanders and winds below like a big serpent, forever watched by many beautiful and some ugly buildings—especially where I live. Green hills and forest stretch out to the horizon. The shores of the river, however, have become scarred from both fortifications and industry. The latter is active in Richmond. We're making guns, cannons, boats, wagons, uniforms, bricks, carriages, milling flour, manufacturing and storing gunpowder, and many other things.

From a distance, mostly everything is pretty. If you look closely at our alleys and back streets though, there is much trash, with dust and bad smells. We have great numbers of soldiers housed close by. Many are careless and throw old bottles, paper, and bits of food anywhere and everywhere. Most conduct themselves decently. However, a few do not. Liquor is easily available, and some become indecent and combative. Several murders have occurred here.

We still have many wounded soldiers in hospitals. Homes were used at first. Private citizens cared for bloody, filthy strangers. They gave good care, except, some men told me, they had their faces washed twenty times a day. Fine ladies learned to look at terrible wounds, and clean them, and listen to the groans and cries at night. Gradually we've become professional, and real hospitals have been created from old warehouses and new wooden buildings. We need space for hundreds and hundreds, maybe thousands, of badly hurt men.

Also, we were all surprised that war means prisoners. Gray-haired Major Wilder is the provost for the city. People are afraid of him: especially his pugilists who do his dirty work. He's turned a tobacco factory and warehouse at twenty-fifth and Main into a prison. Blankets and furniture were hard, but we did find them. Those men aren't very happy, though. They marched proudly out of Washington only to end up behind locked doors. "Those are the fortunes of war," I told a nineteen-year-old private. "We'll get you yet, Reb," he replied. "But thanks for the blankets." He smiled then, and shook my hand. Well, love to all from your somewhat bored son, James.

P.S. Tell Kath, Mary, and Dee that a portico is a nice way to say porch; they needs sum lernin'. And tell them it's about time they wrote. Also, tell Emmie and Annie about the many lovely ladies I see in Richmond. They have a new coiffure with the hair parted in the middle and rolls on each side. That should make Momma and Aunt Sue envious too.

James folded and sealed the letter as he looked about at the contents of his little room—a bed, really a cot, a wash stand, a small dresser, his trunk, a shelf for his books, and a broken mirror, which was good enough for seeing if his beard was well trimmed. "She should be sending word where she is," he said, smiling. "I hope she's all right." He visualized Sarah, his new-found love. She had dark hair, parted in the middle, deep blue eyes, an oval face, bright cheeks, and a beautiful smile. Her rounded shoulders were pleasant to lean against—and touch.

There was a soft rap on the door. "I have a message for you, Master James. From Miss Sarah. She wants you to meet her."

James rushed to the door. "Hello, William. Thank you for coming. I was worried. I hope she's all right."

"She's all smiles, just like you are, Mr. James. But it's all wet out there from the rain this afternoon, so you'd better not wear those good boots. I have a carriage outside. We'll go there now." James changed quickly and put on his most formal coat. He'd been made a lieutenant recently. As he quickly looked in the mirror, he thought he was fairly handsome in his gray uniform. He hoped she would think so, too.

William drove the carriage to Main Street. There were many fine shops, boarding houses, offices, and government buildings there. Sarah's father, Howard A. Robertson, was a counselor for the Tredager Iron Works in the basin just north of the river. James had met Mr. Robertson at the War Office and been invited to his lovely home for dinner. He and Sarah had spent some time in the garden behind their house. It was pleasant there, with trees, flowers, and painted metal benches. She looked a little like his sister, Annie, with a radiant smile and flashing eyes. She had been educated at a nearby small school for women. She knew much about her father's business of general law and his work as counsel for the company.

They were stopped briefly by Provost Wilder's men. James's papers were in order, but he was a little nettled that the provost guard didn't recognize him. He had met and talked with these men several times before, and a month ago he had arranged for providing new weapons for the provost service. "Perhaps they purposely want to antagonize the populace," he said wryly.

They then drove on to the coffee house. "They're not very friendly," said William. "Master Robertson didn't have his papers one time. They were downright nasty to him. At least they smiled at you, when you found what they wanted. Well, here we are, Master James. She's inside."

James stepped quickly from the carriage to the brick walk. "Thanks, William!" he shouted as he entered the open door into a short hallway.

"I'll be back for you both in an hour," William replied.

James pushed through the swinging, wooden doors at the end of the hall into the darkly opulent coffee house with pine-paneled walls and bright paintings of men on horseback and ladies in ruffled dresses. A friend, Mary Echols, was with Sarah when James entered. They both burst into big smiles as he approached. They were having tea, and it was cool inside—much more pleasant than his lodgings.

"What took you so long?" asked Sarah. "And your boots. Look at them. They're muddy." She smiled again. "Did you tell William to return? Our mothers will be furious if we're not home by half-past ten." He looked at the hems of their dresses. They also had walked in the mud. They both laughed when they saw that he had noticed.

"Mary and I were at the Spottswood," continued Sarah. "It's a beautiful hotel. Last week you asked about what people said there during that battle at Manassas. Those women all laughed. 'It was glorious when we won,' they told us. Your new boss, Judah Benjamin, was with them. He sipped wine and enjoyed the day. He said he couldn't help things anyway. And being a cabinet member, he often received reports about the battle. For a while things didn't look good. He told the ladies how the rest of the cabinet were huddled like worried dogs. He said that Secretary Walker damned his office and his fate in front of everyone." She laughed, saying, "Now Benjamin's replaced him, hasn't he, James?"

"Yes. And he's much better organized, and we're getting a lot more work done. I was at the office the day of that battle. We shuddered when each report was received. Most were bad news. Our left flank was being driven back and back. Thank the Lord we finally won!"

"Then the whole city came alive," said Sarah. "It was wonderful. Our prayers had been answered. We wouldn't be a nation if they hadn't been, I guess. Parts of Virginia, though, are still in those Yankees' hands. I hope our army will push them back where they belong."

Mary listened. Her face was serious. "It was the first time I was ever truly afraid. I'm sure it wasn't the fear our boys felt, though. Some have told me they forgot the danger when they charged among all those shouts and cries. In contrast, we women sat there and worried. We were afraid that not only our brothers and fathers and friends might be killed, but that the careers and fortunes of our entire family might be taken away. Everything was at stake. Everything we had worked for. Then came the words:

'It's a great victory . . . We won. We won!' This was followed by: 'Dead and dying cover the ground.' Thankfully, this was impersonal. John, my brother, couldn't be dead. Or could he? No torches or bonfires were lit that night. It was much quieter than earlier celebrations. There was a feeling of thanks as well as sincere gratitude. It was a peculiar contrast of great excitement and deep emotion.

"No marchers filled the streets. Everything had been at stake, and others had determined what would happen. My family and I just prayed and gave thanks. I remember my mother giving me a big hug when we received word my brother was well. She had tears in her eyes, and I knew why."

James smiled compassionately. "I guess I sensed that. There was much happiness, but most of us knew the war wasn't over. The Yankees were back in Washington, but no one was following them. We lost a great chance. Perhaps we could have ended the fighting then, but we didn't. Our soldiers in camps around the city still believe this. So do our politicians. The policy had been for defense. Not attack. It's sad."

"Hush, you two," said Sarah. "Enough about fighting and killing. James, tell us about all those shoes you've been trying to get. Our men's feet must get sore." He felt her gently touch his shoulder, and he saw she then placed her hand on top of his. It was a warm, pleasant feeling. He blushed when he noticed they were both smiling at him, but he told them what he knew. Then they talked about the Tredegar Iron Works, which was the most important manufacturer in the Confederacy—of cannons, machinery, steel equipment—all kinds of things. Suddenly he saw that Mary was carrying one of those little books like Annie, his sister, was always reading—about women. He decided he'd better talk about other things than guns and supplies.

James opened his mouth ready to compliment them both for their lovely dresses and beautiful hair, when a young lady suddenly began to play the violin, accompanied by an older man on the piano. "We'd better by quiet," said Mary. The music then soared around them like a warm breeze. It swelled to heights, then descended to the depths, in singing, beautiful tones.

"That's the 'Andante Concerto in A Minor,' by Bach," said Sarah. "Words can't describe its beauty, can they?" James just smiled. "That's her father. He's a minister, I believe."

"Yes, and she's studied for years. Women are not often allowed to play in public," said Mary. "Thankfully, we can share her great gift occasionally—as we're doing now." She laughed shyly, as if this was something women shouldn't say to men.

"Things will change," answered James. "Probably not as fast as you two would like, but I can see them changing now—in my own home, here, and perhaps in other cities that I've visited. You women aren't only passive doves. Like my mother and aunt and sisters, you're strong people with deep thoughts. And kind hearts, too," he added, smiling.

"Well, thank you, James. I've always wondered why I've liked you. You respect us women, and you're not just looking for love."

Mary seemed pleased, while his face reddened. "Love and loving are two different things," he replied with a roguish twinkle in his eyes.

"Well, Lieutenant Lynn, you surprise me!" Sarah tried to look stern. "We ladies don't talk about things like that."

Mary just smiled. Then she giggled, but didn't speak. James wondered what she was thinking.

Sarah suddenly asked James, "Lee didn't do much in western Virginia, did he? He's even lost the people out there. They're going back in the Union. What's happened? Folks are angry. Not only are our armies here on a 'slow boat,' but so are our other armies in the West. I suppose, as Mary Chestnut said, we shouldn't ask 'awkward questions.' She also said that our generals just 'dilly-dally' while the Yankees get ready to fight. That man, McClellan, whom Lincoln's hired is making a real army up north."

James thought for a moment and looked serious. "I still admire Lee, and he really wasn't in command out there. He had no specific authority. His only means to effect any action were to use tact and reason. The generals in real command were mostly political appointments. When General Wise turned over his command to Floyd, and after General Loring arrived, there were sufficient troops for a limited offensive, I'm told. But supplies just weren't there. That's partly my job. The railway head was seventy miles to Lee's east, and the roads were narrow and knee-deep in mud. When wagons broke down, everything was held up. What we've had here with the rain today is just a shadow of what Lee faced. The Yankees also had retreated farther west, so it was almost impossible to reach them and carry out an extended action. That campaign was lost before Lee arrived." He smiled at both Sarah and Mary. "This is fairly confidential information; so don't speak about what I've said. It'll probably be in the papers soon, though. Also, I believe Lee's on the way to Richmond."

"It's almost ten-thirty, James," said Sarah, smiling. "We'd better go.

But we'll stop at the Metropolitan Hall on the way home. And see what's playing." She spoke softly but with authority. "You said you'd take me there later this week. You did, didn't you?"

"I did. I certainly did."

"And thank you, James, for the good tea and cakes. They were very special. It's nice here, isn't it?"

"It is nice!" agreed James, smiling. "And it was fun. Thanks for inviting me." He turned his head. "And you too, Mary. I've enjoyed being with you both."

Sarah suddenly looked serious. "Some time you better tell me that I needn't worry about that powder magazine just north of my home. We've been told it's too dangerous to store powder near the river where it's manufactured." Her face looked honestly worried. "My father said if it blows up, we won't have to worry about Richmond any more. We'll go up with it." She then laughed and looked hard into James's eyes. "We'll fly like birds," she continued.

"Don't worry. It's safe. And it's well guarded as well as some distance out of the city." The ladies weren't so sure, but in a way, they really didn't want to know the answer to the question about an explosion. He then looked a little less intense. "I'll take you both to the Metropolitan next week if you'd like. Or to the Marshall Theater. The Marshall'll be real theater, not just music. A man named Irving is doing Shakespeare there. *King Richard the Third*, I believe."

"James, either would be fun," Sarah answered.

"Let's go to the play," said Mary. "Two years ago I saw Edwin Booth's brother, John, in Shakespeare's *King Richard the Third* here in Richmond. He was fine, but Papa told me it was nothing compared to his older brother, Edwin. The year before, Momma and Papa had seen them both here in *Hamlet*. Edwin was marvelous in the lead, they said. John went almost unnoticed. He's a handsome devil though, that John Wilkes Booth."

"He certainly is," said Sarah, smiling. "Like a dream. Chambermaids at the hotel here tore his bed apart just for the thrill of making it up again. And women all over the city followed him around. Poor man."

"I wish they'd follow me that way," replied James, laughing.

"Oh, pooh. You'd be too solemn on that stage. You'd probably forget your lines anyway when you saw all those lovely ladies sitting out there beyond the lights," said Sarah.

"Now I might just fool you if I went into acting. I'm from a long line of Shakespeare enthusiasts." He reached over and touched Sarah's arm, then smiled. "My mother and father both quote from his plays. I grew up hearing them. I often listened to Papa emote while he shaved: 'Now is the winter of our discontent made glorious summer by this Sun of York . . .'"

"The timbre of your voice tells much about your skills, James," said Mary, laughing. "Ah, but Edwin. I did see him as Richelieu once." She closed her eyes. "What a wonderful voice and magnificent profile! Years ago his father, Junius Brutus Booth, did his first play in America right here in Richmond. And that *New York Times* writer, Badeau, did a long column about the family, and their home near Baltimore. He went with Edwin to the old homestead."

"Does the family still live there? They've been one of the great theater families in America—and in England, I believe," said James.

"Most have moved away, Adam Badeau told. He was alone there with Edwin, except for the folks who worked the land. He talked about Booth's eyes and that wonderful voice. He also told of Edwin calling from the garden with Sir Edward Mortimer's words: 'Adam, come hither.'

"They washed at the pump, then Hamlet did the breakfast honors with wonderful grace, Lear washed the tea-cups, and Romeo made the bed. Suddenly Booth stood high on his toes, and Cardinal Richelieu's 'curse of Rome' was hurled from his lips. They discussed at length the meanings and interpretations of certain dialogue in the plays, and Badeau often disagreed with the actor. On the stage, though, Booth is transformed, and all the delicate and precise meanings are spoken with a divine fire."

"Well, Sarah, from what Mary said, we have to go to the Marshall. And it'll be exciting. And it is *King Richard the Third*, I hope."

The drive home was pleasant. He was squeezed between them in the carriage. As they laughed and talked, he kept thinking that their perfume was delightful.

They took Mary home first, then went a few blocks farther to Sarah's home. "Here we are, James. Will you come in?"

"Sarah, I'd better not. It's late, and I'm not sure your mother will be very friendly if I visit now. It's been a wonderful evening, though. Mary is a fine lady, too. If my brother Henry visits, perhaps he can meet her. He's a nice young men, even if he is my brother."

"I'll meet him first," said Sarah. "Maybe I'll find him more desirable than you." She, too, had a twinkle of fun in her eyes. She laughed. "If he's like you, though, I think Mary will be most favorably impressed."

William had driven the carriage around to the barn behind the house and was unhitching the horses. Suddenly James held her tightly in his arms, murmuring unintelligible words into her hair. She wrapped her fingers tightly to the sides of his chest and kissed the angle of his cheek several times. As she leaned back in his arms, the moon brightened her face like a flash of sunlight. He smiled as she laughed. "We're silly, James," she said. "But I do like you so much." As James brushed a strand of hair away from her forehead, he saw moisture in her eyes.

"How was I ever so lucky as to find you?" he blurted. His hopes of military prowess were suddenly spilling away like sand in a windstorm. He didn't want to leave her now. Richmond was becoming a better and better place in which to spend the war. "Our lives are wrapped together," he said, smiling. "Perhaps it's fate that we're all mixed up in this big, unending war—and it's not over. We're young, though, like our country, and things will work out. I do love you, and I'm sure we'll find a way to travel together. Won't we?"

"May our dreams come true," she said. Her eyes were deep and dark in the shadows of a lovely big tree. The light of the moon danced around them like sunlight on the water of a pond. She hadn't really answered his question, and he was about to ask it again.

A voice suddenly came from a window of her home. "Sarah, is that you?"

"That's my mother," she said.

"Come in immediately. You're late, young lady. It's about time you were home." The magic was broken. They clung together for another moment, then Sarah turned and walked quickly up the brick path. "Good-night, James," she said softly.

"I love you!" he whispered as she entered the door off the porch. "Some dreams last forever, I hope. I worry that a soldier can't be endlessly away from the battles, however. Can I live with myself if I am? I'm not sure.

"I still have other business tonight, though." He chuckled as he remembered. "It may even be pleasant business. Lil is having trouble with the authorities—Wilder's men. I promised I'd be over. They're going to close her up if she stays open too late. I better find out what late means. It's a dusty door, but there's pleasure inside. Well, none of that tonight. I'll just sip a little wine from behind that Parisian screen in the purple parlor. And watch her lovely ladies until she can see me." There was a dreamy look in his eyes. Madam Rawling provided a fine list of services for the sporting men of the community. She also had good whiskey as well as lovely women. He laughed. "I'll just look and enjoy."

CHAPTER XII
Letters from Richmond

Kath's brother, James, labored at the War Office. His letter of October was received in November. It was read to the family before a blazing fire in the parlor. The cooler days of autumn were now turning the green foliage to a brilliant yellow and red. The misty mountains around them were a purple-gray, the tops just lighted by the pink of the setting sun.

"It's a long letter," said Aunt Sue. She read it aloud.

"Dear family," Sue read, "... I copy dispatches, troop orders, assist with correspondence, run errands for senior officers, and answer angry commanders as to why supplies aren't available . . . ."

"That's dull work," said Papa. "No wonder he tires of it. But we all have to do it. And we gradually learn about the business. And war is a very big business."

"I hope he doesn't have to join the fighting," said Momma. "The army can use his law skills better in Richmond. And, maybe the militia training will satisfy him. You, too, Henry. We need you here. And we don't need heroes."

"Ah, Mother. You want us to be men, don't you? It's the real soldiers that people are proud of. That's what James said. And he's right."

"There are many other professions to be proud of, Henry," said Mr. Raymond. "And you don't have to be killed or try to kill others to gain respect." He hesitated a moment. "I'm glad he mentioned Lee. We've all been a little disappointed with what he's done. I understand he boarded the Virginia Central here just a few days ago. He looked a little grim, I was told. He should be. I hope James is right that he's a capable soldier. We'll find out sometime. We need good generals."

Sue continued reading the letter: "I enjoy the sights of Richmond . . . the Virginia Capitol . . . What a beautiful building . . . perhaps I will someday serve as a delegate in its chambers . . . ."

"Yes, the Virginia State Capitol is a beautiful building," said Sue with a smile. "James has a little poetry in his soul when he describes it. I hope he can someday be a delegate there. We'd be proud. But about the wounded, we know about them. We've seen them right here, haven't we, Ann?" Momma nodded in agreement. "By the hundreds right outside. We certainly know what the people in Richmond went through. And now we know about hospitals, too. We're learning, but it's hard to see men so ill. I never thought, though, about prisoners. Perhaps it'll be a real problem before we're done. I couldn't take care of them, however. I'd be too angry."

"You'd do it," replied Momma, smiling. "Down deep, you have a great big heart, Sue. And they're just boys like our men."

Sue read on about the portico and other facts in James's letter.

Kath's cheeks suddenly became very flushed. "What happened to you?" asked Papa, laughing.

"I'm angry," she said. "I know what a portico is. He didn't have to write that."

"Write him and tell him what you think," said Mr. Raymond. His words were so soft and kind that Kath couldn't help smiling.

"I will!" she replied. Inside she was trying to decide how to write a mean letter, though. As the others went on talking, she was thinking of all the bad words she could use. The letter was never written. She did write a friendly note a few days later.

Kath worked in Richmond some years after the war. She remembered James's words about the uncleanliness of the city. This surprised her then. From her view, now that she was older, the city was clean and sanitary and pretty. "It was the war and all the people," she decided. "But, homes and public buildings still have those little wooden shanties behind, with a half-moon on the door. In the hot summer, these do add to the, ah, odor. No one talks about that much. It's just expected. Maybe that's what my dear brother was referring to."

Momma and Aunt Suellen were intrigued when James spoke about the new coiffure with the hair parted in the middle and rolls on each side. They then gently patted their own obstinate locks. In later letters, he "reluctantly" said that he enjoyed "the pastel complexions of all the elegant ladies in swaying crinolines. They are surrounded by a most pleasant aura."

"I believe he's referring to their smell—perfume, I hope," said Emmie, laughing. "I'm sure it excites many poor soldiers, including our fine brother."

"It's supposed to," replied Mary.

"Is that why it costs so much?" asked Mary.

"No," said Annie. "It's because it's imported, silly. And you stay away from my perfume. I saw you trying it on the other day."

Kath was twelve now and only slightly aware of the strange interest of men for women, and of women for men. She wondered why her brilliant brother whiled time away on such trifles as girls. The sisters knew he loved them, but it was always in an aloof and superior manner. *One's life is such a brief gleam,* she thought, *he really should be involved only in more serious matters.*

When older, she came to realize that nature is remorseless. Basic instincts often control us. Also, perhaps, James was lonely even among fellow soldiers and a circle of friends. "People may philosophize as they like," she said to herself, "but loneliness is a bad experience." She knew about loneliness then. It happens to many in business.

After the war, she had the pleasure of meeting one of James's female friends in Richmond. She was a grave and determined woman with an emblazoned smile and firm discipline. She was no emerald-throated dowager, but a full-bodied businesswoman named Lil Rawling. Kath could then relate to her knowledge of the buying and selling of commodities. Lil was considered to be notorious. She had a coterie of lovely young women who tactfully provided a high standard of services.

Kath wasn't too concerned with ethics, but, like most well-bred young ladies, she had a passionate curiosity about "bad" folks. Lil's hair was bleached, shiny, and woven into heavy chignons matted over the neck. Her cheeks were well-rouged, and her dress was a conservative black. Full seductive bosoms peeked out above a lace flounce. A painted spangled fan hung from her wrist by a velvet ribbon, and gold earbobs tossed as she walked.

Such women, sought and patronized by men, were always mysterious to ladies. If mentioned, they were talked about by innuendo, euphemism, and hushed voices. Meeting her opened an exhilarating new realm of thinking about male-female relationships for Kath. It was a little horrifying at the time. She wondered how men could rummage about for such establishments.

Kath had noticed her mother squinch up her face and sigh as James's letter about scented aura and swaying crinolines was read. Momma softly whispered, "I hope he escaped the grasp of these women!" Years later, Kath realized he hadn't. Even Momma spoke about the Lil Rawlings of this world by euphemism and whisper. Momma did understand these male longings. "Men aren't monsters of depravity," she would say. "But nature is remorseless; the elemental passions of the human soul remain unchanged."

Lil outlined for Kath the perplexities of her trade: " . . . balancing of budgets, keeping records, providing compassionate and attractive companions, being a mother who kisses away the tears, repairing and maintaining properties, dealing with authorities, arranging secretive appointments from prominent guests, decorating the plush green and purple parlors, and providing good food and fine wines."

Ah, these problems Kath, then a businesswoman, could relate to. Confidential entrances and secluded alcoves hidden by Parisian lattice-work screened customers from prying eyes on these very private occasions. Tactfully, Lil's butler acted as Cupid. When a lovely Venus was seen, he arranged for meetings in comfortable upstairs rooms for her guests.

James blushed shyly late in the war when Emmie asked him about Lil Rawling by name, mentioning that she understood Lil was a business acquaintance.

He laughed. "Of yours?" he countered. "I hope business is good." What a wily thing for a brother to say! She stared at his pleasant smile, hoping to conceive a witty reply. Her loss for words seemed to cause a twinge of conscience. "Really, Emmie, you make a man feel positively wicked!" There was a twinkle in his eyes as he spoke.

James continued to keep his family aware of the changing events and directions of the war. Many letters were written in late autumn and through the winter. "Lee is now commander of the Southern coast defenses," he told them. "This is a difficult, perhaps impossible problem to solve for that vast shoreline with its sandy islands and intricate waterways. I'm not sure what he can do."

Lee did his job thoroughly that winter, as citizens finally realized. He developed a strong defense, which endured until near the end of the war. The region was finally conquered by Sherman, who approached from the west, not from the sea. Port Royal and Roanoke had been lost to earlier blunders, but most of the inland towns and cities would now be safe from armed invasion.

During Lee's absence from the storm center in Virginia, the Union high command trained and equipped a great Eastern army. The North had learned that easy victory was an illusion. The folks in the South were also tragically aware of this lesson.

On Lee's return to Richmond in March of 1862, few Southern victories could be cited to bolster sagging Confederate enthusiasm. Great areas of the Western theater had been captured by the Union. Forts Henry and Donelson in northern Tennessee had fallen to a relatively unknown soldier, Ulysses S. Grant.

James wrote his family about this.

Albert Sydney Johnston is in command in that theater. Not only did we lose those forts, which are on major rivers from Kentucky into the deep South, but, also, we lost a small but important battle in eastern Kentucky. Our men were led by Generals Zollicoffer and Crittenden. Zollicoffer was killed and their small army just dissolved. It doesn't sound important, but this was the anchor for our whole Western line from the Allegheny Mountains all the way to the Mississippi. A Virginian, General George Thomas, was the man who beat us. He's a Bluebelly now.

We have lost Missouri, too. The battle was near the southwestern state line at a place called Pea Ridge—one of those back-country places. It was a hard fight, and our men spent an uneasy night on the battlefield. When the Yankees came at them the next morning, ammunition was gone and our troops had to retreat. McCulloch, another of our generals, was killed there.

Another loss is Roanoke Island off the North Carolina coast. It was taken in February. Yankee troops attacked us from the sea. This is only a haunted, sandy swamp, but it has meant that many of our little ships and boats along that coast are being gobbled up like mice.

With all these defeats, we are now literally surrounded. All western Tennessee has been lost except for a few fortified places along the Mississippi. Grant's actions were especially devastating, as I've said before. I wonder if Lee remembers Grant from the "old army"? Before the war, Grant returned to civilian life "under a cloud," I'm told. Alcohol is said to be his problem. He's a soldier, though. He can fight.

The South would hear more about this unsuccessful peacetime officer.

James's enthusiasm was at a low ebb in late March:

The South's arsenal seems almost bare. Gunpowder is gone, rifles are needed, and we're still desperate for factories, even though some machinery is in place in buildings here in Richmond and will begin operating soon, I hope.

Our Eastern commander is J. E. Johnston. He's also retreating, and people are really upset, including the politicians. He moved his army south to the Rappahannock early this month. This is away from, not on the way to, Washington. Now his troops are marching through Richmond toward the peninsula between the James and York Rivers. The new defense line is at Yorktown, and not far from the capital in Richmond. Certainly not far enough. It seems McClellan is transporting much of his Yankee army down there. Their ships and boats and transports seem endless, I'm told.

This, plus Union soldiers near the mouth of the Mississippi River, really does mean we're surrounded . . . We've had one small success over the last few months, a victory at Ball's Bluff on the Potomac. It isn't much.

A terrible battle would soon be fought near a small country meeting house, Shiloh Church. The South would almost win that day. It would be a draw with both armies exhausted, and General Albert Sydney Johnston, the Western commander, dead from a wound. He laughed when a bullet tore the sole of his boot. The second one cut an artery, and no one stopped the bleeding. He was laid on the ground while medical help was called— which came too late. Finally, his Confederate troops withdrew all the way to the border of Mississippi. This was an important Union victory.

"Granny Lee" was back at the storm center. He was still an unknown entity. He was a military advisor "under the direction of the President," a degrading administrative position. This, at a time when the South cried for leaders. In retrospect, people would later learn that Lee, even in an obscure position with no command authority, by suggesting rational minor decisions and actions to President Davis, was able to affect great events.

CHAPTER XIII
The Spring of '62

The days were becoming warmer. The long nights were giving way to the shorter nights of springtime. Drenching rain came often. It was 1862. The dazzle and sparkle of those early days of the war were gone. Gray uniforms showed wear and frequently were covered with patches and mends. Butternut and Union blue were the mixed coverings for many of the soldiers. The latter were from dead and captured Yankees. Leather belts and holsters were tarnished and scuffed, but the men who wore them were alert like panthers and proud.

Gone was the capricious manner and festive parade-look of men home for leave. They were now bronzed and lean, often with mustache and beard. They walked with a certain casual demeanor that you see in those who have been in battle and survived. As Mr. Raymond said, "They have been to the mountain and come home." The Shenandoah Valley was still a relatively unravaged granary for the South.

"The Tamble son, Richard, is home," said Aunt Sue. "He was badly hurt, but he's gradually getting well. Thankfully."

Annie smiled. "He's handsome!" She closed her eyes as if dreaming, then shook her head. "But he can't sleep well. He aches and hurts too much. He arrived home with his arm in a bundle of bandages and a sling, and he still walks with a crutch. His arm and hand are still almost black. The arm was terribly broken. I saw it when his ma changed the dressing. And a piece of a shell hit the leg. 'Clean through,' he said. The leg got better fast, but the arm's taken some time to heal. He fell off rocks when he was hit. That's how his arm got broken."

"I wonder how Annie knows so much?" Kath said to Aunt Sue.

"Perhaps she's visited Richard's home more than we know, Kath."

"Leave it to Annie," Kath mumbled.

Richard stayed with his family one street away. Fever had complicated his illness, and his dark eyes were at first pits in a grim face. He was tall and haggard, with clothing disarrayed and a coarse beard. Youth, though, heals quickly. Kath didn't see him for several weeks. She suddenly realized he was laughing and square-shouldered again, and his beard was neatly trimmed. Pride had replaced longing and indolence. The conceit of new recruits was quickly deflated when they met him on the street.

Richard later spent much time at the Lynn home with Kath's older sisters. They were now expert at pleasing and taking care of the wounded. One evening he told them, "War's not much fun. I can hardly remember how often I've lain in the open fields at night trying to sleep. Afraid. And hungry. Above me were the stars—bright and pretty. The beauty was gone when it rained, however. When your blanket is soaking, you're also cold. It's no fun to lie there and shiver, and have no place to get warm. It was even hard to get a fire going when it poured. I didn't know this when I joined up. I do now. War is dirty and awful. I think I'm pretty good at it, though."

Gone was the old boastfulness and enthusiasm, and Richard's stories tapped a deep vein of passionate feeling in members of the Lynn family. They learned later that he had been mentioned in dispatches. He was a good soldier, and he survived the war. Finally, he joined the regular army, fighting Indians and pushing the frontiers west.

The days were now routine and unexciting. Momma volunteered with Aunt Suellen at the Soldier's Aid Society. They scraped lint, made bandages, helped sew drawers and shirts, and packed healing-stuff. Together they both went shopping one day a week, bringing home bolts of cloth and dry goods, vegetables, flour, and other foods, which on the farm were often provided from their own land. Prices for everything were rising.

On arriving home, Aunt Suellen would often stand red-faced, heart fluttering, with her hand on her rather copious bosom. She was out of breath from the steep hills, and often overwrought with seeing more and more wounded soldiers on the streets of the town. "Oh, our poor boys," she would blurt. She always stashed a "cure-bottle" of good brandy for use when stress was overwhelming.

Kath confided to Momma one day, "The bottle is nearly empty, and Uncle Elmer doesn't help empty it anymore."

Momma sighed, "I know, dear, but Aunt Sue is grown. She's careful." Kath wondered about Aunt Sue, however. It was not only the brandy. She also became so out of breath on the "wonderful hills" in Staunton.

Momma was teaching Henry, her brother, to cook. He was really a poor student. "You don't just add water, but you need milk and lard," she would caution. He seemed to learn a few basic dishes.

Henry approached their father one night, looked him in the eye, then said, "I'm nineteen now, Papa; I'm going to join up."

Papa fumed and advised, then he asked, "Why?"

"I love you, but I also love our country," Henry answered. "I've played soldier for years. I've played with Emmie and Annie and Kath and even with Aunt Sue at times. I've a feeling I'm a soldier, Papa. I must find out. Inside, I know I'm a leader. I think men will follow me." He hesitated, "Please. Please, understand?" He thought for a moment, his face very serious. "Papa, you've talked about pride. So many men of my age have already joined up. I must try."

"Henry, I guess you're right," said Papa, frowning. "I'd do the same, if I were younger. I wish it wasn't needed, but it is. You'll be a fine soldier. I've always known that. God bless you, son."

Momma's eyes were drawn and etched with surprise. She said something that Kath didn't understand. The family knew this was coming, and Momma realized that children must finally do what they think is right. Henry had said it: "I must try." He now made an effort to soften the pain. "I'll be all right," he said, laughing. Momma's face relaxed, and she suddenly smiled. A decision had been made, and she was proud of her son.

Henry went by train to Richmond. Momma packed a bag with loving care. Kath, Mary, and Dee lay by the thorny barberry hedge near the porch of their home. They waved cheerfully as he began his journey to Richmond and the war. His face was beaming with pride as he left.

"Bye, bye, Henry. Get a Yank for us!" they shouted until he was out of sight. They weren't worried that one of their family could be hurt. It was still a game, like Henry's playing with toy soldiers. A border of yellow jonquils close by, sparkled in the warm sunlight. Uncle Jim, the yard man, and Papa drove him to the station. The house was silent that night, though. There was little laughing.

Purple hyacinths, mayflowers, and daffodils were blooming in the Lynns' backyard. The woods were cool and the ground covered with trillium and bloodroot. Later, bluebells and wild honeysuckle abounded. A few weeks later, the gardens were filled with blooming lilacs, banks of brilliant periwinkles, and clumps of Sweet Williams. This surrounding beauty softened the sadness.

There were always bustle and good smells coming from the kitchen. The night Henry left, the family had succulent boiled ham, turnip greens, and cornmeal dumplings. The children would all later reminisce nostalgically about the delicious meals served at their home.

They were a vigorous working people. Later in the war, food was scarce in much of the South, and prices were terribly high. By then, the family had returned to their farm; they again grew most of their own food. They did not eat toast for breakfast. Toast was for the sick. The boxed, dry cereals eaten with sugar, found on modern tables, were unknown. They gorged on plate-sized griddlecakes, made with flour and topped with their own churned butter, then covered with fried apples and sorghum or home-made brown or white sugar syrup.

Occasionally buckwheat cakes or corncakes were substituted. The cakes were always thick, with a slightly sour taste from mashed potatoes thinned with water and allowed to ferment. Corn bread was often served and made from sour milk or buttermilk. Beef hash and biscuits were a fre-quent dish, fortified with scrumptious "light bread," a coarse white bread. This was made with yeast and baked in iron pans.

Fried mush was a treat many mornings. Children shouldn't squinch up their faces about this; it was really tasty. It was also served in the evenings in soup dishes with milk. Another delight was when Momma used graham meal for making mush. She also prepared whole-grain hominy. This was usually fried with strips of fat or else boiled. It first had to be soaked in lye to remove the husks, and then carefully washed. Cook-ing required talent. They were a fortunate family. They ate well.

Momma and Papa were superstitious. The children always tried to go out the same door they entered, and Momma didn't allow telling about dreams till after breakfast. They got rid of warts by rubbing them with potato peels or a slice of onion. These were then buried and the children swore never to touch another toad—an oath immediately forgotten when out-of-doors. Turpentine was put on cuts and scratches; earaches were treated by blowing pipe smoke in the ear, for which Papa used an extra strong tobacco.

Sulfur and molasses were always ready for treating ills from bad vapors to lumbago, as well as many other sicknesses. They always saved four-leaf clovers, and through the summer competed as to who could find the next one. Horseshoes were nailed to the tool shed or barn doors to keep away unwelcome spirits. Uncle Will nailed two on their colorful, out-door privy-house with the fine shingled roof and yellow siding. Kath was never sure if these were to keep spirits in or out. Lest children forget, it was mighty cold out there on husky winter days.

When friends or their sisters' beaus visited, the younger girls helped make fudge or joined in the taffy pull. Sugar was difficult to buy later in the war; so sorghum molasses, the plant grown locally, was used to make taffy. Kissing games were often played; Kath, Dee, and Mary were quickly shuffled off by their older sisters when these began. "Shoo," they would say, or "Momma, it's their bedtime."

Smoke houses were found on most farms. Sausages, slabs of fat belly, hams and shoulders were hung, covered with brown sugar, salt and salt-peter, and smoked for several days with a fire built in a central stone pit. Hickory wood was preferred. The fat belly was later placed in a large brine barrel for salt pork.

They chewed sweet fern on the way to school. They also enjoyed young sassafras twigs, but never touched the May apple roots. The latter were "poisin," they were told. Kath learned later they had a cathartic effect.

Uncle Wen talked about these roots to Momma. "It's an aphrodisiac," he said with a big smile. At the time, Kath thought this had something to do with Africa. Momma just scowled disapprovingly as Wen shrank back in his chair. "Well, it sounds like an aphrodisiac," he mumbled.

"That's enough," Momma said sternly.

Uncle Wen smiled, but decided to change the subject. "Kath, the woods are beautiful; let's you and I go for a walk. We'll have fun."

"Wonderful. Thanks, Uncle Wen," she replied. They did have fun: a bright spring day, and they were gone several hours. She thought it best not to mention the earlier subject. They talked at length about birds and other little creatures, though—fun subjects.

Their brothers, when younger, often found slick, delicious slippery elm for young ones to chew. Pumpkin, onions, squash, many fruits, and other vegetables all graced their table. Wonderful jams and jellies from blackberries, cherries, ripe mayapple fruit, and raspberries were made at home and preserved. Kath's favorite was raspberry jam, which, when applied to course bread, was especially delicious. After a hearty breakfast, her family was ready to face the world and the war.

"We may hear the sounds of cannon," Papa said in mid-April. "The Yanks are getting closer. I hope Jackson's wrong." Papa was holding a let-ter from Tom Jackson in his hand. Their father looked worried, then he smiled with pride. "Jackson still remembers me, even now that he's famous."

The rest of the family never saw this letter. Perhaps it gave Papa an inkling of what was to come. Papa had several reasons for pride. It wasn't just the letter. He now had two sons who were men.

"They were exciting, James," said Sarah. "I never knew how large a division was. Thousands of soldiers right here in Richmond. And they marched smack through the center of the city like they owned it. Look at the clouds of dust." The sun was shining in a blue sky, and the dust billowed up to the east like great banks of smoke from a fire. "We're a little safer now, I think. We are, aren't we?"

"Not much," James answered. "The Yankees have many thousands of troops out there." He pointed east. "I hope these men get there in time."

"Don't look so grim. Magruder's soldiers are in a big fort near Yorktown, I'm told." She was laughing. "You men. You always worry. We'll hold 'em back. And how lean and handsome they've become. They're bronzed, like Roman gladiators. And all those flowers in their rifles and hats and on the wagons—all over. It was a gay march, wasn't it?" She wrinkled her forehead and smiled. "You still look grim. Perhaps it's because you couldn't buy those knapsacks. These soldiers all wore those little bags hung over one shoulder. And their blanket rolls over the other. No knapsacks."

James finally smiled. "They have rifles, too. And those bags are 'haversacks.' They're used by most of our troops now. They're much easier to make than those leather knapsacks. We cut the fabric here in Richmond. Ladies do the sewing. I think the men like them better, too. The straps don't cut in so much, and they're lighter to carry, and easier to march with. Anyway, that's what we're making now."

"That Longstreet and Stuart. They look yummy. Almost good enough to eat. A little more mature than you, I might say. And handsome too. Especially Stuart." She smiled coyly.

"Longstreet's married, Sarah. You can't have him," teased James. "'Old Pete' is dignified, but he's old enough to be your father."

"I know. And he lost his three children with the epidemic. That's sad. He has a lovely wife, I'm told. I never met her, and with his children dying, he's become all business now. He used to laugh more—and tease. Life can hurt people, even without a war." She looked thoughtfully into James's eyes. "Thanks for the bolt of cloth, by the way. And also the eggs and butter. I won't ask how you got them."

James smiled smugly. Lil Rawling had provided them from her

"sources." That bit of legal work with Winder's men had been paid for with some goods, and a few pleasant services. He thought he'd better not mention this to Sarah. She had started on other subjects anyway.

"All they had in the market last Saturday were sweet potatoes, hominy, and turnip greens. Not very interesting. Eggs were gone so fast, you couldn't even touch them. And the few fish left were sick! Also, the meat was all gone, even early in the morning. We aren't starving, but we get hungry," said Sarah.

"The purveyor of one of the hospitals took most of the eggs in town, I was told. And speculators are everywhere—good old-fashioned hucksters out for a good thing—for them. It's been true since America began. And at night there's trouble everywhere now," James answered.

"I'm not allowed out then," said Sarah, laughing. "You men are so lucky."

"Even with Wilder's bully-boys, there are fights and gambling and," he hesitated, "even a few killings. You stay inside at night, my pretty young lady." He gave her a warm squeeze. "There were several shootings last night, too. It's dangerous."

"It'll be worse if those Yankees get here."

"Maybe they can hold Yorktown. Especially with Longstreet and G. W. Smith on the way. The defenses are fairly strong. Lee directed that those forts be constructed last year. But our men can't hold out forever. We'll need something more, I'm afraid," said James.

"It's men like that spy, Webster, that've hurt us. My Pa says they provided the Yankees with all kinds of information: gun emplacements, numbers of soldiers, troop locations, many things." Her eyes were angry. "I hope they hang him real good. He deserves it. What he does helps kill our boys. They should make him, well, hurt for a while. So that everyone can see what happens to spies."

"Now, now," said James smiling. "He'll get what the law dictates. It has to be done legally, or both sides will start lots of executions. Some of our men up in the North might be, well, executed also. Both sides have spies. And there's another problem. Webster was a friend of Benjamin's. He carried letters to Baltimore for our War Department. He's hoping Benjamin will intervene. Benjamin won't. He isn't going to help. Not with all that deceit."

"I thought George Randolph was our Secretary of War now," Sarah said.

"He is. But Benjamin's still here in Richmond. He's our new Secretary of State. He's well trained for that job. He never was very military anyway. He's adamant about being aloof from the Webster case—even if they were friends once." James couldn't help thinking that these political appointments changed like the old game of musical chairs.

"This'll probably be cancelled just as it was for Lewis and that other spy last week," continued Sarah. "I'm told every shady woman in town went to watch. There was a jam of carriages a mile long. Now they're both free. Some spectacle. This will happen with Webster, too, I suppose. I've heard lots of people on the streets talking. They say it makes them angry. Spies get off so easily."

"It was Lewis and Sully. They turned over evidence of Webster's guilt. They're not free, but they'll probably be traded for some of our men the Yankees are holding." James smiled wanly. His eyes were sad. "Webster won't be so lucky. He'll get a chance to know what a rope feels like. It won't be fun." He hesitated, wondering if he should say more. Finally he continued, "And I have orders to attend the execution. Unfortunately." Sarah looked surprised.

"I refused when I was asked. Then Colonel Bledsoe in the War Office ordered me there—as a lawyer and observer. 'It'll not be nice to see,' he told me, 'but you're trained to argue the legal implications, and now you should experience the results.' I won't enjoy it, I'm sure. You work with your father—a lawyer. He's been involved in capital cases, also. And you've expressed all those strong feelings. Perhaps you should see what our courts do at times. It'll go very quickly, I'm told. He probably won't hurt much. It's the waiting that's the hardest. We'll be quite close. Good seats, you might say." He was disturbed by this show of levity. It wasn't intended. "Perhaps then you'll be satisfied with our justice system."

Sarah was shocked. "I really didn't expect that, James." She took a deep breath as she shook her head slowly from side to side. "Life is sacred. Very sacred. I'm not sure any of us has the right to decide whether this should happen. My previous statements were very callous. I'm awfully sorry."

"You needn't be. It's just anger. We all feel it," replied James.

"I am sorry for what I said, though. I guess we all have a morbid curiosity about death. It's one thing, though, to kill another in battle. It's something else to do it . . . ," she hesitated, searching for words, "to do it in a reasoned planned manner, even if it's a court of law that decided. Yet I know it's done. My pa has seen men die that way." She hesitated again. "There's a terrible truth in violence. It attracts us, and yet it repels us. It's a metaphor on human nature. A negative force within all of us."

"That's why all those carriages were in the streets last week. People are curious to see it happen; later they're repelled by what they saw. And by the meanness in human beings."

"If we humans make it happen, we should have the strength to watch it, even if it hurts, I suppose. I'll agonize over it, but since I work in law, I . . . ," she waited a moment, "I guess I'll go with you. I won't sleep well after that, though." Her eyes were directed down, then she looked up into his eyes. There was a mixture of compassion and fearful attraction for what was to be done. It was a deep inner desire to see what men do—perhaps must do—even if it were repugnant.

"Think about it," he said softly. "You'll have to make the decision yourself. And you can always change your mind. I'm almost sorry I even mentioned it. Yet it's going to take place. And it won't change what's happening in Yorktown. McClellan's got a big army out there. We're outnumbered, too, even with Smith and Longstreet. And Henry'll probably be headed that way. He's been sent to join Armstead. I think he'll be part of Huger's Division. They're still at Norfolk, I'm told."

"I like Henry," she said softly. "So did Mary. She told me she wants to see him again soon."

There was a sparkle of light in her eyes. *Maybe*, he thought, *I shouldn't have introduced my handsome brother to these pretty ladies. Sarah liked him too.*

"What are you thinking, James? You look worried again."

"I hope he'll be all right. Sometime there's going to be a big battle out there. All those Yankees have guns—the best. And we can't give up Richmond, or we'll lose everything." He hesitated a moment. "Enough about bad news. Your mother invited me for dinner. We'd better go. She was angry last week when we were late."

Sarah took James's arm. It felt good—firm and warm. "Wives and children are already being sent away from the city," she said. "It's scary. We can hold out, I hope. We can, can't we?"

"I'm not sure," answered James.

CHAPTER XIV
Staunton Is Saved

"Did you ever tell your ma about that spy?" asked Mary. "The one that was executed."

Sarah shook her head. "No. Never. Never. I was too afraid."

"She'd have been very mad at James, I suppose."

"It was my choice. James had to go. He was ordered there officially, as a lawyer. Because of that, we were very close to the front, near the gallows." She nodded her head slowly. "You could see all the lines in the man's face. And he looked ghastly. It wasn't pleasant. He tried to act brave, and he was, I suppose. But you could see his face quiver, and he was trembling. They had to help him up to the platform."

"I think they'd have to help most of us up," said Mary.

"I had bad dreams that night. I cried for a long time, and Ma heard me mumble, 'It's terrible; it's terrible.' I told her it was because of the sick we'd seen that day at the hospital, and because I'd seen a nice man die. I guess he was a nice man to his family. Ma then said to me, 'We may see much more of that. Unfortunately!'"

Sarah was quiet for a moment. Her eyes had a distant look. "A spy is like someone who breaks into your home and steals things. You want something bad to happen to him."

"Or her," said Mary.

"Yes, that's right. Or her. But when it happens, and you see another human being there, you agonize over whether what is done is right. This is the way I felt. Intellectually, I thought it should happen. When I actually saw it, I was revolted. The memory just stays with me. I still see his face."

"A lot of our men have died," said Mary.

"Yes. But not like this. He was alive one moment, then gone the next. He deserved it for what he did, I guess. He was one of those Pinkerton spies. He worked for old Abe Lincoln, and he turned over valuable information to his superior officer. It wasn't pleasant to see him die, though."

"It wasn't supposed to be." Mary's face was somber and sympathetic.

"How frail we are," continued Sarah. "Life can pass so quickly. This took a little more time than I thought it would, though. The trap opened, and he fell through. But the knot came loose. He fell on the ground. 'I die twice,' I think he said. They marched him back up again, while one man made a new, very big knot in the rope. 'This'll hold you,' he smiled at the prisoner. It was grim. As they put the noose around his neck the second time, someone below said it was too short. 'So now you'll choke me to death,' mumbled the prisoner. He looked very afraid. 'You'll enjoy it I'm sure, while I strangle,' he continued. His neck was raw from the previous noose. A rope burn, I guess, and it was bleeding. The black hood was placed over his head again. The trap opened a second time, and he fell through. I can still hear the rope snap, or maybe it was his neck." Sarah shuddered. "He must have died immediately. He didn't move after that. He just swayed back-and-forth like a pendulum.

"James said, 'We'd better go. We've seen all we have to. He's dead now, and not many folks came to see the show. That's just as well. It wasn't fun to see.' I told him I was still shaking. And I was. As we walked away, I looked back at the body. It was being taken down and put in a rough wooden box by Wilder's men. They were cutting up the rope. Probably for souvenirs. Ghastly. They seemed to be laughing and talking."

"That's terrible," said Mary. She shook her head sadly. She suddenly brightened. "There's James." She waved her hand. "Hi, James."

"What have you ladies been doing?" James asked. They were standing on Broad Street just east of the R. F. & P. railroad station. He didn't wait for their answer. He had just remembered the inn in the next block. "My mouth is dry," he said. "We need something to wet our thirst. We'll go to the old Swan Tavern down the street. That's a nice place. Patrick and Henry and Thomas Jefferson received a welcome behind those doors. Perhaps we can have tea—or something stronger."

"That's for men," said Sarah. "You can go, but we can't."

"I think it'd be all right. But we'll go to a hotel instead." He smiled at both of them. "You're probably correct. And the Powhatan is just a block or two farther. We can have dinner there, too."

Suddenly he frowned. "They've given up Yorktown. It's bad. I need a little wine to relax. And there's been a bloody fight at Williamsburg. A rear-guard action, really. The Yankee gunboats went quickly past our position and up the York River to West Point. And West Point is only thirty miles from here. Johnston's retreating. We'll probably have to give up Nor-

116

folk soon. That's where our few ships and boats are. We'll lose them, too, I suppose."

"It does sound bad," commented Sarah.

"Very bad," replied James. He looked grim for a moment. "Richmond isn't safe anymore. Even the river is a threat. That's why they're speeding up work on the fortifications at Drewry's Bluff."

"That's just a few miles from here on the James," said Mary. "Not very far. They won't come by boat, will they?"

"They may. And Drewry's Bluff is the last fortified position on the river before Richmond. It's our main hope for stopping them—their gunboats and ironclads. If we can't, they'll be right here at the wharves in Richmond. At Rockets Landing. Our city'll be lost. And so will the war."

"We saw the sick from Yorktown today. Mary and I visited the hospitals. My aunt, our chaperone, stayed with us until just before you came. She left for an appointment at the Spottswood. For dinner there, I believe."

"I saw her walking away," said James, smiling. "She's a handsome woman."

"Yes, she is pretty. And she told us there are hundreds of stragglers here, too, from the battle. They're in the bars and bad houses, I suppose. Those places line lower Main Street like soldiers standing in ranks ready to attack. Evil folks, many of them. That's what I've heard. They must be. And I suppose a number of them are deserters."

"Just average men, probably," said James. "They're frightened. And we all have a little bad in us. Most of us."

"Some more than others," observed Mary. "But there's an orgy going on in some of those bars, I'm told." She added the last words very quickly. She didn't want it to sound like she'd been inside. "It's a Sodom and Gomorrah right here, with bad women cheering the men on in the midst of all the smoke and sour smells."

"How do you know?" asked Sarah, laughing. Mary didn't answer. She just glanced knowingly at her friend.

James had a remote look in his eyes. He was thinking of Lil Rawling. Perhaps her establishment was a little more elegant than those Mary had spoken about. He hoped so. Besides, since he'd met Sarah, he had little desire to go there anymore.

"I wrote my folks a few days ago," said James. "At least they know what our army's facing. I'll write them again tonight. Maybe." He looked at both young women. They didn't seem very cheerful. He smiled. "Well, enough bad news. We're going to the Metropolitan tonight after we have something to eat and quench our thirst a bit."

"I'm glad you remembered," said Sarah cheerfully. "I thought you'd forgotten."

"Never!" he said smiling.

"What's playing?" asked Mary. "It was Negro spirituals last week."

"It'll be singing and dancing and fun. Something light. None of that serious Shakespeare like we saw at the Marshall before it burned."

"We were just across from the Marshall at the railroad station. It's being rebuilt. It was rubble for a long while after it burned last winter. Like some of the pictures I've seen of Centerville after our army burned the town and came to the Peninsula."

"We can build from ashes," said Sarah. "Thank goodness. But I hope we won't have to very often."

"Like if the war comes right here, you mean," said Mary.

"It won't. It can't. This is the heart of our country. Most of what we fight with is here."

"It is!" James smiled. Then he quickly changed the subject. "I believe two local girls will be singing tonight. They're the Confederacy Sweethearts, I've been told."

"You men. You just love it when they sing 'My Southern Soldier Boy.' You silly boys! You fawn over a pretty face." Sarah was laughing as she looked into James's eyes.

"We love it, too, Sarah," said Mary. "Maybe it gives us more of an identity. We know who we are." She was laughing. "Also, it cheers us up. We need that too. Especially when we realize some of our boys are probably still out there on those fields near Williamsburg—dying. We worry about that, and we're also wondering where Jackson's gone. He's disappeared, my father said."

"He has," answered James. "I hope it's for the good of the South."

"Enough," said Sarah. "Stop all this talk. It sounds like we've given up the beast without a fight. We have good men out there and all around us here. Something will happen. Things'll get better. We aren't lost yet. So there!" She gave James a soft pat on the cheek again. "Here we are, James. And I'll have some wine with you." She smiled pleasantly. They were just entering the handsome lobby of the hotel.

"I'll have some wine, too," said Mary. "And I'm glad it isn't Shakespeare tonight. We're seeing big events right here in our own city. We don't have to go see it on a stage. Shakespeare does bring some culture to Richmond, though."

"My father'd say we need that," said James, laughing.

"I'd like to meet him sometime," said Sarah. "He still teaches, I suppose. He sounds like a fine man."

"He is! And you'll both meet him later, I'm sure."

The Lynns felt ready to face the war, and it was coming closer. They had received James's letter from Richmond. It was the one he had spoken about to Sarah and Mary.

I only have a little space in a dark corner, but I'm now of some use to the war effort. I work with the railroads and with supply lines.

A big Union army is on the Virginia peninsula between the James and York Rivers. Those Yankees are coming west toward Richmond. Their commander is General McClellan—George Brinton McClellan. In 1861, he won that battle west of Staunton in the Alleghenies. You helped care for the men who lost the battle. Most of our troops are under General J. E. Johnston and have been moved from near Fredericksburg on the Rappahannock to the Peninsula. They're fighting to keep McClellan out of the capital.

[The letter continued] James Longstreet's troops, called by many of his soldiers "Longstreet's Walking Division," have recently marched through Richmond. Till that time, our people were afraid—now they have taken heart. It was a fine day in spring with bright flowers, people at the street-side, cheering, bands playing "Cheer, Boys, Cheer" and "My Maryland," hyacinths and daffodils on knapsacks and caps and rifles, and voices singing "Dixie." Our losses farther west at Forts Henry and Donelson and at Shiloh were forgotten for the day. As was Jackson's loss at Kernstown. Thankfully.

When Papa received this information from James, and when he saw facts in the papers about the great buildup of troops on the Peninsula, he shook his head sadly. His voice was serious. "This is what the Yanks should do, I suppose, but we'll be overwhelmed. Especially if General McDowell is able to join McClellan near Richmond. As far as I can tell, we're already outnumbered, even without McDowell coming south. Richmond will be lost. Perhaps the war will be over. Maybe this is good. Maybe we'll be the strong ones who declare peace."

Papa thought for a moment. "I don't want this to happen, though. I want peace, but I also want honor. Why, I don't know. Honor is so trivial, when one has sons and friends who may be killed. God, help us to do the right thing. And God help Henry. He may be fighting soon."

In March, Thomas Jackson, now known as "Stonewall," had savagely attacked Shields of Banks's Corp. The fighting was at Kernstown near the valley town of Winchester. He was said to have been outnumbered two to one. He lost the battle, but it was not a total loss. The Lynns later learned that it caused Lincoln to remove McDowell from McClellan's command. McDowell would later start south and threaten Richmond but would soon be ordered back toward Washington. Richmond, though, was still in danger from McClellan's vast army. And so were Kath and her family, from armies to the north and west of Staunton.

Now Stonewall Jackson had "disappeared." To the Lynns, he was their saviour. He had marched east over the Blue Ridge Mountains. "He's going to support Joe Johnston at Richmond," said Papa.

"We've been forgotten," replied Wen. "Banks is only twenty-five miles north on the Valley Pike. His Yankee patrols were just a few miles away the other day. Then there's Fremont."

"Are those Milroy's troops?" asked Sue. "He's close, too."

"Yes," said Papa. "He commands Fremont's advanced regiments. He's now about ten miles west of here. Moving closer, I'm sure."

"We'll be an occupied town," said Sue. "No wonder people are depressed. We'll be ravaged. It's terrible! And we're helpless without soldiers."

"Are the Yankees bad?" asked Annie.

"Not to pretty girls," said Papa.

"I'll spit if they come near me," said Emmie.

"Emmie, we'll be polite and civil. We'll do what they ask and survive." Momma's face was solemn. "Maybe we can't fight, but we can show inner strength. We're not beaten, and we'll not give in to despair."

Church bells were ringing on Sunday, May the fifth. The sweet scent of flowers filled the air. Kath and her family were at church to pray for deliverance. Music burst from the lips of the congregation: "Our God, our help in ages past, Our hope for years to come. . . . ," but they could not forget the danger.

Papa leaned toward Momma and whispered, "It's hard to believe we're about to be invaded. Things we love are changing. The gloom here is overwhelming. Just look at our people. The Root family were almost in tears. They've had one son injured and a nephew killed. We're all wondering if our town will be destroyed. The Yanks were stopped before, but there's no one out there to fight for us now."

"You told me General Ed Johnson is out there," said Momma.

"Just a few regiments of his. How can he stop them?"

"I don't know. We'll just have to pray. Somehow we'll be helped."

"I hope you're right, Ann Katherine."

"We'll find peace, James. Patience brings many good things." Her voice was filled with feeling with those soft unspoken words that wives and mothers have within them. Kath thought she knew her every expression, but this was one she didn't recognize at first. Then her mother spoke again. "If they come, they come. Strength is not just guns and cannons. It's the power to live through pain and tragedy. Life has always been like that."

Papa smiled knowingly. Momma could always find words of hope. From where Kath sat, she could see a little piece of the sky. It was bright and clear. After what Momma said, she felt there was still much to hope for out there.

Their father sat back and listened as they sang. The music swelled around him like a great chorus, " . . . Our shelter from the stormy blast, And our eternal home."

The minister stepped forward as the last bars of the hymn were sung. "God is with us," he cried. The congregation relaxed expectantly as he continued. "If the Union soldiers come, we will meet them with chin and shoulders high. We are fighting for what is ours—our property and our land. There is goodness and purpose here. Though we are weak at this moment, we will finally prevail. Richmond knows our sorrow, and we are vital to the cause . . . "

Kath saw that the folks about her seemed less apprehensive. The desperate gloom had disappeared.

This reverie was interrupted by the hiss of steam and the harsh cries of whistles from big engines. With the suddenness of a summer storm, trains careened into town. Years later, this would remind people of the valiant work of overland crews during the summer of '61 and into '62. Fourteen big coal-carrying railroad engines were salvaged for the cause during the retreat from Harper's Ferry and Martinsburg on the Potomac. These were from the Federal B&O Railroad. It was Jackson's locomotive adventure.

The engines were ferried south without rails, a difficult but successful effort. These huge vehicles, pulled by a myriad of straining horses, swayed and lurched up the valley, cheered on by the people. They were more like great whales out of water than sleek engines for pulling trains. Old number 199, a Ross Winans camel-back locomotive, one of the last salvaged, broke loose on a hill above Staunton and careened through the streets. This May of 1862, though, the train whistles and steam augured the town's salvation.

A band in the distance began to play. People outside the church started singing "Dixie." The harsh command, "Forward, march," was heard; and the sounds of clanking weapons and marching feet echoed through the streets. Staunton was not pillaged. Jackson's battle-hardened soldiers of the valley army had arrived. They were moving west to meet Milroy. The town's prayers had been answered. The sounds of battle, thought so imminent, were not heard.

Jackson stayed in Staunton for a day, organizing and hurrying his divisions forward. As mentioned earlier, Jackson had known Papa while he was at the Virginia Military Institute at Lexington in better times. Now Jackson visited briefly in the Lynns' parlor that evening. This fire-and-brimstone Presbyterian, described by many as unlaughing and gawky, with a killer's blue eyes, sat pleasantly and relaxed in their home.

"Tom, it's been hard, but you've shown how strong you can be," said Papa. "Our people thank you. I've always known about your inner resources. I saw them blossom in Lexington. Your struggle for health, your religious growth, your fine family, your work with students, with Negro children, with business activities, and not in the least, your good sense as a bank director. I've also seen how patient you can be, when loved ones were lost. We're proud of you."

The family suddenly saw smiling faces at the windows. The children from around the neighborhood crowded in close to catch a glimpse of their hero. "See the look in their eyes," said Papa, smiling. "They know what you've done. I can't ask what will happen next, but may God go with you."

"James, thank you." Jackson laughed shyly as if what Papa had said was embarrassing. Then he became serious. "We're both former professors from Lexington. Now you're basically a farmer and I'm a soldier. How life changes things! I still say little about my work. I guess you know that from our professor days. I pray often—asking the Lord for help. Decisions aren't easy, but I've learned to make them. They must be made, if we're to fight those Yankees and win. I think we can beat them. We're losing so far. I guess you know that."

Jackson hesitated. He seemed to be hunting for the right words. He smiled warmly to the children, then continued to speak. "Where did we first meet, James?"

"I'm not sure, Tom. I think it was in Lyle's store, the bookstore. On Main Street, as I remember."

"We had good times there. All the students and teachers would stand around and talk. Sometimes I think they learned as much in the bookstore as in the classroom. Lyle was a good churchman. His patient counseling brought me into the Presbyterian Church. A good man. These memories make me think of home. It's nice to be with you and your family. It's almost like being home. I've so missed Anna."

"She's a lovely woman," said Momma. "I hope some day we can meet her again. You're a lucky man, Tom, to have such a fine wife."

"James is lucky, too," said Jackson.

Kath saw Momma's face redden a little. "'Many a flower is born to blush unseen,'" she replied.

"'And waste its sweetness on the desert air,'" answered the general. Momma smiled graciously, but didn't speak. He turned to Papa. "We had fun times in Lexington. Remember our trip to the Rockford Alum Springs?"

"Ann never forgave me for not taking her," said Papa. "She wouldn't speak to me for a week."

"I still don't forgive him, Tom," said their mother, smiling. Now it was Papa's turn to blush a little.

The general laughed. "Those waters at the Rockford Springs do wonders. They helped me more with becoming well than anything else I did. I even marched my students there once. Keeping those wild young boys in line was almost as difficult as running an army."

The family didn't remember much more of what he said. Jackson's voice was soft and sincere. Both Papa and he occasionally sighed as they reminisced about the old days in Lexington.

Kath later remembered the general's telling about Papa slipping in a puddle just outside Jackson's small brick home off Main Street in Lexington. "Remember, James, how Anna hung your britches before the fire, while you stood by in that old army blanket of mine? Are your legs still that bony?"

Papa blushed. "I guess they are, Tom. And you children hush about my fine figure. You, too, Ann Katherine. That's why I keep these long legs covered."

"James, you never told me this." Momma had a twinkle in her eye.

"It isn't something one speaks of," said Jackson, smiling.

For a fleeting moment, Jackson was freed of duty, though not from responsibility. He had taken off his mangy old forage-cap with the broken visor, and the children would remember a teasing glint in his blue eyes. His upper lids were shaded by heavy brows, but his eyes glowed happily.

His jaw was firm, and his forehead high and smooth. A few shallow lines radiated out from the corners of the lids. He was at home with a family, not on the field of battle. He spoke lovingly of his wonderful wife, Anna. Kath and her sisters were not afraid of this iron-willed soldier.

For Kath, the memory of Gen. Thomas J. Jackson became indelibly etched in her mind. He was in their home for only a brief time. When she was older and more fully realized his greatness, this became a profound experience. In their home, he had a gracious warmth, which was so unlike the way many people remembered him. In war he was pitiless. Perhaps some men have to be this way. It is necessary for the salvation of order and group survival. Societies must be buttressed by tradition or rely on force.

Jackson was a supreme protagonist. Yet, in private life, he personified the righteous values of family, home, hearth, and church. He was imbued with a gentleness that made children come to him with open arms; paradoxically, in battle, he displayed a reasoned, unemotional ferocity. Papa told his family later, "He also has the ability to look beyond the battles and realize what our armies have done and what they must do."

In the decade before the Civil War, Jackson had lived in Lexington. His native talents were already evident. He traveled widely in the summer months and displayed an increasingly religious fervor. He acquired a house and farm and became involved in successful business ventures and real estate. He was elected a bank director of the Lexington Savings Institution.

Their father spoke often of Jackson before and after the war. They came to know some of the story of his life. Although he was shy, Jackson soon overcame this handicap and became a forceful speaker at public meetings. He carried out official duties in the Presbyterian Church.

In 1855, he organized a Negro Sunday school. A dozen teachers assisted under Jackson's encouragement and direction. Punctuality was paramount. School began at 3:00 P.M. Interestingly, the doors were locked after the three o'clock bell. Latercomers were surprised by this. Soon, there were very few latecomers. The attendance record soared.

In August 1853, Jackson married Elinor Junkin, the daughter of the Rev. Dr. George Junkin, president of Washington College in Lexington. Jackson was devastated by her death in 1854. In July 1856, he married Anna Morrison, daughter of the Rev. Dr. Robert Hall Morrison, past president of Davidson College of North Carolina. He had thus been married to the daughters of two college presidents. In both marriages he helped create a home of warmth and love. Whatever his idiosyncrasies, he was a respected citizen of his community.

During this same decade, his career was primarily dedicated to teaching at VMI. He undertook difficult subjects in the physical sciences, such as mechanics, astronomy, and the principles of sound and optics. His voice was gentle and rhythmic. However, cadets and fellow soldiers rarely saw him smile, and most recalled later that he never laughed.

"He would laugh and smile at home, privately," observed Papa after Jackson had departed that day, "but not during school or business. I believe this was partially from shyness, but he also thought work should be serious. When he was stern, cadets would tell me, he would stare right through them. I knew many of his boys at the school—children, really. I sometimes wondered what they said about me. Most, I'm sure, now appreciate his discipline. They learned what to expect in real battles. And discipline is vital in battle.

"His reputation in the Mexican War preceded him at VMI. And he was known to be a capable soldier during that violent fighting. He was first and foremost an artilleryman." Papa thought a moment. "Fellow professors told me he had exceptional merit as an artillery instructor. I used to laugh as he stood grimly, watching his cadets rush across the large field pulling a heavy brass cannon. They would stop, unlimber, swab-out, fill with powder, packing, then ram home a ball. 'No!' No!' he would shout as they dropped the ball, 'We'll do it again and again, until it's right.' His face would be red and his lips taut. 'We'll stay all night, if we have to.'

"Scores of young men who learned artillery from this harsh man are now scattered throughout our armies. They're better soldiers because of Tom. He's a shy man, but his work has had much influence far beyond the Shenandoah Valley."

In Staunton, Jackson's forces were augmented by a strange military unit. The entire cadet corps from the Virginia Military Institute had volunteered for battle. They were commanded by the VMI superintendent, Major General Smith. Jackson reviewed the cadets on May sixth on the grounds of the Deaf and Dumb Asylum at Staunton.

"Attention! In ranks of four, right wheel! Close-up. Forward, March!"

The band began to play: "We are a band of brothers, native to the soil; Fighting for the property we gained by honest toil . . . " These fine young boys marched across the field before the adoring crowd. Suddenly everyone watching began to sing. Kath stood with tears in her eyes. Flags rip-

125

pled against the blue sky, and folks cheered, "Hurrah, hurrah, for Southern rights, hurrah; Hurrah for the Bonnie Blue Flag that bears a single star . . ."

The girls of the town made much of these trim, well-trained youngsters who marched west with the Stonewall veterans. Jackson, joined by a small force under General Edward Johnson, fought a battle in the Alleghenies near the town of McDowell. The Union general of Fremont's advance guard, Milroy, retreated northward, followed by Jackson.

"It was a brisk battle," said Papa firmly.

"What does 'brisk' mean?" Kath asked. "Was it cold there?"

The adults laughed, while she blushed. Mr. Raymond gave a kind, understanding answer. "It's a term for hard fighting—usually with much killing. Not nice to see. It happens when both sides are determined to win. Your Papa's friend, Jackson, is that kind of fighter. I'm afraid we need him, though."

"The Mountain roads were atrocious, I'm told. But our men fought well. Very well!" said Papa. Kath saw that there was a distant look in his eyes and pride in his voice, as if he were vicariously sharing the glory and the pain. His shoulders were back as he continued. "Stonewall then turned like a gladiator before a bull, and marched back to the Shenandoah. Where he's going now, I don't know. But this was a victory! Fremont's still trying to reorganize his broken divisions." Papa now looked hard at his family around him. "This campaign's not over. It's probably just beginning!"

Another letter came from James:

. . . Many mean things are being said about Joe Johnston. Some call him "Retreat' n Joe." He's continuing to retire toward the capital. He's now at the last major barrier before Richmond, the Chickahominy River. I saw a letter from Robert Toombs the other day. I'm not sure I was supposed to see it. He's a brigadier in Johnston's army and always sounds angry and disgusted, but his letter had a note of logic: "This army will not fight until McClellan attacks it. . . . It will burn, retreat, curse, get drunk . . . anything but fight."

[James continued] McDowell's still at the Rappahannock with 40,000 men, but we have information he's coming south to join McClellan. Things look bad. General McDowell was in command of the Yankee army at Manassas in 1861. He's a good soldier even if we did beat him that time. I'm not sure what we can do. "Little Mac" has over 100,000 soldiers just east of us (Richmond) right now. Folks will probably be afraid again. They should be.

People are leaving Richmond in droves. Even government archives are being sent away. President Davis's family has gone to North Carolina for safety. I recently witnessed the battle at Drewry's Bluff a few miles south of here. I thought I also might see Henry there. He retreated with Huger from Norfolk when we gave up that city. I didn't find him, but he was probably there somewhere with Armstead. Some of the cannoneers from our navy sighted those guns on the bluff, and hit the Yankee gunboats, one after the other. Their boats retreated, thankfully, like dogs being chased by an angry bear. The city was saved again, but McClellan's getting close. There'll be a big battle soon.

"I hope James remains in Richmond," said Momma to herself. Her face was somber as she thought about her two sons. "We could lose both those boys right there in front of that city. Oh, God, help them!" No one else heard this. She thought about what she had said. "What we need is a happy face, not sadness. Grief won't help our people." She then forced herself to smile brightly. "Let's have dinner. And Suellen, perhaps we'll open that bottle of brandy of Uncle Elmer's. It will help us relax. I'll have a little, too."

"Ann Katherine!" said Suellen. "You've never . . . " Suellen didn't end the sentence. Momma had the bottle out and ready. Papa and Wen looked kindly at her. They both were at a loss for words.

CHAPTER XV
Richmond Besieged

"That's an interesting view, isn't it, Lieutenant?" The voice came from out of the shadow beyond a scraggly bush close to where James Lynn was standing. He turned with a start. "It's dingy down there; just brick factories and very dirty, but it's as vital to us as our armies!"

A dark figure emerged from the shadow and was suddenly lighted by the moon. The man's face was harshly lined, and his fine silver hair was blown and ruffled by the fresh breeze coming up from the river. "Good evening, Mr. Mayor," said James. He gave a soft chuckle. "You frightened me. I thought someone was about ready to put a sharp blade at my throat."

"Do I look that threatening?" smiled Joseph Mayo, the aging mayor of the City of Richmond.

"No. But it's dark. I didn't see who it was." James had met old Mayor Mayo several times at parties and in business when he'd negotiated for Richmond city properties that were to be used for manufacturing. "A friend of mine was cut with a knife blade several weeks ago. By one of our brave stragglers. They never caught the man. At least I don't think they have."

"Our streets are dangerous, Lieutenant. For me, too. I'm supposed to have a military escort. They're back there somewhere. Here's the second revolver I've been carrying. We can protect each other."

The Tredegar Iron Works spread before them, like the bastions of a fortified town. There was a glow from the open doors below, and smoke rose lazily from the smokestack of the cannon foundry. The bridge to Brown's Island stood out sharply against the water, which was sparkling in the moonlight.

"We've become a manufacturing town, haven't we?" said the mayor as he pointed to the iron works and then southeast across the Kanawha Canal at the white frame buildings on Brown's Island. The latter were the powder-loading plants for much of the South.

"If things ever explode, it'll make a big hole in our city," James said with a laugh.

"That's possible. But I think we're fairly safe. It's the armies trying to reach our city that worry me. Johnston keeps moving back—then farther back." A canal boat was sliding by below like a small house on the water. Mayor Mayo was interested. "That barge contains archives and some of our gold bullion." He pointed at the boat. "They're being sent west for safety. And the troops nearby will protect things, I hope. Unless someone is pretty determined to get the gold. I suppose a lot of folks would try if they knew it was there. I hope not too many know." He thought for a moment. "But they do know that McClellan is getting close. They're leaving the city in droves. You can hear their wagons and carriages even down here by the river. And it's almost midnight."

They started to walk slowly toward the city proper. Gamble's Hill rose like a tower to their left, and the James River stretched out serpentlike toward the rolling hills to the west of the city.

"People are worried, just like you and me, I suppose," said James. "And they want their women and children safe." His face suddenly was filled with a crafty smile. "If McClellan gets much closer, Mr. Mayor, he'll be able to sit right in your own office."

James saw the mayor take a deep breath before he answered. "I hope it never comes to that, but you're right. I rode out to Rockets Landing today. I accompanied Reagan, our prestigious postmaster-general. It was raining, and we got good and wet. Thankfully it's stopped now. He's done a fine job, by the way, even if he is a Texan as well as an old Indian fighter. He was there a few days ago with Davis. As they came to a low rise with an open view to the east, our president was truly upset. This was just on the outskirts of town. 'Whose tents are those?' he asked. 'Why that's Hood's Brigade,' was the answer. 'No! Hood's Brigade is down on the Chickahominy.' Reagan suddenly realized the president had not been informed of all of Johnston's movements. He explained to Davis, 'This has just recently happened, and that is Hood's Brigade, Mr. President.'

"Davis seemed astounded. 'And General Johnston is in that brick house off to the right,' Reagan continued. I was as shocked as was our president. My city may become Lincoln's property very soon—too soon. It's frightening," the mayor concluded.

"I hope it won't, sir. I hope it never will!" said James. "But what can we do? Could someone like Lee be of help? He's been deeply involved with Jackson in that valley campaign. Now Jackson's a hero, and Banks has retreated north on the Valley Pike from Harrisonburg to Strasburg. Our people jeered and laughed at his men the whole way. This is a big victory, and we've needed it. Also, Jackson hit Colonel Kenly at Front Royal. Now he's after Banks again at Winchester. This in itself is a victory. One of our few. Lee's strategy was a very important factor in all of this. I think Davis knows it. I'm not sure the average citizen knows about it, though."

"They don't. And Lee's reputation has certainly crumbled over the last year. I know he's a fine soldier. But he's still an untried quality. Especially when we're in this terrible, terrible crisis. We need dash and daring. We need someone who can gamble. We're outnumbered, and somehow we have to overcome this by strategy. Also, that man has to be able to handle troops in action on the field. Can Lee do this? Johnston to me seems the most able, and Lee so far has been a loser," said the mayor.

"I understand that, sir. But perhaps he's never truly been given a command," replied James.

"Perhaps! I know he's built fortifications. This was his strong point before the war. In fact he's now known as the 'King of Spades' in Georgia and the Carolinas. He put all their fine troops to work with shovels. Soldiers didn't think that that was very soldierly."

"I can't argue with what you say, but what he did makes sense. He's developed plans for mobility, so that troops can be sent quickly where they're needed. And a few men can hold the danger points for a while, with only a small garrison until the relief columns arrive."

"That's a good explanation, James. Even better than some of your fellow officers have given. Thanks. But I'm not sure Davis can, as they say, change horses in the middle of the stream. He has to stick with Johnston for now, unless everything falls apart. I hope you're right about Lee, though, if we need him," said the mayor.

They saw a small company of mounted soldiers riding toward them. "Where have you been, Mister Mayor? My God, we've been worried."

"Simmer down, Lieutenant Calwell. I'm fine. Lieutenant Lynn here has been protecting me. I just took a stroll near the river to see if that canal boat with our bullion aboard is well protected. We had a nice talk, didn't we, Lynn?"

James nodded that they had. "We did, Mister Mayor."

"Calwell, do you have an extra horse for Lieutenant Lynn? He can ride with us tonight—see a bit of the city. Winder's men aren't the only ones who should be looking around."

"Lieutenant Avery's horse, Mister Mayor. He's ill. He may have to be hospitalized."

"I'm sorry to hear that. I hope he'll be well soon." He turned to James. "But here you are, son. You'll go with me. We can talk a little more." This was not a suggestion; it was an order. Besides, James thought it might be an opportunity to mention some of the things he'd been appointed to talk to the mayor about: old blast furnaces, foundries, and subsidiary iron-works. The mayor also had knowledge of skilled workmen who were older, and who might be available. They were desperately needed.

"You're in supply and railroads, James. I guess you know that if we lose this city, we lose everything. What we need to fight with will be gone, as well as the central hub of our whole railroad system. We make rifles, powder, caps, infantry and cavalry equipment, gun carriages, caissons, artillery ammunition, primers, and many, many other things. And we still make most of the machinery being used to start other factories all over the South. And salt, lead, and coal come from nearby. And the railroads. You know about those," said the mayor.

"We have the only rail line connecting northern Virginia to southern Georgia, with direct connections to the West from this central hub, sir. Most of our food, forage, guns, and ammunition go by these roads. Yes, they are important."

They rode slowly through the streets of Richmond. James could feel the fatigue from being up since dawn. They passed down Franklin Street to the Shockoe Creek area and by the large First Market building. Water lay in big pools from the recent rains. They then crossed over Broad Street to Marshall and headed east again close to the Chimborazo Hospital area and south to Rockets Landing. As they started back into town on Main Street, they passed some of the older, more rundown parts of the city. Skulkers from the armies had stumbled to this area and into the dives and bars.

"This is the region I want to see, James. This is where much of the city's violence occurs." Lieutenant Calwell had stayed a comfortable distance behind the mayor, but he could see him and hear him talking to Lieutenant Lynn. The silence was suddenly broken. It was by the shot of a gun. "My God!" said Mayo. "They're shooting at us."

The sound echoed off the buildings close by, and it was hard to tell the direction. James, however, saw the man who was holding the weapon. He then saw him turn it toward the mayor—and toward him. *It looks huge,* he thought. He had never before looked directly into the barrel of a gun. It was a strange sensation. *And he intends to shoot us. It's real.*

The attacker was hidden from Calwell's view by the corner of a building, and he was in a dark shadow. There was a figure lying close beside him, perhaps someone he had shot.

"There he is!" shouted James.

"I see him!" said the mayor, as he drew his pistol. Another shot rang out, and another. James could hear the bullets pass close by, but he wasn't hit. He noticed the mayor suddenly reach for his right arm, which held the gun. Mayo was hurt but didn't fall.

James was firing now. Another shot passed near them, then the figure in the shadow threw his gun away and started to run. "Get him!" shouted James, as he fired again. "I think I hit him."

Calwell's men quickly reached the assailant. He was firmly restrained, as James and the mayor rode up. Mayo was still holding his arm. "Just a scratch," he mumbled. "So this is the man. If he's not military, he'll be turned over to Wilder's provost men. Well, let's go, Calwell. Two of your soldiers can take good care of him. And that other man. He's dead, isn't he?"

"He is, sir," said Calwell. "We can't help him now." He looked compassionately at the mayor's arm. There was an expanding red spot on his sleeve. "We'd better have a look at that arm, Mister Mayor. Before you go riding off."

"We'd better!" said James, as he tried to see if the injury was serious. The mayor removed his coat. There was only a small crease in the skin. Blood was oozing out over the area, though, and it was quite tender to the touch. He tied the mayor's handkerchief over the wound, and Calwell helped him put his coat back on.

"I look more distinguished with the coat," he said, smiling. "Besides, Lieutenants, a good stout drink will solve all the pain." He laughed. "I know a good place. Lil runs a first-class establishment. We can clean up there, and refresh ourselves."

James noticed that their assailant was groaning as one of Calwell's men twisted his arm. "I'm just a poor man from near West Point on the York, Your Honor. I'm dreadfully sorry, sir. That other man had a knife. I panicked. I had this here gun here, and I shot him. See, there's the knife. He cut me several times. See. You can see where he cut me." He pointed to the blood running down his arm from deep cuts. He also had blood running down his face from a wound below the eye.

"There's another wound on the other arm, sir," said one of the soldiers. "It was probably from a bullet. Just a surface cut, I believe."

"Well, we still have to take him in. If his story is true, perhaps we can take this into account when he comes to trial. If he's willing to join Johnston, though, out there in front of Richmond, and help stop McClellan, maybe we can have him out of jail by tomorrow."

The mayor then rode off with Calwell, James, and most of the troop. "It sounds like a true story, Calwell. I believe him, but we'll have to find out if this is what actually happened. Johnston needs soldiers, too. So take this into consideration. In other words, don't hang him quite yet." Calwell nodded consent.

They were close to Lil Rawling's place. The mayor dismissed his guard and started inside. James followed. "Come back after you've reported in, Calwell," Mayo shouted. "We'll be here a while."

Lil was just inside the door. Her face brightened when she saw them. "Welcome! Welcome, Mister Mayor! This is indeed a pleasure." She then smiled at Lieutenant Lynn. "And you also, James. May I serve you both a little wine? It's the best."

"I'll have whiskey, Lil. And I want it straight, right now," said Mayo.

"Look at His Honor's arm first, Lil. He's been wounded."

Lil helped the mayor remove his coat. She then looked shocked as she examined the wound. "We'd better wash that," she said. "Not too bad, though. Thankfully. And this deserves a free drink, Your Honor." She poured a liberal helping in a large glass, then dampened a clean cloth from the same bottle and began to scrub the wound.

"It's only a scratch," said Mayo, pulling his arm away. He put it around Lil and gave her a little hug. "Thanks for your kindness, though," he said smiling.

"Mary over there is a fine nurse, Joseph. She'll spend some time with you, while I go back to my records and books. Your city requires them. Maybe you should rest upstairs before going home, though. You will, won't you?" asked Lil.

"You've read my mind, young lady," he said, laughing. "But take care of my friend here." He turned to James. "You do know Lil, I hope. She called you by name. I won't ask how you two met, but you can tell me all about it someday." He was chuckling as he walked away.

James saw Lil take Joseph Mayo by the hand and head toward the stairs beyond the Parisian latticework. "I will, Mister Mayor. I truly will." James laughed. "It will be a pleasure." He then smiled at the pretty young woman standing beside him. She handed him a glass of red wine. "Thanks!" he said in a most charming voice.

"Hello, Mr. Lynn," she said, smiling. She gently kissed his cheek. "It's nice to have you come see us again."

*   *   *

Mayor Mayo returned to the waiting salon beyond the French lattice-
work about one hour later. His arm was bandaged and the sleeve repaired
and cleaned. "I am refreshed," he said with a broad smile. "Let's go home,
James." He looked pleasantly into James's eyes. "You look well refreshed,
too, son."

James accompanied him home. Wagons were still leaving the city and
heading west. A few hollow-eyed soldiers from the fighting to the east
were seen stumbling through the streets. He suddenly felt very sad. Sarah
and Mary had both left town. They had gone by canal boat to family
homes about thirty or forty miles away. He missed them desperately.

James had refilled the revolver the mayor had given him with bullets,
which Lil had provided from her office. She had told him about the
refugees who were filling the city from Williamsburg, Yorktown, and
other areas to the east. "Frightened people, James. They've lost everything. McClellan is humane, but his soldiers aren't. Homes were burned,
food taken or destroyed, fields decimated. It's grim. I've provided some
funds for those close by. You'll see them if you leave by the alley behind
here. Perhaps you can even help us a little from the commissary. Joseph
Mayo said he would help. He has pledged to do what he can.

"Those people are hungry. Please look at them. Some are in canvas
shelters; others in the open. With the drenching rains, that's been bad.
And some of the children are sick."

"I will, Lil. Thanks for telling me. Everything we're doing is to provide our armies with what they need. Also, Lee has been working very
hard to bring troops north from the Carolinas and Georgia. We'll need
every man we can get. If the Yankees get into the city, it may be worse. But
thanks for your help. You have a heart of gold. Thanks, Lil!"

"Don't worry," she said, laughing. "I've charged you a good sum,
Lieutenant. Some of it will go to help those people." She pointed toward
the back of the building. "Don't tell folks, though. They wouldn't understand. Especially the ladies."

The mayor and James rode slowly home. It was near dawn when they
arrived at the mayor's house. "The skulkers and the refugees are a real
problem, son. We can put some of them to work, but not all of them. Governor Letcher and I pressed several hundred into service on Capital
Square when Drewry's Bluff was attacked. The whole city was afraid then
and shuddering. We thought we'd have the Federals right here in our own
streets. I'm not sure we could have stopped them if Drewry's Bluff had

134

fallen, but we planned to try. Most of those we impressed wanted to fight. They were angry. They just needed leadership."

"Thank goodness you didn't have to," said James. His face was serious as he thought about what might have happened. "And I'm not sure you could have held out very long against trained troops anyway."

"I'm happy we didn't have to fight. And now we face a bigger problem. Can we win the next battle? It'll be a big one. Well, here we are. Thanks for staying with me, James. Come see me soon. I like your ideas," said the mayor.

As he walked toward the door, he spoke in a whisper to James. "I'm still smiling so folks won't know how terribly concerned I am about how things are going. I say, 'Don't worry!' a hundred times a day. You'd better do the same."

James arrived at his own room at dawn. The sky to the east was bright and pink. The day before, thick clouds and rain had blanketed the city. It had cleared by evening. Now auspicious sunlight shone down. There was a message on his door. "Why am I so urgently needed at the War Office? It says to come immediately. Well, it'll be a busy day, I'm sure!"

Lieutenant Lynn had just led Huger's Division to the bivouac site east of Richmond. He was returning to the War Office, but riding slowly past Armstead's men. His brother was with this brigade. These troops were resting by the side of the road awaiting orders.

"Hey, James!" came a loud shout. "Don't you recognize one of your kin?"

"Henry, you old son-of-a-gun you! I thought I wouldn't find you. Let me look. You've grown a mustache. You look wonderful." James sat back and looked carefully at his sun-tanned brother. His horse suddenly snorted and bucked, then pawed the ground as if it were anxious to be away. "You seem older, Henry. And well. The army's been good to you. I'll write Mother and Father today about my little brother. It's good to see you."

"James, it's nice to see you, too. I've marched a long way in this army since we last met. It was in April, wasn't it?"

"Yes. About a month and a half ago." Henry stretched his long legs, then stood erect. He was lean and lithe, and his eyes glowed like hot coals. James saw that he was inches taller than he'd remembered—taller than he himself. They shook hands.

"Well, tell Momma and Papa that I'm well. I had a touch of the bowels a few days ago." He turned to the soldier beside him. "This is Ben Toggler, by the way. He knew a good old family cure. Awful taste, but it worked. No problems now. Ben, this is my big brother, James." Ben and James shook hands. "Now tell us where you're taking us."

"I volunteered to lead this division to your bivouac, Henry. I hoped you'd be with them. There. You can see the place in the distance." He pointed to the northeast. "That flat elevation." James saw that Ben was also tall and lithe. His face was gaunt and impassive, and partly covered by a short beard. His cap was tilted at a rakish angle.

"Why that's a darn old cemetery," said Ben. "We're gonna sleep there? Damn. I'll have bad dreams."

"That's where I've been told to take you," said James. He was serious, but he suddenly had a polite smile on his lips.

"I'll share the nightmares with Henry," said Ben, smiling. "Besides, the coffee'll be just as good. And probably the ground'll be a little softer on those graves there."

James laughed. "You don't have to sleep right on the graves." He kept smiling. "Well, Henry, Ben, I'll be seeing you soon. I have to go. Lots of things are happening. For one, we're expecting Ripley's Brigade from South Carolina real soon. I think a few of the advanced companies are here already. Lee's trying to bring up all the troops he can put his hands on. Johnston needs every last one of them."

"Alvin Ripon's in that brigade," said Henry, laughing. "I hope I can see him. He's been lucky. After the shooting at Fort Sumter, they haven't done much. Just garrison duty in the city, I'm told. And flirting with all the pretty ladies in Charleston. Lucky guy. That's while Ben and I have been marching all over the countryside and shooting at real Yankees. Well, we'll see you, Brother James. Say hello to our sisters, too, in that letter." James rode off at a gallop. With the heavy rains, the ground was still wet. There wasn't much dust, and the streams and brooks were wild with water.

At least, thought James, *McDowell's stopped marching south toward Richmond. He's going back to the Rappahannock, I hope. We're still outnumbered, but we're not overwhelmed like we would have been if he'd joined "Little Mac." And we have brigades and regiments still arriving. Perhaps Johnston can stop McClellan.* He thought about this for a moment. *But even if he's stopped, he still has those siege guns. He can put shells right into the city. Poor Richmond. She'll be hurting. She is besieged!*

136

CHAPTER XVI
Deep Turmoil

General Jackson had again "disappeared," but he had a habit of reappearing where he was least expected. On May 23 he shattered Colonel Kenly's command at Front Royal, at the northern end of the Massanutten Ridge in the Shenandoah Valley. He then viciously attacked the Union army commanded by Banks, which had been outflanked and was retreating north. At Winchester on May 25, he struck Banks's quickly drawn-up defensive line. The Union forces were driven back to the Potomac.

This general, who had marched his soldiers mercilessly, and as some thought, almost "to death," had led them to a dazzling triumph. The North's recruiting stations, which had been closed in anticipation of victory, were reopened.

"The Union," said Mister Raymond, Papa's friend, "was like the man (who) . . . sold the lion's skin, while the beast lived, (and) was killed while hunting him."

The rest of this campaign is well-known history. Banks's men were huddled near the Potomac. Jackson put his "foot-cavalry" back on the road and marched south along the Valley Pike. Yankees in the lower valley outnumbered him by at least two-to-one. He passed through Strasburg only hours ahead of converging Federal columns ordered to intercept him. Jackson's men fought several brisk battles near the southern tip of the Massanutten Ridge, which stood between the Union forces like a great dike. They were unable to mass their troops and destroy this meddlesome soldier. Stonewall's forces prevailed. He then positioned his army in the valley east of Staunton and awaited orders from Richmond.

Like a volcano about to explode, the large armies before Richmond portended fighting. Johnston had directed that all available troops be brought to the capital. Both armies were poised for a "final" struggle—the Confederates to save the city, and the Union forces to capture it and end the war. Many would wonder about the tactics and strategies of the army commanders. No one would question the valor of the common soldiers who fought.

A deluge of rain swept down the Chickahominy River the night of May 30. Thunder crashed and rolled like a thousand cannons. McClellan had two corps south of the river. His other three were north, with his right flank close to the Virginia Central Railroad not far from the city.

Johnston had an opportunity. With most bridges over the river out of service, he could attack the isolated forces to the south with vastly superior numbers. Near dawn on May 31, his divisions were on the road marching east to attack McClellan. His plans for attack were excellent. Staff work and communications, unfortunately, were primitive and difficult.

Longstreet, for unknown reasons, had directed his troops to the wrong road, the Williamsburg Road. His orders were to march east on the Nine Mile Road. A frightful traffic jam resulted. Three full divisions were marching toward the enemy on the same one mile stretch of highway. The time of attack had been delayed. The minutes ticked away like grains of sand in an hour glass. The advantage of surprise was being lost.

Henry was with Armstead's Brigade of Huger's Division. That night of May 30, they slept near Oakwood Cemetery at the northeastern outskirts of the city. They arose before dawn and marched. "Well, what do you think of our army now, Henry? I don't even know what day it is."

"The last day of May, Ben."

"We've been waiting here on this hot road for hours. What happened to our orders? Our generals don't know where to take us. We slept near that gruesome cemetery last night, and not only did we get a big rainfall, but I swear I saw ghosts all around us."

"That was the lightning, Ben. It came close, but it didn't hurt us none," replied Henry.

"I guess not. But we got awful wet. Then they rushed us down that muddy hill, only to have us stand and watch while all those Longstreet fellas crossed that little creek before us. It was supposed to be just a small stream, you told me."

"It usually is, I guess. But not when we've had a storm. Gillies Creek is the name," Henry added.

"Then we waded across in water up to our waist. Little Sid, my friend up there"— he pointed forward to the company in front of them—"dang near got washed away. Why old Longstreet let us pass by him after that, I don't rightly know. He rushed ahead of us at that creek, then he let us walk right past his whole dang division while they stood and watched us. That's no way to win a war. Then he ordered two of his brigades detached. And they marched right by us again. Damned if I can see the reason. Somebody's daffy. Then they turned about and marched right back agin—like they's retreatin'. Now here we sit. Nothin' to do but wait. And where're those Yankees? I'd like to git me a few Bluebellies. Danged if I wouldn't." It was past noon. He held up his rifle, which he called "Big Berta." He laughed. "I's a damn good shot, too. But you gotta have somethin' to shoot at."

"You will. And I'm sorry, Ben, but in an army, you always have to wait. It takes time to get everyone in position. Yet it's strange. I'm not sure who's giving us orders. I guess Longstreet's directing Huger—or is supposed to be. I saw Captain Sykes's map. We have three columns marching east toward McClellan's lines. We're the right flank of the whole darn army. That's important. I think we're supposed to protect Longstreet's or D.H. Hill's flank from being turned."

"Turned where?" asked Ben.

"It means we prevent the Yanks from coming in on the very end of Hill's or Longstreet's battle line. If that happened, their few troops there would be greatly outnumbered. They'd have to retreat, and there'd probably be much confusion. That's how battles are won."

"That's bad?" Ben questioned.

"It is! They'd be rolled up like a top. Many would be killed." Henry was silent for a while. "Our trouble is partially the roads and streams. It's hard for the commander to send us orders. It's also hard for us to send requests to him for orders. That bad storm last night also hinders our wagons and cannons. It's difficult to bring them forward for the battle. Then there's that swamp ahead of us. You can't see it, but it's there. Hill's or Longstreet's men are probably knee-deep in water out there—or deeper. Like when we crossed the Gillies. I just hope we get there in time for some of the action."

"Your pa was a teacher, it sounds like. I guess you told me that. Maybe this soldiering stuff makes sense to you, but it don't to me. We ran away from Norfolk like scared rabbits," said Ben.

"It was a strategic retreat. We were outflanked."

"Well, we left in a big hurry for Petersburg. My feet are still sore. And my friend in the Fourteenth Virginia told me we sunk all those little boats we'd been protectin'. At least their gunners could join us and shoot at those damn Yankee's comin' up the James."

"At Drewry's Bluff, you mean. Yes. We stopped them, didn't we?

They turned like an old dog with his tail between his legs." Henry had a broad smile on his face. "They didn't get Richmond by water. Now they're trying to do it by land—and we're in the way. And maybe we can push 'em back a little."

"Yeh. If we don't get killed tryin'. Or die from the heat. I'm like that old cur of a dog. I just hope my tail doesn't turn under, too."

"We'll get 'em, Ben. Here comes another courier. Maybe it's our orders." A few minutes later, Henry saw Sykes approaching. "We're ready to go, Captain. Too much waiting as it is."

"Yeh, let's go get 'em," said Ben.

"You're right. We're marching," said Sykes. He pointed east. "Henry, follow our other companies up forward there—behind Armstead. We're gonna get those Bluebellies. You'll see."

They marched east along the Charles City Road, then turned north, following a muddy path toward the Williamsburg Road. They could hear the roll of musketry to the east and the deeper throb of artillery. There was heavy firing to the northeast too. "Somebody's fightin' out there," said Ben. "It ain't us."

"It will be," said Henry laughing. "Don't fret so much." Then his face hardened. He'd played with toy soldiers. With them you knew where everyone was. No guessing. Here you didn't know. He also thought they were being poorly led. "Was it Joe Johnston? Or could it be Longstreet? Well," he said to himself, "what's the difference? Maybe we soldiers can make it work. We'll do our best. At least I saw James for a few minutes. I wonder where he is now. He said we'd lose the whole war if we lose this fight." Henry thought for several minutes. "Well, at least I'm doing what I've wanted to do for a long time. I'm a soldier. And I understand a little about what's going on." He smiled. "And it's exciting."

"What's exciting?" asked Ben, laughing. "My feet are damn sore. And you stop that mumbling. You always come up with bright ideas when you mumble." Henry just smiled.

"Halt!" shouted Sykes. "Those're incoming shells! We'll deploy here," he continued. There was a great crash among the men in the company just in front of Henry and Ben.

"Damn!" said Ben. "I hope they didn't get my friend, Sid."

"We're in the fight now, Ben!" said Henry. His face was covered with a wry smile. He didn't feel afraid. "You wanted Bluebellies. Now's your chance."

"But I can't even see 'em, Henry. Where the hell are they?" Another shell crashed close by.

An artillery battery stood some yards to their front. They were returning the fire from the Union artillery on the far side of the swamp before them. As each cannon fired, it jumped back like an angry hound, tearing and throwing pieces of wet earth into the air. Fire belched from the muzzles as if from a dragon.

"We'll form a line of battle to the right of the road," shouted Captain Sykes. "Company, forward. MARCH! By file right. MARCH! Double quick. MARCH!" Ben and Henry went forward with the regiment. "Company, HALT," Sykes continued. They were in four columns with the other men of their company. "Left, FACE!"

The even-numbered men of each platoon stepped quickly forward and to the left. The soldiers were thus formed into two ranks, one behind the other, facing east. They were now in a line of battle, ready to go forward into the swamp. Two paces back stood a third line. These were the sergeants and lieutenants. They were called "file closers." To their right and left were other companies of the regiment.

The captain was to the far right of the company. Henry laughed as he looked from the captain to Sergeant Wilkin behind him. "The sergeant'll keep us moving."

"Yah," said Ben. "And they have to shoot right through us before they can get him."

Their regiment was in contact with another Virginia regiment to their left. Henry could see their battle flags. The long shadows of darkness were creeping over the field as they prepared to charge.

"We still don't see those damn Yankees," chuckled Ben. "Where am I supposed to shoot?"

Henry had then been wondering if he'd mastered Hardee's movement from line of battle into a "column of fours, by the right flank." He had just decided that that maneuver would have to wait for now. Ben's words sounded far away as if he were just awakening from a dream. "Well, don't shoot behind us," he said, laughing. "You might hit the sergeant."

"I heard that, Private," growled Sergeant Wilkin. The sergeant and the lieutenants looked intent and serious. Then Wilkin burst into a big smile. "We're ready to go, Henry. I'll be watching the two of you." Henry swallowed hard. It was thrilling, but he suddenly had a twinge that his dreams of being a soldier might end right here.

"Forward!" came the command. After passing the line of cannons, they walked slowly toward the water, which glinted in front of them like an evil pool. They entered it and quickly felt the black ooze at the bottom suck at their feet and draw them deeper in with each step forward. Water lapped at their knees and thighs. Bullets whistled around them like small insects. Several men in the company fell forward and had to be pulled from the water to prevent them from being drowned. A man in front of Ben fell, his whole head shattered apparently by a shell fragment. The man was dead. As he collapsed, the advancing column stepped around him.

"Damn!" said Ben as he wiped the man's blood from his face and eyes. They had just reached higher ground where it was easier to march. They continued going forward. Suddenly men in gray came running back through the tangle of woods to their front. They passed through Armstead's column and kept retreating.

"Steady," shouted Sykes. "Keep going." They advanced another forty yards as bullets whistled close by and men to their right and left were injured and fell.

"HALT," shouted Sykes. "Fire at will!" Henry and Ben both stood and fired time and again. Often there was no target they could actually see through the smoke, but the Yankees were out there and shooting one round after another. Henry swore as he dropped a percussion cap into the black water at his feet.

Other men in the company staggered and fell. With the tangle of trees and scrub brush, it was impossible to see the other regiments to their right and left. "We're retreating," said Sykes. "We'll go back slowly and keep firing. We need to get to higher ground."

"Slowly!" shouted Wilken. "Slowly, men. That's the way." He looked like a tiger that had just roared and was now licking his lips.

Armstead finally sent word that the regiments to their right and left had already retired. "We're in danger of being isolated or turned," said Henry. "This is a holding action now."

"Damn!" shouted Ben. "It was just becomin' fun."

"It's nice to have you come along with me, Lieutenant," said General Lee.

James wasn't sure if Lee wanted an answer. "It's a pleasure, sir. I can't stand to stay in an office when our whole army's marching. I did that when that Mannassas battle was fought. It darn near killed me, waiting for news.

Thanks for letting me ride out to Johnston's headquarters with you, General."

"Son, I felt the same way. We've done everything we can in town. Now it's up to Johnston. And much is at stake. With that big storm, the flooded Chickahominy'll be in our favor. McClellan'll have trouble bringing any troops across to strengthen his two corps in front of us. Maybe we can drive 'em back. Perhaps even destroy them. We'll see." Lee smiled at James. "You were the officer who got Huger into position last night, I'm told. Thanks."

"And Ripley's close too, sir. I have a friend in one of his regiments. Most of his men are still on the other side of the James, though." Lieutenant Lynn had briefly seen Alvin Ripon. He was with Ripley's Brigade from South Carolina. The had been called up to Richmond by Lee. Alvin told James that his brother, Dan, had been killed in the defensive action before Williamsburg. James suddenly had felt very sad. "Little Dan Ripon. We grew up together," he said silently, "Now he's gone." He had written his family about this the night before. *That was Emmie's friend. She'll be crushed,*" he thought. "*But I guess that's war. How foolish men are!*"

James turned to Lee. "My friend's brother was with the Twenty-fourth Virginia at Williamsburg. He was killed there. It was a sad meeting."

"Brave men," said Lee. " They were in Hill's division. D. H. Hill. He held our left flank there. Many were killed charging an artillery position. Those Yankees were hitting Fort Mugruder across an open field, when the Twenty-fourth came out of the woods and attacked. They were delayed, though, by stout post-and-rail fences. Their charge was finally aborted. It probably didn't hold McClellan back much, but it showed how fine our soldiers can be. We can do a lot with them if they're handled properly, son."

They rode on silently. Perhaps Lee was thinking about the letter he'd written to the army's commanding officer, Johnston, asking if he might be appointed to an active command. James didn't know this, but Lee wanted to be in the field and fighting. He wanted a chance to lead troops in action—any troops in the coming battle. Johnston had sidestepped Lee's wish. He wrote back stating that more regiments were needed. Now all those available were being hurried forward. The paperwork and planning were done, and only time would give answers.

A dull, cloudy day surrounded them. James watched Lee ride forward and begin talking to other officers in his small troop. They were on the Nine Mile Road, heading east toward Johnston's headquarters three miles from the city. This rutted, well-traveled thoroughfare led to McClellan's main position south of the Chickahominy River. Deep wagon tracks and the flotsam of war marred the surface.

Johnston was not at his headquarters. "He's gone forward," an aide shouted. Lee and his attendants continued on in that direction.

Confederate soldiers were in a line of battle across the highway a short distance ahead, near where the New Bridge Road went north. They found Johnston at Magruder's headquarters there, just off the Nine Mile Road. Everyone seemed tense. A general movement was evidently going on, and Johnston appeared to be repositioning his troops and moving them forward. He gave Lee a brief explanation. James thought he seemed very abrupt, but he finally decided that this should be expected, considering the intensity of the moment.

They waited. Couriers came and went. None of Lee's small group knew what was happening. James heard the faint sounds of guns to the southeast. It was near three o'clock. Lee smiled. "That's musketry."

"No!" said Johnston. "It can only be an artillery action." He explained no further, but he soon hurried off in the direction of the guns. He was following troops that had just moved forward along the Nine Mile Road.

The strange, indefinite sounds continued. They became more intense. James saw Lee smile. He then saw the familiar figure of President Davis approaching. "Welcome, sir," said Lee. Johnston could still be seen riding across the field and disappearing on the road beyond. "Have you heard it?" asked Lee.

"Most assuredly, General. What does it mean?" asked Davis.

"I believe it's musketry, Mister President. Johnston told me it's an artillery action, though." As they listened, they decided it was either a heavy skirmish or a battle, probably near where the Nine Mile Road turned south toward Fair Oaks Station on the Richmond and York River Railroad.

Lee and Davis hurried forward toward the sound, following Johnston. The others followed close by. James began thinking about how he had accompanied Lee the day before across the Chickahominy and along the Virginia Central Railroad tracks. They found that McClellan had moved his right flank eastward, back from the rail line. Could the Union general have anticipated Johnston's attack? If so, would this influence the outcome? He didn't know, and Lee had not commented on the significance.

They continued on for about a mile. There were dense woods on

144

their right. An open flat field was to their left. As they continued farther, they came to a lane that probably led to the Chickahominy. It was surrounded by a thick tangle of trees. The troops they had followed up the road were deployed on farming land just beyond. They were evidently driving back Federal pickets.

There was great confusion. Suddenly a shell exploded close by. James nearly fell from his horse, but he had enough sense to realize that their president was coming under a hot fire, too, from the musketry nearby, as well as the artillery. "You'd better get back, Mister President," he shouted. His voice seemed to be shrill and metallic. Hidden Union batteries were now sending in an intense fire of well-directed shells. These Union forces seemed to be in the rear of the Confederate lines. To their right, another Southern column was heavily engaged. Clouds of smoke were everywhere. Johnston apparently was somewhere beyond this point in the thick of the fighting.

Lee was only an observer without authority. Davis made a quick reconnaissance, then sent a message to Magruder to hurry troops over beyond the Federal right. Magruder could not be found, but fortunately Smith's division was coming up. Griffith's Brigade of that division was formed into a line of attack. They prepared to advance on the left. Before they could go forward, Confederate troops to their front came streaming back from the woods. There was no one now for Griffith to support. Further loss of life would have been futile. The attack was cancelled.

James waited with Lee. There was no counterattack by the Federals. Southern wounded were staggering back from the woods now. Postmaster-General Reagan rode up. He had been farther to the south to cheer Hood's Texans. He told them that he'd found Johnston in great danger and taking unnecessary chances. "And you, Mister President, are needlessly exposed." Davis wouldn't leave, however.

A courier arrived at a gallop. He skidded to a halt near the president. General Wade Hampton had been badly wounded. Another courier arrived moments later. General Johnston was, also, seriously injured. Perhaps the wound would be fatal.

Confusion surrounded them. Neither Lee nor Davis had time to plan any statement about what this might mean to the South, however. Just then a litter was seen to be approaching from across the battleground. Johnston was being carried from the field. The litter-bearers were passing between all those other wounded and discouraged men. Many were limping. Some were without rifles, probably dropped in the heat of the battle. A few were bandaged. Others had fresh, clotted blood over uniforms and faces.

Most in Lee's small troop were silent as the litter carrying Johnston approached. He was conscious, but in severe pain. Davis showed great compassion for his friend and chief officer. He offered any help he could give. He even offered his own home until Johnston's wounds were healed.

Lee made no mention of what he thought the future course of the Confederacy should be. It was a desperate hour. No one but Johnston knew the dispositions of the troops. Fortunately, both armies were quite content to leave things as they were.

James rode back to Richmond some yards behind Davis and Lee. Those two distinguished men talked for a while, then both were quiet. Then they talked again. Words seemed to come slowly as James watched. They rode past tangled woods and by small streams where reserve troops were bivouacking and sleeping. Lines of ambulances surrounded them. Fires flickered on both sides of the road as men rested and prepared meals.

The two riders ahead of James and the small group of officers lapsed, finally, into a long silence. Then they heard Davis speak. His voice was not very loud, but they could understand his words. "General Lee, I shall assign you to the command of this army. Make your preparations as soon as you reach your quarters. I shall send you the order when we reach Richmond."

The direction of the war had changed. Lee was now in command of an army. It would soon be known as they Army of Northern Virginia. Many great battles were still to be fought. The war would now last three more years.

James suddenly realized he was shaking his head from side-to-side and taking deep breaths. Perhaps it was from the strong emotions he felt. He had always idolized Lee. He had often thought that Lee had never really been given the chance to command. He also realized he was thinking of Sarah. *How beautiful she is,* he thought. *And how I miss her. War is a tragedy. It kills good people. We've seen them die today. But love builds civilizations. It doesn't tear them down. God, how I miss her. What will happen next? Will she and her family be able to come home? Can Lee stop them?* They were entering Richmond now. Wagons, ambulances, and hollow-eyed soldiers surrounded them.

Henry had just dozed off. The ground was wet, and so was his blanket. He ached from head to foot. He was uninjured, but very tired. He awoke with a start. "Dang!" Ben had shouted. "We's right back to where we started. And all our friends killed or hurt. Even those cannons have gone back. And where is the rest of Huger's Division? They ain't even with us, I heard."

"I don't know, Ben. I guess they've fallen back. But we held!"

"We sure did. We sure did." Henry couldn't see Ben's face. He wasn't sure if he was proud or sad.

CHAPTER XVII

The Army of Northern Virginia

James's letter about Alvin Ripon and the death of his brother, Dan, had been received in Staunton. Emmie was crushed. She cried often. "It's terrible, Momma. I can't believe he's dead. He just can't be dead. I've seen so many of our soldiers in Staunton die, but I never thought it would happen to a friend who was so close."

"It happens, Emmie. A terrible war. And we're going to hear about it more often now. We'll know of friends in Amherst as well as new friends here in Staunton who'll never come back. It isn't only the bullets. It's sickness. We've been lucky so far, but I hope your two brothers are safe. Where are they now? Since that big battle near Fair Oaks and that railroad, we haven't heard a thing. James wrote his letter the night before the battle." She shook her head slowly. Her eyes were distant. "I just pray they're both well."

"I just pray they're both alive, Momma," replied Emmie. She saw her mother close her eyes. Her lips were taut. There was a slight quiver of the muscles in her cheeks.

"We'll both pray, Emmie," said Momma as she returned to dusting and rearranging books on the oak shelves before them. The wood was graylike, as if imbued with the dust that was being carefully wiped away. Emmie began to help her mother. She cleaned each volume, then smiled as she ran her fingers over the leather covers and around the golden tracings embossed on the surfaces. Each book had a musty smell after years of use. There were many notes in the margins, and large sections were underlined.

There was other news—from Amherst. Annie's friend, George Green, had been badly hurt. He wrote the letter himself. He was back in the town after a long siege of illness in hospitals at Charlottesville. He had been injured in the fight with Jackson at Kernstown. "I lost an arm, Annie. I still have the right one, which I use for writing. I wake up at night and think the other one's still there. When I touch the spot, it isn't. It just hurts and burns when you feel where it used to be. At least I can still work with my pa. He says I'm needed. I also do work with the regiment forming here. Our boys are learning to march in a right good way . . . "

Annie wrote him that afternoon. For all her enthusiasm about soldiers, Kath noticed her eyes were sad when she came down from her room.

McClellan's Army of the Potomac had been slowed but not stopped. This vast Yankee army was positioned just east of Richmond.

Lee renamed Johnston's Confederate forces the Army of Northern Virginia. It was outnumbered two-to-one by Federal troops. It would defend the capital. Union balloon observers could easily see the buildings of Richmond. The plum, the heart of the Confederacy, was within McClellan's grasp. A fortnight later, he had been defeated.

Many thought the South would lose that battle for Richmond. This did not happen. Their best generals were in command. Lee's strategy was to attack. For seven days the two armies fought. Battle lines bent forward, wavered, retreated, then attacked again. It was a violent struggle, and thousands of men were lost. McClellan was finally driven back to Malvern Hill, a hundred-foot plateau near the James River. He hovered under the protection of his gunboats. People cheered this victory throughout the Confederacy, but there was much sadness in individual homes, in the North and South.

The name, Army of Northern Virginia, was fortuitous. Many battles would be fought there. For three long years, it would hold the Federal armies at bay. Mister Lincoln later observed, " . . . woe to that man by whom the offense cometh . . . blood drawn by the lash shall be paid for by another drawn by the sword . . . "

The Lynn children had been taught that slavery began North and South for one reason: profits. Blood had been drawn by the lash; it was to be paid for with blood drawn by the sword. Years later, Kath realized how true these words spoken by Mister Lincoln had been. Economics may have been paramount in the origin of the war, but the South, where slavery continued, suffered a system that some thought foreboded defeat. Still, the South rallied and fought; it was a sacred trust. Most thought they could not lose.

Political leaders extolled the Confederate cause and noble purpose to newly inducted troops trained by Papa. Kath would remember one of the men who spoke; "Each of you knows what the fighting is about. Our ways must be defended, sometimes even with life itself." The man's face was veined and his body rounded, as if culinary enjoyments were not unknown to him.

Mister Raymond commented to Kath's father, "I wonder if this man's life has ever been in danger." Papa did not answer.

The politician continued, "War is a demanding school, but we shall continue to do battle for what we believe. When we return to our homes, we will say with pride, 'I fought for my land.' I'm proud of you all. You will be fine soldiers. God be with you. You will serve with honor."

The unmentionable word, "money," which motivated those "rational men" who were striving to create a "Cotton Kingdom," was realized by very few. Also, the South had misjudged the enemy. The Yankees were far from being cowardly.

Martin Stiles, who was visiting the Lynns' neighbor, Mister Raymond, sat with them late one evening. Momma had ordered the young ones to bed. Kath stood in the hall and listened. Martin was a professional soldier and had fought against Grant at Shiloh. "They're tough," he said, smiling. "There are capable Yankee soldiers out there. You all talk about the Eastern armies, but the Bluebellies are cutting us in half at the Mississippi. They'll have us in the end, I'm afraid."

Suddenly, pandemonium broke out in the parlor. Even calm Mister Raymond nearly shouted in a high, unfamiliar pitch, "We're just beginning to fight! Watch Lee! Maybe Davis will send him west."

"We need him more here," Papa countered. "The war can be lost quickly without Lee near Richmond."

Kath later thought that she should have returned and looked at the faces of her family. She had never heard them so excited, and she had always believed they hated war. Now she, also, realized they couldn't face losing it. They all disagreed, however, on what action the South should take.

The talk in homes and on the streets was now mostly about the war. "Men like war; it fills a need," said Mrs. Larkin, one of Momma's friends in town.

A group of women were standing with Momma at the streetside, on a dusty warm day. "We'll hurt a whole generation if this goes on," another woman answered. "Yet, we can't stop fighting. We're different," she continued. "We love the soil—not factories."

"Yes, but there must be better ways," Kath's mother said. She was frowning. "All people have problems. Why kill thousands to find an answer?"

"I think it's our politicians," said Mrs. Larkin. "For three decades they've failed to find answers. Now we're fighting. Also, our boys become bored with ordinary things. They want thrills and flattery. To be brave becomes a virtue in their eyes."

"Foolish. Foolish—we humans. You can't eat bravery—yet it becomes so plentiful that it smothers you," said Momma.

"We women hate war," said Mrs. Larkin. "We'd stop it if we were in charge. Each generation of men seems to crave fighting till they find it's terrible and dirty and hurts; still they continue."

Kath would hear for years how much women had hated the war. She spoke with hundreds after it ended. Still, patriotism was imbued; the rolls of the paupers were augmented, as their loved ones faced enemy guns, and fell "gloriously" on the field of battle. Many women wondered, "Were the reasons ever sufficient to kill so many?"

In much of the South, however, there was a universal effort to believe in its final triumph. This was true with most of the people in Staunton. They questioned, though, if the violence was truly justified. They had heard no guns fired in anger. Yet, below the surface there was a vague uneasiness; nerves were stretched and muscles taut. Friends spoke sharply to friends, then later apologized.

Papa often listened to others on the streets when he was in town. Kath was with him one day. They found three men arguing.

"You have no sons in the war; why should you care about the battles?"

"I love our people," the man replied. "Besides, I have a brother-in-law and two nephews with our Western armies. I care!"

"Stop it, you two," said the third man. "We all care. Don't fight each other."

The first two were red-faced and angry. Suddenly, one smiled and extended his hand. They shook hands, then walked on together.

"There is much pain beyond the battlefields, Katherine," Papa said. "You've just seen some of it. We'll see more."

Staunton, Kath would remember, like other towns throughout the North and South, hungered for news. The fact that a large battle was happening far away seemed to be known by all. She always wondered why. "Could the word have been carried by the wind?" she asked her mother.

"It seems that way," Momma answered. "So often, no one has to be told. Maybe it's sensed, as is the life of those we love."

To Kath, birds seemed to change their songs, and the wind spoke with a different tone. "But we all listen," she said time and again to herself. "We hope we're wrong about a battle. So often we aren't."

Kath continued to listen to her family. "We won a fine victory at that little stream we call Manassas," said Uncle Wen that evening. "That's where the first big fight took place. You know," he continued, "where Jackson stood like a stone wall." Manassas had been the site of a previous great struggle. The second battle there was no less desperate. The South won that second battle too.

"Lee is over the Potomac in Maryland now," Papa answered. "I'm not sure where. I can't imagine that McClellan will let him go rampaging about in the North. I guess you know McClellan was relieved of command for a while. Now he's back in charge. Lincoln was just as frustrated with his other generals. Thankfully, our best team is in there fighting. Lincoln should be worried now."

Following Manassas, Lee had crossed the Potomac and met the enemy at a little town in Maryland. They faced each other across a small, sluggish stream known as Antietam Creek. Reports of the battle were sent via Richmond to Staunton. It took time.

In front of the newspaper office, the Lynns waited with others for word about the battle. Reverence, mixed with the anticipation of sorrow, had crept over and hugged the town. The pall blanketed them all. It pushed aside their usual enthusiasm. Kath noticed that many folks were looking upward. They seemed to be praying. The blue dome above was bright and dotted with fluffy clouds. The minutes, then hours, became piled, one on top of the other, like Spartans in battle. No official news was heard.

Kath would later remember the worried, patient faces of those around her. As the years passed, she could no longer identify most of them. The personality of each person and memories about them had become shaded, one into the other, like the soft colors of a rainbow, but when blended together, however, they become a triumphant whole. This was an assembly of caring, working people. She would always love them.

"Please help him be alive, Lord," an aging women near Kath said. "Please! Billie, you're my only son. Your family needs you." All prayed their men would survive. There was dread expectation that great pain would be caused by those lists for which they waited.

Loving mothers stood patiently, faces wan and solemn. They remained calm and attractive, but careless, straggling locks over foreheads and necks betrayed deep turmoil. The demeanor of these women added an element of eloquence to the milling crowd.

Dust rose from the dry streets, clogging throats and nostrils. Rumors spread like intoxicated flies.

"The Yanks are invincible."

"God has forsaken us."

"Our army has been pushed into the river; it's been destroyed."

"The Yanks have retreated, driven almost to Washington."

"'Jeb' Stuart's cavalry has been broken."

They cried for news. What had really happened? No one knew.

The crowd grew; they were restless. As people were pressed together, anger occasionally overcame patience. Hardly a person there had not sent a husband or son away to the war. This battle was in Maryland and north of Virginia soil. People thirsted for revenge. "Virginia has been trampled and burned," one man said. "Now the Yankees can feel the heel of an invader. They deserve it."

"We should destroy their fields and ravage their homes," a second man said.

"We'll turn out their women," said another.

Groups of neighbors and friends stood on porches and walks, as well as in the streets. To Kath, they seemed to move to and fro as if listening to a somber Bach cantata. A close friend of Momma's, who lived nearby, stood quietly in a doorway off the street. The children called her "Aunt Mary." What a fine caring person! Traces of wrinkles swept out from the corners of her eyes and mouth. Glasses with small rims rested on her nose, partially covering her weathered skin.

Aunt Mary was a quiet person who asked for little, but she gave much of herself. She had no family—no son or daughter or husband. Some thought she had a brother, somewhere, but never visited. She was basically alone, yet she was always cheerful. She seemed to be there when friends or neighbors needed help or just an ear to hear about a difficult problem. As these people talked about their troubles, they suddenly realized Aunt Mary was listening.

Her house was fresh like a clean piece of denim. She cooked plain meals. Kath and her sisters knew that. They'd been there. What wonderful cookies and tarts she hid, in easy-to-find places. Her eyes were kind. She undoubtedly was lonely, but she compensated for it with a warm heart.

153

Things were often left at doorsteps for less fortunate families in town. Food, old clothing, a prayer, somehow seemed to be placed on the right step.

Kath thought for years that Aunt Mary was the source of these kind deeds. She finally knew it was true. Her mother often helped. A few days before Momma passed away, years after the war, she whispered this in private. "Kath, remember Aunt Mary, that very old lady in Staunton? She did much for many people. She never let them know. I helped once in a while."

Momma hesitated, searching for words. "She seemed to know about everyone. She had limited funds, but she used them for others. There are people like that in the world. She always said, 'My wants are simple.' We should remember her, Kath. Tell your children about her."

Kath was always glad that Momma had told her this. Someone like Aunt Mary should be remembered.

Aunt Mary's heart that day went out to all those standing around her. She spoke to Kath. "We must help them," she said. "We'll find ways. Talk with them, Katherine, and smile. We all need friends when we're worried."

Kath did, and folks smiled back.

Hatred of the enemy and fear of the expected casualty lists made anger bubble to the surface. Oh, the horrors the Yankee armies had perpetrated! Children in the South could recite stories about the fear and the fires. Some of these stories were true, but not all of them. Children had been taught to believe them, though. People had "seen" what had happened in Virginia. Careless testimonials and hateful recollections by others from Tennessee and Mississippi fueled the anger.

Mister Raymond, the Lynns' neighbor, pleaded for moderation. "Many of the tales aren't true. Some are imagined. Their boys and ours are probably equally bad and good. It's the war. When you're frightened, it's hard to be nice. It brings out the worst in most of us."

The people waited. Hours passed.

CHAPTER XVIII

The Lists Grow Longer

Kath always remembered the terror of those long lists. The door of the newspaper office opened slowly. Suddenly, everyone was quiet. The squeak of the hinges of the heavy door sent a shiver of fear through those waiting outside. People winced and looked away. It was as if a dreaded executioner ascended the scaffold, watched painfully by the accused.

"Here he comes," said a man close by.

"Tell me he's safe," answered the women beside him.

"Now, now, Mary, he's all right. He's strong."

"Not against guns," she said.

The editor, an ancient, white-haired man, stepped cautiously out onto the walk. He was carrying the list of names. His face was tense. His deep eyes were a soft gray but sharply drawn from worry. He was not the professional examiner standing aloofly over the remains. He was a caring townsman bringing tragic news. Men had died. Many were injured. Others were missing. These were not unknown names. They were brothers and fathers, neighbors and friends.

A member of each family reached to receive the galley copies still fresh from the press.

"My hand's shaking," whispered Mrs. Larkin, Momma's friend. Her face was flushed and worried.

Reluctantly, the names were read by all. Tears welled up.

"No, no, he can't be gone," said an anguished father close by. "He's our only son. Why?" He shook his head sadly. "This must be wrong, Mary. John is so fine. He can't be taken away."

The Mitchells, who lived near the Lynns, as well as other friends and neighbors, looked at the lists with consternation. "These awful papers," Mrs. Mitchell choked. "I can't see them, Father." She squinched up her face, then handed the sheets to her husband.

"His name's here, Mother. I can't see it well, but I'm sure that's our George."

155

There was a name of a loved one. It could not be erased. "Oh, no," she whispered. "He's a good boy. Tell me it's not our son, Lord. Please, help him. Please!" She cried softly. Her husband drew her gently to his shoulder. There was a stoic look on his face, but his hand trembled slightly.

Pride and patriotism were seen in but few of the faces of those in the crowd. Most seemed sombered by dismay and anguish. Kath saw Aunt Mary walk to Mrs. Mitchell, smile compassionately, then gently grasp her arm. "We'll find out," she said softly. "Lists and figures can be wrong. Don't give up hope."

Aunt Mary was right. The Mitchell's son lived. He finally returned home. He was ill but very much alive.

Ann Lynn breathed a deep sigh as she said, "Thank God, James! Henry's name's not here." Henry Lynn had fought in that battle. When they next saw him, he had matured greatly. His face had been scarred; a dark angular line wrinkled the corner of the mouth. It was here that a shell fragment had cut the skin.

Though their brother survived the battle, many others had not. The tragic losses at Antietam were reported in the North and South.

Henry wrote weeks later, "I'm well. My face was scratched a little, but I'm a veteran now. Momma, thanks for teaching me cooking. I do a fairly good job for the company. We eat on the ground; not many tables."

Momma shuddered when she read this. Cooking. He's not a cook. I hope they get something edible."

"They're strong," Papa murmured. "They don't need much, and they probably find ladies to cook, anyway, or someone."

Momma glared at her husband. She wasn't happy about this conclusion. "He better stay away from that kind," she said caustically.

I sleep on the ground, wet or dry [Henry continued]. Then I wrap all my things in a poncho and blanket; these are tied over my shoulder down to the waist. When we march, we travel light. I have no roots; no home place to stay. We have lots of stories, though. Like those apples we took from the Maryland farmer. He was furious. Especially with the chickens we got later. He chased us with a horse and an old saber. We finally turned around with guns at the ready. He stopped very quickly. The captain said angry things about our doing this, but the whole company ate very well that night.

I gamble a little at cards. I'm getting pretty good at it. Also, Papa, I'm getting better at checkers. I'll take you and Uncle Wen on when I'm home. I play chess, too. The battles are terrible. No pen can tell the horrors. We forget the dangers when in it, though. I told a friend, "You're a hero." He

156

answered, "And here I lie bleeding." His leg was badly hurt. It's sad.

Many deserted before and after Sharpsburg, but most are coming back now. We lost many good men in that fight. We're strong again, and we're near Fredricksburg. From the beginning, the war has whirled around this town. It has been occupied by both armies, and the countryside is devastated. Dark chimneys stand like lonely soldiers. Crops are trampled and stock run off. Stragglers terrorize the few who remain. Those who can afford to leave have already left.

The area to the Potomac is a wasteland—strange and empty, I'm told. Virginia certainly is hurting. In contrast, farms in Pennsylvania bulge with food. Stuart rode there to find the Yankees. I have friends who rode with him. Not all people are suffering, I guess. The life in the cavalry is exciting. They eat better too. Maybe the difference is the cook. Also, they can ride and get supplies. I'll write again soon. Love, Henry.

The battle at the Antietam (Sharpsburg) in which Henry fought was a draw. *Perhaps,* thought Papa, *we hurt them a little more than they hurt us.* Just before that battle, a copy of Lee's general orders had reached the enemy. It makes one believe that a supernatural being alters what we humans do. Lee was in Maryland. His marching orders became known by McClellan, who then advanced with startling precision toward the Confederate troops north of the Potomac.

These columns were stretched over miles of rutted roads. Mister Lincoln is said to have thought that "so long an animal must be very thin somewhere." He wanted that animal broken. Troops had to be brought together en masse. Lee stood valiantly. He held the passes in South Mountain, giving his troops time to concentrate. He then sidestepped and retreated to the strong position behind Antietam Creek. There he resisted a horrendous offensive by Union soldiers. The losses for both armies were staggering.

The Confederate lines held—barely. Lee then waited a whole day for McClellan to continue the attack. In some places only one small brigade stood between McClellan and Sharpsburg. The Yankees could have easily broken Lee's thin line of exhausted men. They had fresh troops (V and VI Corps) in reserve. Lee watched. His back was to the Potomac River—a dangerous position. He then sensibly retreated across the river to Virginia soil. Except for raiding parties, the Yankees did not follow for many weeks.

As usual, McClellan had hesitated. He was soon removed from command by Mr. Lincoln. These cautious generals were being replaced.

Future battles would be hard. The battle at Sharpsburg was fought in September 1862. It was followed by a frightful struggle along the Rappahannock at Fredericksburg in December. The South won a great victory there. Southern troops seemed irresistible. The Lynns wondered if this were a prophecy of final victory. It wasn't.

They were still in Staunton. A cold winter was beginning. The new year, 1863, approached. In the Confederacy, spirits were high; they were in the ascendant. The reverses and panic of the spring had been overcome. "Richmond has been saved, and the Yankees have been pushed out of the Valley," said Papa. "It's been a good year for the South. Maybe we are tougher than they are. We won that Fredericksburg fight, too. I hope Henry's all right. I'm sure he was in that battle. Let's drink a toast to his health." Papa raised his glass.

"Here. Here!" said Aunt Sue. "And to the success of our armies!" she said, smiling.

The Lynn family was sipping Uncle Elmer's brandy before a large fire. It was snowing. "I pray the war is nearly over," Papa continued. "I'm glad I don't know what the future holds, but by the way things are going, it should end soon."

"We hope!" said Annie. "The Yankees are still strong and mean, though." She smiled. "May I have some brandy too? I'm almost eighteen."

Papa looked her straight in the eye and shook his head. "Wait a while longer, Annie. It's a dangerous drink. We sip it occasionally to relax."

Momma was more emphatic. "No! Annie. Not yet."

Henry was in the battle at Fredericksburg. He never wrote about it.

The new year, 1863, dawned auspiciously. It later brought sadness to the Lynn family. In that year, a loved one was injured in Pennsylvania and later died. The South won great battles. Others were lost. The high tide, the apogee of the Confederacy, was reached and passed. The South had not nor would it become victorious. Yet, the winter and spring of that year were filled with many bright memories for Katherine and her sisters.

They never suffered much for the lack of good food. Momma's fine management overcame the scarcity of most necessities. The blockade by the Union Navy, though, produced progressive problems for the conscientious housewife.

"Prices are so high, James," Momma complained to their father. "Sugar is fifteen times as expensive and coffee forty. I can't afford to buy them."

"Fifteen from when?" Papa asked.

"From just before the war. We can hardly afford to live. It's not easy. It's good we saved some money."

"Elmer sends us a little," Papa commented. "Very little, I might say."

"He's honest, James. You'll see."

Papa shook his head. "I'm sure he is. I just hope he's a good manager."

"Merchants in town say there's an awful lot they don't have, James," said Uncle Wen. "There're many necessities they just can't get anymore." He looked hard at Papa. "Our armies also need a lot of things. We're a farming land. There aren't many factories or machine shops. That's what you need to fight a war. We've talked about that."

"We have talked about that. At least it helps us understand what our soldiers face," Papa replied. "Also, with thousands of men gone from farms, food is short in some areas. A few planters even refuse to grow what's needed. They continue to plant money crops and find ways to send what they grow to the North. I guess that's good business, though. They make money."

"'Dishonest' is a better term," said Wen.

"Still, we can purchase many things from others," Papa continued. "Europe is glad to have our business. And we can still supply many of our needs from the North. It's surprising how a Yankee will sell goods to the enemy. Money rules most of us, I suppose. It's sad. There are more important things, like the lives of our men."

"We're buying all kinds of goods right now, I'm told," said their uncle. "Surgical instruments, medicines, shoes, blankets, lead, many rifles and cannons, saltpeter. Mostly it's for fighting men." He began smiling and rubbed his chin. "But we do get some luxuries for civilians. Especially for the ladies. They're expensive. Just what we need—silks, satins, trinkets of all kinds. You can't feed people with trinkets, can you?"

"Men risk their lives to bring them in," said Momma. "We're lucky they're willing. It's just too bad it's for money."

"You men want your ladies dressed prettylike," said Aunt Sue. "Now you stop that talk about satins and trinkets. They lift our morale. Yours too. We also save money by making things from what we have here. Ann used that old mosquito netting for her dress there—and it's beautiful."

"It is pretty, Momma," said Emmie, smiling. "Can I do it with the fabric you gave me last week?"

"Certainly, Emmie. It's upstairs. You know. In our sewing room. I'll get it later."

The Confederacy could survive without luxuries, but the equipment for fighting was vital. Blockade running was the only means for the South to supply many of the vast needs of its armies. The coastline extended from the Potomac River to the Rio Grande—a distance of about 3,500 miles. When the war began, few Federal ships were ready for action, and sneaking past the Yankees was "easy." However, the cordon of military vessels vastly increased as the war continued.

In 1863, three out of four ships successfully bypassed the blockade. In late 1864, though, only one of two vessels avoided capture or destruction. One by one the most important Confederate ports were sealed off or captured—Beaufort, New Bern, Charleston, New Orleans, Mobile, and others were lost. Finally, Wilmington, North Carolina, was the last major port open to the blockade-running fleet.

"Some of our family lived near Wilmington," Papa told his family. "I visited there when I was a young'un—years ago. I had no beard then. I was smooth as a peach, not gray like now." He smiled, while he stroked his whiskers. "Old sailors used to tell about the cape in that area. Cape Fear, down-river from Wilmington, has always been a terrible place for ships to pass. The Frying Pan Shoals reached south from there. Those moving sands are like tentacles. They can tear out the heart and soul of a ship, and kill all inside. Many good men have disappeared in those waters.

"I can still hear the winds that blow over that tiny bit of sand," he continued. "When I was young, I thought I heard the faint voices of maidens, like the sirens of mythology, that lured sailors to a terrible death. Seductive women, Ann. They can lure men to eternity."

Momma thought a moment. She laughed as if trying to find something funny to say. "I agree, James. We women are strong—seductive, too. Even good men respond, I'd say. I hope this helps with eternity. Some of you need lots of help."

"Hmm!" Papa chuckled, blushing slightly. "You're right. You're, also, strong—and fascinating, too. I guess that's what seductive means."

"Well, thank you, James," said Aunt Sue, brightly. "It takes time to draw out these compliments. We need this support, occasionally. You keep it up," she said, laughing.

Kath lived in Wilmington soon after the war. She remembered her family talking about that region and the blockade. She, too, was told that the waters down-river from the town had consumed many brave folks over the years. This bar of sand extending into the sea was properly named the

160

Cape of Fear. During the war, Fort Fisher and those lethal shoals protected the approach to the Cape Fear River and the vital port of Wilmington.

James, Kath's brother in Richmond, knew much about this region. It was a major port for receiving military equipment from overseas. Also, he provided his family and some friends with valuable imported items like bolts of pretty fabrics, spices, some coffee, and other treasures, which he seemed to have acquired surreptitiously. Kath would remember the stealth and hushed voices when he arrived home with these luxuries.

"Where is this from, James?" Papa asked. "Not dishonest, I hope?"

"The blockade fleet," he replied. "I have friends. Don't ask too much, Papa."

His father shook his head, knowingly. "Be careful, son," he cautioned.

Kath thought these treasures might have been stolen, not by James, but by others. Thankfully, they were not. They were brought to Southern shores by daring men aboard fast ships. These ships were side-wheelers, which burned hard, smokeless coal. They stood low in the water, and their color was lead gray or "foglike," making them almost impossible to see even at short distances. By furtive methods, they outwitted Mister Lincoln's coastal blockade.

Some of the treasures came to James during his negotiations with private shippers for the War Office. Also, Emmie later told Kath that their brother periodically provided legal services for friends in Richmond. "One of these folks was the notorious Lil Rawling. As payment for his professional consultation, Lil supplied him with some goods and certain pleasant benefits."

Emmie smiled. "I'm familiar with the goods that reached our family. They were delightful. As to the 'benefits,' I'm not so sure." James spoke of them near the end of the war, but only by innuendo. His sisters finally concluded they were probably of a sensual nature. "Ah, the habits of men," said Emmie, laughing.

Kath sold lumber to Lil after the war. In business negotiations with Madam Rawling, she found out the source of these fine imports. "Where from?" she asked, after speaking of her older brother and the good things he had acquired.

"I had a lively sister named Maggy. She was a good businesswoman. She lived in Wilmington," Lil retorted. Long after the war, Kath saw the building where Maggy did business. It was used for more accepted ventures then. It still had some of the plush Victorian parlors and shaded nooks. It was exciting to see. She later dreamed about the lusty activities that took place there.

Maggy, too, purveyed worldly pleasures. She was described by Lil as, "A delicate women, but firm; very firm. Excellent business sense. Till near the end of the war, she managed a good overseas trade. She finally owned many fine vessels. Good seamen sailed them, and good wages. Also, she gave other favors. You know, her other interests in men trade—all pleasant. Honey, you don't understand men, even the very good ones. They like these, uh, soft, uh, things a woman can provide."

Kath smiled knowingly, but her lips quivered, and she supposed her cheeks were scarlet.

"Honey, I'll spare you the pleasant details, but I know men. Maggy's earnings were not small," said Lil.

Kath was impressed that Lil's sister knew her business. "These men were lavished with very delicate pleasures to gratify the senses. They purred with contentment," Lil commented. "Then they enjoyed that nice softness that suddenly surrounded them, following a hard voyage. This wasn't all." She broke into a glowing smile and laughed. "After being satisfied with these pleasantries, her men found parlors with games of chance and liberal amounts of good liquor. It helped to while away dull hours, I'm sure. Yes, Maggy was a fine one, I'd say."

Kath always believed this was how great ships came under Maggy's control.

Even with James's help, many home supplies were seriously diminished. Coffee was nearly gone. Sugar was hard to get. They had to conserve. The blockade was felt by all. There were some substitutes, though. Roasted rye, mixed with just enough coffee for flavor, was quite tasty.

However, it was difficult to replace sugar. Honey and maple syrup were found in limited quantities. Also, the juices from the stems of sweet sorghum (sorgo) were used.

"Mrs. Robinson said her son's planting sorgo," Ann Lynn told her husband. "I talked to her yesterday. I know you grew it on the farm. Perhaps we can grow it here, too." From sorgo, a thick molasses-like syrup was made. The plant is still used today in the South for the syrup and for silage and fodder.

With the help of friends, Papa planted sorgo in Mr. Jones's fields close to their home. Kath always remembered the rhythmic movements of the tasseled tips of the canes in the fall. The stems were cut and ground, and the juices were boiled down to the thick syrup, in big boilers.

Candy was gone from stores; the children made taffy from the sorgo. Also, they cut the sorgo stems after the first frost; these were peeled and they chewed on the sweet pith inside. It was good! Momma and the Lynns' cook, Joansie, made wonderful gingerbread from sorgo syrup; for fruitcake and Christmas cookies, though, real sugar was needed. "It can't be replaced," Momma told her children.

Raisins were also difficult to obtain. The older members thought cherries covered with sugar and soaked with a strong alcoholic drink were a fair substitute.

"It's sad, though, to use brandy that way," said Uncle Wen.

"We have a fair stock," replied Momma. "Elmer had the foresight to purchase it some years back. He told me not to tell Joan. I can assure you, my sister would have been furious."

"Even she liked your cherries, Ann. Remember. She said nothing about the brandy; she just wondered about all the sugar."

On the farm, the children helped Momma dry the cherries. These were then drenched with Uncle Elmer's brandy. She never told him about this. Laughing, she once said, "I hope he doesn't mind. It's better for people this way. The bad part goes away."

Even before the war, their mother used sugar sparingly. At that time, when Mary, Kath's sister, tasted the cherries, she squinched-up her face. "Terrible," she said. Dee and Kath agreed. As the war went on, however, the cherries preserved before the war tasted better and better. It helped the children forget raisins.

"We could preserve the cherries right here in Staunton, if we had sugar," Momma said. "We still have the brandy."

"Well, we can't get it," Sue answered. "We'll just have to dream." Fortunately, she was not entirely correct.

"We'll be gone for days," the children's playmate, Mark, said mysteriously one evening. Mark was embarking on a trip.

"Where to?" they asked.

"It's a secret," he said in a whisper. "We'll bring you some sugar, though."

Sugar for Christmas delights would come in modest amounts after Mark's daring mission with his pa.

CHAPTER XIX
Men in Gallant Ships

Mr. Mentron and his family lived close to the Lynns in Staunton. His son, Mark, was the children's good friend and playmate. In early December of 1862, Mark and his father traveled north to the Potomac. It was near freezing. They left horses with friends near Martinsburg in the northern valley, then crossed the Potomac by rowboat into Maryland near Williamsport. Kath and her family were very worried. "I hope they get back," said her father. "It's terribly dangerous."

Mark later told his story: "We was goin' for sugar in Bluebelly country. I was shivering right down to my toes. The wind blew cold air the whole way. It was exciting, though. Uncle Bill met us by an old oak. He and Pa used to sit by that tree fur hours and fish a long time back."

His eyes glowed. "We hid behind bushes and rocks after we got over the river. We was on the way to my uncle's house. About five miles, I suppose. We saw Yankee patrols. Hundreds of bluecoats rode by. They came real close. They all seemed to have rifles and sabers. An old sergeant stopped and looked around. Skeered. You can't believe how skeered I was. He looked like a vulture. Red and mean. I think I saw blood on his shirt.

"'He probably ate children for breakfast,' said my Uncle Bill. Big. He stepped right by us. I could almost touch his pistol. It looked as large as a cannon. He finally rode off."

"I bet you were frightened, Mark," said Papa.

"I sure was," mumbled Mark. "We heard shots a little later—down the road a ways. I'm still not sure what they meant. Thanks to Jesus it weren't us. Neighbors of my uncle said they found a spy or something. They wondered about my pa and me.

"'Where're they from, Bill?' I heard a neighbor ask my uncle.

"'Why, from the western counties of Virginia,' my uncle answered. 'They've gone back in the Union, or goin'. Many of my family live out there.'"

"This was part right," Mark continued. "My pa lived there years back. He lived in uh small log house with my great uncle. They hunted their own meat. It were uh little farm on a mountainside with lots of rocks. You'd fall right off that mountain if you warn't careful."

"Did you have any more troubles?" Papa asked.

"Naw. It were easy from then on."

"Was easy," corrected Papa.

"That's what I said," replied Mark. "We went back over the river that night. It was dark. I thought fur a while we weren't headin' right, but we got across easily. Then we cum home." Mark's family was originally from eastern Maryland. They "moved-on" over the years, some to the western counties of Maryland. Others moved beyond the Shenandoah. Those in western Virginia became real mountain men, Kath was told later by her father.

"You're heroes, Mark, you and your pa," said Mr. Raymond. "You deserve medals, I'd say. I also thank you for the good supply of sugar. Spices, too." He gave Mark a warm pat and a squeeze of the arm. The children's friend glowed.

"Here's a big medal, Mark," Annie said several days later. Kath and her sisters had helped Annie carve it from a block of wood. His name was on it, and the word, "HERO" with a bright blue and red ribbon attached below. "I'll kiss you if you'll let me," she said, laughing. She leaned forward and tried to do just that.

"Stay away from me, Annie," he said, frowning. "You're too anxious to kiss us men. Ain't you?"

"Only when you deserve it," she teased.

Mark was happy with all the attention. He delighted in telling and retelling about his adventure. "We're goin' back again soon," he said with pride. They did, some months later, and returned safely.

"Mark, you're one of those daring men in gallant ships," said Papa. "We're mighty proud of you. You outwitted Mister Lincoln's blockade."

"It were only a rowboat," said their friend.

"That doesn't matter. It's the man. You're one of those strong people." Papa then turned slowly toward Momma and Aunt Sue. "Now you ladies git to work. Your men are hungry." He had a big smile on his face as he licked his lips.

Momma and Aunt Sue looked stern, then laughed. "We will, but you're going to help a little. Get out and cut some of that wood. We'll need a roaring fire. You can carry it in, Kath. Now git!" The family all went to

165

work. They were sure the delights would be wonderful.

"What do you think they're planning?" asked Papa, smiling. "I'm sure that I'll be outvoted by you girls."

There was no finely granulated sugar in convenient paper bags on store shelves in those days. Sugar, when they could get it, came as a loaf, usually in the shape of a large cone. For cooking, these cones were broken up and pounded into a powder, using a mortar or other strong vessel. This was a job for the little ones.

"Now you young ladies break that up carefully," Momma warned. "Mark risked his life, so don't you go spilling any, or I'll be very angry. We'll filter it through that cloth to get all those big lumps out. It has to be fine for cakes." It took a long time until Momma was satisfied. She finally smiled. "Well done, girls. Now get started on those spices." The kitchen was hot, but the smells were delightful.

For Christmas of '62–'63, the children would remember the delicious black walnut pie, the sponge cake, and the luscious sugar cookies. "Yummy, those cookies are good," said Mary. "I helped make them, Papa," she exclaimed proudly. "I chopped nuts, too. Cook even let me lick the pans."

"You're lucky, Mary," her father said, smiling. "They chased me out of the kitchen. I was told that they had enough folks helping. By the way, thank Mark again. It wouldn't be possible without him."

The Christmas of 1862 was one of those bright memories Kath would have for a lifetime. And they did thank Mark and his family many times. They ate these good things while bathed in the warmth of a roaring parlor fire next to a lovely big Christmas tree trimmed with boxwood strings, sprigs of holly with blood-red berries, bits of mistletoe, pine cones, dried fruits, candle ends on small metal plaques, and ornaments.

The Lynn children had made many of the ornaments from wood shavings, paper, yarn, and pieces of wood. Henry was the artist, though. Before the war, he had made beautiful animal carvings, which he carefully painted.

Annie always remembered the fragrances that permeated the room. There were candles set about, centered in laurel wreaths to honor the many brave soldiers. She also cherished the stiff, thorny leaves of the holly and its glowing berries. "It's so beautiful, and everything smells so good," she said, smiling to Papa. Then she broke into her silly clown smile. "I'd pick more of those holly leaves, if you'd let me."

"We have enough," Papa answered. "I don't want to strip our holly bushes of all their leaves. They might not survive the winter." He smiled. "They are beautiful. Pagan tribes in Europe in the Middle Ages kept sprigs of holly close to ward off evil spirits. We keep them nearby 'cause they're pretty. Maybe they'll protect us too. We may need lots of that come the spring."

"Let's forget what may come," replied Sue. "We'll talk about things we can do something about." She smiled deeply as she looked at James's face.

Suddenly he laughed. "I did sound somber, didn't I? Well, Merry Christmas to our whole family!"

"That's the way," she said. "It is Christmas!"

Friends visited, and the children traded gifts with their friends: knitted things, fruitcakes, homemade dolls, whistles, gingerbread, carved figures, and dried fruits. It was fun! Some of the boys in the neighborhood set off firecrackers, to the delight of all the children. Momma nearly jumped over a chair one day when Mark visited and burst a bladder behind her.

"Leave!" Momma shouted. "Don't do that again. Hero or not, next time, you'll find it's hard to sit for a while." Mark left sadly. He was back soon, though. While he was a friend, he usually managed to get into trouble.

Annie was always cheerful, especially with the Christmas holidays. "Look what I got from Willie Jones," she shouted. Her face was creased with a big smile.

"What is it?" Emmie laughed.

"A gargoyle," answered Annie. "He carved it himself. He's good at it, like Henry."

"That looks like one of James's friends," said Emmie, smiling. She was referring to a friend of James whom he had written about in Richmond.

Mark, their neighbor, was a playful friend but also a jokester. "Look what I found," he announced to Annie one day. It was a little round disk. "Here, hold it," he said.

"What is it?" Annie asked.

"A knee bone," he said, laughing.

Annie dropped it with a shriek. "Eeeek!" Her face was angry. "It's not a person, I hope." She swallowed hard and stared at him.

Mark had found a flat animal bone in the woods. He scared poor Annie half to death when he told her it was from a real person. "From that hangin' place up that uh way," he said, pointing north. "You know, where they let 'em dance and choke. Not far from here. The man kicked it right off tryin' to breathe. Here, take it." Annie held it a moment, then dropped it again as Mark began to gambol around with his fingers at his throat, making gruesome, strangling sounds.

Annie watched grimly, then bent and picked up the specimen. She glowered and slapped him hard when he came close. As he backed away, she threw the bone hard at his face. Her aim was good. "There," she said, "take your old bone." She picked up several rocks and threw those, too. Mark had big blue spots on his face for several weeks.

The younger girls had bad dreams for several nights. Momma later said to Mark, "You stop scaring those little ones."

"Yes'um," he answered as he always did. He didn't stop, though.

The ominous name, "Gallowstown," was given to the far north side of Staunton, the "northern end of the Stuart Addition." Mark played this for all it was worth and scared the britches off his young friends. Even after Momma spoke to him, he would often run around with his fingers at his neck, making raucous, strangling noises. Finally Papa took him aside. "Stop that!" he said. "The war's bad enough. I mean it, Mark."

Papa did. Mark knew he meant it. "I never knew your pa could get so mad," he later groaned. "I was just havin' fun."

In Kath's wanderings and hikes in the fields, a habit of a lifetime, she visited the north area of town. She was never sure if she ever found the wicked old gallows. She did find a high, squared timber topped with a short lintel and brace. It passed in her fantasies for an old English gibbet. When she was older and employed at the Virginia legislature, they used to joke, "Nothing concentrates one's attention like the imminence of being hanged or like the imminence of being reviewed by the legislature for a political position."

When she remembered that old post and lintel, she understood the reality of this statement. It was a long time before she recovered from the shock of seeing this "execution device." She imagined the faces of the crowd that came to see the final minutes of the accused—lips dry, jaws tightening, then relaxing then tightening again. Faces would show ambivalence; mouths would open as lungs drew deep, enjoying the sweet freedom of breath. Eyes would look hard, then draw away, then flick back again to view the man who stood stark against the sky.

Kath thought about those final seconds, as the accused experienced the inefficiency of this mode of transport into the world beyond. "Mark's antics with strident breathing and jumping about," she decided, "were probably a reasonably accurate portrayal of those last desperate seconds."

Papa commented, after talking to Mark, "We all worry about death, young man. It is an omen of man's future. That hanging place is for mean people, though. By the grace of God, most of us will avoid that way of dying. Now stop frightening those children."

"Mark sure scared me," said Annie wryly. "I keep seeing a man standing before a big crowd. Suddenly his body drops, then jerks, as the rope tightens. It's not much fun. There must be an awful time of being awake, before the darkness stops the hurting."

"But, Annie, isn't the hurting the reason for this method of punishment? It is meant for bad people who do bad things." Emmie thought for a moment. There was a pained look on her face. "It's an eye for an eye—one's life for another. It seems like the right thing to do when someone kills someone else."

"What about war?" Annie questioned. "There's all kinds of killing. Are those soldiers bad? Most of them are pretty good—like Henry. Where do you draw the line?"

"That's for lawyers to decide," answered Emmie. "That's why James is reading law. We'll ask him."

Death and dying have always been fervent topics for discussion down through the ages. We all can imagine why. We fantasize about ourselves undergoing the agony. Are we ever sure the debt is truly paid, or that this is the answer to what some persons owe society? Kath later learned that the real gallows in Staunton had been used very little. Only two persons had been dispatched there over many years.

She asked Annie one day, "Why does Mark talk so much about hanging? It's not much fun to be choked. It's for bad people, as Emmie said."

"I guess we all think about it, Kath. We wonder if we're bad too. Mark also plays at war," she said. "He wouldn't jump around that way if he were a little older like Henry and in the fighting. He wouldn't need to tease as much and show how strong he can be. Boys need pride. He'll be brave if he does become a soldier. It's hard to see, but he has strength inside. Boys change. They grow up quickly. He wants to be like Henry. He told me that."

CHAPTER XX
Mist from the Valley

Mail came most mornings for Kath's older sisters. There were notes and invitations for walks, parties, and also for "seances," whatever that meant. Kath wasn't sure. What a great deal of flutter they caused.

Emmie and Annie each had their beaus. Annie was the lively and happy one; she was always laughing and teasing. She had so many young men calling for her that Kath often couldn't remember their names. How she saw one, with another coming an hour later, she never quite knew. Somehow their paths almost never crossed.

"Annie, how's your boyfriend? The one with sleepy eyes. Did he really fall asleep that last time?" Mary, Dee, and Kath would tease.

"Yes, he did," she said smirking. "Now you be quiet and leave, you mean little chirps. Go. William's coming. I think it's William."

Emmie was more serious. She had only a few young men calling—all fine. She could cook, sew, and do all kinds of domestic things. "Look, Aunt Sue, see what I've finished."

"What lovely embroidery," said her aunt as she looked carefully at the stitching. "You should be proud, Emmie." It was lovely.

When the older sisters were deeply involved socially, Momma slowed things down a bit by adding extra jobs for them to do. "Annie, get these stockings mended. Carefully. Your sisters play hard. Also, they need tending out there. They're going to the store. You be nice to them."

"But, Momma, they're almost grown," Annie complained. "They can take care of themselves."

"No, they can't today. It's all right when they're close, but they're going into town. They need direction. You get at it, Annie." Their sister went with them. She, too, had fun shopping.

Their workbaskets became filled with stockings and socks to mend. Then they were out with the younger girls, playing games, reading out loud, and assisting with lessons. During this time there was much havoc created. Both sisters would come out with long faces. Once there, they, too, began smiling and laughing, and even helping with the havoc and noise. They had lots of good ideas, like trying to hit the chimney with rocks or throwing mud and sticks close to Momma's laundry line.

"Stop!" Momma would shout with fire in her eyes. They did till the next time.

Many of the sisters' beaus visited in the evening. The whole family then sang songs, except Momma who found this difficult. Some of these boys had fine deep voices; others, like Momma, could hardly carry a tune. Strains of "Weeping, Sad and Lonely," "The Yellow Rose of Texas," and "The Bugles Sang Truce," could be heard well into the evening. They learned all kinds of tunes and words. Scarcity didn't diminish basic pleasures and the warmth of human relationships.

James, their brother, was home in January 1863, with all kinds of stories. He revered General Lee, and he worried about the scarcity of supplies and manpower for the armies. "I hope we can win," he said to Mr. Raymond, their neighbor, who visited often.

He countered sympathetically, "James, be thankful if we're left, finally, with a modest bit of pride."

James spoke of buggy rides, charitable fairs, laughing soldiers, farewells, toasts, piano playing, and, of course, one of his favorite subjects, pretty girls. With the latter, Kath heard Momma's distressed whispers in the background. When he told about Sarah and her family, she was much more impressed. "She sounds like a fine girl," Momma said. "That's the kind you should look for."

James loved to hear music and sit and read. He "painted" with nice words the beautiful arching trees, gaily decorated wagons, bonnets, embroidered shawls, parasols, enticing smiles, jokes, secluded corners, and flowered walks. "I'm having so much fun in Richmond, I'm not sure I want to march off," he said. "We eat at fine homes, and I'd miss all those pretty daughters."

"Be careful what you say, James," said Mr. Raymond with a laugh. "Our country is fighting for its life. People might wonder what you mean. We know you're doing what's best, but maybe you shouldn't talk about not wanting to march."

"I worry about your marching off," said Momma.

"I'm sorry. It did sound funny," James replied. He hesitated, eyes glowing. "I guess girls do something to me."

"It's about time you admitted it," teased Annie.

"You should know, my little sister," said Emmie. "With all the boys you twist around."

"Well, I can't help it if you only have a couple of men friends," replied Annie with a teasing smile. "Don't be so serious, and you can twist a few boys, too."

"So that's what you women do, Annie," said their brother. "I always thought we did the twisting."

"Stop it, Annie and James," said Momma. She seemed serious. "And, Emmie, you just be yourself. You'll do fine. Now go on with your stories, James."

Their brother sat in the ruddy glow of the fire, which was intensified by pine knots placed on top of the coals. These lightwood knots gave a pungent fragrance to the flickering shadows. He talked about recent news stories, then, at Aunt Suellen's request, he read a poem he had written that day: "The wolf crept close, beside the door; He could hear the princess cry; She cast herself beside the fire, Prepared that she would die. But the walls were thick, And the doors were stout, And her will was strong, Didst keep that evil out."

"That's kind of a silly allegory," said Annie.

"I know, Annie, but we have to start somewhere. I'll get better. I wrote it while I was sitting here by the fire listening to the wind. It sounded like a princess crying," said James.

"How did you know it was a princess?" asked his sister.

"Just imagination. It's fun. It sounded like a young woman."

"It did, did it? That's just like a man to say that. Men cry, also." She took a deep breath. "We listened to you. Now maybe you'll listen to me. I write a little poetry, too," she said, laughing. "Maybe you'll sit and hear mine sometime." She was blushing slightly, which she rarely did.

"We'll all listen," said Papa.

"I can't read to the whole family," she said, with a squinched look on her face. "I'd be too embarrassed."

James smiled at his sister. His face showed great empathy. She smiled demurely back. It was as if each, suddenly, had a deeper understanding of the longings of the other. "I'd be happy to listen, Annie. It would be an honor and a pleasure." He did later that week. Emmie sat with them. They laughed and talked. All had private writings. It meant much to each of them to have someone listen to their deepest thoughts. Momma came in the parlor often that day. She would smile and look satisfied when she saw them talking on the far side of the room.

Kath never remembered what happened to the princess in James's poem. At a young age, though, she was impressed with her brother's talent. Later, she wasn't very taken with that particular poem. He did write some good poetry later on. This perhaps was the start. He also helped Kath with some of her writings.

Momma and Aunt Suellen sat in the background, with knitting needles flying silently over rows of stitches. The children's socks and all their gloves and under-flannels were knitted. These kept them warm in winter. The marble-gray skies of January were brightened by family. All the grouchy little children were made to smile.

Later, Henry also arrived home on leave. He stayed for about one week. He told how, after Momma's cooking lessons, he truly had become one of the cooks for his company. "I hope some of the meals can be eaten," said Momma, smiling.

Henry could make two dishes. His sisters never remembered what they were. He could also make rolls and bread and fry meat. He observed how his "innards" became "corroded" by the black coffee and fried foods. "The men want fruits and vegetables. We get these from the fields. We're right good providers at times, which is not easy with thousands of other soldiers doing the same. My bread is good too. It helps to prevent that awful corrosion."

He turned to his father. "Several officers in my regiment have been killed, Papa—or injured, that's how I became a lieutenant. I replaced Lieutenant Owens, Bob Owens. He was very badly hurt. I think he's getting well, but he won't be back for a long time. I think the men like me. They're my men now. There aren't too many complaints," he said, laughing. "There are always a few, but I've learned to give answers. It comes with practice. See, I wear braid now." He held up his arm proudly and showed them his sleeve. "I have two bars on my collar, too."

"We are proud of you, son," said Papa.

"The day I was hurt," Henry continued, "began as the morning mist from the valley around the creek (Antietam Creek) gradually cleared. We saw 'ghosts' coming toward us. We were exhausted, but we were ready. I had to literally kick some of my men awake that morning. They had dropped where they stood. We had marched for miles. It was eerie when the Yankees came. The sun glowed through the trees. Their men looked like shadows, shoulder-to-shoulder, row-on-row, coming closer. Scary! I almost ran. They would fade in the fog, then appear again, then fade away. They looked like survivors on a lonely island rather than an army. We heard guns begin to fire. They weren't ours initially. We tried to wait till the enemy got close.

"There were only a few guns at first, then thousands. For hours they kept attacking. Our lines were pushed back, then moved forward, then fell back again. We held, though. I could see battle flags twisting around us like frightened animals. Many of our men dropped. A few got up again. I saw that some were bleeding. I think the bullets had knocked them down. What did you say it was like, Papa? Like being kicked by a horse? You're right. That's what some of the men told me later.

"Arms grasped my legs. I didn't know what they were at first. I kept thinking we were surrounded by snakes. It was like a dream. Gun powder and dust clogged everything—eyes, nose, mouth. Our skin and clothes were covered.

"Finally the Yanks fell back. Regrouping, we thought. We then heard the guns from other parts of the field. It must have been loud, since we were almost deaf from the noise by that time. A man spoke to me. I couldn't hear a word. He pointed at my face. I suddenly knew I was covered with blood. I remembered thinking how sticky it was. My shirt and trousers were red. A surgeon later sewed up the cut. He said I was lucky, and that it wasn't deep. It makes me smile a little more now."

The scar from the cut twisted Henry's mouth a bit, but it had broadened his smile. He truly enjoyed being home. He looked hungrily through the windows as pretty neighbors passed and smiled. He took his younger sisters for several walks in the town. It left them in a fine glow. Kath curtsied and mumbled, "Thank you," when they arrived home.

"You're welcome, Mademoiselle," he answered. There was a twinkle in his eyes.

As they walked away, Kath's sister, Mary, growled, "Oh, fiddle, you're so smart." She didn't talk to her for the rest of the day.

Poor Henry was overcome with fumbling awkwardness when a pretty young neighbor with silky black hair, Caroline, stood shyly at the doorstep. She asked for a loan of sugar. "I'll ask my ma," he struggled to say. "And, please, won't you come in?" Kath was standing in the hall close by. "She's nice," he whispered as he walked toward the kitchen. "You entertain her, Kath. Make her stay awhile."

They, too, took several long walks later that week. Basic instincts were emerging. He was a boy no longer. He was a man. He had become self-reliant and confident—except when he was face to face with a pretty young girl.

Henry's shoulders were square, and his eyes were deep and glowing. The holster at his side was scuffed, and his belt broad and worn. His gray vest had three buttons open at the top, showing a crisp linen-collared shirt with a checkered pattern. He had a dark blue neckerchief coiled at the neck and tied. His face was unlined except for the scar. Over the vest, he usually wore a coarse, homespun "butternut" jacket—a mixture of cotton and wool. "It's ordinary but comfortable," he said smiling. "My coat and the braid are for show."

A mustache accented his upper lip, projecting down over the corners of his mouth. He wore a sword on formal occasions at home. This slapped briskly against his high boots as he walked. He had become handsome; ladies' eyes slyly turned to enjoy his lean figure and casual movements as he walked. He was with his family such a brief time; he then returned to his company in Longstreet's Corps of the Army of Northern Virginia.

Henry had stood with Pickett at Fredericksburg. "Above a rail line, near Deer Run, a little stream," was all he related about the fighting. "Some good friends in another regiment put up a big sign after the battle. It was right at the bank of the river on an old railroad tressel. I believe it added salt to the Bluebellies' wounds. We'd hurt them bad." Henry had a big grin on his face. "The Yankee pickets spent a lot of time shooting at that sign."

"What did it say, Henry?" asked Uncle Wen.

"This Way to Richmond!" he replied with a laugh. All but Momma and Aunt Sue laughed with him.

"They'll try again!" said Sue with a look of disgust. "Soldiers keep fighting."

Momma and Daddy found great warmth and pride at having the family assembled. "It's nice they're home," said Momma.

"I wish they could stay," Papa replied.

Momma sat daintily aloof in the evening, displaying an authoritative air over her brood. She was always neat and fresh; an occasional wisp of hair was awry after the daily bedlam of a large household. Her clothing was always freshened by a sweet-smelling sachet. Her eyes moved slowly from face to face. "I'm just admiring the blossoms of my garden," she told them. "I treasure you all."

James stayed with them for three weeks, much to their delight. He often led evening conversations. Mr. Raymond, their neighbor, would sit quietly and listen. He visited often, and he and James became good friends. James began calling him, "Robert," which Papa thought was excessively familiar toward a respected senior friend.

Mr. Raymond and James would walk together, talking about poetry, politics, philosophy, love, and, of course, about the war.

Robert was the analytic and interested sounding board for James's ideas and occasionally his writings. Mr. Raymond, bless his soul, was very patient. Their brother often made careless statements. With a few astute, tactful words or observations, Robert would show James how he had erred.

Emmie remembered when James talked lustily one evening about a damsel in Richmond. "Robert," he said, possibly with tongue in cheek, "she's truly been created for my personal entertainment and joy. A lovely thing. Long, dark hair and a wonderful smile. I must have you meet her someday. She enjoys men who are discerning, like you and me."

Emmie recalled Mr. Raymond's serious answer. "James, it may not be proper to talk so openly and lustfully about female attributes. Also, descending to fantasies of possession is frowned upon by many. You should win her by love, not possession."

Momma was standing silently behind James at that moment. "You'd better listen to Robert," she said firmly. "Any woman you win that way won't be worth her salt. Also, Robert's name is Mr. Raymond to children. You're still growing, so be respectful."

"Yes'um," James replied, timidly. He quickly retreated to other topics.

Mr. Raymond would bristle when James was overly self-centered or careless with words. Their brother needed this guidance in a home where he was treated with caresses by a loving family. Kath liked her brother very much, but she was impressed that he thought he was becoming a very important person. Perhaps he was at the War Office, but it irked her when he said, "I'm now indispensable in this railroad work."

Emmie, too, was annoyed. "Well, you do sound pompous," she said.

"No one is indispensable, James," said Robert, smiling. "Just keep doing your job."

"Hear, hear," Papa agreed. He looked hard at his son, who was blushing slightly after these reprimands. "James, I'm elated that your legal background is helping with the war. This is what I hoped, when I wrote your preceptor, Jason. He gave you a fine start. Keep working at it. You're more valuable at a desk than behind a gun. I think you'd also make a good soldier, but there're many other important things besides fighting. Perhaps you've found your niche."

"I hope I have, Papa. I do help with negotiations between the government and the railroads. Equipment can be confiscated by the government; sadly, it isn't always returned. People representing the private corporations tell me this causes great losses. I think I help them to limit their losses. We'll need these private businesses after the war. Their people operate much more efficiently than we government servants."

James experienced much of the war at the storm center in Richmond. He was in daily contact with professional soldiers. "The character of the war is changing," he said late that evening. He then continued to tell his family what this meant.

CHAPTER XXI

The Winter of '62–'63:
Lace Ruffles and Pretty Dresses

While James was home, one evening he discussed at length the many problems the Confederacy faced. His vision about the future was not auspicious. "We suffer in many ways," he said. "For one thing, the Yanks have repeaters. They can shoot faster than we can. They don't have many, but enough.

"Also, many basic items are hard to get like niter for gunpowder, mercury for percussion caps, cloth for uniforms, leather, heavy machinery, lead. We're gradually solving these problems, but much has to be imported. Another seemingly trivial difficulty I've worked on is canteens."

"That's not trivial if you can't get water," said Sue.

"Exactly," he replied. "It isn't always easy to find water on a battlefield. Also, most of our canteens are wooden with a metal band and pitch inside. Our men don't like these. They prefer the metal ones, which they get from dead Union soldiers. The reason they prefer metal is because they stand up better. Also, they can be cut into halves like two bowls and used for cooking—or eating." He looked caringly at Momma and Aunt Sue. "These are a few examples. You know about others like coffee and sugar. Bonnets too."

"It's nice to know you fight with bonnets," Sue said laughing. James just smiled.

"We won those battles at Sharpsburg and Fredericksburg," said Papa. "At least we hurt them a little more than they hurt us. It sounds like we're doing something right. We haven't lost battles because of lack of guns. Also, our men have the heart to fight. There's a glimmer of hope."

"You're right about the weapons, Papa," James answered. "We have the guns and powder. We also have the heart to fight. That isn't entirely true about Sharpsburg, though. After the battle, our men stood bravely and waited, then came back to Virginia. It looked like a victory. Some good soldiers disagree. They think the Yanks won this one. The big offensive stopped. Our men retreated. They didn't go forward. They were worn out and in tatters when they recrossed the river (the Potomac), and they were desperate for what was needed with cold weather coming. Also, forage for animals is in short supply, as is food for our men. We're refitting, but transporting what is needed is difficult even when we have the supplies."

Kath saw Uncle Wen shake his head. "They outnumber us, too, and they have more money and factories."

"That's right," replied James. "Another real problem is that the character of war is changing. It's difficult to see this. It's like watching the movement of a fly on a small pin."

"That's a good simile," Papa whispered. "My eyes'd have trouble seeing that fly."

"It sounds bad, doesn't it?" James continued. He was being very patient, often repeating things he had said. "It is. We depended for so much on those people we're now fighting—the Yankees. A tough man's helping us though. He's a transported Yank. We're learning under his direction, but it takes time to put plans into use."

His face brightened. "We have a few successes. We're very slowly becoming a modern workshop with skilled workmen and good managers. We make guns, cannons, armor plate, powder. This is a revolution for the South. We now make things to kill. Later, we'll do it to keep people alive and to make life easier—I hope."

"What's the man's name?" asked Momma.

"Gorgas, Josiah Gorgas. He's head of ordnance for the Confederacy. He expanded the Tredagar Works in Richmond—our mother industry. We can make anything now, including machines for other factories. We've already lost some of our shops, though. Nashville. New Orleans. It's sad. It took so much effort to get them started.

"Another big problem is our Congress. In its wisdom, it allows skilled workmen to be taken into the army. That's because of our conscription laws. Those laws help keep armies in the field, but they hurt our efforts to provide what those armies need. Some of our expert craftsmen, also, move away when they're called. They're immigrants. They're from Germany and England and are familiar with machines and handling molten metal, but they aren't willing to die for our cause. The North needs them, too.

"Local towns decided who goes. That's what 'state's rights' means. Still, we're good with guns and machines, but men can't eat guns. They need food. We're a farming land, but many planters still grow only money crops. Others grow the food we need as you do, Papa and Uncle Wen, but we can't get it to our soldiers. Train track sizes differ; lines stop; the next one is across the town. Wagons, mules, and horses are all scarce, and food rots on sidings, while our men starve."

Mr. Raymond and Papa shook their heads sadly. Neither spoke.

"That sounds terrible," Momma murmured. She spoke for all of them.

"Also uniforms are needed. Individual states use most of their cotton and wool for their own militia. North Carolina, for instance, has thirty or more mills, but much of what they manufacture is used within the state. These are problems Congress must solve. The cloth we get is cut in Richmond, but it's sewn in homes all over the South. The problem again is transportation. We can't get it to the men. They're cold. Also, they march in bare feet. They need shoes. Raw leather is from Tennessee, which is now in Yankee hands. As you said, Papa, we're resourceful. At least we have guns, but we need much more.

"There is something else," he continued. "Lincoln did something very right. His Proclamation. It changes the war. The slaves, he says, are free. 'Emancipation,' he calls it. Europe probably won't help us now. They'll not help us fight to keep slaves. Sharpsburg was a battle we had to win, but lost."

"Go on, son." Papa smiled wanly, but there was pride in his voice. His son had grown up.

"I guess I help some with supply and providing what we need. Railroads are my special interest. They're vital but frustrating. I've mentioned a few of our problems. What we can't make or grow, we buy. Much comes from overseas, but Yankee gunboats surround us. Not all ours get through. Also, we have fewer men than the 'Bluebellies,' and they aren't easy to lick like we thought they'd be. We're tough. They're also tough. Our people forgot this early in the war. We thought it'd be easy—a battle or two. We're still fighting, and no end in sight. We'll keep going, though. We have good generals." He turned to Mr. Raymond, then thought for a moment.

"Keep speaking, James. You have the floor. We're listening. What you say makes sense; we'll stop you when it hurts." Robert closed his eyes and smiled sadly. "Hmm," he chuckled. "It hurts already. I guess we can take it, though."

"Robert," said James, frowning.

"Call him Mr. Raymond," Papa interrupted. "He's older than you, and we all respect him."

180

"I'm not that old, James. I guess the mister part is more proper though."

"Mr. Raymond," their brother continued, "you said, 'Be happy if we're left with a modest bit of pride.' I agree. I've done much thinking this winter. Where do we go from here? How? There are no easy answers. Perhaps we can try again in the North. It's the only sensible idea I've heard." James shook his head slowly. "You know, Robert—sorry, Mr. Raymond, we started a big move north this summer. Not just Lee. Others too. It didn't work."

"What others?" Momma asked. "We know more about the East. Evidently you're talking about the West. We've lost much ground out there. The Union holds large parts of the river."

"You mean the Mississippi?" Papa asked.

"Yes," she said ruefully. "The Yankees sting us like a serpent." Momma then spoke slowly, "'What! Wouldst thou have a serpent sting thee twice'—to death? While our boys fight at one door, the serpent's coming in by another. I suppose it's our vast shoreline. It's so hard to protect."

"True, Momma. Much Yankee travel is by the rivers and the sea. Some think our tide has ebbed." James stopped talking for a moment as if wondering what to say next. "Old Scowling Bragg, General Braxton Bragg, marched north into Kentucky last summer," he continued. "He also failed, as did Lee. In October, he came back. He expected recruits from the people, but few joined up, and not much was accomplished."

"Maryland and Kentucky are border states," commented Robert. "It hurts one's pride when they don't come to help. It's too bad pride pushes us on. It kills a lot of fine men. There are bad times ahead. A long darkness, I'm afraid." He turned slowly to Momma. "Ann," he said, smiling knowingly, "'The night, me thinks, is but the daylight sick.'"

She smiled in return. "'. . . Blessed candles of the night . . . ,' I hope, will light our way. 'Tis not the night from whence the sickness comes, Robert."

"So much for our bard," said Papa, grinning. He then looked seriously at his son. "Go on, James."

"Our grizzled Earl Van Dorn also made a valiant effort," James continued. "He tried to knock out Grant's defense line in Mississippi. There was an enormous fight at Corinth. Muskets became hot; the field was strewn with dead. On October fourth, he retreated. There may be terrible battles ahead, but we have just made a supreme effort. I hope we can mount another. Three armies attacked. Now they've all retreated. I'm not sure what it means, but it's not good."

Kath's mother, father, Mr. Raymond, and her whole family sat dazed. The conversation stopped. Papa struggled to say, "It doesn't look good, James." No one heard him, and he didn't repeat it. James talked quietly across the room with Robert and Uncle Wen. Most of the family didn't hear that either. Mr. Raymond soon went home, and they all went to bed.

Momma came to Kath's and Mary's bedroom later and kissed them both. "Good night, children. We love you," she whispered. "We have problems, but they'll finally be solved."

Winter did not miss Staunton. Much snow fell. Kath made many long treks over rolling fields and through bleak woods. Fluffy clouds of snow blew from the hillsides. The carnivorous predator, the hawk, often circled overhead, searching back and forth, the streams and crevasses, for an unsuspecting animal out of its protective den.

"Katherine, don't stay out so long," Momma would say.

"I'm never cold," she answered. She was soon back in the open fields, which bordered on woods and copses of trees, bare in the cold winter air. Intricate lacy patterns of the black locust trees moved against the gray sky. The giant white oaks stood like great multi-armed soldiers, straining, but bearing patiently the gusts that surrounded them. A few brown, wrinkled leaves still clung tenaciously to the swaying branches.

"It is beautiful out there," she would tell Momma, when she seemed worried. "The orange bark of the pines is so pretty against the white hillsides. Their needles grip the snow like a cradle. Then it falls from them in big puffs as the wind blows or as you brush them aside. All those trees seem so unconcerned with the cold and the wind. It's fun to be amongst them."

She heard Aunt Sue mumble, "You're growing up, Katherine. You're learning."

She also noticed the weaving branches of the hawthorn being moved by the wind. The long, brown, delicately curved thorns seemed ominous as she walked between them. She was exhilarated, though, by these hikes, and Kath later treasured such moments alone. It was a time to think and plan and sort out ideas.

The winter of '62–'63 seemed long, but not all was dreary. It was filled with much brightness and fun. The battles in the coming spring and summer would be seismic, and long lists of dead and wounded would be received. This was still in the future. For the present, pleasure filled those cold days. The planning went on for weeks. They forgot about the war. Some of the pleasure was anticipation. The whole town was involved. Friends visited and talked.

"Where should we have it?"

"When will most of our men be home?"

"Oh, she'll be lovely in that beautiful dress! It's pale blue watered silk. She'll be devastating. It complements her hair."

"It's raven black," said Emmie, smiling. "Lovely. Silky."

Cheeks were pink and eyes twinkling as wrinkled brows foretold of the planning of fun ideas and pleasant delights.

"Why not use the old barn? You know, the one with the hand-hewn beams, there on the edge of town. I think it belongs to the elder Mr. Fraser."

"Our father knows Mr. Fraser," said Annie.

"He must let us use it!" argued Emmie. "What a great, quaint place. We can whitewash the walls. And, oh, the decorations we'll think up!"

"It's so dusty," said Annie. At times she seemed very squeamish.

"Yes, it's dusty, and it has holes, but we can clean it and mend all those," said Emmie.

"We can, and we will," answered Mary Jane Revels, Annie's friend. She was pert, with dark hair and slate-gray eyes. "And I can see it now. Lighted. Filled with happy people. It'll be wonderful."

Annie thought for a moment. "I guess you're right. And it's the one place we probably can get." She grinned. "Most of the other buildings not used by the Army are warehouses, storing all kinds of nasty things. Why not the old barn? I think he'll let us use it without a charge. I'll talk to him this afternoon," she continued with her most alluring grin.

"Annie, you look positively seductive," said Mary Jane. "That smile would trap any man."

The planning went on. The old dusty barn became magnificent. Bright-colored cheesecloth booths were constructed. Large wooden and brass stands filled with candles were set about. Holes were plugged by the men and boys. China and silver candelabras were placed on shelves and tables. Plants and flowers from many families were commandeered and ensconced in alcoves and along a central platform for the musicians.

Spicy pine branches were wound on rafters, around doors and windows, and at the edge of the stage. Old wagon wheels were suspended from the large beams and woven with boughs of pine and grape, and accented with flowers of yellow and blue and pink. Bunting and flags completed the decor. A picture of scowling Stonewall Jackson had somehow been contrived.

"Why's Jackson up there?" asked Mary Jane. "He's not handsome. It should be Lee—yummy."

"He's our Valley hero; he saved us from those dreadful Yankees," Emmie answered.

Yes, there was Jackson, gazing out over his loving, thankful people. The frame was flanked with banners, and two old sabers were crossed above. Pots of shrubs were set at the sides of the banners. This embellishment would probably have embarrassed such a dedicated soldier.

There were lots of snuggle nooks and crannies for the younger ladies and their special beaus. Ann Lynn, Momma, sighed when she saw this, then said, "I'm sure they can sneak in there and, uh, talk." Annie blushed a little as Momma looked steadily at her. "Did you hear me, Annie?"

"Yessum, Momma."

"That isn't what you told me, Annie."

"Now you just hush yourself, Mary Jane. Wait till I tell your family about you."

Kath would later dream about that evening. The music sounded and the hall burst into life. Choruses were heard of "The Bonnie Blue Flag," and "Your Letter Came, But Came Too Late." Handsome soldiers, some on crutches and some with a limp or with a missing arm, walked about and smiled and danced. Uniforms were mended and pressed. Gold braid decorated many sleeves, but had often become tarnished. Swords swung at men's sides and tapped at the tops of boots.

"My, they're beautiful," Kath gasped, as she saw pretty girls gliding about as if on the surface of a smooth pond; bare backs and lace ruffles topped dresses with billowy hooped skirts, floating over lace pantalettes that peeked out below.

"They are beautiful," Momma answered. "You young'uns are pretty, too. Not as tall, but important. A big part of the color here." This made them proud. Momma didn't pass out compliments freely; she meant them. "Also, you're our heritage to the future. We want you here. You didn't want to come last night, did you, Mary?" She looked softly at Kath's sister. "You said it wouldn't be fun with old folks. There are many of your own friends here. Look, there's Mark and his brothers. Also, the Henry girls over there. Aren't you all glad you came?" She didn't wait for their answer. "You'll have fun, and look at all the people who are smiling at you. It's wonderful.

Now have a good time. However, you're still growing, so I want you off to bed early. Kath, you lead the way in an hour or two."

"Ahh, Momma," smirked Kath. "I'm near grown. I heard Annie say she doesn't want us prowling around when she's busy tonight. I know why she's busy. She's after that Reginald again. Poor man. She's like a spider. Ehh! I like boys, too. I'm getting big."

"Hmmmm," Momma answered. "You are, are you?" She looked hard at her middle daughter for a moment. "Katherine, you have grown, bless you. You're still going home early though . . . " She hesitated, searching for a word. "Now you chillen plan right now that you're still growin', or your Momma will become an ill-tempered old crone. Do you hear me?"

"Yes'um," they squeaked.

Watered silk and taffeta were decorated with rosebuds and little ribbons and scrumptious foamy material. Some dresses were created from old drapes and other cloth, and embellished with mosquito netting in place of lace. Fabrics were harder and harder to get, but ingenuity prevailed. Shoulders were soft and pink and graced with smooth, dark hair, rings of blond curls or plaited locks in many styles. Fragrant scents wafted in the convivial air. Paisley shawls and delicate silk scarves draped shoulders and were tied around slender waists.

Momma and Papa and the whole town came. What a wonderful evening! Uncle James, who lived twenty miles from their farm east of the Blue Ridge, was there. His son had died in the war, not from wounds, not as a hero in battle with a sword raised toward the enemy, but silently, in a wet, uncomfortable bed, from fever. He had died of the measles. So did many others.

Uncle James never spoke of this. He came that evening; he smiled and laughed, shook hands with the soldiers and their fine ladies, talked with the children, praised them, and told them stories about the family, about his early days in Virginia and about the war.

"Dee," he asked, "when do you start school again?" He knew Dee was their scholar.

"We've been off this week for the dance, she answered. "I can't wait to get back. Kath doesn't like school much. Do you, Kath?" Her sister's face burned as she heard this, but Kath saw Uncle James smile compassionately at her. She didn't speak.

He also winked at Kath and put his finger to his lips. "She's our naturalist and philosopher," he said softly. He continued to smile. "Kath, you're our practical one, too. We need your skills and Dee's, too. We need both of you."

Kath glowed inside. He knew how to make them feel good. "There, Dee," she scowled. "He likes both of us." She then whispered to her uncle, "Thank you, Uncle James." Then she hesitated for a moment, hunting for the right words. "Uncle James, why are there so many Jameses in our family?"

"It's a name our family just likes, I suppose," he said, laughing.

The little girls now watched and talked and occasionally teased. They slyly ambled around the tables of good things to eat, furtively taking bits and morsels. "Now you small children wait a little," Emmie said sternly. "That's for everybody, not just babies. You've been back five times already."

"We're not babies," Kath said, her face all squinched. "Momma said to try everything."

"Not everything." She frowned, then finally smiled, and walked off toward a "pretty" young man. "Children!" she complained laughingly to her friend.

After several hours, Kath saw Dee yawn. "I'm tired," she blurted. "Let's go home, Kath."

"Not yet. Mark said he wanted to dance. I've never learned how, but he'll help me. I've got to start sometime."

"That's the way," said her uncle, smiling. "Get out there and glide over the floor. Say hello to Mark for me. Your father said he has all kinds of deviltry inside. See what he's planning." As they danced, however, she, too, saw, as had Annie, a serious side to their friend.

"I'm old enough to be a soldier," he confided. "I'll be a good one too. My pa says 'no.' He won't even talk about it."

"You stay with us, Mark," she said. "We sisters need protection. You've been our real friend. Silly at times, but nice."

"That's not what you said yesterday."

"That was when you were a real bore, and not very funny."

Mark didn't answer, but he smiled and held her firm. Dancing with boys was fun, she found.

The mayor of Staunton was there and spoke of their great cause and future. Mr. Raymond listened intently and looked incredulously at Papa, as if to say again, "We may be left only with a little pride."

Many compassionate faces watched and savored the evening. Pretty girls, protected by dresses of black crepe, sat quietly at the side. They were properly sedate in memory of lost husbands and sons, but the rhythm and syncopation of the music caused many a toe or heel to beat fervently against the floor.

"I'm glad Mark's not too persistent about being a soldier," Uncle James continued. "Young boys get killed. Our land needs them for the future. You keep telling him to stay home. Girls have more influence than fathers and old folks."

Uncle James looked at the pretty girls in black crepe. "The period of mourning must seem long to those fine girls with warm hearts. Their veins are still filled to bursting with normal desires. Those are basic instincts, Kath. Glamour, passion, all still to be savored. The deep meaning of life has hardly been tasted. You tell Mark to stay home. We don't need news from the War Office about him. We have enough tragedy in our lives."

Uncle James stopped for a moment. There were tears on his cheeks. He grasped Kath's shoulders, and he turned about so he could face away from the folks around them. "Sorry," he said. "A grown man shouldn't cry. Don't tell your father. He'd probably understand, though. He's a sensitive man. We've all seen a lot of hurting." He took several deep breaths. "Kath, go sit with those ladies there. Find out how they feel. Much of life is still before them."

"What should I say?"

"You don't need to say much. Smile, if nothing else. Tell them about the woods and the trees. Your momma said you're full of words about trees and flowers and wonderful things. And, also, let them know we care."

Kath did sit with them. They were kind. They let her talk, which was always rewarding to a young lady.

Outside the decorated hall, a chill wind blew. Little creeks and streams and beaver ponds spotted the surrounding land. The heavy beat of music, with the piano tinkling loud, lasted well into the night.

These sounds were heard for miles. People wished they would never cease, but nature is remorseless and time passes. The pristine environment and rich soil bring a fervent spring into life. Ponds give rise to aquatic animals; marshes provide food for herons and egrets. The eagle flies high overhead hunting fishes and other flesh. The human imprint on nature's glory must continue amongst the peeping heads of crocuses and minnowy streams.

Violence permeates nature's gentle mantle, as all animals search for food and sustenance. Plants probe the earth for nourishment. All this is necessary for survival. Only man strives to destroy his fellow being for ethereal, difficult-to-understand ideals unrelated to necessity. Thus the war continued. As armies again began to march, illness came to the Lynn family.

"He's sick; terribly sick," Momma told her children.

"Henry?" Annie questioned. "Not Henry, I hope."

"Papa's sick," she said. "Not Henry." She hesitated a moment, wondering what more to say. "Thankfully, only one of us is ill."

CHAPTER XXII
Tomorrow's Blossoms

Momma's face was pale. She struggled to talk, but her voice was barely audible. "I received a note from Uncle Elmer at Doria, children. Papa's badly ill." She tried to look unconcerned, but her hands trembled a little as she lifted the letter close to her face. "I'll read it to you."

She squinted her eyes hard so she could read the scribbled text. "'James collapsed yesterday while walking the fields in the north quarter—looking for Annie, that rumpled excuse for a Jersey cow.

"'James has a shaking fever and he talks foolish. He's out of his head. Dr. Mast is treating him with a very bitter brown medicine. I know because I tasted it. He's also done many bleedings. It makes James very weak, and it's hard for him to lift his head. I sometimes wonder about this bleeding idea. Mrs. Mast and Mary, your cook, are with him day and night. His bed is clean now. It was soiled from nasty vomit and other things. The ladies are giving fine care. I think he'll be all right.'"

Papa had visited their home at Doria several times each year. He went again in early March of '63. He had written his family a few days before his illness: "The farm's well managed—a compliment to Elmer. The books and records are exemplary, Ann. My apologies for having doubted. Elmer is in good fettle; he looks younger even with the extra load. It was cold here, so I built a big fire, and had several glasses of brandy with Elmer. He likes to talk. This was fine with me, since I was very tired, and I could just sit and listen. I'll be home soon. Love to you all, Papa."

Momma now started making plans to go to Doria. Aunt Sue was to manage the home in Staunton; all of the children were given jobs. Kath was to help with cooking and fetching water, Mary was to dust the parlor and clean their room each day, and Dee was told to straighten books and feed their new small kitten. Emmie and Annie had constant jobs, such as making beds, sewing and mending, and getting milk from Mr. Holman, who lived half a mile to the west of their home.

Just before Momma planned to leave, they received another letter from Uncle Elmer.

> James is much better. He talks sense now. He said to have Jim, your yardman, accompany either Annie or Emmie to Doria to help him home. He has a rash all over his neck and body and arms. It's clearing, though. The fever suddenly was gone. It left James limp and tired, however. He took broth and bread today, and started walking with an arm around my shoulder.
>
> Your pet, Annie, that silly cow, was probably taken by drifters. She never returned. James said she always comes back. She didn't. I hope she tasted good.

"Can I go, Momma? Please, Momma. I'm used to sick folks now," said their oldest sister.

"Yes, Emmie. You certainly can. Hurry, though. The train leaves in two hours. Be aboard. Use that old carpetbag of mine for packing. You don't need much. Take some victuals too, and tell Uncle Elmer we appreciate what he's done."

"Thanks, Momma." Emmie smiled; then she thought a moment before rushing upstairs. "Poor Annie. She was a fun pet—even though we teased her. I can't believe she's been eaten." Kath could see Emmie shudder a little. "It's gruesome. She was most likely cut into little pieces. It served her right, though. She was always getting in trouble. That's kind of like our friend, Mark."

"We don't want Mark in little pieces," said Annie. "He probably wouldn't taste good anyway."

"Girls, don't speak so disrespectfully. Mark's nice underneath."

"We know that, Momma. We're just joking," continued Annie. "We've been so serious lately with Papa sick, we're trying to change the talk a little. We'll have fun again, now that Papa is gettin' better."

"Girls, we hang on to life by a thin thread," their mother cautioned. "It's easily broken—then we're gone. I've been so worried about Papa, I guess I've forgotten to smile. We need to laugh."

"We've worried too, Momma," said Emmie.

Their mother stood for what seemed minutes, then said softly, "Thank you, Lord—for helping us." As Kath looked at her face, she noticed that her eyes were closed in reverence.

"I think God was listening," whispered Annie. She had been holding their kitten and petting it gently. She had just handed it to Mary to hold.

Suddenly her face burst into what Uncle Wen called her big "clown" smile. "Hurrah for Papa," she said, laughing as she clasped her hands above her head.

"That's what we need," said Emmie. She put her arm about her mother's shoulder and gave a good squeeze. "He'll be home soon. He'll want happy faces. We're practicing."

"Keep it up, girls," said Momma. "That's what he wants."

Weak and tired, Papa returned to Staunton and Momma's care. Emmie and Uncle Jim, their yardman, had gone to Doria to help Papa home. His ghostly pallor shook the whole family right to the tips of their toes. Kath looked at him as he came up the steps. He seemed to drag his bent torso along, and he was very out of breath. She didn't have Emmie's and Annie's experience with ill people, but she realized now that he was still very sick. Emmie had been a great help during the trip. Her experience in the hospitals meant a great deal.

Papa improved, but slowly. Suddenly, he was struck down again. It was as if a giant hammer had hit him. "He can't breathe or talk," said Aunt Sue. "Your momma's with him. Run quick, Annie. We need Dr. Prine. Hurry, girl; his face's gray! Oh, Kath, he looks so bad!"

The prostration was frightening. He coughed violently and held his hand to his side, writhing in pain. His eyes became glassy and distant. Reddish fluid from his mouth ran out over his blanched cheeks. It looked like blood. Their local doctor was away for the complicated delivery of a female friend. His assistant, Jacob Merns, arrived at the Lynns' door, puffing and apologetic.

Kath sat with Aunt Sue while Momma was upstairs with Jacob. They had great trust in Jacob. He was soon to be degreed by the local licensing board. He had but a fragmentary background of formal education in the mountain country to their west. He had learned spelling, writing, and ciphering by the rule of three from itinerant schoolmasters when they passed through town. Otherwise, he had taught himself from books.

For lonely years, Jacob had "consumed" all the books his father owned. "These were few," he said. "We had a Bible, a book of hymns, *Pilgrim's Progress*, and a romance about knights and bad people. I must have read all of these a hundred times. One of my early successes was memorizing eight or ten lines of a poem a neighbor had lent me. I don't remember the name of the poem, but it was about pretty ladies and undressed dwarfs living in a forest.

"Finally, when I was fifteen, a friend loaned me Guthrie's *Grammar of Geography*. I think this is when I began to sense how big our world was. I wanted to see more of it. My mother worked so hard, though, I couldn't leave her to struggle. I decided then, I would find a way to go on to other things. I wasn't sure what, at the time."

During this period, Jacob toiled in the fields and farmyard with animals and plants. He loved green things, and his heart blossomed as they grew. His interests leaned to the natural sciences. His father was a true pioneer and moved when others came too close. The farm was self-supporting of all needs except for salt, gunpowder, and whisky. The syrup of the maple was used for sugar. His mother, father, and sisters worked from dawn to dusk.

"On weekends," he had told Kath and her sisters, "our family occasionally went to town. Our mother always insisted on church, on those Sunday mornings. I remember how I enjoyed the peace and quiet in church. I still do. Pa, though, would sit and fidget and turn. Finally, Ma would look sternly at my father. She didn't have to talk. He knew what she meant. He would then sit quietly for a while.

"Saturday evenings were disgraceful with whisky, however. This gave Ma a chance to tell us about the wickedness of drink. I still don't touch a drop. I use it for sickness, though. At times it helps."

A failing physician had provided Jacob with an aged volume by Dr. John Rush. It was Jacob's first encounter with medicine other than local vermifuges and powders. He later disapproved of Rush's methods of depleting vital fluids, but it brought him to Charlottesville, where opportunity beckoned and he began training under senior doctors.

Jacob later came to Staunton. His descriptions of death and healing seemed macabre at that time. When Kath later reflected on his stories, this still seemed true. "The man twisted and hurt while I probed him," he said. "He screamed and screamed. You should have heard him scream! Finally, I found the ball. It was big as a rail spike, almost. This was a hunting accident in the mountain just east of here. He had fallen over rocks and brush and was badly cut up. I spent hours sewing up the cuts.

"I didn't have to bleed him anymore. He'd done enough bleeding. Besides, I'm not much of a bleeder. I've never much agreed with those doctors who do it. I don't think you really let the bad humors out, as they say. They just let all the good fluid out." Jacob was trained to use stimulants rather than purges, and he generally opposed Rush's methods of bleeding.

Kath didn't sleep that night for worrying about Papa and, also, the memory of Jacob's medicine talk, which she had heard some weeks before. When she finally feel asleep, she had bad dreams about cuts and wounds, and people with bad coughs and rust-colored fluid running over their pale cheeks.

Jacob's use of stimulants seemed to work with Papa. He also used Peruvian bark and cool cloths for the terrible fever. "It's awfully expensive," said Aunt Sue as she came back from the doctor's office with a new supply. "It cost over two dollars for this little bottle."

"I guess it's a small price to pay for James's health," said Momma, smiling. "He looks much, much better. Wellness is a blessing, Sue. It certainly hurt bad to see him so sick."

Nux vomica was the strong stimulant Jacob used. He told Kath the name when she seemed interested. She never could remember it for sure, though. In later years, she tried to learn some of the remedies used in the old days. She found that name. She never did know what the vile brown liquid was that Papa had taken so reluctantly for the gruesome coughing.

"Your husband has pneumonia," Jacob told Momma with a stern face the day after the coughing and high fever had started. "He was already weak from his first fever. This often happens when folks've been ill for a while." Momma hadn't asked about pneumonia, but she had suspected it.

Pneumonia was a terrifying disease in those days. It still is, but at least we know now about bacteria and other minute wiggly things that cause sickness. Koch and Pasteur were just beginning the revolution of medical thought about infection. Cowpox methods were being used, but the whole science of immunization was unknown. Lister, the great English surgeon, first wrote about his studies in antiseptic surgery in 1867. Many young men would die in the Civil War because his methods were unknown at the time. Some perceptive physicians suspected minuscule living things were causing these terrible problems called putrefaction, but they were in the minority.

James Lynn was still very weak, but he was definitely getting better. Others in Staunton died that winter from pneumonia. The oppressive pall of illness worried the Lynns as winter ended, but their father's recovery was the perfect counterpoint to these apprehensions. Illness and the threat of dying, however, were not gone.

Tragedy struck again. Dee, the youngest sister, became deathly ill. Momma was exhausted, but she steeled herself and sat for days with their sister. A friend named Nancy came to help Momma. For this, the whole family was thankful. Nancy stayed with Papa, while Momma cared for Dee.

"You just lay right there, Master James," Nancy would say, smiling. "I'll do the turning. There, that was easy," she would tell him. She was jovial and rotund, and she turned their father like a feather. "Now you finish the soup and those crackers, or I'll tan you like I does my children." She would sit patiently with Papa, talking pleasantries and then threats if he didn't obey. He was gaunt and wasted. Kath thought that even she could have rolled him over easily. She did help Emmie and Annie on occasions when Nancy wasn't there.

Kath was sitting on the porch at the back of the house, reading. "Vile," she heard her father shout.

"Now don't you go spittin' that out again, Master James," Nancy ordered. "It's good for you. Here's more. Take it. Now keep that mouth closed. That's better. Fine!" Kath could visualize Nancy's satisfied smile.

"Awful," was Papa's reply.

The children were kept at a distance from Dee. For only short periods were they permitted to look into her sick room. She was pale and flaccid. Papa also had that gray pallor in his face and hands. Kath would then sit downstairs, thinking about what she'd seen, and praying that both would live through all this. For the first time, she truly sensed the grisly meaning of death. She worried about sin and about the life hereafter. She wondered how often these furrows in their lives would suddenly become an abyss, and swallow those they loved.

Dee was sick from diphtheria. The disease was unknown by many doctors at the time of the Civil War, or it was not considered to be a separate entity from other severe throat inflammations. It killed thousands. Jacob had seen similar cases, but he had no specific treatments. His methods were supportive—control the fever, provide fluids and nutrients, and assist breathing if possible. Diphtheria had been accurately described by the French in 1826. The causative agent was not identified until after 1870, however.

Momma nursed Dee night and day. Gauber's salts were used as purgatives to help the awful throat-swelling, and the fever was kept down as much as possible by medicines and cool baths. An arm and foot were paralyzed. She couldn't stand. Also, she couldn't swallow and could hardly cough. Jacob himself sat with her and spelled her mother. They often held her for hours in their arms, walking about and gently rocking her back and forth to help her breathe.

194

The younger sisters, Mary and Kath, didn't talk much to Momma during these days. Aunt Sue reported, "Dee's breathing is so hard, and she can't swallow. I don't know what we can do for her, poor tike. Mary and Kath, you stay well. It's best not to go too near her."

"Can we help, Aunt Sue?" mumbled Kath. "I'm strong, and I can at least help turn Papa more."

"Kath, do what you're doing in the kitchen. Tell Uncle Jim outdoors thanks for that nice doll he made. That's the first time Dee's smiled in a week. You two write notes and try a poem or two; she likes words."

"I'm not good with poems, Aunt Sue. Can I send a picture? I have those nice crayons from Christmas."

"Mary, you do that, darling." Her Aunt smiled.

Water and juices were carefully poured down Dee's throat. Sometimes one or two hours passed while she drank from a single glass. Her throat was terribly sore, and there were gobs of matter finally coughed up as she improved. None of the rest became infected, much to Momma's relief and many, many prayers.

Their sister lived! She was soon running about and laughing. Papa seemed to take much longer before his strength returned. This made him very discouraged. He was overwhelmed even by simple walking or stairs. Dee also tired quickly for weeks. She loved to run upstairs, climb into her father's arms, and let him read to her from his many books.

"Please read to me again, Papa. That story about the little dog. Also the one about the princess and that bad knight." They would sit together for hours. Kath always considered this the time when her sister became a dedicated student and began to think about becoming a teacher. "I can do this when I grow up," she would say, smiling. "I'd love to read to little children, Papa."

"I hope you will," said Papa. "Now get up here, pumpkin. Sure we can read. Mr. Raymond brought over another story too. It's about dragons in old England. It has pictures. See!" He held up the book so Mary and Kath could also see it. Papa's face was gaunt, but color was returning. "Mary and Kath, you can stay too. We'll all read together." Mary and Kath soon tired, though. They needed to be out-of-doors. Papa then heard their laughs and shouts through the open windows.

Mr. Raymond began to visit them daily, and it was therapeutic to have someone of Papa's generation come by. "You need meat, James. Good red meat. I'll get you some. I used to be a pretty good shot with a gun."

"You may be a little rusty," Papa said.

"I don't think so. We never forget once we've learned."

Kath saw him stalk out toward the woods for game. Papa was stronger. He laughed when Robert came home, black-faced from the powder. "The gun didn't work well," he said, frowning. "I shot at a deer, though."

"It was a good shot, I'm sure?" Papa said. "Don't tell me, though. You must have missed a few times."

Robert just laughed while Papa looked at him with a faint smile. "Robert, thanks, but we don't want you to be another casualty. I think we can still buy some beef and pork."

"It's harder to get than you think, James," Momma said firmly. "The staples for the South are still cotton and tobacco. There are some cattle and pigs, but so many of us are competing for our share that there just isn't enough. Much of our meat came from Tennessee—and Kentucky. They're in Yankee hands now. The man at the market told me there's not much fruit or flour either. And our trains are in such bad shape that whole shipments are rotting on loading platforms. James told us about that. He can tell you much more than I can."

"I'm sorry, Ann. Being ill has drained my mind, I'm afraid. I didn't know what you had been facing. Thanks for all you've done, you and Sue. And Wen and Robert too," said James.

As the days grew longer and warm, Papa did get well. About this time Mr. Raymond surprised them with an announcement: "I'm gonna be married. Now I know what you're thinking. I'm too old. But I don't feel old. And I need a friend and a partner."

"We all do," said Aunt Suellen. "I'm happy for you Robert."

Mr. Raymond hesitated, as he smiled at those about him. "She's a widow and lives in Hagerstown. She's a handsome woman. And very nice."

"Wonderful, wonderful, wonderful!" their father shouted from his bedroom upstairs. "Robert, I'm just thrilled with your good fortune! We must meet her soon." He was so elated that he literally ran down the stairs to shake Robert's hand. They then knew their father was well.

Mr. Raymond's previous wife had died of fever. He thought that her illness had begun following a passionate argument. He was a peaceful soul, and the Lynns never quite believed that this interchange was as violent as Robert suggested. She had washed all his pipes in soapsuds. "Wash everything else I have," he recoiled, "but never, never, never my pipes." Robert always felt guilty about this incident. He never talked much about it, though. Kath heard it from Annie, who always found gossip to pass around.

"There's no connection between the fever and that disagreement," Papa told him.

"I know," said Robert, "but still I think I'm to blame. I can't forget it. She was so kind and sensible, and I loved her very much. I should have been more careful." He thought for a moment. "I will be this time."

"All of us have sacred views and fetishes that should never be profaned," said Papa.

He tactfully advised Robert's wife-to-be about this "whale" in his personality. Robert called it his "Jonah and the whale fetish."

"Perhaps these should be reformed, but carefully," he said to her with a laugh. "We all have them."

She answered, "Well, he's still the same person. Possibly the cover's a little different, but I think I can handle that. It's nice to know he's not perfect." Later, however, she was careful about pipe-washing.

It was a warm day in April. Papa and Dee were almost completely well. A lazy sun burnished mellow clouds near the mountain crests. "Climb up here, Kath," said Papa, smiling. "You're my practical one, my sweet; you argue, but you act. That's good. I'm not sure you'll make the dutiful wife, but you'll find a place." Papa's palm was warm as his fingers circled around hers; his fingertips were cold. She, too, was invited to the treasured space beside him.

Papa told her, "Kath, I saw your gray eyes often at the door, cheering me on when I was ill. Thanks."

They talked about the world: elephants in Africa, tigers in the back country of India, how Europe was not likely to support their cause, and about the changes the war would bring. "We need inner stability so we can change as the world changes," he observed. "We've grown up in a culture civilized by progress. We should be proud of that progress. We pale, though, in our effort to equal God's work. However, we've brought some light to the world." His voice was now very soft. "People have tender feelings, create art and music, speak softly and, until recently, have wrestled sensibly with problems. Thus a high level of social order has emerged.

"The war has negated much of this advance. We have become animals, like the tigers we spoke about. Humane usefulness and caring beget a strong nation. We must return to these fundamentals."

That day, Kath was puzzled by his metaphor: "The canker in the core of the apple is beginning to show in the skin." She later believed he was suggesting that the economic system in the South foretold defeat.

"Kath," he continued, "coarseness and bitterness will fill our land after the war. Be ready for it, as we work to recover. We will survive, though. I hope this will be a better place in which to live after all of the pain and the terrible loss of life. Perhaps this suffering is because of many, many past sins against others.

"We will survive our injuries, though," he continued. "Even from dust we can rebuild. Now off to bed with you. It's getting late. Kiss Momma and Aunt Suellen. The armies are restless. We'll soon hear the sounds."

Kath began to sense Papa's understanding of their problems and his confidence in their future. His insight would prepare her a little for the time when they would "bind up their nation's wounds."

A shadowy mist and the sweet smell of flowers filled the yard and woods about their home that night. Kath lay awake for hours, thinking about Papa's words. She was then at the advanced age of thirteen. She could foresee much hope for the future. The surface was wrinkled, though. They would experience many problems. Tomorrow's "blossoms" were still far off.

CHAPTER XXIII

The Armies Are Restless

Papa ran through the front doorway of the house, waving an envelope. "I have a letter from Henry," he shouted. "I got it from Pudgie Townes's father. You know—Henry's friend. Pudgie's home on leave, and he brought it with him. He's been ill. It probably was pneumonia, like I had. He's getting well, his father said. He apparently felt just as bad as I did. You ache all over, and you can hardly move. It hurts so much to breathe, you think you're dying. I guess you almost do."

"From your little brother," said Aunt Sue with a big smile. "He's not little now, though. He's bigger than I am. James, I hope he's well."

"He is. And the news is good."

"He's our hero brother," said Annie.

"I hope not too heroic," Papa said. "Heroes get hurt. And killed."

"I met Pudgie at the dance," Emmie said. "He's a nice boy, but he is pudgy. The army's taken a little weight off. Not much. Henry likes him. That is, he likes everything except his ideas about eating. He consumes so much food that it's a wonder he doesn't burst. I don't know how he stays as thin as he does." She shook her head in wonder. "Maybe the men didn't have enough to eat in camp this winter. That was good for Pudgy. I know his sister, Margaret. She's nice. I'll be seeing them both soon. They'll know things about Henry that we don't know."

Henry had grown mentally as well as physically. He was now writing long, newsy letters home. He mentioned details about the war, which gave his family some feeling for what their men faced. Momma read Henry's letter out loud: "Dear Family, Captain Sikes was seriously injured in a fall. This wasn't in battle, but during an evening reconnaissance. He was up in a tree looking for Yankees. He landed hard on his head and received a deep cut. More importantly, he can't move his legs. I've now been appointed our company commander with the rank of captain. Sergeant

Wilken said I'm strict, but that the men appreciate this. They want to know their limits."

"That's good news," said Papa. "Too bad about Sikes, though."

I had to punish several of my men yesterday [Henry's letter continued]. I tried to act very serious. They had plundered a farmer's orchards and taken eight or ten chickens. I've never seen a man so irate. I said I'd take care of it, but he wanted to see them whipped. He repeated this several times, then he said: "I'll go above you if I have to."

"Are you threatening me, sir?" I answered. "I can have you arrested, if need be." He left without a whimper. I did feel compassion for him, though, and I later paid him in Confederate scrip for his loss. The men then hiked with hands tied for half the day. The farmer saw us march off that way. They marched behind Sergeant Wilkin. Each had a little plaque hanging about the neck. "THIEVES," it said. I commended the sergeant for what he had written. The sergeant ordered them to extra duty for several days. I think what we did was fair. The sergeant thought so too.

Papa, you said our armies would begin to move again when spring came. They have already started. My division's on the way to Richmond. We're following our corps commander, Longstreet. He's a good general, slow to start, but when he gets going, he fights hard. He's tough. When we reach Richmond, I hope I have time to see James. I received a letter from him last week. He told me to visit.

Expect big battles along the Mississippi. Some of our high officers worry about Grant out there. He perseveres like a hound dog. They respect this odd man, and captured Yanks say glowing things about him. He drinks a little, but not when he's fighting. He sits quietly with a big cigar and thinks. They wonder what he's dreaming up. It's not good. If we lose Vicksburg, we will also lose Texas, which we need for hogs and other foods. Also, James told me about mercury for rifle caps. The ore comes from there, and it's important. It's sad to see, but our country may be cut in half.

Papa looked thoughtful. "What's happening to our country is sad, as Henry writes. But I'm proud, though, that he's developing as a leader. He's serious, but he's always been good with people."

"I've watched him with the workers on the farm," said Momma. "He seemed to have the right words to explain what should be done as well as why it should be done. Then he'd work right with them until they got the idea. After that he'd compliment them. He didn't seem to have to drive folks to do the work. And he'd learned much from you and Wen, James. He's had book-learning as well as an example of how to get along with others. That's good. But with the war, he's certainly a worry.

"Yet we have to let him do what he wants to do," she continued. "He's always wanted to be an officer. Now he is. And that's good. And he's working with other officers, making plans and anticipating what's needed. I hope this contact will make him want a little more formal education. Perhaps college. I suppose now, though, he's realized he can do the job as well as anyone. Even without formal schooling."

"Well, those worries are for the future, Ann. Go on with the letter," said Sue. "For now, he's doing all right, and we're proud of him."

[Their mother continued] The Eastern Yankees are also restless. We get reports that they're active and taking long marches. They're better fed than we are, and they drill endlessly. They have a new commanding general. Hooker's his name. He's supposed to be a real fighter. Some call him "Fightin' Joe." Of course we men do the fighting. The generals push us on, then watch. Very few of them go up front when the bullets are flying.

Burnside was relieved of command. He helped us kill a lot of Bluebellies at Fredericksburg. He sent his men forward right into our guns. It would have been wonderful, if it hadn't been so terrible. Also, his men suffered badly in winter quarters. Maybe worse than we did. The first thing an officer should do is take care of his men. Burnside didn't. I'll write more later about where we're going. Love, Henry. P.S. Don't worry about me, though. We're moving away from the big Yankee army. If I don't see James, tell him I'll be close by.

As Henry related, General Hooker, "Fighting Joe," was a tenacious fighter. He was now in command of the Yankees in the East. On paper he was excellent, in the view of the Union high command. Lee was at Fredericksburg; Hooker made a long march up the Rappahannock; he then crossed that river with three army corps, the Fifth, the Eleventh, and the Twelfth, forty thousand men. His soldiers were pushed forward across the Rapidan, which flowed close by. It was a clear night, with moonlight on the banks and the whippoorwills singing. His army continued southeast to the clearing at Chancellorsville. That day, even grim General Meade of the Fifth Corps was laughing: "We're on Lee's flank and he doesn't know it!"

"This first step by Hooker was very smart," Henry wrote later.

Their older brother, James, agreed. "Henry's right. This was brilliant. The Yanks could have destroyed us—especially with much of Longstreet's First Corps far to the south. Lee, though, can look deep into a man's soul and find his weaknesses. He did this at Chancellorsville.

"With Hooker on his flank, Lee turned and faced him. He then gambled. He split his few regiments into two parts and sent Jackson on a long march around Hooker. He marched around their whole darn army. Papa, your friend, Jackson, reached the Union flank late that day, but in time to attack before dark. While Lee held the main line, Stonewall rolled up almost their entire Twelfth Corps. The Yankees were in a panic. I bet Lincoln's angry. He's still searching for a general. We're lucky to have great commanders. This was a fine victory. Maybe Lee's greatest. Jackson was seriously injured, though. He lost an arm, I'm told. I hope he gets well soon. The South needs him badly."

Jackson's tough divisions did attack near dusk in early May 1863, at Chancellorsville. The men of the poorly anchored Federal right ran in panic. They became a confused, yelling, running, stumbling horde before Jackson's troops. The moon that night was high and clear. As Stonewall reconnoitered his lines, his own troops accidentally fired upon him.

Jackson's terrible injury at Chancellorsville resulted in the amputation of his left arm. He too was weakened, as was James Lynn from fever that spring, and he became sick from pneumonia. Papa recovered, but for "Stonewall," this was a mortal illness. Each breath became agony, and delirium developed. With Anna, his wife, at his side, at the end "of a Sabbath Day's journey," his quiet voice was heard: "Let us cross over the river and rest under the shade of the trees." Mrs. Jackson wrote this to Kath's father. It meant much to James that she remembered him during this time of great trial.

There was gloom throughout the South with Jackson's death. Staunton was in mourning. "Who can ever replace Jackson?" asked Mr. Raymond. "A great man is lost—forever."

Papa had similar thoughts. He wrote in his diary that day:

> The South won an important victory at Chancellorsville. Our people were ecstatic when they heard the news. We're somber now. In this battle, we lost more than we could afford to lose. We not only lost thousands of brave boys, but we also lost that great commander from the Shenandoah, the man who was Lee's right hand, the man who saved Staunton from depredation, Gen. Thomas J. Jackson. I'm afraid his loss is irreparable. He truly stood as a "stonewall" in many battles.
>
> Also, I lost a fine friend. Anna must be very frightened and hurt. She's a lovely woman—warm and kind. I'll write her tonight, if I can find the proper words. I'm often fairly good with words, but ideas seem to stick in

my throat today. I must send her a note, though. Perhaps I can lessen some of the grief. I'll tell her about those good times I remember—before the war.

Papa read these words to the family that evening. It was a few days following the reports of Jackson's death. "You should write Anna," Momma said. "He's meant a great deal to our people. I'm sure she's proud of him. She should be proud of herself, too, though. What he was, she helped create. Tell her about our pride in both of them. Don't mention that we've been crying. She'll know."

Their father went upstairs to his desk. The family never saw the letter to Mrs. Jackson.

Henry didn't fight at Chancellorsville. In the letter to his family, he had told them that he was marching south toward Richmond, away from the main army. The Lynns later learned why. "Pete" Longstreet in February of 1863 had been appointed to a strange semi-independent command, and an even stranger campaign. First-line men from his First Corps were headed for a region south and east of the capital. These troops included Pickett's and Hood's divisions. Henry was in Gen. Lewis A. Armstead's brigade of Pickett's division.

James wrote further about Longstreet's campaign:

I heard briefly from Henry. He's with Longstreet. It's lucky he was away from that battle at Chancellorsville. Many, many were killed, and I've seen hundreds of the wounded who survived. Our hospitals are filled to overflowing. I went through the wards the other day. It's frightening. Men were moaning and crying, and the odors were abominable—like sour milk.

I was happy to hear that Henry is with our divisions at Suffolk. I don't know why Longstreet was ordered to that district. I believe there was a worry about tough Union troops being sent there, and Lee responded by sending Longstreet.

Pickett's and Hood's battle-hardened soldiers were finally involved in commissary functions in the Department of Virginia and North Carolina. The reason for sending first-rate fighting men to that department was the report of transports moving down the Potomac to Hampton Roads with Burnside's old corps, the Eleventh. This region south of Hampton Roads was a country of hogs and corn, as well as an important district for purchasing needed supplies for the armies.

Longstreet also attempted the investment and siege of Suffolk, an important town in the district. Henry wrote: "We didn't capture much. We pinned some of the Yankees down a bit, and many of our troops helped harvest the grain. This took good men away from the real war. Lee should have used militia instead. In any case, not much was accomplished. My men were well fed, though. They're gettin' fat and lazy. We're going back to Richmond soon. I'm not sure where after that. I'll try to see James."

Henry got his wish and did see his brother in Richmond. James wrote: "It was a stimulating event in the town. I think Henry would like to stay here. He said that we eat better than they do. When I'm home, I'll tell you about the shadowy moonlight nights and other things."

"I'm not sure I want to know what that means," said Momma.

"They're just boys," said Sue, smiling. "They'll tell us about it some-time."

"It's about girls," said Emmie. She looked serious, then she chuckled. "Henry's always quiet like a mouse when a pretty young lady smiles his way. But he's handsome. Someone'll find him one of these days." She was right. Shadowy moonlight had to do with love and attractive women.

"My, you're pretty," said Henry. His words were a little slurred. He and his brother had consumed some of the fine wine at Lil Rawling's establishment. "But, Sarah, why would you ever think that? You're very special. My feelings for you are totally different. My brother and I do have other lady friends whom we enjoy, but it's only been in a mature and aloof manner."

"Like heck it's been mature and aloof," said James, laughing. "We've loved in a very basic and pleasant way."

"My, my, that's interesting," she replied. "I can see how you've con-quered so many lovely women." Her eyelids flickered up and down as she looked coyly at Henry and then at James. "Also, your success is probably because you're both so handsome and manly. Especially, James, your brother here." She reached over and gently patted Henry's cheek. "I know about you. You're the one who's been hurt in fighting. Just look at that scar. Where did that come from?"

"Antietam Creek," said Henry.

"My cousin was there, too," she said. Her voice was soft and caring now, and she wasn't teasing. "He was with A. P. Hill. He stood at the crest of that ridge as the Yankees crossed the stone bridge. They were coming over by the hundreds. He told me how he wanted to run, but he didn't. Our boys stopped 'em, by God. We're proud of you men, even if you are a little romantic when you're on leave. Now tell me about all those interesting women on your list that James introduced you to. Then we can talk about other things, like the fine banquet we're going to tonight. I hope you meant it, James. I'm famished! And we still have to pick up Mary." She smiled again at Henry. "And she's really looking forward to being with you, Mr. Lynn. Captain Lynn, I should say."

James just laughed. His reference a year later to "naughty ladies" and "shimmering hair over bare shoulders" probably explains some of their other activities. He told Annie about this confidentially, but Kath overheard the conversation. His references to Sarah and Mary, however, were always respectful and enthusiastic.

From Chancellorsville, the Army of Northern Virginia headed west for the Shenandoah. Henry's regiment marched with them. He wrote infrequently now, though the family did receive one note in mid-June.

A friend on Pickett's staff told me about "Jeb" Stuart's wonderful review—his cavalry. That's what I'll do in the next war. It was at Brandy Station a week ago. The people were thrilled. They sat on Fleetwood Hill as thousands of horsemen charged by. Pistols and cannons were fired, and ladies swooned. Perhaps those folks got some idea what war is about.

The cavalry has the best of things. They even had a ball the night before. Dancing in the moonlight with hundreds of candles and many pretty ladies sounds exciting. This doesn't happen in the infantry. We're going west now. I'm not sure where, but I'll write soon and let you know. Love, Henry.

James in Richmond confirmed what Henry said about a colorful review:

It was held in early June. Lee wasn't happy about it. "A waste of powder," he said. Also, only a few tallow candles were used. Though some women swooned, the married and unattached ladies were a little more dignified and watched somberly. There was a similar review a few days later, which Lee attended. He directed that powder not be used and that the horses walk and not gallop. Both would be needed for battle very soon. This second review was much more sedate.

Brandy Station is midway between the Rappahannock River and Culpeper [James continued]. The following day, firing was heard from Beverly Ford on the Rappahannock. General Pleasanton's Union cavalry was attacking Stuart. It was vicious. The battle was a standoff, however, and Pleasanton retreated. To "Jeb," it was a humiliation. The pale-red horizon at sunset ended an ugly day. Some say, "He was unhallowed!" I agree. He should have been ready. I'm sure he knows that now.

The vigor of Pleasanton's attack was no accident. The Yanks had finally developed a very strong cavalry corps. Their men had become well trained. Southerners were "born" in the saddle, according to Stuart's men, but " . . . the Yanks are learning. We rode around them once. This would be hard to do now."

The *Richmond Examiner* initially lessened Stuart's chagrin with smooth words, then puckered his wounds as with salt by reporting, "The country pays dearly for blunders."

It was said openly in Richmond that "Stuart's headquarters had been fired into before the enemy's presence was known." Fleetwood Hill was so covered with blood stains, blue flies, dead horses, and the bodies of men that a tent could not be pitched there for Stuart's headquarters.

Lee's army was again invading the North. To the northern Shenandoah and across the Potomac, they marched. Ewell had replaced the honored "Stonewall" as corps commander. Ewell's Second Corps led the Army of Northern Virginia into Maryland and Pennsylvania. Federal outposts in the valley had caved in before a whirlwind of Confederate soldiers. Winchester had been evacuated by the Federals, and 3,400 Yanks had been captured by "Old Bald Head" Ewell.

In Pennsylvania, Ewell scoured the country for horses, cattle, and flour. Thousands of animals were sent South with wagon trains as well as thousands of barrels of flour. The land was ripe and "fat." His dust-covered, wild-looking men scared ladies in the North. They were unused to the ragged, footsore, butternut-clad soldiers. Many stragglers lolled behind, wandered about, some sodden from whisky, others stealthily entering homes for food and barns for horses. Still others of a more dependable nature also stayed behind. They would defend their own homes, but not enter those of the enemy.

Longstreet's First Corps advanced north, following Ewell. Henry was with the First Corps and wrote his family some details about this march. He didn't mention crossing the Potomac River. Old soldiers later told a funny story about this experience, however. It was crossed at Williamsport. "As the long, long columns reached the river, trousers and shoes were removed, bundled, and carried with cartridge boxes on shoulders over the waters. Maryland ladies that day, mostly young and guileless, were making a pilgrimage to the southern Potomac shore, to Virginia. In mid-stream they encountered these half-naked men."

"Their faces were probably beet red," said Momma laughing, when she heard.

"You and I would have enjoyed it, Ann," said Aunt Sue with a smile. "We've been changing these boys' diapers and clothes since they first lay in a crib."

Momma smiled at Annie and Emmie. "I can imagine the embarrassment of these young girls. They're kindred spirits. I, too, would have blushed and covered my eyes. I probably would have peeked a little between my fingers, though, to pick out the handsome ones."

"Momma. I'm shocked. You wouldn't!" said Emmie.

"Oh yes she would," Sue replied. "You didn't know her when she was younger. I did."

"Momma!" said Annie sternly. This was followed by her big clown smile. "I'd have looked, too. Several times."

As was written by Adjutant Owen of the Washington Artillery, "50,000 men without their trousers on can't be passed in review every day of the week." With this, the Lynn family agreed.

Henry's company in Pickett's Division continued north through Hagerstown and into Pennsylvania.

The days are hot and oppressive with clouds of dust. There is growing enthusiasm in the air. We're in enemy country now, living off the abundance. Rolling fields are covered with nodding tassels of grain.

We've encountered no organized resistance as yet. But if looks could kill, we would have died a thousand times. Faces are grim in towns and at crossroads as our brigade moves deeper. We fill our needs using Confederate money. Many Yankees don't like this, so we write requisitions to the towns. The land is full of everything we need.

Our bands play "Dixie" as we march along silent streets lined with natives unused to any invasion. Occasionally mean words are heard, but most residents submit without questions. My men joke about taking a few pieces of silver and other trifles; they don't. They are well-behaved. There've been few reprisals for the damage by Yanks in the South, I'm told, and I haven't seen any.

Our First Corps pushed into Chambersburg today. We're in fine spirits. It is June 27th. Soon A. P. Hill's Third Corps will be up. Ewell's columns are farther north and have reached the region of York near the Susquehanna

River. I don't know where the Yanks are. I don't think they're close. Spies bring in information constantly, I'm told, but Stuart has disappeared. He's usually the eyes of our army. We trust Lee, but we're in the enemy's land, and there aren't many friends to give us information.

Spies did provide the vital information that the Federal army had left Virginia. Henry never spoke of this. He probably was unaware of it. Lee decided to concentrate his army east of the long ridge of South Mountain. This was to be in the area of Gettysburg. Hill was thus ordered to march east, and most of Longstreet's Corps followed on June 30th. Pickett's Division was left to guard supply roads at Chambersburg; Henry's company of Armstead's Brigade remained with Pickett.

Shoes were a major accoutrement in war for armies on foot. Near Carlisle, General Johnson, "Old Allegheny," of Ewell's Corps, had lined up captured well-shod militia prisoners in fancy uniforms and relieved them of their shoes and socks. The wretchedly dressed Confederate soldiers gazed with curiosity at the resplendence. It was a work of necessity for Johnson's barefooted men.

General Heth of Hill's Third Corps similarly needed shoes for his men. He asked permission to take his division to Gettysburg to "get those shoes." He wondered if Hill had any objections. His commander replied, "None in the world." Fate hangs on simple phrases. Heth's Division marched to Gettysburg and into history. It was July 1, 1863. The day was warm. Water was scarce. Two armies collided on that fateful field. They left deep marks on the broad panorama of history.

A letter from Henry arrived a week after the Battle of Gettysburg. It was written near Cashtown in the early morning hours. He wrote:

> . . . Our regiment has crossed South Mountain. We are being hurried east.
>
> We were rushed quickly away from Chambersburg yesterday. It was before dawn, and the roads shimmered faintly in the distance under pink clouds. We marched up very rugged trails to a mountain pass, then down toward the farming lands below, which spread before us like a fairyland. In the sunshine, the road became a white, knobby finger pointing the way to the fighting. We've rested now, but the sun will be up soon, and we'll be on the road again. We should arrive at the battle later this morning. It's usually a sleepy place, I'm told. It's not sleepy now. The name of the town is Gettysburg. . . .

The Lynns would remember that name.

CHAPTER XXIV
The Third Day—Gettysburg

The ground about Capt. Henry Lynn was dotted with round and angular boulders. Some were piled into irregular lines as fences separating the corn fields close by. Split-rail wooden fences were scarce now. They had been used for cooking fires by troops who had passed by here in the last few days. South Mountain was still a purple shadow to the west against a pale gray sky. Its peaks were just lighted by the morning sun. Patches of mist were rising off the earth like lace veils. It was quiet. The glowing embers of camp fires studded the surface, and the men of his company were preparing to march. Many were camped in a stand of oaks nearby.

Henry could sense the presence of a vast army about him as he walked among his men and looked and listened and remembered the faces and the sounds of voices. Their expressions, the incessant chatter among them, gave him a feeling for their enthusiasm and fears. He smiled and nodded, but he spoke few words. They seemed in good spirits. In the past he had always been introspective. Now he tried to enter the thoughts and cares of those for whom he was responsible. These were his men. They would fight for him, rather than for vague ideologies. They would be moving out soon. They were ready.

He picked up his metal cup from beside his bedroll and walked over and sat beside Wilken, the sergeant, a harsh, rounded man with a broad face and strong shoulders. His beard was short and dark, and his cheeks were ruddy and veined. The sergeant poured a steaming cup of coffee for Henry. "Thanks, Wilken." He tasted the coffee. It was bitter, but he could feel its strength circulating through his veins. "Have the men finish up soon, Sergeant. We'll be marching within the hour." He looked and nodded east. "That way. That's where we're needed."

"We are, sir. And these boys will give us a good fight. Wiggins is ill, but he'll march. And many have bad feet from the hard roads here in the North. Especially those mountain trails we came over." He looked toward the blue hills to the west, then smiled. "But that's not new, is it? The Shenandoah roads are much easier. And softer." He then pointed toward Gettysburg. "It's quiet that way now, Captain, but we've had a real fight out there, I'm told. Old Longstreet's other divisions have lost a lot of men. Thousands. And the Yankees don't attack us. They're like those buzzards up there," he continued. There were hundreds moving back and forth far off. "They just sit there and wait."

"Well, we can't lick 'em by sitting down," said the captain, smiling. "Here comes a courier." The order to advance soon came down the line. "Let's line 'em up to march, Sergeant. We're on the way." Henry could hear the grumbling and swearing as men stamped out fires and grabbed bedrolls, haversacks, and weapons. They assembled in ranks of four. Canteens had been filled from a dirty stream close by, over which hundreds of feet had walked. A stone bridge crossed the stream, and a caisson and several dead horses were to the side of the road just beyond.

The division marched toward the east. In the distance, Henry could see a peach orchard to their right, with fields of wheat beyond. Cows were seen farther off, separated from the fields by stout neat rows of post-and-rail fences. Evidently Lee's men hadn't camped right there. He could see Pickett's whole division stretching out like a great serpent along this rutted highway. The land was gentle and rolling and green. They were on the Chambersburg Pike a few miles from Gettysburg.

Dust rose in great clouds, covering faces and uniforms. Colors bobbed and rippled, and the rising sun glinted from metal as if from sparkling gems in the mist. Vultures still circled far off. He could visualize their evil eyes as they hunted for food. "I suppose some of the food they're eyeing may be dead soldiers and friends," he said grimly. The men about him were lean and dusty brown. They had an earthy look. There were hardly any complete uniforms, and what there were, were often mixed with Union blue. Many feet were bare. "They don't look like much, but they're good soldiers. The best. And they'll fight," he continued.

His mind wandered. He thought about his family. They were hard working and honest. Good folks, he decided—like those on the farms about him now. His eyes closed to slits as fatigue and the boredom of marching overcame him. He could hear birds singing in the trees, the clink of metal, occasional laughing, harsh voices, and a band playing far off. The shuffle and clomp of feet on the rutted road was ever present. "All places look alike," he decided. "Just rocks and dirt. The soil in the Shenandoah is more rusty in color, though. This here is just a golden, smudged brown." It crumbled beneath his feet as he walked.

A few of the local people stood along the fences as the division passed. They were the enemy, but they looked just like folks anywhere. A little more grim perhaps. Some waved slowly, but few spoke. They watched sadly. Neatly painted homes and barns were beyond them, and animals grazed in the fields. "Why am I here?" he said. "They don't look very threatening. Ordinary people. All just trying to make a living—like my family."

Henry thought about the letter written in camp late last night. They had just passed gaily through Cashtown with hoots and shouts and gone into bivouac several miles to the east. In the early morning hours, the division had been hurried out of Chambersburg toward Gettysburg. When they were finally over the mountains, the distant sounds of the battle were heard. The crash of cannons and the roll of muskets became more and more intense as they continued east. It was an exhausting day, but the pace had suddenly slowed, and the march was finally halted. As darkness fell, the grim sounds of the fighting then gradually lessened and finally stopped. A ghostly silence fell over the field.

It was a time to think and write. Some of the men, though exhausted, had been singing songs around the camp fires. Stars sparkled in the sky, and the moon was shining. "This is the way war should be," he had decided. "No fighting. Just friends together. And singing."

[He had written] Dear Family, It is early July . . . The roads are dry and dust cakes everything. We've walked far since leaving Chambersburg. It was more than twenty miles over mountain trails. We finally heard the sounds of the battle in the distance. Late in the day, we bivouacked in this field near Cashtown. This is a small village near Gettysburg. Thousands of troops have been here before us, and the ground is covered with things like bits of food, ashes from fires, and combs and buttons and other objects soldiers have dropped. The moon is still shining, but it will be light soon. I'm used to sleeping on the ground, and the stars are beautiful. Tonight I couldn't sleep well. I was too excited.

When we left Chambersburg, we waved to pretty girls. In a lifetime they've only been a few miles up this road. They stood in small groups in the shadows watching us as we left. They were possibly too embarrassed to wave. We were the enemy. A few smiled a little as we marched by. I think they had found that we weren't real bad or mean. It was early morning, and some of the older women seemed very happy to see us go. They can't forgive what the South has done. "Now you'll meet a real army, Reb!" several shouted. "And they'll get' ya for destroying our factories," others laughed.

I'm lucky to have seen a little of the world. We've marched hundreds of miles over the last year. I've also reaped a few of the honors—including command. It's not always easy to lead men, however. They trust you, but you know you're not always right. Humbling. In peace, one loses money. In war, we lose men. I'm not sure which is better—to take one's means to live or to take one's life. These burdens may outweigh the privileges.

By General Order No. 73, Lee had outlined orders for the guidance of individual soldiers in the "enemy's country." No officer below the rank of general was allowed to enter Chambersburg without a pass from Lee personally. Henry knew this.

[His letter continued] We were under orders not to enter Chambersburg. I was fortunate, though, with Sergeant Wilken's help, to meet several fine ladies. I was unable to be with them in the daytime, but the nights passed quickly. We watched the beautiful sky. Kathryn was my special. She has sparkling blond hair that touches the shoulders and moves as she walks. Sorry to have enjoyed "the enemy," but she was fun. I thought of you, Kath. She was nice like you. [These words made his sister, Kath, feel very proud.]

Couriers now led them off the Cashtown-Gettysburg highway. The roads twisted and turned, but they were gradually approaching the battlefield. Though it was still early in the day, it was becoming very hot below a vivid sun. Yesterday's march over the mountains had been tiring. Then the pace had slowed. Henry still wasn't sure why. He began to mumble to himself: "Perhaps, after reporting to Lee, Pickett found our division wasn't needed yesterday." He later was told that this was true. He also learned, as Wilken had suggested, that McLaw's and Hood's divisions of Longstreet's Corps had been badly handled in that second day of the fighting. They had hit the Yankee's left side very hard, but without success. The enemy line had held.

"We're moving away from the battle," Wilken suddenly said to Henry. He was just behind Captain Lynn and had been talking with Lieutenant Edwards. They had been laughing about the hostility they had found near the pass in South Mountain. "Bushwackers," Edwards had said.

"We won't be moving away for long," Henry replied. "We'll get there, and I'm sure we'll be fighting today, Sergeant."

"I agree, Captain," answered Wilken. "Bobby Lee can't let us sit here forever with a long supply line. We'll either have to go forward or back. And he won't retreat without a good fight first." The sergeant laughed. It was a deep, threatening laugh that gave men courage.

"Those bushwackers had popguns against this whole division," Edwards then continued. "Old Ben back there is an excellent shot. He may have gotten one of them on that high crag above the pass. That'll teach 'em."

Henry, also, wondered if Ben had hit one of the bushwackers. He laughed to himself. "It took courage to take on our whole division, though. But maybe it just took being a damn fool." He thought a moment. "They must have known we'd go after them. And Armstead did. He sent out that small patrol. He'd probably have shot them if he'd caught them. Those locals know the ground well, though. They'd be hard to find on those mountains. At least none of our men were hit." He listened. He could hear the harsh throb of artillery and the roll of thousands of muskets to the east. "The battle's not far away now," he said grimly.

Gradually the division moved southeast on back roads and narrow trails. There was no sense of urgency. They were in good spirits. It was a fairly sheltered march as they neared their lines, but they were already parched from the heat and the dust. Shade from lots of trees covered the roads. Kemper's Brigade was in the lead, with Garnett second, and Armstead last. They now entered a shallow valley with low ridges to their front and behind them.

They halted for a time in a little woods. It was dark there. Sunlight filtered through the trees and glinted off their guns and faces. They now moved forward into a field. The main Confederate position on Seminary Ridge wasn't far off. Close by was a shallow creek, which could be used for filling canteens. "I'll get yours, sir," volunteered the sergeant. Henry handed him his canteen.

"We'll rest here, Sergeant," said Lynn. "Have all the men fill their canteens. This'll be a hot day, and there may not be much water out there." He looked hard at the sergeant. "And I think our lines are just over that ridge." He pointed east. "That rise ahead of us."

Wilken turned. "All right, men, you heard the captain. Put your gear down and get those canteens filled. And, Jones, that means you too. Get moving!"

Jones stood and laughed. "Yah, Sarge. I heard it. So what?"

Wilken, his eyes gleaming like hot coals, took several steps toward the man. "I mean it, Jones." The man took off like a rabbit toward the stream.

This creek flowed into Willoughby's Run, which ambled south just west of Seminary Ridge. Henry's men were protected from artillery fire by the low rise to the east. Water was plentiful in this valley that fateful morning, and there was still some briskness in the air. It would become very hot as the hours passed. The division was less than half a mile from the main Confederate line.

They piled blankets and extra gear in high mounds. Ambulance men and doctors were setting up a field hospital nearby. This didn't help enthusiasm, but most didn't think they would be the ones to be hurt. Thus, no one worried. Men attended to needs such as canteens. It didn't smell good there. There were no privies around, but few seemed to notice this. It was just expected.

"I was bone dry, Sergeant. Thanks for the water. Foolishly, I didn't fill my canteen before we left this morning. Thanks again!"

The rumble of cannons and the crescendo of rifle fire was heard to the east. "That's around that big hill with the cemetery, Henry," said Captain Palmer. His company was just to their right. The sounds didn't disturb the men. They were veterans. Most didn't even seem to hear them. All this pleasantness didn't last, however. They were there for a reason. Orders soon came to form for attack.

"Sergeant Wilken," Henry called. "Double-rank formation. Form our men to the left of Captain Palmer's company." They could hear orders being shouted up and down the lines. Sergeant Wilken and Lieutenant Edward, Henry's second in command, plus the corporals, formed a partial third rank as file-closers. They would keep the men in line and moving—sometimes with the tip of a sword or a bayonet.

The sergeant was in his glory. "Straighten those lines, men. Larkin, get back in line or I'll use this boot. Jones, what'do yah think this is—uh picnic?"

"Yeh," said Jones. The sergeant started toward him. "I'm sorry, Sergeant. I was just foolin'."

Ben Toggler walked up to Henry. He was his old friend from when they'd fought together at Seven Pines and in the Seven Day Battle before Richmond. He'd been injured at Antietam, but he was back now. "This'll be that big one you told me about, Captain. I'll get me a few of those Bluebellies. I think I got me one in that pass back there yesterday. I saw him fall."

"That's good, Ben. We need you. Glad to have you back. And take care of your part of the line over there. You're a veteran now. And a good man." They shook hands, then Ben went back to the left side of the company's formation.

"I'll stay with you," Ben shouted. "We've been together a long time now, Captain." Henry just smiled.

Captains were in the front rank at the far right. Henry's sword was out and ready—not to kill but to lead. The men could see it above him as they marched forward. Their personal gear still lay in piles behind them.

They were ready for battle; no need to ask questions. Their pockets and cartridge boxes were weighted with ammunition. "Forward," came the command. They marched east toward the guns. It was into the sun. A few swollen bodies of the dead lay about the fields. The enemy was not in sight. A low ridge still hid their formation. Fighting had occurred there a day or so before. Killed horses, broken wagons, ammunition boxes, shattered cannons, and other things partially blocked the march.

For a while their lines were disordered. This was only temporary, as they stepped around broken boxes and wagons. "Steady, men!" the sergeant growled. His face had a hard look, like that of a lion devouring a lamb. They were again halted with the ridge close in front of them, still sheltering their ranks from the enemy.

Orders came down the line from Armstead to the company. "Everybody stay low," ordered Henry. "And silent!"

"Do you hear that, men?" the sergeant shouted. "Low and silent! You, too, Larkin. I heard that. Don't call me that again. You neither, Jones." They stretched out on the ground and rested.

Henry laughed. "I wonder what silent means with all that racket around us." The guns were still firing in the distance. A lull, however, soon came over the field, and it became quiet except for sporadic cannon fire. *There's something wild and uncanny about this*, he thought. *It's as if a fuse is burning toward a great big keg of powder, while everybody waits. And maybe we're that big keg. The final huge explosion. It's like ghosts and goblins are circling about. And the silence is more frightening than the noise.* He laughed. "I sure get dramatic at times. That's what old Ben told me once. I guess he's right."

Lee, accompanied by Longstreet, rode slowly by, examining their position. The men stayed quiet. Pickett followed shortly behind Lee. As was ordered, all of them refrained from cheering. Suddenly, as one, the entire brigade got up. This was because of their respect for Lee, their commander. They removed their caps and hats and stood quietly. Henry suddenly realized that he was wiping his forehead. The sun was high now, and it was becoming very hot. "I didn't think it could get any hotter," he mumbled. His mouth was dry, and his lips felt raw.

"Dang, it is hot, Captain," said the man beside him.

"It is, Abner," Henry replied. "A lot of battles are fought in the sun, though. This is the way it's supposed to be, I guess."

"I guess you're right, sir," said the man, laughing. "But it's not sensible."

As they stood there, Henry suddenly realized he could see only a small part of the big attack that was planned. Their lines stretched in both directions and seemed to have no end. The battle lines truly disappeared into the woods to their right and left. A lieutenant in another company told him that Garnett's and Kemper's whole brigades were to their front. Henry could see part of them. Kemper was to the south and Garnett to the north. These two, plus Armstead's, made up Pickett's division. They were part of Longstreet's big First Corps. Longstreet's other divisions were exhausted, though. They would watch the attack, but not go with them.

"They're lucky," mumbled Lieutenant Edwards over Henry's shoulder.

"They had a bad day yesterday, though," Henry replied. "They're fought out, I'm sure."

"They lost a lot of men already," said Wilken. "Hope my friend Jake Gibbons got through. He's from my ma's town in Georgia."

"We're still fresh," said Edwards. "I guess you're right. We have to be used."

"Part of Hill's Corps is to go with us," said Lynn. "I have word we're heading toward a little clump of trees across the battlefield. That, unfortunately, is the center of the whole Yankee line, I'm told. Well, Lee knows what he's doing, I'm sure."

"I hope you're right, Captain," said Abner beside him. "I just . . . " He hesitated and shook his head. "I just hope you're right. Their entire dang army's out there, I'm afraid. We'll need Hill's troops. And maybe lots more than that."

Captain Lynn's men couldn't see Hill's soldiers, but they were there—to their left. They'd been in the fight since the first day. In fact, they had started it. And some of their men had already been fighting this day farther north—the Union right.

A. P. Hill's men were to the left of Garnett. They would go forward with Pickett, as Henry had said, extending the column far beyond Pickett's brigades. Pickett's division was in Longstreet's First Corps. The two other divisions of this corps would not go forward with them. Many of these men, the divisions of Hood and McLaws, had died on the slopes of Cemetery Ridge and Little Round Top.

A double-ranked assault column of two brigades, Kemper's and Garnett's, would lead Pickett's advance to the Union lines. Armstead would follow some yards back and directly behind Garnett.

Heth and Pender were the division commanders under Hill. Both men had been injured earlier at Gettysburg. James J. Pettigrew and James H. Lane now led the divisions. Interestingly, Isaac Trimble would take command of Pender's men, who would make the attack. Though recently injured, he was known as a ferocious fighter. He was the man Lee had chosen. Thus, forty-seven regiments of nine brigades of two corps of the Army of Northern Virginia made ready to strike the enemy. If they had been successful, where would the next battle have been fought? No one will ever know.

"The enemy is in front of us," said Henry to Lieutenant Edwards. "And we're ready to fight. It's so hard to lie here and wait."

"These men are desperate to start moving, Captain. So here we stay."

"It's always a wait. Always will be. It takes time to organize several divisions. I sometimes wonder how they can be organized at all." He looked over at Ben on the far side of the company. He could see sweat running down his face in a stream. When Ben saw him looking, Henry laughed. "Like we did at Seven Pines, Ben. You and me. Just waiting."

They lay there as ordered—joking, swearing, laughing, and teasing. It seemed like hours. The low ridge was to their front. They thought they would see the Yankees once the brigade passed the crest.

Henry could hear men close by talking and spreading rumors. He laughed softly. "They don't know any more than I do," he said as he listened.

"Stuart's been destroyed."

"Hill's been killed."

"Ewell's divisions have been beaten. They're retreating."

They also talked about other things, including pretty girls and families. He began thinking again about Katherine, that pretty girl in Chambersburg. He wondered what his family would think about this recent interest. "Annie would probably laugh and say it's about time."

The division finally advanced over the ridge and down into a thicket of trees on the eastern slope. The two leading brigades broke from the woods into a shallow swale. An easy slope rose before them to a low crest of ground. Pickett's division had arrived at the main Confederate line.

A farmhouse and barn stood out against the sky. A line of cannon was in position but sheltered just under the crest of the ridge. Rail fences zigzagged up the slope. Armstead's brigade was halted just within the cover of the woods. All the brigades remained hidden. Again they waited. It was tiring, and it gave them too much time to think.

As in all armies, interminable waiting is the plight of those who fight. The men had been told of the difficult work ahead. However, morale was high. They would fight courageously. Lee was a man they could trust.

Orders came for skirmishers to be sent forward over the ridge. Henry ordered this. Reports then came back that there was just rolling farmland beyond. It was green and golden with farmhouses, barns, and fields of wheat, which stretched out all the way to the Yankee lines. It sounded so peaceful.

The two armies watched each other expectantly over that quiet, rolling countryside. It was a deadly game, though. Both were well armed, but only one would be victorious.

By noon, stillness lay heavy and the heat was intense. Above them stretched a blue summer sky. Canteens were empty; the trees of the woods lessened the circulation of air. Lynn's men ate some corn dodgers and little bits of bacon. It wasn't much. "At least it's something," Wilken said to several of them. His face was firm, but there was a twinkle in his eyes. Suddenly, close by, came the crash of a cannon. It was a signal. The gunners before them stood to their guns. They were ready.

Two puffs of smoke twisted and turned and floated into the sky. Suddenly, the whole Confederate line exploded. It was like one big crash. Edwards said something to Henry, then shouted, "This is like being struck by a lightning bolt."

Henry smiled, then became serious. "I just hope it slows those Yankees down a bit." He wasn't sure Edwards heard him. Hundreds of cannons fired on and on. Fire and smoke were everywhere—all around them. Lynn was sure the Yankees were being torn to pieces across the valley. His face was a little sad. He could imagine their horses running about like scared ants, and their men trying to crawl into the ground, as pieces of rock and hundred of shells buzzed about like insects.

Several of the observers from the ridge in front of Pickett's division came back and told what they had seen. One talked to Henry. Actually he shouted as loud as he could, "We're hitting them hard. It should hold them down a little. I was amazed though. There were still folks in those farmhouses in the valley out there when the firing started. They ran from their homes like frightened birds. God, why did they stay—with armies on both sides?"

Those were their homes, Henry thought. He didn't say this, though. He just shook his head in amazement as the officer went on to the next company.

The Yankee guns finally answered them. They didn't do much damage to the Southern cannons, though. The Yankee gunners overshot their mark—the top of the ridge. The shells hit the Confederate infantry instead. They were badly hit! There was no time to dig trenches. Stones and little mounds of dirt were all they had. Also, a few logs. "Everybody down, as low as you can," Lynn shouted. No one heard this, but they knew what to do. They lay as flat as they could. Henry suddenly realized he was trembling as he tried to scrape up dirt with his fingers. Kemper's and Garnett's men were in the open. They were hit worse than Armstead, who was with his men beneath the trees. This gave some shelter, but not much. Branches fell all around them. Splinters flew from fences, and shells and pieces of broken rocks came humming over them like bees.

Henry saw several of his men try to crawl into the ground. He had tried that too, with his fingers, but the dry soil made it almost impossible. Now they used their bayonets, those who still had them. The shelling went on and on. It seemed like hours. It was deafening. No one could talk much with all the noise. If they talked, they shouted. Henry was amazed at Armstead. He walked around as if he had the nine lives of a cat. He didn't seem afraid. It did mean that all his men were just a little less scared. Men and horses in front of them were literally blown to pieces, and gun carriages flew into the air. All the brigades were badly hit, but Kemper's men got the worst. He lost many men—killed or badly wounded. The other brigades also suffered.

The crashing increased as the Yankees to the south started firing. Then slowly it faded. At first it didn't seem to be slowing, but suddenly it was gone. Just a memory. It was time to march. Henry heard himself saying, "Out, out, brief candle. Life is but a walking shadow; a poor player . . ." He wondered if he was that poor player. Or were they all?

The final thrust by Lee's army at Gettysburg was beginning. People across America awaited the outcome. The prayers of both sides could not be answered.

Pickett's troops were to the south and Hill's men to the north. Chaplains moved among them. One helped Henry and Abner beside him with a prayer. Henry saw that Abner's and the chaplain's faces were grim. He supposed his was too. "Forward!" came the command. They were aiming for a little group of trees across the valley. The group had a distinctive umbrellalike shape. Everything was quiet. The brigades moved out of the shadows into the open.

"It's beautiful," Henry mumbled. "Lines straight as an arrow."

"It's as if we're going to a picnic," answered Abner. "And we're wide open in front of their whole dang army. This'll be a tough one, Captain." Henry just nodded.

An old soldier would later tell: "For those who made the charge and for those that waited and watched, this was the supreme moment of their lives. It was splendid, but it was frightening—for both armies."

Dense banks of smoke were rising off the meadows. The pageantry of color was majestic. The sun was shining. Confederate soldiers in double-ranked formation, elbow-to-elbow, battle flags unfurled, drawn swords, polished musket barrels, and lines as straight as on parade, were coming on through the meadows at a steady pace. Sunlight gleamed on metal, and banners of slashed red and blue moved in the breeze.

The line stretched over half a mile in a north-south direction. The blue flags of old Virginia were to the south. The call "Rally round the flag!" was no misnomer. These flags led men into battle. They were the essence of pride. To lose the flag, even in death, was unforgivable by some. Unknown to most of the men under Pickett, the prestigious Second Corps of the Army of the Potomac stood near that little copse of trees. They would defend their honor. They had never lost a battle flag. They, too, watched anxiously as fourteen thousand Southern veterans marched toward them.

CHAPTER XXV
Blood Drawn by the Sword

"James, why did Secretary Randolph resign from the War Department?" Sarah looked intense. Her brows were drawn together, and her voice was hesitant. "He was a handsome man, and I miss him. I asked my father why, but he was busy. He murmured something about respect, which I didn't understand. Did he do something wrong?"

"Politics, I guess. I know that he felt he was just a clerk. Davis makes most of the decisions. He still decides policies and authorizes the troop movements. Even Lee communicates his plans. Davis pretty much follows Lee's advice, however. In the west, Seddon, our new secretary of war, has had some influence, I believe. He's a forceful man."

"He's a sickly man, isn't he? Emaciated. Sunken eyes."

"Gray hair and pale too. A man in our department said he's a 'corpse exhumed.'" James laughed.

"That's not very nice," said Sarah. She then looked serious. "My father told me about James Seddon. He's a fine lawyer. He also served in the U.S. Congress as well as our Confederate Congress. Now he's in Davis's cabinet. He's accomplished a great deal in life. And he can't help how he looks."

"He supported Joe Johnston out there near Vicksburg. Grant pushed Johnston east, while he held General Pemberton's forces in the city. Vicksburg's a terrible place now. People living in caves. Shells falling all around. And they're starving. Even eating rats."

"That's terrible. And I suppose they've eaten the mules and their horses, too. Our food's not much better at times. That was horsemeat we had the other day. Pa told me so."

James squinched up his face, then smiled. "I've had my share too. It's really not so bad when you're hungry. A little tough, perhaps. I'm not sure about the rats, though." He then shook his head sadly. "And now Vicksburg is going to surrender. We've lost that city. And also the whole darn Mississippi, as well as the states west of there."

"Are you sure?" asked Sarah.

"Yes. Absolutely! Pemberton will formally surrender tomorrow. Vicksburg gone. It's devastating. It'll be official in the morning. The South is cut in half. I only hope Lee can win in Pennsylvania."

"That's a dreadful fight up there. Just awful. I hear we've lost men, even generals, like a scythe cutting through wheat in a field. Just mowed 'em down. Can we even continue the war with so many gone?" She hesitated—wondering. "And should we continue?"

James shook his head, then looked thoughtfully at Sarah. "Henry's there, I'm sure. I hope he survives." He was at a loss for words for a moment. "You're almost fortunate not to have a brother."

"My cousin, Will, is with Lee. He and I spent many summers together. He's almost a brother. I pray for him every night now. We even visited together at the Seddon estate years ago. It's west of here on the James. Sloping hills going down to the river. Blue sky. We were good friends. James Seddon is distantly related to Will's father. It's a small world. And a sad one now."

"I hope they both live, Sarah! I should be out there with Henry. I always thought I'd lead the way. Not my little brother." He squeezed her hand.

"Stop that, James. We need a few young men here at home." She kissed his cheek gently. "I need you too. Stay here."

Henry's company had moved out of the shadows into the open fields. He still couldn't see the ends of their battle lines. They disappeared in the distance. The sun was very hot, and both armies were surrounded by an eerie silence. Thoughts filled his mind, one after another, like vivid dreams. *I wonder if God at this moment has already decided the outcome. Should we even go on with the battle if he's planned what will happen? We've crossed the proscenium, though. We're on the stage.* He laughed. "And my winter of discontent has been made . . . glorious summer. I'm in battle now. It's where I've always wanted to be.

"Foolish. My legs feel like saplings. They seem to bend as I walk. And we've hiked many miles since Richmond." He saw Garnett in the distance mounted on a greater charger. "A horse! A horse! My kingdom for a horse! And still we walk." He squinted his eyes. "Where are those Yankees?" He looked carefully across the field. There was that peculiar copse of trees—green and stark, umbrella-shaped and ominous. It was the goal to which they were marching. He suddenly heard his voice shout: "Keep moving, men. Forward! Forward!" His sword was still high, so that everyone could see it. "We're headed for those trees."

His reverie was quickly broken. A soldier close by said, "Damn!" The man had struck his toe on a large stone. Several others around the man laughed and uttered bad words.

Mundane things, thought Captain Lynn as he returned to reality.

He heard Wilken close by growl, "Keep movin', men. Keep movin'. Any laggards and I'll use this boot. We're goin' to a fight!" Henry turned and saw the sergeant's long arm pointing across the valley. "The enemy is there. And we're goin' there to get 'em. We'll break them Yankees in two." A proud, threatening laugh followed.

"That's the way, Sarge," shouted Lieutenant Edwards. "Go get 'em!"

"Yah, Sarge, go get 'em!" Others laughed. They all relaxed. The sergeant would point them right.

They began to see the faces of the enemy—not the details—just the outlines. The Union regiments were still far off. But they knew they were there: tough, battle-hardened troops, waiting and watching. A private, Beryl, marching near Henry, wiped his mouth and swallowed hard as if spit stuck to the sides of his throat. Others grinned and swore softly. Some blustered out loud, probably to help forget their fear.

"I can see them," one man said in the rank behind.

"You'll see 'em run," a voice threatened.

"Close up, close up," Wilken yelled. The men were ready. Their fears seemed to have disappeared.

His troops were silent now. Henry smiled. *These are men I have lived with. We're together. We help one another.* They continued on for another hundred paces. He could see determination in each face. *We're a solid company again and ready to fight. We'll beat those Yankees yet.* "And there they wait." The last sentence was mumbled loudly.

Abner, marching next to Henry, spoke: "We'll get 'em, Captain. They look evil out there, but we'll get 'em. You'll see."

"Good man!" Captain Lynn said smiling.

It was silent again. He could hear men nearby breathing hard. He was relaxed now. His mind was clear. This wasn't a dream. He no longer felt afraid. He could hear about him the noises of an army moving to attack. No one was speaking. These were soft sounds, but very loud to him. Leather groaned on ragged uniforms, sore feet scuffed the ground, voices hummed far off, and canteens and weapons gave a soft clinking sound.

Thus Henry Lynn began the charge with Pickett at Gettysburg. The future of their country was in the balance. Not all that was said or thought could be recorded. There were a hundred stories, perhaps thousands, out there. Each man was an island alone. A thinking, caring, frightened human being. Each man suffered a little differently, but each one suffered. Their worries and thoughts were covered by bravado and that ill-defined something that clothes a soldier as he goes into battle with others whom he trusts.

Gunners in the Yankee lines made ready. They watched the ranks of gray soldiers approach. Their cannons, though, remained quiet. Henry and his men thought that many of their guns had been stopped. There were puffs of smoke and the bang of rifles ahead of them. Skirmishers were fighting for those green fields of Pennsylvania.

Their lines moved forward. Henry could see a road angling toward Gettysburg. "The Emmitsburg Road," he said, smiling. On both sides were solid fences with rails and posts. It was a stone's throw ahead. Suddenly, like thunder, their ranks were hit by shells. It was a great burst. Fire flew up around them like lightning. Hundreds were hit at once. Big holes were torn in their lines. The gaps closed quickly and the holes disappeared. They became a solid front again.

Henry laughed. It was a forced, desperate sound. Then they were struck again as if by a giant. Private Beryl nearby groaned and fell. Three others beyond him also staggered and dropped like sacks of corn thrown from a wagon. Someone in the third rank also fell. He prayed it wasn't Wilken or Lieutenant Edwards. As they got close, they'd need these leaders. It's hard to keep men moving when the going is tough. He smiled. "I wondered what tough means. It's already tough."

"It is!" said Abner with a low growl. He was angry. "But we're doin' all right. I'll get me a Yankee yet. Damn those cannons anyway. And them Bluebellies are still far away." Southern smooth bores and other guns were firing overhead now. "I hope they get them a Yankee cannon or two," Abner said. "Kill 'em flat. Break 'em in half."

"Close in, men. Close in," Wilken shouted. His voice sounded like the snarl of a wolf. Henry smiled. The sergeant was heading them right. "Jones, I heard that!" Wilken continued. "Now get in close. You, too, Wilson. And dress up those lines. That's better. We're not goin' to no dance. Larkin, I'm gonna use this here bayonet on you. You get back in line. I mean it, Larkin. And, Jones, pick up that pace there. Your rank's laggin' behind. Lieutenant, put your sword into that man there." Even Edwards was smiling now.

"You have my permission, Lieutenant," shouted Henry. He heard Jones give a yelp like a stuck pig.

"I's just foolin', Sergeant," Jones answered.

As they reached the road with fences on both sides, the straight lines became tangled from stepping over bodies and weapons and all kinds of things. "Get over those fences, or knock 'em down," shouted Henry. They were soon scrambled over or pushed down. This was done in a hurry. Shells were now falling all around them.

They halted; their lines were again dressed. "Forward!" could barely be heard above the crashing. Even the sergeant's gravel voice was drowned out by the explosions.

If Hell could be seen, thought Henry, *perhaps this is what it would look like.* A few low spots gave some protection for his men now. These were only little hollows in the ground, though. There were few places to hide, and most of the Yankees' cannons had not been stopped. Especially those to Pickett's right.

The Yankees then began an accurate fire of long-range shells. Pickett's soldiers were being hit badly. Henry, too, now had anger in his eyes. "Those on the hill don't feel the pain. They push home charges and fire and fire again. I'm sure they stand with pride to watch their work. They watch us as our men die. 'That got 'em,' or 'Did you see 'em fall?' or 'We'll get ya, you dirty Reb.'" He could see their faces in his mind, and he imagined he heard them shout. It was likely, though, that but few of them could hear what anyone said. There was too much noise. They just pointed.

A stream of wounded now were walking back. He looked once behind the company. He wished that he hadn't. Men lay there in pain. Some crawled and others tried to rise. Some lifted their heads and their bodies and seemed to be shouting for help. Others lay twisted and very still. Were they dead or living? He never knew. Some vomited and held an arm or a leg. Several had their hands to their chest or their stomach, while they twisted and moved about.

The Confederate charge continued.

The command, "Left oblique," had been shouted before they reached the road. Each man in the division had turned forty-five degrees. The whole line thus became angled to the left. It didn't change the straightness, but they were now marching directly toward the little group of trees that was the central point for the attack. There were more fences, but these were easier to climb over. Most were on people's farms. They finally reached the last slope. Garnett was ahead. The Yankees stood ready. They weren't far away now. Their rifles glinted in the sun, as their battle flags wagged about them like the tongues of hungry animals.

Cannons hit them again. Kemper's men were pushing left. Someone was on his flank, their right. They were becoming all mixed up with Garnett's troops. Armstead was marching on their rear, and his men couldn't go around. It was frightening. It gave Henry's company some protection, though, since Garnett was to their front. A seething mass. Disorganized. Like swarms of bees.

The whole Union line then fired. "That's canister and rifles," Henry supposed. It hit them like big hailstones. Armstead's whole line staggered, then fell back a step or two. Many of their battle flags were dropped, and hundreds of men fell. Henry was sure he stepped on some. With all the chaos and smoke around them, it couldn't be avoided. The flags were taken by other hands, but many who were down would never stand again. Henry's eyes seemed glazed but intent. They burned from the acrid clouds. He stared off into the dimness and the smoke.

He suddenly heard hundreds gasp, "Oh, Jesus. No!" as General Garnett was hit. He fell forward onto his horse, then slid slowly off to the ground. He didn't move after that. *Garnett was a good man,* he thought. *One of our best. Now perhaps that shame has been erased. Why must this happen to fine soldiers?*

The Lynn family would remember Garnett. Captain Lynn's father had once met him before the war. "He was disgraced at Kernstown," Papa had told them. "He lost his command."

Years later, Kath would mention Garnett's name to an old veteran of the Stonewall Brigade. The man thought a long while before he spoke, then replied, "He was a fine and brave soldier. He never lost our trust. Jackson was wrong that time. Perhaps that's what war is about. It hurts so many. He was brave at Gettysburg—and at Kernstown." The old gentleman stopped talking. Garnett had died in the war with many others. Kath would remember his name.

Pickett's battleline now halted for a moment, then continued forward. Their heads were low as if they were in a hailstorm. Armstead was directly to Henry's front. He could see him through the smoke. Somehow, he broke free of Garnett's and Kemper's tangled lines. Their men were like ants that had been poured out of a jar and spread over the ground.

Armstead's formation was also disorganized. Henry could see his commander, though, and he followed him. Somehow. He was not sure how, but they moved around Garnett's men who were before them and leaderless.

Henry soon saw Armstead lift his hat. He put it back on the tip of his sword. That was where it had been since the charge began. It was black with several holes punctured through it. It kept sliding down over the blade. Since they had left their main line (Seminary Ridge), he had kept it up high to show his troops the direction. Now Armstead shouted a command. Henry couldn't hear the words with all the noise. But his gray-haired commander was standing on a low stone fence, waving them on. *Probably,* thought Henry, *he said: Follow me, men. Follow me. Over the wall. The enemy is there!*

His hat had again slipped down over the sword, but the blade glinted in the air. Smoke covered the field and surrounded the little copse of trees. These were beyond the wall. Thousands had died to get near them. Captain Lynn shouted as loudly as he could, "Charge! Charge! Follow Armstead. Over the wall. Charge!"

Then suddenly, like the flash of a falling star, Henry, too, fell and didn't move. Several others fell beside him, and one man lay over his legs. Though the captain was alive, he was dazed. He couldn't think. He wasn't sure who the man was. The whole face was gone. He knew his men, but the shell had completely destroyed this soldier. His head and shoulders were just a mass of red.

Henry's family would later shudder as they spoke about this. "That's terrible. Just terrible!" Aunt Sue would say.

Henry fell into a dreamless sleep for a while. As he woke, he couldn't remember at first that he was hurt, and he didn't feel pain right then. He knew something bad had hit him. He hoped it was just one of the men falling against his side. He tried to think what had happened. Deep down, he realized that he had been injured, but it was only a vague feeling at first. He wasn't thinking clearly at all.

He then tried to tell himself it hadn't happened. *How could it happen to me? I felt the blow. I straightened up as best I could. Then I fell. I knew I was falling, but it seemed unreal—a dream.* He now tried to stand, but he couldn't. He reached for where he had been hit. It was sticky, but it still didn't hurt. He looked at his hand. It was covered with blood. It was funny, though. He still found himself denying it. He again saw old gray-headed Armstead surrounded by smoke—and fire. He looked like a Greek god standing in the clouds. A moment later, his commander looked more like a lonely survivor on a broken ship. Not many butternut-clad men were at his side.

Henry saw cannons standing beyond the wall. There were no gunners near them. They were Yankee guns, of course. He was able to lift his head and chest a little. He then saw the artillerymen on the ground near the guns. Their horses had all been killed.

"Fine animals, and so sad. Both armies need them." He then smiled. Some of the Yankees who had hurt his men, now, too, felt the pain. "An eye for an eye," he said. "I shouldn't want that, but I do. You're filled with hate at times—like now. Anyway, I feel better having seen them. Or do I?" His arm was numb, and the pain was becoming intense. He groaned as he rolled slightly to one side.

Suddenly he saw a Yankee soldier close in front of him—some ten feet away. He didn't know how he got there. He was evidently trying to stand. Henry blinked his eyes hoping to see him better. He saw that the man was raising his gun to shoot. Lynn groped for his pistol, but the Union soldier fell back before he could fire. He had made one last desperate effort to fight. A pool of red was around him.

Henry looked very pale in the dim light below clouds of smoke. Sweat ran from his face, and his hands felt cold even in the heat of the day. He searched for words. He couldn't think of any. The smoke had cleared a little. He again saw Armstead. His commander was now close to the cannons on the other side of the stone wall. Henry felt a bad pain in his back and side this time as he lifted himself up to see if any of their men were with him. There were a few. Not many. It was sad. He suddenly felt like a broken toy soldier that had been thrown down hard by a little boy. "I played with toy soldiers once," he mumbled. "Now I have played with real ones. It isn't fun anymore."

He struggled to rethink what had happened. "It must all be a dream," he said to himself. It wasn't. He touched the spot again where he had been hit. It had become very sore. Again he tried to stand. He couldn't. Suddenly, he was aware of all the noise about him. He had ignored it for a long while. There were shouts and cries everywhere as men tried to kill one another. He looked at his blouse. He hadn't really looked before, and he wasn't sure why. He supposed he was afraid. There was a big red stain near the armpit. It covered a large part of the sleeve. It was slowly getting bigger.

Henry would remember seeing Armstead fall near the cannons just beyond the wall. Many Confederate men stood before that pile of stones firing, reloading, and firing, again and again. Not many went beyond it. He thought the few who had were dead. Suddenly, several of Armstead's soldiers came back across it. Each one was ragged and limping, and most were helping a friend. They were retreating, and few were left unhurt. "They stopped us, those Yankees!" he said.

He shouted at the top of his voice, "Take me! Take me! Please take me!" No one stopped. They hadn't heard him. He realized this, and called to many others. They continued without pausing or with but a brief glance. Finally he sighed: "We put up a good fight, but they beat us. Those Yankees beat us fair. Damn. And I'll probably be their prisoner."

The battle was over. Armstead had become the spearpoint for the Confederate attack. He was the spearpoint, but there was no spear behind. The mark he reached, though, was important. It was the high tide of the Confederacy!

How long Henry lay on the field, he wasn't sure. He vaguely realized that it was becoming quieter and that men were still going back. He knew he had lost much blood.

Henry was startled when he saw a rounded figure approach. He wasn't sure who it was. The man had a broad face and strong shoulders. Suddenly he realized it was the sergeant. "Wilken, you've come back. Thank you. Thank you!"

"I've been looking for you, sir. Thank God you aren't dead. I got over the wall with Armstead, but they beat us back. Not many lived. Ben's here with me. He's a good man. He helped me when I was hit back there. Then we both've been looking for you. Ben, he's over here. He's been hurt bad. I'll need your help."

"Howdy there, Captain. We was sure worried. You'll make it, though."

"Ben, you've been hurt too." He could see a big red spot around his ankle, and he was limping.

"Just a scratch, sir. Don't hurt much. The sergeant got hit too. Look at his head. Like a cow stuck in a jugular with a knife."

"We're all invalids now." Henry's face suddenly brightened. "But we're alive. Thanks for coming back. Both of you." As his eyes cleared, he could see that all three of them were bleeding.

They helped Henry walk. It was a blessing. They reached a high rail fence, then fell across it. Henry heard a loud crack as he dropped to the ground, and he felt a terrible pain in his thigh. He was aware that he may have broken his leg, but he didn't mention it to the others. He grimaced, then laughed. It was a harsh, forced sound, more like the groan of a bass viol. "We're like a couple of drunks, aren't we? You didn't know your captain was a hard-drinking man, did you?"

"You aren't," said Wilken. "Ben and I here have tossed a few. But not you very often, sir." While the sergeant was talking, Henry noticed that Ben had become very pale. The red on his pants was getting bigger. Wilken, in contrast, was covered with clotted blood. The head wound had stopped oozing, but there was a large open cut from the brow to behind the ear.

"Sergeant, Ben's still bleeding. We'd better stop. I don't want to lose him. He's a good man, and we need him."

"I'm all right, Henry," said Ben. "We'll just get you back first." They kept walking. It seemed like miles. The captain heard both men occasionally groan. He couldn't see their faces well. It was hard now to lift his head. He did see the killed and injured on the field. There were mounds of dead and arms and pieces all around. It was frightening.

They limped on until they seemed to be very close to their lines. Henry suddenly realized Ben wasn't there. "Where's Ben, Sergeant?"

"I'll have to go back for him, Captain. He just couldn't go on." The sergeant tried to smile. "I'll have to rest a moment first, sir." They both then collapsed in the woods and brush. The sergeant lay exhausted for a long while. He then struggled up and seemed to be returning for Ben and also for help. Henry didn't remember much after that. It was like being in a cloud. Just blank.

Henry lay in the woods for what seemed a whole day. He wasn't sure. The sergeant never returned. Henry actually remained there for almost two days. Ladies who were searching the fields for those who were still alive found him there. They had covered their faces with scented cloths to mask the smells of the thousands who were dead.

He thought they were angels when he saw them. They were beautiful and bright. Through the branches, they seemed to be coming toward him from heaven, and descending between the trees. Suddenly one of them spoke: "He's alive. He's alive! Get help. Hurry!" No one spoke after that for a while. The woman had looked at his wound and felt his pulse. He stirred and tried to talk. "He's so young," she said. "He's an officer too."

"And he's handsome," said another woman. She was looking into his eyes and at his face. He smiled gratefully. "But he's still bleeding," she continued.

230

The ambulance ride was one of terror. It was like being on a board on a bucking horse. There were several others moaning beside him. They were left at other places that were filled with wounded, and, evidently, didn't have room for him. The men in the ambulance always argued, but this rebel wasn't accepted.

Henry remembered coming to a little church. It was raining hard. He saw the steeple through the mist. When he was carried in, someone said, "With that chest wound, this one won't make it. We should have left him." They slipped once on the way in. It was a narrow board, and Henry fell off. "Damn!" the man said. "We certainly should've left him. I'm soakin' wet now, and he's only one of them Rebs. He's almost dead already."

Inside, he found himself with many Yankees. He was a prisoner, but they were nice to him, a terrible rebel soldier. He felt the doctor probe the wound at the side of the chest. "It didn't hit the lung," the doctor mumbled. "But there may be a shell fragment here below the scapula." Henry winced with pain. "And there's no exit wound. The leg's broken too, but we can splint that later. And the wound's bleeding again. We'll have to stop it. Let me have that clamp."

The softness of the doctor's voice soothed Henry's mind. Suddenly, though, he felt the searing pain of an instrument below the skin. It was humbling, that fright, that feeling of mortality. He moaned and twisted and tried to speak. Then everything went blank.

"Hello, Mr. Robertson, Mrs. Robertson. It's nice to see you," said James. It had rained that day. They were standing before the War Office. He tried to smile, but his lips twisted wryly. "Hello, Sarah."

"Why are you so sad, son?" asked Mr. Robertson.

Sarah reached over and touched his arm. Her eyes were warm. "What's happened, James? You look like a ghost."

"We've been beaten. It was hideous. Pickett's Division is destroyed, I'm afraid." He saw Sarah draw back and close her eyes. "We lost thousands of men. Now we're retreating toward the Potomac. The battle's over, I hope. Unless they catch Lee with his back to the river. And the Potomac's very high right now. It could happen."

James turned to Mr. Robertson, Sarah's father. "My brother, Henry, is probably lost. So is Sarah's cousin, Will. He was with Kemper's troops, I believe. Pickett's whole line marched across the field in the open. They were hit by all the guns the Yankees had." He shook his head sadly. "Annihilated. Apparently the Yankees couldn't miss. I'll go back later and see if

I can get more news. It's been a bad week for the South. This, and also losing Vicksburg."

"James, come home with us," said Sarah's mother. "We can talk. It helps." She looked into his eyes. They were moist. She patted his arm gently. "They're in God's hands now, son. He'll know what to do."

James saw that she and Sarah both were crying. Mr. Robertson took a deep breath. He, too, was badly hurt by the news. He wondered what to say. "Soldiers may be missing, James, but not gone. We'll find out. Let's go home, son." His eyes were soft. "We can sip a little wine and have dinner."

"We'll also break bread and pray, James," said Mrs. Robertson. "This will be a sign of our love and faith. We're lost if we lose that." Sarah gazed upward as she listened to her mother. The blue of the sky was reflected in her eyes. They were caring and deep, Lieutenant Lynn noticed.

Mrs. Robertson continued, "Blood has been drawn, some say, by the lash. Perhaps we're now paying for that." She spoke slowly, then she looked kindly at her daughter and the young soldier beside her. "James and Sarah, what we see and feel perhaps was meant to be!"

CHAPTER XXVI

The Ways of the Lord Are Not Easy

Captain Lynn had written a letter to his family in the early morning hours while his company was camped near Cashtown, just off the Chambersburg Pike. Before the letter arrived, the Lynns knew there had been a major battle at Gettysburg. They were sure their son had been in the fighting. With mixed feelings they waited for the lists of the missing and dead.

Suspense and dread hugged the town like the claws of a serpent. It was a hot summer day. A few fluffy clouds were scrunched together in an otherwise clear sky. Hours had crept by before the galley copies of the long lists came from the newspaper office.

"His name is here, James—on this terrible list," said Momma. "There it is: CAPT. HENRY LYNN." She pointed. The print was poor, and she squinted and looked again, then handed the papers to her husband. She didn't speak at first, but she took a deep breath and closed her eyes, as if time would erase his name. It did not. Her face, though fair, was clouded and pale like the moon. "I pray it isn't Henry. I hope I've read it wrong. Please, Lord, please, have it not be our . . ." Her voice hesitated. "Our son!"

"His name is here, Ann," Papa said softly. "I'm sorry, dear, but it is Henry. Lord protect him. He's not listed as dead—but missing. There's hope, God willing."

"Oh, Lord, how can he be gone? Such a fine man. Please! Please have him still be alive." She stopped talking, but her lips continued to move, and her eyes were moist and distant. Suddenly she understood. "Our soldiers have become professionals, haven't they? They've learned to destroy. Now thousands of fine men are gone." She looked caringly at her husband. "But I know Henry's still living. I must go to him."

Papa squeezed her hand. He said nothing at first as he gazed compassionately at her. "Our land has lived with slavery. Perhaps we are being judged. Every home feels sorrow. Why should we be different? We must first find where he is." He thought a moment. "Be patient, love. We'll find him."

"I pray you're right, James!" said Momma softly. "I pray you're right."

Much has been written on the Battle of Gettysburg [wrote Papa in a letter sent to a cousin in Boston after the war. They were comparing wartime experiences]. A myriad of books tell the story. They record valor; they analyze failure. Children can learn from these books: how "Jeb" Stuart, the eyes of Lee, our commander, was off attacking wagon trains when he was desperately needed; how Longstreet disagreed with Lee's orders to take the offensive; how Ewell hesitated before Cemetery Hill and lost the day; and how there was utter absence of coordination in the movements of the various commands. Some contend Lee would have vanquished Meade, if my friend, Jackson, had lived. We will never know, however. Jackson was dead. My friend was gone.

What you cannot glean from history books, though, [he continued] and the prosaic listing of events, are the feelings of helplessness of people living through this dreadful time. My family saw and heard of the devastation. We witnessed much tragedy. We held the hands of friends and relations who lost sons and fathers. We saw homes and fields that had been burned and destroyed. We wondered if we could live through more. We did. We human beings are resilient. There is great power and strength within us, if we have the patience and determination to find it.

I was sure Henry was gone. I prayed this wasn't true. I told my family, "Be patient, we'll find him." I really didn't believe this myself. I wore a "painted smile" as best I could.

Momma accepted Papa's advice. "Be patient, love." She did wait patiently. She talked but little. She scrubbed, cooked, managed, and prayed. There is healing in such employment. Angry rainstorms wetted the dusty roads.

We are not alone with our troubles [Papa wrote at that time in his diary]. Other families suffer. Few are left untouched. The papers have confirmed the death of the Morgans' son, a few houses down the road. Jesse Chandler, Emmie's special, has also been killed. His cheerful smile is gone now. What a fine man he was. I wanted him as a son. I cried tonight when I heard of his death. I still can't believe it's true. I held Emmie's hand for a long time. We didn't speak at first. Then she told me how they had met and what he had meant to her. "We were in love, Papa. I now have a glimmer of how you and Momma feel toward each other. Why does it take such hurting to really find this out?"

I couldn't answer this for my daughter. I thought for what seemed minutes, while she looked sadly into my eyes. "We learn much with time, Emmie," was all I could think to say.

The Lynn children helped at home. They were well educated in domestic responsibilities. In this time of pain, they were of great help, but for all of them, it was an effort to keep smiling.

"Momma, you're crying," Emmie said softly one day.

"Yes, I am," she answered. "The men and women of our family mean much to me, Emmie. You'll find this true as you grow older. Friends of childhood become distant with time, but one's family, one's flesh and blood, is there, always. They help us face life. We love them. When tragedy takes them from us, we hurt inside."

"We love you, Momma," Emmie whispered.

The rain passed, but the storm continued. Religion helped lessen the sadness. The glory of music filled the sanctuary: "God is my strong salvation; What foe have I to fear? In darkness and temptation, My light, my help is near . . . " The Reverend Barkan arose before the congregation. He stood silently until the music ended, then walked slowly to the raised platform from which he preached. There he stood for a seemingly endless moment in quiet, looking searchingly over his people.

The minister's face was firm, yet compassionate and handsomely composed. He was tall, black hair salted with gray, piercing blue eyes, rough hands and shoulders of great strength. He had reached middle age, and, though heavy, possibly even a little rotund, he was still a good-looking man. His words began softly and rumbled out over the assembly, seductively but with reason. "There are lost souls here today. They have allowed the world to dismember their lives; they have lost touch with who they are and why they are here in God's world. We must all put ourselves under influences that restructure our lives and give us purpose. We cannot know the significance of tragedy until we know what is intended. We are not yet privileged, though, to view the total plan. Still, we must look forward to light, not darkness. We must believe in a caring God, or all is lost."

Reverend Barkan stood pensively for what seemed minutes, then continued, "Why does the Lord allow appalling disaster to fragment his people? Can we find meaning beyond the grave and the wreckage of lives?

The burdens carried by quiet folk, the losses amidst calamitous events, try us, and for most, bring from the core those qualities that work for the betterment of all. When the base of the apple tree is gashed deep with an axe, the tree harbors energy for the growing of beneficial, edible fruit. Are we like the tree? Does God have plans for our future?"

Reverend Barkan waited, and his eyes moved slowly over the assembled people as if trying to sense their feelings. "I truly believe the mold is prepared. We must find patience till we cross the mountain. We too will view the fruit on the other side. For now, let us find comfort within ourselves, within our faith and with the doctrine of love!"

Barkan continued emphasizing service, hope, and caring. Suddenly, what he said, much of which Kath had heard before, clothed in different words, struck a chord within her. On a wrinkled pad with a stub of a crayon, she took notes. That faded outline exists today.

The Reverend Barkan continued: "We are in a great conflict. What we do here in this world will finally become right. We know who guides the way. What we have done thus far may not be what God wills.

"The ways of the Lord are not easy," he said in a thunderous voice. "Patience and love, dedication and service will heal us. We speak of liberty. What do we mean? Do we speak from the soul with the true meaning of God, or do we speak from past comfortable self-interest and the status quo? We are set free when we have mastered a great and good cause. Have we as a people mastered the right cause? God, give us insight and perseverance to know your will! Forgive us for that which has not pleased you . . . " The words Reverend Barkan spoke seemed to agree with the philosophy Kath's father had shared with her some weeks before. It caused her to wonder if they were truly fighting for the right cause.

For all her new maturity—and she felt she had aged considerably— she daydreamed intermittently during this earnest oration. Perhaps this is a fault of all young people. She wondered about the rightness of their cause. She also wondered about the rightness of Annie's new special. He had recently proposed marriage; he was most acceptable by Momma's and Papa's standards. There was excitement in new love! However, Annie's answers were evasive; the family was never sure if she had said "yes" or "maybe." She advanced elusiveness to a fine art.

Men always have been attracted to Annie, thought Kath. *She probably worries that an engagement would stifle all her fun and play with other boys. And it is play.* Kath chuckled. Annie, who was sitting in front of her, turned and gave her a stern look. "She is beautiful," Kath said to herself. "Even when she's angry. I wish men'd look at me the way they look at her." She smiled wanly. "John, her new beau, is certainly handsome, though. And interesting."

John Ingram was also tactful and persistent, with a reasoned modest disinterest. Annie couldn't hog-tie him with smiles, then wish him "Good-bye."

The family thought Annie was nearly won. So did Kath as she sat astir in the house of the Lord and admired John's handsome profile. He was large-boned and muscled. His forehead was pale below flaxen hair; his bright pink cheeks were hidden behind fuzzy sideburns extending to the angle of the jaw. The skin of his neck wrinkled slightly as he turned his head and smiled. He winked at her. His eyes were gray-blue, and his hair smooth except at the lower cheeks where the ends twisted a little. Kath liked him very much. *He's a fine man!* she thought.

Annie sat beside him, hands fidgeting a little as the sermon continued. John saw that Kath was staring at him, and he whispered something into Annie's ear.

"Oh, John, you're silly," she said, smirking. "This is serious. Now listen." She tried to look stern, but then smiled. "She's only my little sister. How would she know?" Ringlets of Annie's dark hair peeked below a luscious green-white bonnet, tied below a firm chin with a band of watered green taffeta, which outlined her pale oval face. Her cheeks were colored by a trace of delicate pink.

Annie often seemed flighty, but this was for show, as if submitting to male dominance. "John, you've been naughty," she would say, giggling, or "John, you remembered the anniversary of our first meeting," she would tease. Then she would smile shyly and lower her eyes. This wasn't demureness, Kath knew; it was to hide the glow of achievement. She devoured newspapers and books; she could be conspicuously dominating when circumstances required it.

With their prayers came an answer. They received a letter from Cornelia Hancock, a nurse, in Gettysburg. Aunt Sue read it out loud: "Dear Family, Your son, Henry, is beside me. He has been badly hurt, but I believe he is getting better."

"Thank you, Lord," said Momma. "Thank you for finding him." She looked at their father—a peaceful, caring look. "Oh, James, he's alive!" She then sank back and listened.

We are in a little church just east of Gettysburg. The whitewashed walls are stained by heavy use. Hundreds are being cared for here. He has a broken leg, and his right arm has been torn by a piece of a shell, but the arm is healing. The doctor says there is still some metal deep inside. He has had a high fever. This is improving. He is now able to talk a bit. He sends you his love.

Henry lay for days in the brush close to Seminary Ridge. There were many dead around him. He talked of angels when he was rattled with fever. He now speaks of you and the ladies who found him there. The scented hankies covering their faces were needed because of the terrible odors. Perhaps that is what he remembers. These ladies were angels. They searched for the men who were still alive amongst the thousands who had been killed. Most of the latter are still unburied.

Momma left the next morning for Gettysburg, a long journey in those days. Uncle Jim accompanied her. She was not afraid. "A mother going to an injured son is safe on the road," she said.

"I hope so," replied Papa. "I'm sure we can't stop you, Ann. You'll be in enemy land, though. It won't be easy."

She had shown this strength and compassion during Papa's and Dee's recent illnesses. To spend nights awake, as she did, suggested a stature of seasoned oak. She could be gentle, but she could also be very firm and unyielding.

The children all jammed aboard the wagon for the drive to town. They were as excited as a tree full of chickens, but there was an underlying sense of worry. "She'll be all right," said their father.

"We know she will," answered Emmie. There was a ring of uncertainty in her voice.

The girls had grown, and they didn't fit as well into the wagon as they had on the day they had arrived in Staunton two years before. Their home would seem desolate without Momma.

Papa still tired easily. He was "flabby, like an old sponge," he said. As they bounced along, however, he sat straight as a fence post. "Take care of yourself, Ann," he continued. "Don't worry about home. We'll be fine. Henry is your job now."

Rain still lay in pools along the way and splashed the wagon. The water gleamed in the sunlight, like a bride in her looking glass. A regiment of militia with pompons and color crossed before them as they entered the town. Bayonets glittered in the light. The train whistle was heard in the distance. Usually it was an exciting sound to hear. This day it caused sadness. It beckoned their mother to Gettysburg. The battle was over. The ruins and pain were still there.

Momma would describe what she saw.

"Man's folly!" said Papa years later.

CHAPTER XXVII
Sadness at Gettysburg

Their mother departed on the Virginia Central Railroad among whistles and a cloud of steam. Her gray eyes were bright, but as Kath kissed her good-bye, she noticed that, although she was smiling, Momma's cheek was moist.

"Bye, bye," the children shouted until the train disappeared around the bend. She waved slowly from the window; they couldn't understand her words.

"She's gone," said Papa. They too tried to smile. "She'll be fine," he continued. The others weren't so sure. On the way home, they didn't talk much. Perhaps silence best expressed their feelings. The wagon wheels crunched on the rough ground. These noises didn't drown out the sniffling and soft coughing by the younger daughters.

Finally Annie spoke. "She is gone. Please take care of her, God."

Aunt Suellen met them at the door. She saw the tears. "Welcome home, children," she said, smiling. She hugged them all. "Momma's strong. She'll be all right."

Momma's journey north was mostly by train. Uncle Jim was with her. He had talked to Emmie and Annie about many things the night before they left, including the trip. "I lived near Alexandria years back," he said. "Friends and kin there will help us. We'll get along."

"I'm sure you will," said Emmie.

"Take care of our mother," said Annie, smiling. "She's strong, but she'll need some help."

"We'll care for each other," he replied. "And I'm happy I'll be going along. Since your Pa arrived in Staunton, I've always felt like I's part of the family. It's a good feeling. Sure, you have squabbles, but there's love inside. This has kind of washed over into my life. I'd never felt this with other folks before. Your pa has helped me with writing. You and your sisters

240

have sat with me and talked. Dee has read me stories from her books. She and I have kind of learned together. It's helped me so I can scribble down a few words. Now I can remember what we've done and seen. It could be hard, but we'll manage."

Emmie grasped his hand. "Good luck, Jim. We'll miss you both."

They traveled partway in open railroad cars among boxes of creosote, tin cups, stretchers, alcohol, permanganate of potassium, nitric acid, bandages, bed sacks, tents, food, clothing, and other types of equipment.

"Jim, what do we do now? The Federal lines are that way." Momma nodded toward Alexandria, the terminus of the Orange & Alexandria Railroad. "It's not many miles, but they may not let us through. Perhaps we should go in another direction. Maryland isn't far, the women at the last station told me."

"Miz Ann, I can get us a wagon so we look like we belong. No one'll worry about you and me goin' slow along these roads. There's a ford we can use some miles from here." He pointed north. "Another way over that big river is by Chain Bridge. I'm told there're soldiers there, but they're not as particular. We'll be in Maryland then, and we can head for Mr. Lincoln's city. It'll take us a while, but we'll make it. I lived around these here parts some years back. I probably still have kin here somewhere. Perhaps they can help a little. It's a pretty bumpy ride, though."

"The bumps don't matter, we'll just keep moving. I think you're right about that direction straight north. It's the safest way. That is, unless we meet stragglers. With all the rain, though, the Potomac's probably pretty high, even at the fords. We'd better try that bridge first," said Ann.

"If we meet stragglers, we'll hide then, Miz Ann."

Uncle Jim sat at Momma's side. He smiled courageously. His eyes showed the inner pride that he deserved. Through friends, he had found a wagon. It was a very old wagon, but it was holding together pretty well. It was a long day, that day, while they wound along endless roads. There were many places Momma hadn't heard of before: Springfield Station, Back Lick, Annandale, Munson Hill, Falls Church, Pimmit Run, Mackall's Hill, and Fort Marcy.

They crossed several streams that were swollen by the recent rains into formidable rivers. It was a more difficult trip than Jim had thought. "Will we make it, Jim?" Momma asked.

"I think so, Miz Ann. It's a mite deeper than I remember. I'm sorry your shoes are getting all wet." He cracked the whip sharply over their aging excuse for a horse. "Adeline, you keep moving there." He turned to Momma and smiled. "I hope you can swim if we have to."

"Jim, I've never been swimming in my life. Thankfully, though, the water's not as deep here. I don't think I'll have to. I don't want to start learning today, anyway. Good job, Jim, we're almost there. Whoops! Sorry! I didn't expect that bump."

"Adeline, you wrinkled old horse, you keep pulling. Up that bank now. That's the way. Come on, you wrinkled old thing That's it. Sorry about that last bump, Miz Ann. It was a big one."

"I'm shaking a little, but we're safe. Thanks!"

They were able to pass along the outskirts of most towns. Some good people helped them with food. There weren't many folks left on farms, though. The wandering stragglers and groups of men from both armies made life on farming lands dangerous in war areas. Burned barns and homes along the way stood like lonely sentinels.

Momma and Jim hid several times from rough-looking men with uniforms of mixed colors—unshaven and coarse. Drinking water was not a problem. There were many streams. In contrast, the forests of northern Virginia had been cut by troops of both sides, leaving scrub trees, stumps, and a stubble of brush and prickly bushes.

"Better keep her quiet, Jim. If she neighs again, we may be lost." The pounding hooves above them on the bridge numbed their ears, and dust and dirt came through the cracks, covering their faces and clothes.

"They's mean men. We better not meet up with them, I'm afraid. That last one with the sword, . . . it looks like it just cut someone bad."

"I didn't see that, but the buildings in the distance are smoking. They must have been burned. Then those were hogs they were driving in front of them. And one of them was carrying a goose. Someone's farm's been destroyed, I guess," said Ann.

They traveled on and on, staying that night in an old partially burned barn sleeping on a little straw. Jim had fluffed it up for Momma, then used an old sheet to cover some sweet-smelling grass and leaves for her head. "You need a good rest tonight, Miz Ann. It's a big day tomorrow." She made tea in the morning in an old can. They sipped it as they nibbled on crackers Momma had brought from home. Then they were off on the road again heading north.

"We made it," said Mrs. Lynn. "But I'm exhausted. The rest of the way fortunately is mostly by rail. I think it'll be easier. The man in the station said our train will be by in several hours. We'd better be aboard. It's going to Baltimore. Thank goodness the soldiers at the bridge let us go through. I was scared to death when that one soldier said, 'Where you goin', Ma'am?' I held my breath. He certainly looked mean, didn't he?" Momma chuckled softly and shook her head.

"He sure did. I didn't think he'd let us pass, Miz Ann, and I was angry too when he laughed at Adeline. She's not much to look at, but she got us here. He was pretty nice—finally," said Jim.

"I almost put my arms around him when he smiled," said Momma. "I was telling him about Gettysburg and Henry. He has a son who fought there, too. He wondered if his son was all right. I guess kin bring out the best in us folks." Her eyes were soft, as she remembered their crossing over the swollen Potomac River and the rutted, well-traveled roads in Maryland. She had a look of great satisfaction. "It's been difficult, Jim, but we've made it this far, and I have the tickets for the train. I'll hold yours if you like. We'll be on the B&O Railroad and two other lines. We'll have to make a transfer when we get to Baltimore. And one more after that."

"At the bridge, you spoke so nice to all those soldiers, Ma'am. You sounded like a mother. I don't blame them for smiling. You care about soldiers on both sides. They knew it too." He hesitated. "I worry about the train ride, though."

"You do look worried. Why?"

"Miz Ann, here in the North they'll think I's still a slave. Folks by the road told me that several times. They said slaves are emancipated. I's a free man. You know that."

"I do, Jim. You are a free man, and I'm still learning more and more about you. You're capable. And you're kind. You deserve to be free," said Mrs. Lynn.

Momma, too, was worried. The presence of a Southern woman aboard a train possibly wouldn't be excused. Momma's pale face and unassuming smile got them through, however. She was always honest about a son injured at Gettysburg. She also tried to help people where she could. An elderly woman near Washington shared her crackers and a jar of jam, which she had bought near the train station. The woman was hungry, and she was also going to see a son who was ill in Baltimore.

Momma later marveled at all the activity at railroad stations. Wounded soldiers by the hundreds were embarking and disembarking from the trains. Dedicated women had established aid centers and hospital facilities for the men while they awaited transfer to the larger cities. Those centers were way-stations with tents, cooking facilities, and a surgeon.

Loaded ambulances came and went. These women, some still fairly young, had been recruited by the Sanitary Commission, which had agents in many Eastern cities to interview applicants and organize working units.

Miss Dorothea Dix of the regular army refused to accept women who were too young or too pretty. In contrast, the Sanitary Commission searched for plain as well as pretty women. Ability was the critical factor. As these women patiently worked night and day, ancient tradition quietly died. Society for ages had supposed nursing was a job for the sullied hands of trollops beyond the pale of decent folks, or for enlisted men with little training.

"Miz Ann, you've been in here for a long time," said Jim. "Why aren't you tired? I helped those men outside with loading those bags and boxes on to a wagon. They thanked me for it. Now here you are still working in this here tent. It's been hours. You should be tired. And just look at all those boys. They're all bandaged and hurting."

"They are hurting, Jim. We have to leave now, though. It's getting late, and those boys are in good hands." They walked slowly down the road, Uncle Jim with his satchel and Mrs. Lynn with her big carpetbag. Momma continued talking. "What injured men need is what they left at home—mothers and sisters and wives. Where else can you find the love and caring young men should have when they're sick? We women for years have shouldered these burdens. This's what soldiers look for. Most are still careless boys. They don't know a plugged nickel about scrubbing and cleanliness. And on their recent travels on the train, they couldn't do much—and every bump was torture. The wagons are even worse when you're hurt."

"You're kind, Miz Ann!" said Jim. "And those other women in there, are they mothers and sisters, too?"

"Most are. And we're seeing the mobilization of a whole country of folks. We may not know all the reasons for the fighting, but the people of this land are helping those who get hurt or sick. Perhaps that's the solid rock on which our world is founded. The home. I wrote a letter for one of the boys in that tent. His name's Billy. He asked me to tell his parents about the lady taking care of him. It wasn't me," Momma said, smiling. "It was that elderly woman on the far side of the tent. I told his family she's a grandmother, and that she deserves praise. She's worked hard for many days." Momma looked at her watch. "We'd better hurry now or we'll miss that train."

At each station, while waiting for the next train, Momma was in the station hospitals "elbow deep" in wounded soldiers, helping with bandages, brushing away flies, washing faces, holding hands, and speaking softly. She was treated with kindness by the doctors and others. There was one misfortune while they traveled. It was at a station beyond Baltimore.

"Jim, the train won't come for a while. We'll wander toward the town. Then we won't have to answer so many questions. I'll get us some fruit and bread for our dinner." They walked around the station building and storehouses toward the village a short distance away.

Momma was several yards in front of Jim, passing an old, unused shed. The roof shingles lay about amongst broken slivers of glass. She heard a moan from inside the shed, then a soft cry, "Help me. Please help!" The voice suddenly became muffled.

"Quiet, lady. No one'll hear you out here. You and me are going to have a nice quiet time. Don't make me choke you. I will if I have to." The door was slightly ajar, and the upper hinges were torn off. Momma peeked cautiously inside.

"It's a young girl in there," she said to herself. "How terrible. And that dirty soldier." It was later established that the man was a deserter. He had never been in a battle. His filthy hands were covered with wisps of hair pulled from her scalp. His face was streaked with jagged lines. Her fingernails had gained some revenge while she fought. Blood oozed over the lower parts of his cheeks. In his effort to ravage her, he didn't hear Momma enter.

Mrs. Lynn saw the bruises on the woman's face. Her multitude of petticoats were torn and ragged, and her undergarments shredded and almost completely off. Also, the corset cover was ripped, exposing flesh above. A pistol was lying on the floor beside them.

God, this makes me angry, thought Momma. *How can anyone do this to such a lovely person?* She lifted her carpetbag and brought it down with all her strength on to the man's head. He shook his head as if dazed, then turned on her, an angry look in his eyes.

"Women," he said in a growling voice. His stained trousers were torn and loose at the waist. There was fresh blood on one side.

He lurched toward Momma, his large hands settling at her throat. She couldn't scream, but she twisted sideways and he followed. There was a terrible thump. His grasp relaxed, and they both fell to the floor. There stood Uncle Jim. He had struck the man hard with a log of wood, which he had found beside the door. "Thank you," Momma whispered. "Thank you, thank you!"

Jim was bashful and apologetic. "I'm sorry, Miz Ann," he struggled to say.

"Sorry, Jim? You saved my life. Thank you. And thank you again!"
She then turned to the young woman beside her. Jim stepped out while
Momma tidied her clothing as best she could. She had a few pins in her
bag. She suddenly noticed the inside of it was stained and sticky. Mrs.
Lynn had broken the jar of jam with the hard blow to the soldier's head.
He was bruised, but not bleeding much.

"Jim, I've patched and mended what I can. Let's help this young
woman to her home. But I don't even know your name, young lady."

"Jane. Jane Winder, Ma'am. I live close by. It's not far. Thank you for
saving me. I went to the station to welcome home our returning soldiers. I
made these little cakes and things to pass out. That awful man caught me
as I walked near the shed."

Momma and Jim missed the train that day, but they spent the evening
with Jane's family. The clean sheets were a delight. Jane's father and
neighbors, though, were white with anger. Momma, too, was angry, and
she thought that the authorities should be notified. One neighbor left for
this purpose. Others went soon after. "It's been taken care of," Momma
heard outside her window late that night.

In the morning, Momma and Jim continued their journey. This
would be the last leg of their trip. They were well rested now. Before they
left, they thanked the Winders for the fine meals and lodgings. Jane was
there and smiling. Her cheeks and arms were bruised, but she appeared to
be in good spirits.

They boarded an open freight car surrounded by stretchers, tents,
bandages, and bottles filled with powders and colored liquids. There were
no passenger trains that morning—only freight trains. A mile west of
town, they saw a lonely tree. A dark figure hung from a lower limb. It
swayed to-and-fro in the gentle breeze. The face was dark and reddish
lines marked the cheeks. The neck was sharply bent. "Oh, God. Jim, it's
him." Mrs. Lynn shuddered and could hardly talk. "Violence often meets
with pain," she struggled to say. She shook her head sadly. "That man paid
a price."

"The Lord speaks at times with anger," replied Uncle Jim. He thought
a moment while shaking his head slowly. "The ways for bad ones is hard.
We're rid of him now, Miz Ann."

At the Gettysburg station, Momma met charming Georgeanna
Woolsey, a vivacious, exuberant young woman of the Transport Service.
She gave Momma directions through the town to the church hospital,
which was undoubtedly where Henry was being treated. Cornelia Han-

cock had recently been a nurse at that church. She had written the letter that started Momma on her trip. Georgy knew her personally.

Georgeanna warned Momma about the shock of seeing hundreds of painfully wounded men lying on hay-covered boards laid atop the backs of pews. The terrors of hospitals in wartime were not new to Mrs. Lynn. She had worked with the wounded in Staunton. This, however, was different. Her son was there. "I pray he's getting better," she whispered. "Thank you for everything, Miss Woolsey."

"I'll pray for Henry and for all of the men, Mrs. Lynn," said Georgy. "Good luck to your son."

Momma and Jim headed for the church. The damage to the town was seen everywhere. "I'm appalled at the devastation, Jim," said Momma. "Just look. Houses and yards destroyed. Furniture in the streets. People's treasures all over. How can men do this to others? It's dreadful. Till a few days ago, Gettysburg was a peaceful town. Look at what our politicians have caused. They should all be brought here and made to stand and see what they've done. Their sadness should be like a heavy chain that stays with them always."

"Perhaps they know that already, Miz Ann," said Jim.

The town looked as if it had been thrown about by a storm. Houses were destroyed. Walls were torn and scarred by bullets and shells. Broken furniture lay against houses, on barricades, and tossed as feathers in a wind. Life's possessions were gone. The people of Gettysburg had suffered. Stoves, rockers, bureaus, fence posts, rails, wagons, rocks, logs, tools, and sofas were mixed in great piles. They seemed to have been stirred by a big hand.

Ann Lynn later told her family, "These folks were strong. Trouble brought out the best in most of them. They walked with chin up and a courageous smile. A few, though, were dour and quiet and watchful, and didn't talk to strangers. There are always a few people like that in any community. I guess one has a right to be that way."

Annie commented later on, "There probably were more grave looks in town than fleas on a hound dog." She was rereading some of Momma's notes about Gettysburg.

Emmie pieced together other things her mother had said and written:

The bad odors of the unburied men and animals filled every nook and cranny in the town. The countryside was warm and soft, but the smells were like venom, and the air was heavy. To all this, dusk gave a somber, weird cast as I walked through the town that night. Lacy shadows of gray and purple crept across the golden fields as the sun set over the mountains to the west. Distorted forms lay upon nearby fields like rag dolls in a nursery. They lay quiet and aloof from worldly cares—discarded "clods" of "turf" in a meadow, patiently awaiting a caring human hand and a word of benediction. The bodies were in every position, singly and in mounds.

In the tedious days ahead, Momma would walk these fields. Even that evening, she could see some details of the remains of the animals and men who had died there. She wrote: "Eyes were open, gazing at the sky. Faces were black and bodies were swollen in the warm air, causing the dead, North and South, to look like giants. Clothing was torn, probably by their own hands during the agony of death. It is a hard war, which neither side will win!"

It was to an improvised hospital, with beds of straw, that Mrs. Lynn and Jim were walking that evening. They were just east of Gettysburg. "I think that's the church there, Jim. I can see the entrance to the sanctuary that Miss Hancock described. It has those big, heavy doors. My heart feels heavy too. It makes me ache inside." Their steps became slow, and they stopped several times. "What will we find there, Jim? Death is all around us. Perhaps we shouldn't have come. Will Henry be there? We don't know."

"It seems peaceful enough," said Jim. "But it's dim and from this distance, it's hard to be sure. Those are people moving about, I believe. Unless they're ghosts." That made Mrs. Lynn smile.

"There are no ghosts, Jim. Just men. And we're nearly there. We have to go on. Let's go find Henry."

CHAPTER XXVIII
An Injured Son

Mrs. Lynn approached the little church near Gettysburg. Would Henry be there? She wasn't sure. Neither she nor Uncle Jim spoke as they neared the sanctuary entrance. Outside the doors she was horrified. There were bad things she hadn't seen from a distance. Possibly she knew they would be there, but she wasn't ready for the fright of seeing them.

"Jim! Jim, it's terrible. I'm afraid to look any further. That's a pile of arms and legs over there."

"They're being removed, Miz Ann. They're piling them in those carts."

"Probably for burial," said Momma. "I hope none of them belong to Henry."

Wooden surgeon's tables stood outside in a small wooden shed. Black streaks were upon the wood and on the ground around the tables. Soldiers still sat about, along the fence. Some were slumped over, others were lying flat; a few crawled on all fours like weak animals.

"They're loading those other wagons with some of the men," said Jim. "I wonder where they're going." A sergeant, looking frazzled and tired, stood close to the wagons directing the loading.

"Sergeant, where are they going?" asked Mrs. Lynn. "I had a son inside the church who was hurt. Maybe he's already been taken away."

"These men are going to larger hospitals right close, Ma'am. A few are on the way to the rail station and bigger cities. Most inside can't be moved as yet. They've been too badly hurt. There are still some outside here that won't live. Head and chest wounds. They never make it." He smiled and shook his head as he pointed to his face and chest. "They're bad wounds, I'm afraid."

Axles creaked along rutted roads with puddles of rainwater still about. Women with calico skirts puffing around them were kneeling among the men with food and water. The surgeon's tables, thankfully, were not being used for their bloody work as Mrs. Lynn arrived. "Our medical corps is setting up those large hospitals right close to here. If you can't find your son, ask where he was sent. I'll help you find him. It won't be too hard."

"Thank you, Sergeant. What is your name?"

"Warren, Ma'am. Sergeant Warren."

"I'm glad there aren't hundreds of injured men around this little church, Sergeant. I thought there might be many more than I see here right now," said Mrs. Lynn.

"Ten days ago, the injured and dying covered the ground everywhere, Ma'am. They filled this little church to the walls. It's hard to believe, but most have been sent on—or have died."

Momma walked up the steps to the heavy sanctuary doors. Uncle Jim waited outside. "Call me if you need me, Miz Ann."

"I will, Jim," she said. Her voice was soft and she smiled wanly. As she was about to enter the church, a ghastly cry came from the yard. "What was that? Jim, it sounded terrible. Like a laugh in Hell. Lord Jesus, what was it?"

Sergeant Warren looked up and smiled. "It was expected, Ma'am. One of them just died." He spoke with little emotion. "It's a common thing here. We'll take care of it; don't worry yourself." Momma's hands were trembling, and her smile was gone. One of the wounded men, who had clung patiently to life, had died. He vanished like a spark on a sheet of paper. Those around him showed as much feeling as rocks in the sea. Sad! There was little meaning there to the loss of a life.

Momma entered the church. She felt deep distress. After the experience outside, she wondered what might be waiting for her indoors. She left her carpetbag just inside the door. She put her hand to her chest to still the throbbing of her heart. "It's fluttering like a loose wagon wheel," she said to herself. Her lips quivered, and she felt dizzy. "I hope I don't fall right here on the doorstep."

It was some time before she could see in the dimness inside. She shook her head, trying to clear her eyes. Gradually she saw pale forms and distorted bodies on rough boards and a little hay. Many were quiet, exhausted. Others were moaning and moving about. "What a frightful chamber!" she mumbled.

"I suppose these men are like our James. They've dreamed of glory. There may be glory here, but there's also hurting. It's all around me."

The walls of the sanctuary were stained and scratched, and except

250

perhaps for the nurses who were about, working with the men, there was little glory. Momma's heart was filled with empathy when she saw these tired women. They had struggled for days. Why they had not all lost interest and caring during this strain, she never knew. Some months later she said, "I thought I could see the faint glow of a halo in the dimness, around their heads."

Several months before, Momma had talked about the pain seen in war. "Emmie, Annie, you've both worked with soldiers who have been hurt. You started soon after we came to Staunton. And you've seen what it's like to be wounded."

"Often. Too often, Momma. In hundreds. They hurt from wounds. They also hurt from worry about their families," Emmie answered.

"The men keep coming, Momma," said Annie. "Many are carried here from places far to our north. Some from Winchester. There's much fighting there, I'm told." She then laughed, and broke into her big "clown" smile. "That town's changed hands so many times, Pudgie Townes wrote his sister, they don't even move the maps and papers anymore. They just hide them."

"Be serious, Annie. I'm trying to make a point about the war."

"Sorry, Momma," Annie mumbled in a not-so-sorry voice. Momma looked sternly at her for a moment, then turned toward Papa and their uncle.

"James, Wen, you men see less of the real pain our soldiers suffer than we women do. You say war is bad. We women see what it does to so many. Do you wonder why we hate the fighting? Except for the doctors, we women are the ones left with the injured. You men forget. You see only the honor."

"Perhaps you're right, Ann," Uncle Wen answered. "We know about what happens, but we don't have the patience to sit and listen. Women do—and we thank you for it. I mean that."

"In battle, those who are hurt are stepped over by those left standing," Mrs. Lynn continued. "Henry told us that. It's only later when these soldiers are taken to care stations, that men see and hear what the wounded feel. These men then leave them and go back to the fighting."

"Ann Katherine, we men are learning," Papa said. "It takes time."

"Centuries have passed already, James," said Momma. "It hasn't changed. Men are still fighting." Papa smiled sympathetically.

Ann Lynn remembered that conversation as she entered the church. She waited until her eyes cleared; then she looked carefully about at the

251

attendants in the sanctuary. There was an older man on the far side of the room near an exit door. He was working with instruments on the leg of a soldier, who was moaning and moving about. There was fresh blood on the boards beside him. One of the women was helping to restrain the soldier. A lantern was held close by. "Stay quiet, son. We're trying to help you. That's the way. Hold that light up a little higher now, Mary. That's it. We've got it clamped. The bleeding's stopped. Now hand me that tie." He lifted up one end of the clamp he had put into the wound. "Here. Hold this now. And keep those tips up so I can see where to tie. There. That's the way." His hands moved quickly in the dim light. "We got it. It's stopped. He'll live."

This elderly man was the doctor. His head was mostly bald like an egg. A few strands of hair dangled about his ears, and his face was deeply lined. Mrs. Lynn later learned he was an army man; he had been one for many years. He had treated the injured and sick for more years than she could remember. Momma summed up her thoughts about him long after the war: "He was a good man."

The women tending the wounded were mostly in stained calico dresses. Some had the soft accent of New England, and a few had the flat, drawling voices of the South; the latter were mostly from Baltimore or the Washington area. Some were from Pennsylvania and New York, and others from Illinois and Ohio.

Mrs. Lynn's entrance into the church did cause astonishment. Cornelia Hancock was not there. She sensed a reserved politeness when she explained to a woman close by, "I'm Henry Lynn's mother from the Valley. I'm sorry to bother you, but Miss Hancock wrote me he's here. I'm also sorry I look so disheveled, but I've traveled a long way. Do you know if he is here? Perhaps I can see him for a few minutes. I won't stay long if it bothers you."

"I'm not sure. I don't know Henry Lynn," the woman answered. She hesitated and looked hard into Mrs. Lynn's eyes. "You're from the South— a Confederate," she said. "Look what your men have done to our boys here in the North. It's terrible."

Ann Lynn felt very alone. A wavy curtain seemed to cover her eyes. It was like moss on a live oak. "I'm sorry," she said. "I have a boy here, too. He's just a boy, and he's been badly hurt and has fever. We're proud of him, as I'm sure all you ladies are proud of your sons." Her eyes filled with tears. She couldn't talk for a moment. "I'm truly sorry," she struggled to say. She could feel her hands tremble. "I hate war. I'm not really sure which side I'm on. I'm Southern, but I've held the hands of men on both sides; then I've written to their folks. Please, is Henry here? I won't bother you long."

Another woman nearby walked up and gently held Momma's hand. "We understand. I'm sorry about the anger, but we see so many injured boys. Jeannie just lost a son. At Vicksburg—not here. Perhaps we have to strike back once in a while. Miss Haines has a list of those in the church. She's sleeping in town right now. She'll be back, though. I don't know your Henry either, but I'll help you find him. Say some good words to the other boys as you pass."

The battle was over, but even in this holy place, a church, feelings ran deep. There was great ambivalence, both caring and hate, toward the enemy from the South. Momma was the "enemy." The Lynn children's wonderful mother, filled with feelings of love of people and embitterment toward war, was looked at with suspicion. Some drew back. Momma understood this, but she was deeply hurt.

Most of the women were very hospitable. They were not concerned with what cause was followed. They saw Mrs. Lynn in coarse, unprinted cotton clothing as a person like themselves, a mother who loved her family. They stepped forward to help her.

Momma found Henry. It took time. There were several Henrys among the two hundred men in the sanctuary. She went from row to row and peered carefully at emaciated faces. She smiled and spoke softly—a few words of encouragement.

She seemed angelic to the men. Lips smiled back as she said, "Son, get well. Your family needs you. Bless you."

"Thank you, Ma'am," several answered.

She awakened many. Suddenly she turned; she recognized that voice. "Thank you, Lord," she said. Then she nearly shouted. Tears ran down her cheeks. "Henry!"

"Over here, Mother! You're here! My God, you're here in Gettysburg! Why?"

That last statement needed no answer. However, she had walked right by and not recognized his familiar square face. She laughed a little, when she thought of that. It was almost a giggle. Thankfully, Henry didn't see her tears.

"What are you laughing at?" he said. "Do I look that bad?" He then also laughed. "You should have seen me a few days ago. I was really bad then. My leg hurts now, but my arm's much better. I hope you can stay here tonight."

"I'll be here till you're well, Henry. Don't you worry. I won't leave."

Momma shook her head as she looked down at her son. She saw how pale he was. His skin was washed but almost blue in color. He looked very tired. His right shoulder and upper chest were swathed in cloth; an irregular yellow stain wetted the surface of the bandages close to the armpit. His right leg was splinted with a wooden splint—very crude. Probably a slat from an old fence.

For all his discomfort, his face shone with light as he said, "I can't believe you're here. But you are. I never thought I'd care to see family so much. Thanks for coming to Gettysburg, Momma. I'm sure the trip was hard. Is everybody well?"

"They are, Henry. Now we have to get you well." She patted him gently on the shoulder. Henry rarely cried, even as a little boy. Now Momma saw tears well up in his eyes. She couldn't help touching him. The skin of his face was warm and moist. He responded with a thankful smile.

Henry didn't talk much for a while. However, he was in good spirits with family again beside him. He seemed to be in deep thought, but he finally looked up again at his mother's face. Her eyes were soft, and the tears were gone. With a rush, all his experiences of the last weeks welled up and came tumbling out like water over a falls. "I should be with my men. They're like little children at times. They need me. I hope they're safe." A moment later, he continued. "There're probably few left." He hesitated again. "I hope a few of them lived!"

Henry's company, a few fortunate souls, had marched southwest with Lee into Virginia. The Lynns later learned of the horrendous trial his soldiers faced, especially the wounded, in a line of wagons fifteen miles long. We needn't mention that further. There was enough pain to see and think about in Gettysburg.

CHAPTER XXIX
A Little Church

Henry had been injured, but he was very much alive. His mother had reached his side in Gettysburg. It was night. The bright moon lighted a clear sky. Momma was very tired, but she listened as he talked on and on, faltering occasionally when he drifted into sleep. He would abruptly awaken and begin talking again, but for a time, his words would be slurred, and one thought would interrupt another. His story finally became coherent, and a picture of the battle emerged.

Momma suddenly realized that the doctor was behind her. "Let him continue," he said softly. "He needs to talk. He's getting better, slowly. I think he's over the worst. He's a nice young man, Mrs. Lynn."

"Thank you, Doctor. He is a good young man. We need him at home." The doctor held Ann Lynn's hand for a moment and squeezed it gently. She knew in her heart that he was a caring person. "You look very tired, Doctor Stevens, but you continue to work on all night."

"We have to keep working. These men need so much. The last days have been better, though. I have fewer patients now than before. I feel sorry for our nurses, however. Most of them have hardly slept." He looked kindly at Mrs. Lynn. "Henry's fever has lessened now, but you stay with him for a while yet. It'll help him to talk about what he's been through. He needs encouragement, too. That bad drainage from the wound is much improved."

The doctor walked across the sanctuary to examine another patient. Several minutes later, Momma heard his voice again. "Son, that leg's infected. You've got to stop pulling those bandages off."

"I gotta scratch it, Doc," the man said. "It's drivin' me out of my head."

"You'll lose it if you don't stop. I'll wash it again and irrigate it, but keep those dirty hands away."

Henry had again fallen asleep. Momma sat beside him and saw how he winced and groaned as he turned from side to side. "What will happen, must happen, Lord," she said, "but please help him, if this is your plan. Thank you for letting me reach his side."

Henry suddenly mumbled, "Katherine, I'm going to miss you."

"Who's Katherine, Henry? Do you mean your sister, Kath?" He was now partially awake. "Who is Katherine?" she asked again.

"She was pretty, Momma. I liked her very much. She lives in Chambersburg. I hope you can meet her sometime." Henry related again how he had met a fine girl. He had spoken of her earlier in a letter. "She was always cheerful and interested in me and our family. She was much like Kath." His sister, Katherine, would later sparkle when told these words. It was so nice of him to say them.

Henry spoke mostly about the days leading up to the battle. His mother kept notes about this. "Papa wants to know," she said to him later. The rest of the family wanted to know, too. Uncle Jim now cautiously entered the church. He was the Lynns' yardman and had accompanied Momma to Gettysburg. She saw him and beckoned him over. Neither spoke. They sat on boxes and listened.

"We could hear the sounds of cannons and thousands of rifles and muskets. It was like thunder. We were with Pickett. Our division didn't reach the field on those first two days. The march over the mountain had been hard, and we were tired. Then our pace was slowed. I didn't know why. I thought we were needed. We were finally ordered to halt, and we bivouacked for the night.

"The sun the next day was very hot, and the guns started again. The Yankees were much closer. Gradually we got nearer and nearer to the battlefield. Suddenly we were directed onto a side road, and hopefully, were headed away from the fighting." He laughed softly and shook his head. "This was true only for a short time. We were soon marching east again toward our lines. There was no sense of urgency, though, and we were in good spirits. It was a fairly sheltered march, thankfully, with lots of trees. We finally were very close."

"Go on, Henry," Momma encouraged. "You reached the battlefield. What happened next? Papa wants to know everything."

"We were halted for a short time in a little woods. It was dark there. I remember the sunlight coming through the trees. It seemed to sparkle off the faces and guns. We weren't there long, though. The command came to move forward into a field. Our main Confederate position was on Seminary Ridge, which wasn't far off. There was a little creek close by, which we used for water.

"We put our blankets and extra gear in big piles," he continued. "Ambulance men and doctors were setting up a hospital nearby. This didn't help our enthusiasm, but you never think that you'll be the one to be hurt, so we didn't worry. My men attended to canteens and things, while they laughed and talked. And I remember how bad the smells were there. So many men had passed by, and left all kinds of . . . waste and trash." He continued on about the double-rank formation formed to the left of Captain Palmer's company, and how Lee and Longstreet had ridden slowly by, examining their positions.

"Suddenly our entire brigade stood up. It was because of our respect for Lee. We all knew why. As I stood there, I could see we were only a small part of a big attack. Our lines went in both directions. They seemed to have no end. They disappeared into the woods on both sides of us. Garnett's whole brigade was to our front with Kemper to his right. These two brigades plus ours made up Pickett's division. We were part of Longstreet's big First Corps. His other divisions were fought-out, and they weren't to attack with us."

"You were with Armstead, weren't you, Henry?" asked Mrs. Lynn.

"Yes. With Armstead."

"Longstreet's other divisions were lucky, weren't they?" continued his mother.

"Not really," he replied. "They had arrived at Gettysburg the day before and had fought pretty hard. They had lost a lot of men, already. We were still fresh. We had to be used. Brigades of another corps, though, probably Hill's, were to attack with us. They were just to our north. We were all heading toward a little group of trees across the battlefield. We couldn't see Hill's men, but they were there to our left. They'd been in the fight since the first day. In fact, I was told they'd started it."

Momma didn't make a good record of much of this part of Henry's story. She didn't know the names of the many officers. She did understand that Armstead had followed some yards behind Garnett and that Hill's men had gone forward with Pickett, extending the column far to the north. She later knew that many men of Longstreet's other divisions, the divisions of Hood and McLaw, had died on the slopes of Cemetery Ridge and Little Round Top the day before.

Henry now slept restlessly for a while. Momma watched quietly.

When he awoke, he started talking again. She wrote the names of Heth and Pender, who were the division commanders under Hill. She wasn't sure what they had done.

"The enemy was in front of us," said Henry. "We wanted to fight, and my men were ready. We were desperate to start moving. Still we lay there as ordered, joking and talking. It seemed like hours. There was a low ridge in front of us. We thought we would see the Yankees once we crossed it."

He continued, "The division finally advanced over that crest and down into woods. There was still a small slope ahead of us, but we were now at our main line—Seminary Ridge. It really wasn't much of a ridge at all. It was just a little higher than the valley between us and the Yankees.

"There were a farmhouse and a barn close by, and a line of cannons in position near the top of the slope. We got word that farmhouses and fields stretched from there all the way to the Union lines. It sounded so peaceful. And it was peaceful for a while as we and the Yanks both watched each other. This didn't continue for long."

Henry told about the signal guns that fired and the terrible shelling that followed. "It seemed as if our entire line exploded. It was like one big crash. I'm still not sure how we and so many Yankees lived through it. I couldn't hear myself talk. Hundreds of cannons fired on and on, and shells burst all around us. It was awful, but the worst was yet to come.

"Finally the shelling was stopping. You could hardly tell it at first, but it did. It was time to march. I found myself saying, 'Out, out, brief candle. Life is but a walking shadow.' Then I laughed. I'm not sure why. Perhaps it was just good to be doing something. We had been lying on the ground trying to stay alive."

Henry's mother listened patiently. She wasn't sure what to say. The doctor was standing close by as Henry's voice raced on. "Here come the rebels!" he said. He then blushed as he explained; "I was watching from high on Cemetery Hill. As the shelling stopped, the charge began. There was a shout from our lines, 'Here they come!' It was as if one great voice spoke, then we all watched."

"I understand," Momma replied. "You were there, too. It had to happen—the battle." She looked searchingly at the doctor, then out into the sanctuary. "I just pray that one day it will all have some meaning."

Henry slept for a while, then continued his story about the final thrust by Lee's army at Gettysburg: "Pickett's troops were to the south and Hill's to the north. I was with Pickett. Chaplains moved among us. One helped me with a prayer. 'Forward!' came the command. We were aiming for a little group of trees far across the valley.

"Everything was quiet. Our brigades moved into the open. It was beautiful. Our lines were perfectly straight—like an arrow." Thus fifteen thousand Southern veterans began the attack across the fields.

The old physician stood wide-eyed listening to Henry talk. He had watched Pickett's charge from Cemetery Hill above the battlefield. The thrill of the battle was afire in his eyes. Momma suddenly realized how much men love the excitement of fighting. Even for a good man, there was awe and enthusiasm. Few ever experience these emotions in actual battle. Most relive only what others have done. *We women hate this instinct,* thought Momma. *Our loved ones are consumed!*

While these Southern veterans marched with a cadenced step across the meadows, Henry's voice became slurred and irregular, then he fell into a deep sleep. His mother recorded some of his words: " . . . the cannon, . . . enfilade, . . . hundreds of men were falling, . . . a stone wall, . . . canister, . . . 'over the wall,' shouted Armstead, . . . he fell . . . "

The doctor was standing beside Henry. "What happened next, son? What happened?" He gently touched his patient's shoulder. Henry didn't answer.

"We better let him sleep now," said Momma, smiling. "We can listen again tomorrow. I'm tempted to wake him, too, but perhaps it's best that we let him rest."

"It is. But I keep wanting to hear the end, even though I know what happened. I was there, and it was terrible, but I really wasn't in it. I didn't fight. I still want to know what those who were in the battle felt and thought. I was high on a hill. I watched real soldiers, and I felt a little like a coward up there. I still do."

"You should have been hiding, Doctor. We need you as you are. If men keep fighting, we'll need all the doctors we can get," said Momma. Her eyes were filled with compassion. "God put you where you should be. Stay there. You have enough danger from fever and illness. You don't need more."

"Thank you, Mrs. Lynn," he said. "You're right. We need to be told that once in a while." She saw he, too, was smiling. It was a satisfied smile, like that of a little boy who had been praised by his mother.

The moon was still high in the sky. There were a few clouds. Henry's mother helped the nurses and the doctor with some of the injured. They bandaged wounds and cleaned faces. Most of the women had left the church, probably to sleep for a few hours. The Rev. James Amars awakened Momma. She had rested a while on a wooden box in a corner and fallen asleep. He gently shook her shoulder. "Thank you for all your help," he said. "I saw you working with many of the men. They can't thank you now, but they will later. For the rest of the night, you'll be more comfortable at Mrs. Jordan's. It's only a few blocks from here. A straw sack in a corner is better than a box or a hard floor in the church. It's not far. Here's the address." He smiled. "Again I thank you, Mrs. Lynn."

"And I thank you for your kindness, sir," she said. "Where is Jim?" She suddenly realized he was no longer beside her.

"He's out by the cooking tent. He's fine. He was helping with boxes and other things. Don't worry. He's sleeping now, too."

Ann Lynn looked about the church. It was dim, but she suddenly knew she belonged there. Though she had had much experience in the hospitals in Staunton, she realized she wasn't trained as a professional nurse. These thoughts encumbered by fatigue came with difficulty, but they wouldn't go away. "I think I'm an administrator," she said to herself. "Also, I can cook. I've been doing that for years for a family. I've also cooked for many of our field hands when they've been sick. That's what I can do here.

"The food I saw them eat tonight was bad—terrible. I pity them all. That's how I can be of some help. Jim will work with me, I'm sure. He's probably already been helping outside. When it's light, we'll find out what we can do."

The sun was high above the hills when Mrs. Lynn finally awoke. The minister, Reverend Amars, ambled across her field of vision. "Vicar," she mumbled, "where is the storehouse of the Sanitary Commission?"

He smiled and bent forward, answering, "Morning, Ma'am. I didn't understand."

"I'm sorry, Reverend. I was partially asleep." Momma suddenly was fully awake. She inquired again about the storehouse.

Reverend Amars gave a brief answer, then laughed. "You did enough yesterday. You'd better rest today."

"There'll be time to rest," she said. "Don't worry. I'll be all right." After he left, she arose quickly and headed back to the church.

"I'm ashamed to say how long I slept last night, Jim. This usually is not my weakness. I guess I was tired. It sure stops ambition, though."

"Miz Ann, you had a right to be tired. Your eyes were so red. I was worried."

Momma smiled. "That's kind of you to say that, but let's get started. We have lots to do."

She was filled with disappointment when she talked to one of the cooks. "This here's what the Army provides. No, I ain't had much trainin' in this here cooking. I set guard over there at Fort Henry for the last three months. What do you mean you don't just add water . . . ?"

Momma was shocked. In happier times she had taught Henry about cooking a few dishes. " . . . You don't just add water, you also use milk and lard." He had learned a little; his meals were even a "delight," one officer had commented. In the cooking tents just beyond the church in Gettysburg, hardtack, grainy, hard-to-chew meat, cold coffee, and vegetables, more related to cooked "rubber rain covers," were the usual selection of the day. "No wonder sick men are famished, Jim. They can't even chew this gristled meat. This would dampen the appetites of healthy soldiers."

With a firm jaw and shoulders back, she set to work. She first spoke to the doctor. "The quality of the meals here is very poor," she said. "Wounded men need proper food." This fact to Ann Katherine Lynn meant war. "I believe this is the firm rock on which good health is founded. At least it's a start. And I think this is a way I can be of help to you now."

"It will certainly help these men." Doctor Stevens was smiling. "Anything you can do for them will be sincerely appreciated, Mrs. Lynn."

She grinned. "I'll get started today. On my trip here, I saw the wonderful work being done by the Sanitary Commission. I was astounded. Perhaps they can help me with food. I understand they do have a warehouse close by."

Momma had seen the hospital tents and cooking facilities of the Sanitary Commission at railway stations in small towns and large. These were staffed by nonmilitary people who seemed well qualified for the work they were doing. This was the response of a caring nation to the war.

The woman in Baltimore who had shared Momma's jar of jam told her: "The Sanitary Commission was organized by private persons, all civilians, and all separate from the army and the government. They've helped our boys from one part of the country to the other. It's something we're proud of. They provide nursing, medicines, and food. They have large warehouses for supplies. They're efficient and prepared to help good people who are willing to work." Uncle Jim and Ann Lynn visited the warehouse.

"I knew they would help us get started," said Momma, smiling to Uncle Jim.

261

"They sure did, Miz Ann!"

Georgeanna Woolsey wrote the Lynns years later how Momma and Uncle Jim had commandeered a small, hand-pulled wagon and brought food from the Sanitary Commission storehouse—fresh vegetables, good meat, flour, milk, and other edibles.

Mrs. Lynn was a skilled craftsman. The results of her cooking were excellent. Not only the sick were fed, but also others in the vicinity of the church. The doctor, Mrs. Jordan, and the Reverend Amars were also frequent guests. Momma had overcome the hard feelings of those who had displayed such formal courtesy when she arrived. She was no longer thought of as "the enemy."

The days passed. She continued to assist with the cooking. She also helped where she could with the injured and sick. She later told her daughters, "I cleaned faces, helped with the dressings, wrote many letters, comforted those who were too ill to eat and some who were expected to die. And I was with Henry when possible. He slept much of the time. He knew when I was about, though. If I wasn't there, he often asked where I had gone."

Mrs. Lynn read to Henry from papers, books, and an old, browned copy of the Old and New Testaments: "The Lord is my shepherd, I shall not want . . . " She also read to many others in the church. Henry was improving slowly. The drainage from the wound decreased. The doctor still thought a shell fragment was within the muscles of the back below the bone he called the scapula. Because of its proximity to the lung, he advised against removing it. As a seasoned army doctor, he had vast experience with wounds. "I agree with him," Momma said firmly to Henry.

Ann Lynn kept a diary. She also wrote detailed letters home. Most of these were never received. As Henry talked, his story about Pickett's charge unfolded.

CHAPTER XXX
An Eerie Stillness

Captain Lynn awoke with a start one evening. "Henry, that was a chill you had an hour ago," said his mother. "You're exhausted. You should sleep a little longer." He was getting better, but he was having intermittent fever and pain. The latter was when he coughed or moved quickly. He had walked a little with one crutch, and even sat outdoors on warm afternoons. Drainage continued from the wound below his shoulder.

"I'm all right now, Momma. Besides, I've slept too much. Where is Jim? He was going to help me take another walk this evening. One of the nice nurses is working outdoors. I said I'd see her later."

"You can see Miss Hawkins some other time. She's not going away. And, also, you just had that chill. You stay flat for a time." She laughed. "A few days ago, you said you were still in love with Katherine who lives in Chambersburg. What happened to that affair?"

"She's too far away," he said, smiling. "Miss Hawkins is here." Momma now knew that even with the fever, her son was definitely improving. It was late in the evening and very hot. He fought sleep, but he finally dozed off for a while. When he awoke, he was talkative and alert. His mind roved outside on the battlefield. He spoke slowly, but seemed determined to tell his story.

"We moved out of the shadows into the fields. Our battle lines went north and south as far as I could see—thousands of good men. A bright hot sun was above us. And all was quiet. It was an eerie stillness, and very weird. Smoke was coming up off the valley, and the Yankees were just a gray haze far off. They didn't look very dangerous." He hesitated. "My legs seemed to bend as I walked. Then I heard my voice shout, 'Forward, men!' My sword was still high. This was so my men could see it."

Henry told about the bravado and bragging, and about the sounds of an army moving to attack. "Sergeant Wilken in the third rank growled, 'Keep up, men. Keep movin.' Any laggards and I'll use this boot. We're goin' to a fight! . . . ' A harsh, threatening laugh followed. Lieutenant Edwards answered him, 'Yah, Sarge, go get 'em!' Others laughed too. We all relaxed. The sergeant would point us right."

"He sounds like a very strong man, Henry. What happened to him?"

"I don't know. After I was injured, he helped me back to our lines. I think he then went to find my friend, Ben. He and Ben were both wounded. They never returned. Perhaps they're dead." His eyes stared upward. He looked sad. "They were both fine people, Mother. Someday I'll learn what happened." Ann Lynn shook her head slowly and patted Henry's hand. She didn't speak.

He was silent for a while. Then he told about the Emmitsburg Road and the solid fences with rails and posts. He mentioned the shelling, and how big holes were torn in their lines. "Hundreds were hit all at once, but the gaps closed in quickly and the holes disappeared. We became a solid front again."

His mother winced and for a while tried not to listen. His words grated in her ears like a scream. He mentioned how Private Beryl close by had groaned and fallen, and how others had dropped like sacks of corn thrown from a wagon.

"We climbed the fences or pushed them down. We halted then and our lines were dressed. The command 'Forward!' could barely be heard above all the noise."

"An angry enemy watched," said Momma with a grim smile.

"We were like fish in a bowl," answered Henry. "A few low spots gave some protection. There were only little hollows in the ground, though. There were few places to hide, and most of the Yankee's cannons had not been stopped. Especially those to our right."

"I looked behind us once. I wish I hadn't," he continued. "Our men lay there in pain. Some crawled around and others tried to rise. Many just lay still."

Some of what Henry told, he mentioned several times. He would do this, then lie quietly, staring off into space. He was awake and thinking. "The thoughts don't go away, Momma. They won't go away. I sleep better after I talk. I seem to forget for a while."

Henry told how they finally reached the last slope and how the Yankees stood ready. "They weren't far away then. Their rifles were shining in the sun, and their flags wagged about them like hungry snakes.

"The whole Union line then fired, and hundreds of our men went

down. Our flags were picked up by other men, and we continued forward."
After pausing, he continued: "I saw when General Garnett was hit. Papa
has talked about him. He was the commander of the brigade in front of us.
He slid slowly to the ground. He didn't move after that. The Yankees later
told me he was dead. Garnett was a good man."

"You're a good man, too," said Momma. "You mean a lot to your family, so get well. Perhaps you should stop for now. You're tired, and I can listen all day tomorrow. There's plenty of time."

"I must tell it, Momma. It's inside of me. It's like an ache."

Momma looked at Henry. She thought he was right. It would help
him to go on talking. She wasn't sure how to stop him, anyway.

"We halted for a moment, then went on. Armstead broke free from
the tangle in front of us. We were also completely disorganized, but we
could still see Armstead, and we followed him. Somehow.

"I soon saw him standing on a low stone wall. I couldn't understand
what he shouted. He was probably saying, 'Follow me! Over the wall. The
enemy is there! Charge!'

"I heard my voice say, 'Charge! Charge! Follow Armstead. Charge!'
Then I fell, and several others fell with me. One of the men fell right over
my legs. I'm not sure who he was. His whole face was gone."

His mother gasped and closed her eyes. Then she shuddered. "That's
terrible. Just terrible!" She took several deep breaths while she tried to
find words to divert his attention to other things. "You fell, Henry. Did you
know you were hurt? When we're injured we often don't feel much at first.
Could you get up? Did the others go on?"

"That's right, Momma. I didn't know I was hurt at first." He told
about the gradual onset of pain, and how he had finally realized he was
badly hurt and couldn't rise. He mentioned the shouts and the hatred and
the complete loss of a sense of time and place. He told several times about
Armstead falling, and how he thought his commander looked a little like
his father—white hair and older.

Papa grinned when he heard this. "I guess he's right. Time marks us
all."

Henry looked very pale to his mother in the dim light as he searched
for words.

"We had been stopped," he continued. "I saw our men, those who
were still standing, going back toward our lines. I shouted at the top of my
voice, 'Take me! Take me! Please take me!' No one stopped. They probably didn't hear me shouting. It was Sergeant Wilken and Ben Toggler who

finally found me. They helped me to stand and walk. They both had been hurt, and Ben was bleeding badly. He finally dropped behind us. I didn't know it at the time.

"I think I broke my leg when we fell across the fence at the road. That was when I heard the bone crack and felt the pain. Evidently I had also been hit in the leg by flying metal. I didn't even feel that. The doctor said it went right through and didn't hit anything important. We kept walking and walking. It seemed like miles. The sergeant finally let me rest in a little woods. He evidently went back for Ben. Things just went blank then. It was like a cloud about me until those ladies found me there."

"I know about that," said his mother. "You talked about angels, and they were angels. I've tried to find out who they were, but I wasn't able to. You can thank the ladies right here, though. They're fine people, too. Now tell me about the ambulance ride. You mentioned that in your sleep last night."

"It was a rough ride. Very rough. Then I fell off in the mud when they carried me in. I heard one of them mumble: 'With that chest wound, he won't make it. We should have left him. Besides, he's only one of them Rebs.'" His mother looked sad and was shaking her head. "They carried me inside. Suddenly I was aware that I was surrounded by Yankees, and that I was a prisoner. But they were nice to me, even if I was a Rebel soldier."

"Just remember to thank them," said his mother.

The doctor was very interested in Henry's description of the complicated "left oblique" maneuver executed under fire. He was an old military man. "Tactically, that was a triumph, Henry. Frederick the Great would have been proud." He had listened to what Henry had said. Also, he asked Momma questions about what he had missed. "I could never be a hero," he said to her. "Yet I've worked for years with fine men who are."

Momma thanked him and his staff many times for all the healing they had done. She later told her family, "He had peculiar ideas, though. He disagreed with cutting off all those arms and legs on the battlefield. Also, he demanded fresh water in small pans for each man when he cleaned the sores and covered them. We had pots and pans of all sizes, piled around. Another thing he did, he kept washing his hands all the time. Peculiar. Most doctors don't do that," she said, smiling. "He knew something we didn't know."

This washing of hands was not something most doctors did. They went from bed to bed with the same bucket of water, the same unwashed

266

hands, and the same instruments and tools. Doctor Stevens had trained in Europe. He had visited England and France just before the war. Perhaps he knew about some of the discoveries there that would soon shake the medical world.

From high on Cemetery Hill, he had watched the Confederate charge. He was a Union man. He tried not to emphasize this to Mrs. Lynn. They had become friends. He did argue that he wanted a great nation. "We can never be strong till we're united," he had told her.

Ann Lynn couldn't answer for a moment. She shook her head. The doctor wasn't certain if she nodded agreement or if she had disagreed. She finally whispered, "We must be strong."

Doctor Stevens continued to talk: "During the battle, I heard an awesome, mournful roar above all the din of the rifles and cannons. It was a terrible sound—a frightening rumble. I finally decided it was the cries of those thousands of desperate men. It accented all the terror and the violence and the tragedy. You and me, we can be friends. Good friends. In war, men forget this."

He reached over and held Ann Lynn's hands. They were warm. She later remembered he had held them once before—on the night she had arrived in Gettysburg. "You're a kind man, Doctor," she said, smiling. "I've seen what you've done with all these soldiers. Thanks! Thanks ever so much. Many have lived because of you."

"That's what I've been trained to do," he answered. "I wish I could do more."

Doctor Stevens then talked about the attack by the brigades to the north of Pickett's division. These had been commanded by Pettigrew and Trimble of Hill's corps. Henry had spoken of them briefly, but he had no knowledge of how they had fared. From Doctor Stevens's position on Cemetery Hill, he could see that part of the attack.

"I admired the trimness of the Rebel battlelines," the doctor said. "It didn't seem possible in the heat of all that fighting."

"We aren't rebels, Doctor," Momma replied softly. "We have grievances, but we love this land just as much as you do. It's too bad it's come to fighting to the death."

"I'm sorry, Ann," he said. "I'm aware of that." He hesitated, then went on with his story. "We all waited expectantly. The Union soldiers watched as your men approached. I could see them aim and threaten, but our officers walked back and forth, shouting and cautioning, 'Steady. A little longer. Steady. Wait. Steady. Steady. Now!' Suddenly, every rifle and cannon opened fire. The whole approaching battleline disappeared in a huge, dirty cloud."

Veterans of the war would later tell the macabre tale that "parts of arms, legs, caps, knapsacks, blankets, guns, and flags literally flew into the air within this cloud." Others related how "the cloud boiled around these men. They became a twisting shadow in the smoke—like a big animal."

"Your men continued forward, though," the doctor continued. His eyes were sad and drawn. "It didn't seem possible. Our Yankee soldiers fired again and again without mercy. Finally, the Confederate line seemed like a crippled animal. It was torn to bits and pieces. Small groups reached the stone wall and fought with Henry (Pickett)—what was left of those troops. The anger and the firing soon were dying down. Your soldiers were going back or dropping their muskets and raising their hands."

"With time, I hope we can forget all this horror," said Momma. "I pray we forget."

"It will be hard to forget, Mrs. Lynn. We've been too close to it." Ann Lynn didn't reply. The doctor was right.

"The men who fought marched into history," wrote Papa to Emmie some years later. "As you mentioned in your letter, they've become immortal in the eyes of our people, and have been glorified in books and papers. We must remember, though, they were not immortal. Like Henry, they came from the clay of ordinary people. They faced a job that had to be done, and many died. Also, we should not forget the terror and the pain that your mother saw. This was not glory."

Mr. Lincoln later spoke upon that field. His gnarled sentences lent meaning to the eerie stillness that marked the battle's end. It is still quiet there today in Gettysburg. His words still echo among the cadenced steps of heroes, North and South.

CHAPTER XXXI
Thin-Planked Coffins

James Lynn stood before the open door. "Lawrence, it's nice to see you," he said. "Sarah and I are going shopping. At least I believe we are. She told me Williams will be driving us."

"Good morning, Lieutenant," answered Lawrence. He was a house servant for the Robertson family and was courteous and dignified. "Won't you come in, sir?"

Sarah's mother was just inside the door. "Hello, Mrs. Robertson. Sarah's ready, I hope."

"James, she's dressing. She was up late last night and reading. Come sit down." There was a smile on Mrs. Robertson's face, but it was shaded by distress. She took a deep breath. "Will, our nephew has been killed. We've been very, very sad. It was at Gettysburg as you suspected. It was that charge by Pickett's men. It's official now. We'll grieve for a long time, I'm afraid. I'm happy your brother, Henry, lived through it. He's a nice young man. So was Will."

James was at a loss for words for a moment. He closed his eyes and shook his head sadly. "I'm sorry, Mrs. Robertson! So sorry. I never met him, but Sarah has spoken of him often. He was like a brother to her, I believe."

"He was! And it will do her good to go shopping today. Perhaps help her with a new bonnet, or something else nice to wear." She turned toward the arch that led from the hall. Lawrence had returned with tea and bread spread with jam. "Thank you, Lawrence. That looks nice."

Mrs. Robertson began to pour the tea. "This was made specially for you, James. There's not much tea left in our cupboards." She smiled. "Lawrence's been with us for years. So many others have left over the last few months. The war, you know. They're working for the army now—digging forts and trenches. It's hard to run a household this way.

"Amanda, our cook, has stayed. She's a jewel. Varina Davis, the pres-

269

ident's good wife, tried to take her from us. Twice to be exact. She has trouble with help too. Just like we do. She's also suffering from the high cost of food and clothing, many, many things, like the rest of us. We evidently don't pay our president very well. And everything we need for a family costs a fortune. Even needles."

Sarah had told him about the many households in Richmond that were short of help. Also, she had mentioned several times how the servants had become less dependable. Finally, some just didn't come to work, leaving the poor housewife stranded with many chores undone. From personal experience, he also knew about the high costs.

"You seem lost for words, James. What are you thinking?"

"About what goods cost. It affects me too. You know, meals and things. I'm able to get some items from the army, but hardtack and rancid butter aren't much help. I did go out of town a ways. I got some fresh milk and eggs. Here. You take the eggs. I don't have many places to cook them." He handed her the package he had brought with him, then laughed. "The milk's gone. I gave it to the Arnolds, who own the home where I live. They have several children. They're wild but a lot of fun. They like the stories I read them in the evenings."

"That's nice of you to do that," she said, smiling.

Just then Sarah rushed down the stairs. "Mother, what can I do? That lovely green ribbon is gone. I need something to tie up my hair before James comes." She stopped with a start. "Hello, James. I didn't know you were here." She moved quickly back behind the archway.

"Young lady, that's no way to come downstairs. And not even with your dress on."

"I'm sorry, Mother. And, James, please accept my apologies." She had a wan smile on her face, and her cheeks looked tense. He noticed, though, that even without her usual attire, she was lithe and lovely.

James could hear her footsteps hurrying back up the stairs. "I've often seen my sisters only partly dressed," he said. "I'm really not very shocked." Her hair was also undone, but there was a budding pink softness about her face that made him want her—not only for her mind but for her beauty.

He stopped talking for a moment while Mrs. Robertson stared into his eyes. His face was suddenly sad. He saw she was looking intently at him. "My mother's gone to find Henry in Gettysburg. I hope she's even able to get that far. It's terribly dangerous, and I'm helpless to help her. At least my brother, Henry, is still alive. Thankfully!"

Mrs. Robertson thought for a moment, her gray eyes directed down-ward. Then she looked carefully at him. "From what you've told us, James, your mother's a strong person. She should be all right. We women aren't weak sticks like some men have thought over the years." There was pride in her eyes. "Women are doing much of the work all over the South while you men are away. They'll survive. So will she."

"Thank you, Mrs. Robertson. I'm sure you're right." He hesitated. "I, uh . . . I'll be away for several days. I haven't told Sarah yet, but I will be telling her later on today. Lee's over the Potomac and safe now, and he's desperate for food. I'm going north with a trainload of flour. It was ground in the mills close by here in Richmond. We have some bacon, too. His men need that also. And I have a thousand pairs of shoes to take along. There are a lot of sore feet in Lee's army. What's left of it." He suddenly turned to the hallway. "Sarah, you're lovely," he exclaimed. He stood up and gently held her hands. "I heard about Will. I'm so sorry!"

It was the first day of August. Dust rose about the wagons in clouds. James was near the head of the column with Major Allen. Sunlight lighted their faces as they rode north toward the Rapidan River. It had taken much of the night to load the thousands of bags onto wagons. They were headed for Lee's troops in the angle between the Rapidan and the Rappahannock, just east of Culpeper.

Suddenly scouts came galloping toward them. Their horses were lathered and foaming. It was a hot day. James could see what appeared to be another column of horse soldiers in the distance. They too were riding hard. One Confederate scout skidded to a halt, his face red and earnest. "Those are Yankees out there, Major. They're after this column. They know the trouble Lee's having with food. We'd better pull off to the right. Those rocks and logs up there can be used for cover. We have a regiment of our own horses headed this way too."

"Ours! Sergeant, are you sure?"

"Ours, sir! They're riding fast. If we can hold the Yanks back a while, they'll be into them from the rear. I hope."

"Get those wagons up that slope near the farm," shouted the major. "We'll fight them from there. Move men. Move!" Horses and wagoners and the protecting column of cavalry raced quickly up the hill. The house and barns had been burned. The Yankees had been there before.

James could feel a lump in his throat as he galloped up the slope. They were on high ground now. There were several big rocks near the top, and he began helping the troops bring logs and boards and anything movable that they could hide behind. He heard the command, "Charge!" in the distance. The Yankee line was surrounded by smoke. They had unlimbered a cannon, and a shell exploded behind him. He had his pistol in his hand.

"Let 'em get closer, Lieutenant. Then shoot as straight as you can. We just have to hold 'em for a little while. That cloud off there is a regiment of our men. They're comin' fast, I'm sure." The major smiled. It was a wry, knowing smile. He was an experienced officer, hardened by years of fighting. "You've been in Richmond for the war. This'll be a brisk fight. You'll get a chance to see how the other half lives." He winked, then turned and shouted, "Fire, men! Fire! Let 'em have all you've got."

James aimed at a horseman thundering toward him like a charging tiger. He heard his pistol explode and felt it kick back. He saw the man fall then slide close to the foot of the rock before him. The far side of the Confederate line had been penetrated by the charge. Men were swinging rifles, and several had swords that they were using effectively. The sergeant fell, and others were also down. James kept firing and firing. Then he reloaded and fired again. A horse crashed into him from behind, but he managed to stay on his feet. The horseman then turned and fired two shots as his horse reared. James fired at him and saw him lurch forward and fall to the ground.

He saw the major rushing toward him, stop, then shoot over his head. Another horseman fell close behind him like a sack of grain. The Yankee's face was filled with blood. James wiped the sweat from his eyes and saw that his sleeve was covered with blood. His arm was burning just above the elbow. It felt as if he had been seared by a hot poker. Through a tear in the sleeve, he could see a long cut in the skin. "You look like you've been fighting," the the major said with a laugh. "It's over now. Thank, God! Our other troops arrived in time. The Yankees destroyed several wagons, but most are safe. We lost a few men too. But the Yanks lost more."

James looked over the field. Blue and butternut-clad bodies lay still and grim. One Yankee close by was moaning. "We almost got ya, Reb." James saw that the man's shooting arm was limp. He helped him to his feet.

"We're hungry," James said quietly. "This is food Lee needs very badly. You wouldn't want to make his men starve, I hope. Then you Blue-bellies wouldn't have anyone to fight." They both laughed. "Let me see that arm, soldier," James continued. He suddenly noticed that his own left arm was limp and bleeding profusely.

"That was my shot that got you, Lieutenant. Now I'm glad I didn't hit you too bad. I hope you know your forehead's bleeding too, like a stuck pig."

James felt strong arms directing him toward a rock close by. "We'll have to patch you up a little, Lieutenant." It was one of the privates from the cavalry column, which had reached them just in time. "These wounds aren't deep, sir. We'll just wrap 'em up a bit."

They soon continued on to the north. James's horse had been killed; he was sitting by one of the wagoners on a hard seat, which seemed to writhe up and down like a bucking mare. His arm was hurting now, but there was a look of pride in his eyes that most of the men didn't notice. Major Allen rode up. He, however, was aware of James's feelings. "You put up a good fight there, Lieutenant. Thanks! I didn't know War Office soldiers could shoot that straight. That first man would've killed me dead if you hadn't gotten him."

James smiled. "I practiced a little. Maybe it paid off. Thanks, Major." He then saw the major go up and down the column and shake hands with the men and the wagoners. The cavalry regiment was a ways to their rear, but coming on like demon avengers. James felt that Lee's men were in good spirits and proud. They had lost a great battle at Gettysburg, but they weren't beaten, as many folks in Richmond seemed to believe.

"James has been hurt, Mary, on that trip with supplies for Lee's army. His forehead was badly cut, and a bullet hit his arm, and it's infected. He says he's improving. Ma and I visited him today at the hospital. His arm still hurts, but he had a smile on his face when we arrived. And he was glad to see us. He looked ghastly, though, with his head all bandaged, and his arm in a sling.

"And he had a shaking fever while we were there. I put blankets all over him. At least that made me feel good. Then I washed his face. He didn't like that very much, but he finally appreciated the fruit I brought him. He said he'd enjoy it later on."

"He's getting well, Sarah," said her mother. "He was in battle and loved it. I guess you feel that way when you're still alive. Now maybe he'll be less enthusiastic about getting into the fighting. Sarah and Mary, men have to show how brave they can be. And Sarah, even your pa talks about joining up once in a while. He's as bad as a young boy. At least age is an excuse to make him stay home, but it hurts his pride. Well, you two sit here and visit for a while. I have work to do inside. We'll have tea later. Whatever's left."

Her mother walked quickly indoors. Sarah looked pleasantly satisfied, even radiant. "At the hospital, when Mother stepped out, he asked me to marry him," Sarah whispered. There was a gleeful note in her voice.

"He did? Wonderful! It's about time too. You two have been more than friends for a long, long time. Too long. Have you told your mother?" asked Mary.

"Not yet. I will!" She seemed to shiver with delight. "I want to think about it first."

"Now don't play difficult to get, Sarah Robertson. You've loved him since the first day you two met. Just tease him a little. Not too much." Mary chuckled. "Last week you were worried about his being away. And you wondered if he'd ever ask the question."

"I wasn't sure then what was happening between us. I knew he loved me, but there was always that distance, that something holding us apart. Maybe it was what Ma said. He had to prove himself in battle. When Henry was hurt, it was almost as if James thought that this is what men needed to go through, like a christening or a secret ritual. Now it's done. I hope forever. When he came into my life, I was used to being lonely."

"With all the people who are around you?" asked Mary.

"Well, it was always different. Men then seemed attracted by my looks, I think. It was like being a pretty vase on a shelf. James was different. He liked me for what I thought, and what I was inside."

"Were you scared? You were a little scared about that once, I remember. You thought he knew you better than you knew yourself."

"Perhaps. And maybe I was even a little angry. He always seemed to know what I was thinking. I couldn't manipulate him the way I could a few men. It was a surprise, but it felt good. My body felt good. Yet, it was baffling and bewildering. I just wanted to let things happen and enjoy it all. But sometimes, I, uh, I wanted to break it off. I wanted to be without feeling again. Aloof. I had more control then. Now, I, uh, I, well you know . . . as with your cousin whom you loved, but couldn't marry."

"He was in Vicksburg. Captured, I suppose. We haven't heard a thing. I hope he's alive. I pray he is. And my brother's still with General Lee. I love him too," said Mary. "In a different way, off course."

"James's seen me horrible. He's seen me ugly. And angry. Like when we were going to the theater, and he was late. He'd been sipping wine with friends. That tavern on Broad Street."

"The Swan Tavern?" asked Mary.

"That's right. I was furious. It was a wonderful sensation, though. That's the way it was for a moment. It was something real. Something deep was going from me to him. Yet he didn't get angry. He seemed to accept it—and me. He thought I had a right to be angry. He apologized. That completely disarmed me. I stopped ranting and laughed. 'You would say that,' I said. Then he kissed me, and I got angry with myself for acting that way. Now I have to think for a while before I say yes."

Sarah took a deep breath, and her eyes had a dreamy look. She could still visualize his lashes, the sunburned surface of his face, his grave mouth and firm jaw while he listened to her. She was very happy that he hadn't seen the hurt and longing in her eyes.

Mary looked at Sarah. She saw that the sun had given a fine blush to her face and shoulders. They both smiled. "You know what to do, Sarah Robertson. Don't wait too long."

His story finished, Henry relaxed. It was as if a great weight had been lifted from him. His soul was free. He slept restlessly, though, and often complained that his shoulder hurt. One morning he had another chill. It went on and on, until he was exhausted. His mother shook her head compassionately and closed her eyes. "I thought he was getting well," she mumbled. She covered him with a blanket and her shawl, then piled straw around him. He now rested for a while, but he felt very warm to her touch.

When he awoke, he seemed delirious, and he didn't talk straight for nearly an hour. He moaned and moved about like a sick animal. "Oh, God, it hurts! It hurts awful!" he kept saying. He pointed toward his shoulder.

There was a big lump near the shoulder blade. He jumped as his mother pressed there. The doctor was away. With the help of the nurses, she applied cool towels. Then they gave him an opium pill. This settled him for a while.

"What's wrong?" asked the doctor when he returned at sunrise. He felt gently over the back near the shoulder. "That hurts bad, doesn't it, Henry? We have to do something about it." He had scissors in a small pan. He poured a blue fluid over the blades and wiped them dry. "This is going to hurt a bit," he said. "Grit your teeth, son. Hold still. Very still. It'll hurt more if we don't take care of it. And you could become even more ill," said Doctor Stevens.

The scissor-points were jabbed deep into the swelling. Henry almost jumped off the rough boards on which he was lying. Then he sank back with a deep sigh. The doctor spread the scissors wide and drew them back.

"Oh, God!" he shrieked again. There was a burst of bloody, yellow fluid, which ran out over the skin.

"Help wipe that away, Mrs. Lynn," said the doctor. "That's the way. Now take that old towel. Good. Very good. That's what's been hurting. Keep wiping. And sponging. A little pressure now. Good."

"It just keeps coming, Doctor," she said. "And it looks just awful. No wonder it was sore."

The doctor then began to probe the wound with a clamplike instrument. Henry again writhed and turned. "There's metal here somewhere," he said. "I can't find it. And I'm afraid I might push it deeper. Well, he's had enough." He put a loose dressing over the opening. "You rest now, son. It'll feel better soon. This will help the fever too." He patted the captain's arm, then squeezed it gently. "It's good we got that out. It can fill the blood with poison and kill."

Mrs. Lynn would later describe the operation to her family: "It was the simple lancing of a boil," she said. To her children, it sounded ghastly. Yes, it was only a minor operation. Imagine the description of an amputation. This would sound much more frightening. Many, many were done during the war.

Henry did improve. Several days later he was moved to another hospital. Clusters of government tents had been assembled around Gettysburg. "They rose like monstrous weeds about the town," said Ann Lynn later. "There were so many sick and wounded that I was overwhelmed by the numbers. At the church, I had seen only a few of them. But there were thousands.

"A Union flag was run up to the top of a flagpole; nurses, cooks, and orderlies arrived in great numbers. Ambulances carried men from the emergency shelters in barns and houses and churches, over the rough roads to these pleasant new hospitals. The doctors were different, though. My trusted friend, the old doctor, was gone. He had been ordered to serve with Yankees just south of that high hill known as Big Round Top."

When much older, Mrs. Lynn would look back over the years of the war with a knowledge of modern medicine. She would know that the ambience in these places was dreary for sick soldiers. During the war, no one seemed to realize this. To them, these hospitals were shiny and clean. Grisly, sallow figures, though, lay in rows. For all the "modern" equipment of the period, most surgeons with their unclean knives and saws and little sponges continued to practice their trade among the heavy odors of rot and death.

The operating table was where the worst of this macabre trade was carried on. In dressing stations and field shelters, the table was often an old door torn from its frame. It was wiped clean of bits of flesh and bloody stains. Nearby, amputated arms and legs and even swollen corpses might be found in ghastly, grotesque piles.

Doctors stood with sleeves rolled up, bare arms, and aprons smeared with blood. These grim apparitions could terrify the devil. Imagine the fright of a young soldier when the doctor shouted, "Next!" The patient's mind was often clouded by opiates and liquor. His haggard, struggling form would be carried by attendants to the table. It was truly an instrument of pain.

These experiences caused inexpressible and unsolaced horror and hurting. There was a loss of identity and dignity, as the men twisted and turned about. "It was like being forced into an abyss of slimy mud," said Mrs. Lynn. "Many said it seemed to draw one into eternity. Finally, often, they would fall into a tortured sleep, a shock from which some never awoke.

"The examination began amidst shrieks and cries. The torn skin and muscle and bone were entered by strong fingers pressing deep inside the cut. Bits of cloth and wood and rocks and soil and even pieces of bone would be taken out and thrown into a pan. Parts of cannon shells, bullets, and all kinds of ghastly objects came out. It was awful," she continued.

During the war, the Lynns, and in fact most of the world, didn't know that unclean hands, probes, forceps, and instruments of all kinds including sutures carried infection deep so that thousands died.

Antiseptics were available for cleaning hands and instruments, but these were mostly used after infection took hold. If surgery was needed, it began immediately. Thankfully, chloroform or ether was usually administered, whenever it was available. In the days of the Civil War, a knowledge about sepsis and bacterial contamination was just beginning to be understood in Europe. The principles of asepsis, so important a generation later, were followed by very few.

Instruments were clenched in teeth, sutures were moistened with

277

saliva, sponges were rinsed in a communal pail of water, which was often bloody from other cases and contaminated with pus. These sponges were used immediately for mopping wounds or instruments or tables. It is little wonder that a day or so later, "laudable pus" filled the wound.

Ointments and salves were applied on lint scraped from cotton cloth by unclean hands. Poultices of moistened bread or flaxseed were applied to wounds for healing. Suppuration abounded. Cold water helped relieve burning pain. Whisky, tincture of opium and, later in the war, morphine, "salted" on the wounds, caused fine young men to drift into a dreamlike state and forget the pain and terror. To these "pristine" pavilions, gallant men were carried. As we know today, gangrene, tetanus, lymph node infection, general blood poisoning, delayed bleeding, and pneumonia were frequent visitors.

When Ann Katherine Lynn was much older, she would say to her own children, "I tell you all this because you'll probably find it fascinating. Frankly, it makes me a little sick, but maybe it adds spice to the story. It all happened. Battles were exciting; the aftermath was agonizing. Most wounds were caused by bullets that spread when they struck, or by pieces of shells. Flesh was terribly torn and often infected. So much bone was gone that the only avenue of treatment for many was to remove the limb entirely."

In spite of these terrors, though, these "fine hospitals" were a place where a man was fed and cared for and washed clean. The men arrived hungry and unattended after a jarring, excruciatingly painful ride in an ambulance, often a square box on an axle with a single pair of wheels. Kath mentioned this to her mother after the war. "I know," Momma replied. "I saw it. I was there. I used to think, 'How brave men are!' Ladies could be just as brave, though, and we were! We suffered with these men. We would grit our teeth and tremble. Some died while being carried. Sad. It's so sad. Others died after they arrived at the hospitals.

"These places were a haven, however," she continued. "The men, after past days of neglect, crude field amputations, delirium, gashes by musket balls, and advanced infections, yielded to the sleep caused by morphine or whisky and brandy. Little ceremony, though, was paid to those who died. Thin-planked coffins were loaded onto a cart; it rattled off." Mrs. Lynn never could forget these experiences. "Life at times meant so little, even to caring people. I guess we just became used to death when there were hundreds dying."

She also remembered the cries and irrational behavior of fine young men. "They were still alive, but fever, pain, and all the medicines they were given placed them beyond rational action."

Mrs. Lynn was very impressed and pleased with the nursing. "We timid females have grown into lions with our new professions and services. Institutions such as the powerful Sanitary Commission have become household words up North. They have by-laws and large donations of money—from caring people. Enormous and efficient storehouses and other services have blossomed. The people of this land should be proud! Whether men agree or not, this great war has brought light to the women of this land. This 'light' is service. Though we women do not fight, we've developed a vast system to care for those who do."

Henry was transferred into this milieu. A general hospital, known as Letterman Hospital, was established at Gettysburg to care for those too seriously wounded to be moved to major facilities in the bigger cities. Dr. Jonathan Letterman was the medical director for the Army of the Potomac. This taciturn, sensitive man was instrumental in developing the ambulance corps and vastly improving the efficiency of providing Union forces with surgical and medical supplies.

The Letterman Hospital where Henry was sent was considered a model, well-run place. It was a city of tents. Medical knowledge, however, was still primitive. Only one generation later, such fine institutions were considered abominable.

Before Henry was transferred, the old doctor at the church had counseled no surgery or exploration of the wound, which seemed to be healing despite the metal piece next to the ribs. He stated this repeatedly to Momma and Henry. Her impetuous son, however, wanted a body free of that sore. He wanted to be whole.

"He seemed so reasonable in other areas, it was difficult to understand his reasons for wanting surgery," Momma said later to her family. "He was told about possible bad bleeding, and that the metal might be pushed deeper, even into the lung. 'This is very serious,' he was warned. 'And the lung pus might kill, but not until there's much fever and dreadful pain.'" His mother looked sad as she related this.

"The old doctor also told us: 'In my experience, patients respond more quickly if surgery is not performed, unless the reason is great. That's where judgment is needed. I think you can live a fine life without surgery, young man.' I wish Henry had listened better, but your brother was determined. I should have known he wouldn't stop asking about it when he was transferred."

Henry was sent to Letterman in one of the newer four-wheeled ambulances. Without springs, the ride was grim. Momma remained in the home of Mrs. Jordan, but she visited Henry daily. The most important skilled service he seemed to be denied was the good cooking prepared by his mother. She continued to work at the church until all the patients were moved to other hospitals. She didn't forget, though, to bring Henry some of her delicacies.

Henry truly did feel better. He smiled, and he walked a little with difficulty. He walked much better when being assisted by the gentle hands of several pretty women who worked at Letterman. One of these young ladies had deep dark eyes and brown hair. All had apparently avoided the careful scrutiny of the senior nurses. Good looks met with disfavor. These senior women preferred mature females who would be safe from lecherous men.

Momma would tell her children, "I really don't consider your brother lecherous, but he had the usual male longings. He became perky, and his mustache was longer now and twisted up a little at the ends. He was a dashing cavalier. All he needed was a rakish cap with a bright feather.

"He, also, walked unshod in a ridiculously long flannel shirt, which went part way to his knees." She chuckled. "The contrast between his handsome face and the bony knees was shocking. He did it because he couldn't don his trousers over the wooden splint. This didn't seem to interfere with his social desires, though, and the pretty women didn't seem to mind. He somehow made friends everywhere."

"Henry, of course I'll walk with you tonight," said the young nurse with dark eyes. "Now you be good, and I'll show you that little hideaway I spoke about. I love to sit there and read on my days off. And I'll tell you stories. We'll have fun."

"She had lovely eyes and shiny hair," Momma related. "Henry had a good friend. And she had a delightful smile. She was very nice. Her father also had taught school."

CHAPTER XXXII
The Grass Covered All

Bad pain emanated from the muscles below Henry's injured arm. It went up under the shoulder blade like a knife.

"It's that metal that's still there. I can feel the lump. The doctor says it's a scar. I think it's part of that shell," complained Henry to his mother.

Momma still noticed some pus coming from the wound, but the hole was almost closed. Also, his fingers tingled and often felt numb. He constantly questioned the doctors about these problems. He had become friendly with a young physician, Bill Abrams, from Baltimore. They joked frequently about manly escapades and fun. His friend also answered some of Henry's questions. "It's dangerous to explore it, Henry, and, unless it continues to bother you a lot, I think you should leave it alone."

Henry told his friend about the fun he and his brother, James, had had with the pretty ladies in Richmond some months before. Momma listened. "He's getting well," she told herself. She knew he would soon be sent to one of those prisoner camps farther north, unless he was fortunate enough to be exchanged.

"I'm not sure they were always ladies, though," she heard Henry say to Bill in a low voice.

Mrs. Lynn saw the doctor ridge his brows and smile. "We can't always find the right women, Henry. It sounds like they were nice, though. It also sounds like your brother, James, may have led you into some of those shady activities." The last few words were whispered, but his mother heard them. She didn't speak. She just smiled knowingly. Parents worry about hushed voices and laughs. Sons grow up, though, and she was happy that he was getting better. He now had color in his cheeks, and the doctor was a good influence.

"Thank you, Lord! He'll come home to us some day," Momma said in a low voice.

James and Henry both enjoy being with women now, she thought to herself. *They didn't when they were children—except their sisters. They have grown. It's almost frightening how fast. Henry's been more shy and self-examining. I guess that's good. But they both have that certain sensitivity about people, and how to put others at ease and make them feel better. I'm certainly proud of the two of them."* She hesitated for a long moment. *And they're usually so logical and careful, now that they're older. Except Henry, when he thinks about his injury."*

After listening to Henry's stories, the young physician countered with tales about his medical training in Baltimore: dissecting the deceased, hearing long lectures, taking out barmaids, scaring his family with bits of human bone and flesh, fresh from the dissecting theater. *Oh, what fun,* Momma thought as she smiled compassionately.

She related to her family: "Your brother paled a little with these stories about dissection. Henry was the hero, though, in the eyes of the two. He had fought bravely; he had shown his mettle and leadership. This didn't mean much in Gettysburg. There were heroes galore.

"And the young doctor was still learning his trade. He told of tricks they played on some of the senior physicians at the hospital in Gettysburg. There was a large locker, housing all the old and damaged instruments awaiting repair."

Momma didn't know the names of the instruments. She imagined there were blunt knives and saws, scissorlike fasteners, small dull round saws with wooden handles, a strap to tie the limb during amputations, and bent hooks and rakelike tools. She worried about how they were used.

"On several occasions, I met a Dr. Aldon Coppersmith who was one of the senior physicians Bill Abrams told about. Coppersmith had a sharp nose, and he was skinny, proud, and demanding," she continued. "Haughty—he looked like an eagle standing over its prey. He didn't smile much, and he often threw defective instruments across the tent in which he was operating. Deep inside, though, I found him to be a caring person. But this was hard to see.

"Imagine his surprise one day, when, unbeknownst to him, all his instruments had been rescued from that locker. He was furious. Instruments 'sailed' across the tent. His assistant didn't dare breathe a word about what had happened. However, somehow, the surgeon-in-charge had found out. He was a handsome man. He stood back and chuckled and watched with rakish glee as instruments galore were hurled. No one was hurt, just feelings. It was nice to know that serious doctors could be human. They could laugh and tease and for a moment, at least, forget the tragedy.

"After talking with the surgeon-in-charge, the doctor responsible for your brother's care decided Henry should be operated on. I believe his name was Traymour or Trymore. I never really wanted to know who he was or anything about him," said Momma grimly.

This name became an anathema to the Lynn family. They often spoke it when they talked about something bad. Kath was not sure the doctor deserved this hatred. Like many people, he was just trying to satisfy another person, their brother, who could be very demanding at times.

Momma was aghast when Henry decided on surgery. Her friend, Doctor Stevens, was now with the Second Corps hospital some miles south of the town. He was conservative and sensible. "You do surgery, but you first decide what is best for the ill and the injured." Unless the reasons were strong, he would watch and give supportive care. "Skillful neglect," he called it. "Patience, son," the doctor had counseled time and again. When Henry insisted, the doctor continued, "I'm sorry to find you so resolute." He had then patted Henry's good arm.

Mrs. Lynn started south along Cemetery Ridge, past the Peach Orchard and Devil's Den and by Little Round Top where thousands had died. She saw the Angle, the Stone Wall, the spot where Henry had fallen. The ground was still covered with swords, guns, and those remains that once were men and animals. It was horrible. She turned away as she saw long trenches that were being dug and others in which bodies were being placed in neat long rows. *Oh, God!* she thought. *Why? Why must we kill so many? They were men once, and loved by families and friends, and now they're gone. Please bless them, Lord. They deserve much praise.*

She walked, then ran. She was not sure if she were running for Henry's sake or out of sheer fright. Hot tears streamed down her cheeks. When she reached the hospital, she felt foolish, but she couldn't stop crying. A young officer saw her distress. She told him about the old doctor and her injured son. He smiled a little as she explained: "I worked with him at the church in Gettysburg—as a nurse and helping with the cooking. He's a good friend. Tell him it's Mrs. Lynn. Please! I need his advice very badly."

"I hope my mother worries about me like that," he said, smiling. "We'll find Doctor Stevens. An old army man, you say. Yes, I know him. So you're the one who did all that wonderful cooking. He keeps talking about that. He's told me at least five times. Come this way, Mrs. Lynn."

They found the doctor. He saw instantly how distressed she was. He realized her grief was genuine. She was not clamorous, yet not subdued. He looked at her face. He knew that she was desperate. Something bad had happened. He was sure it was about her son. "What's wrong, Ann?" he asked softly.

Mrs. Lynn told him the story. "They may be operating now," she struggled to say.

The doctor and Mrs. Lynn returned to Letterman in a borrowed shay. The horse was lathered, and its saliva wetted the dust when it was tied to the hitching post near the hospital. They ran to Henry's side. With a sigh of grief, Momma found that Henry had already undergone surgery.

His face shone with light, though. When she looked more carefully, the brightness was only in his eyes. They were set between lurid cheeks—like a ghost. Momma couldn't talk at first, then she blurted, "Why? Henry! Why? You were getting better."

"I had to, Momma. I wanted to be whole again. I had to try. I'm still here—a little weak, but it's out. They got it." He hesitated, then spoke brightly, "I bled a little, but it's done."

It was done. He had not bled a little but a lot. That night he shook with chills and his body writhed with pain. He awoke, sobbing from the fitful sleep of laudanum.

Each breath came with great difficulty now; a dull area was found over the back and side of his chest. It was painful for his mother to watch, but she couldn't leave him. She was not sure then if he knew she was there.

Mrs. Lynn said several times, "It can't be true!" Later, she said this again, then continued, "I can't criticize his judgment, though. A decision made must be lived with." She sighed deeply. "Or died with!" She then wrote in her journal: "The terrible fever. It crept into his flesh like a rock beneath the water that tears . . . the life of a ship."

The site of the surgery continued to bleed. The wound was looked at again and again. Blood vessels were tied, but this didn't stop the bleeding. "Necrotic," she heard one of the doctors say. "There's nothing to tie."

Mrs. Lynn sat and wished her son had listened to the old doctor. "However, Henry did what he thought was right," she mumbled to Uncle Jim. "Maybe I would have done the same."

"We all must decide for ourselves, Miz Ann. Master Henry made this decision. Not you!" He was shaking his head slowly from side to side. "Our Lord says how it comes out."

How I need a friend, she thought. *And here he is beside me. And he's been here all this time. Or helping with the cooking at the church, or some other job.* Uncle Jim was a tower of strength. He sat with Henry for hours. He hardly ate. Finally Momma insisted he eat something, but he consumed only a little food. "About enough for a small bird," Momma later told her family. "I became aware of how much he had loved and respected your brother."

Emmie listened to her mother's words, and she knew that Henry's life was about to end. She had thought her brother childlike at times, and indestructible. She finally remembered how much he had changed when he joined the army. She later told Annie and Kath, "He became a man!"

Many at the hospital felt great sadness when Henry died. It emphasized the tragedy of war and of the state of medical science at the time. Both Mrs. Lynn and Uncle Jim were crushed. As his final words were spoken, they both were at his side. Uncle Jim reached over and tenderly closed Henry's eyes. "They's the windows of the soul, Miz Ann."

Momma watched him as he spoke. *Every line of Jim's face seems clothed in sadness,* she thought. *And what a hot day on which to die. It's so humid. Jim's clothes are hugging him like a wet sheet. I suppose mine are too.*

She listened as he continued: "Hear that echo, Miz Ann." He took a deep breath and sighed. "It's the power of the Lord, Jesus; he's in our midst. He's here with us now. Henry's not alone!"

Momma could hear the whispering of the wind through the trees outside the tent. She shivered as she understood the meaning in Uncle Jim's statement. She suddenly realized that what had happened to Henry would some day make sense to her. Jim's words were wise and thoughtful for a torn, doubting soul.

Henry's friend, Dr. Bill Abrams, was with them at his death. This good young man spoke tenderly to Mrs. Lynn and Jim: "He's dead. I'm sorry. You see, he was a friend of mine; not just a patient."

"You were a good friend," said Momma.

"We try not to be too close to those we care for in medicine," the doctor continued. "A little reasoned aloofness is necessary. Doctors seem stoic, but they suffer the same feelings as the rest of you. I, too, am crushed."

The lovely nurse with dark eyes and brown hair came and spoke to Momma. "Mrs. Lynn, over the past weeks, I've been with many who have died. Mostly they've been alone. Henry was not. His fineness lives on in my heart and yours. Also the hearts of your family and many others whom his life has touched. Perhaps these thoughts will soften the hurting a little."

The elderly doctor, Momma's friend, sat without speaking. His face was deeply wrinkled. He was a renaissance man, literary, musical, scientific, social, and compassionate. Momma early on had sensed this. He finally turned to Mrs. Lynn. "Ann Katherine, I worry that my yesterdays have ushered many folks 'the way to dusty death.' We have much to learn of healing. I'm truly sorry." He choked and couldn't speak for a moment. "We tried so hard. Your son was a good man." The doctor's cheeks were moist.

"Shakespeare was wrong, my friend," said Momma softly. She hesitated a moment, then continued. "These days have been full of sound and fury, but they signify something. If nothing else, they show the fineness inside most people. We all differ in personality, but there is goodness about. Thanks for everything, dear friend."

Henry's remains were placed in one of those thin-planked coffins. A cross, whittled tenderly and smoothed by hand, was placed on top. As with most deaths within the hospital conclave, this death passed unnoticed by most. His remains were trundled off. However, he had family and good friends to see him go. He was not forgotten. These people wrote Momma and Papa later that summer.

The old doctor would even take time to visit them once. He had admired Henry. He felt partly responsible for his death. He also relished Mrs. Lynn's fine cooking. At that table, Kath would remember his astute statement to her mother: "As you told me in Gettysburg, Ann, when someone is remembered with love, their spirit never dies. That's true of Henry." Doctor Stevens had become stooped. His heavy shoes scuffed the hardwood floors as his feet moved over the surface in short, shuffling steps. One hand trembled a little. Despite all this encumbrance of age, he spoke beautifully.

Henry was buried a half mile east of Benner Hill outside of Gettysburg. He lies there today. Emmie and Kath later searched the countryside for the grave. They did not find it. The grass covered all, and new hardwoods were growing. The wooden cross that their mother had described was gone.

The family's business in Gettysburg was done. Armies would fight. Appomattox was far off. "On earth, peace, good will toward men," was yet a dream. There is a time to die. For young men, this seemed to be the time.

CHAPTER XXXIII
Ghosts and Goblins Circle About

Ann Lynn returned to her home in Staunton in a borrowed wagon. Her shoulders were drooped forward and her face clouded. Fine lines stretched from the corners of her mouth and eyes. They gave her skin the texture of old parchment. Her gaze was directed down. She was very tired. She knew the war was continuing, and she wondered what she should say to her family. In spite of worries and sadness, her thoughts gradually shifted. She had lost a son, but there was pride deep inside her—for him and for those that had done so much to help him. "There's much love in the world," she decided. "Even with all the violence."

She heard Jim beside her stir. As her eyes moved up, she saw him smile. "We're home, Miz Ann. There's your family out there."

"She's here! She's here! Papa, she's home. Oh, Momma, you are home. We've been so worried." Mary ran to the wagon and jumped onto the step. She literally fell onto her mother's lap. "Thank you, God, for keeping her safe." There were tears in Mary's eyes.

Momma's face beamed brightly, and the lines disappeared. "Jim brought us through, darling." She kissed her daughter, then put her hand on Jim's shoulder. "Thanks, good friend. Thanks so much!"

Mary turned to Jim. "I thank you too, Jim. We thought we'd lost both of you."

"Child, how could I ever be lost? I had to get back here and hear more of those stories you chillen tell me." There was a smile on his face as Mary hugged him.

Uncle Wen had arrived running. He pumped Jim's hand as he talked to Momma. "We know about Henry. We got your wire. My God, how you've suffered. And you too, Jim." He continued to shake Jim's hand.

"I failed with Henry," Momma said softly. "I met many fine people up there, though. I also saw a land coming to life, both here in the South, as well as in the North. People are taking over. They're mad at the politicians and at what they've done. There's much pain in my heart about Henry, though. Jim was a mountain of help from the time we left. And somehow we survived."

"We did what we could for Henry," said Jim. "He knew that. He told me one night how much he loved his family, Miz Ann. And that he hoped you wouldn't blame yourself for what happened."

Momma squeezed Jim's arm. "Thanks!" she mumbled. There was now a strong bond between them that humans have when they have lived through a great and common experience. It was a warm, deep feeling. No one but Jim and Momma would ever know the whole story.

They had crossed the Potomac River again at Chain Bridge on the way home. She and the sergeant there had both cried. His son, too, had been killed at Gettysburg.

Uncle Jim had comforted Ann Lynn with kind, well-chosen words on the long trip home. "They died with a purpose, those fine boys. Master Henry didn't want no cryin'; he told me that many times. We both feel sad, but don't you fret none about what you did for all those people back there. You were kind and wonderful."

"Ann Katherine, you have not failed," said Aunt Sue in a firm voice. She had arrived running and out-of-breath. "You helped many soldiers— North and South. Hundreds of them. Yes, you can make mistakes, but your judgments are never without sense. Henry died. It was not you, but the times. Few families are left without sorrow. Welcome home, Ann. We need you. We'll talk about the living now. We won't forget Henry, though. He was a fine young man. He deserves to be remembered."

As Aunt Suellen said, Momma had encouraged a son and many others who were there. Her son had died, but this was not a failure. The war and the primitive state of medicine had killed Henry Lynn.

Papa was very serious as he shook Jim's hand. "Thank you for all you did," he said. Then he smiled compassionately and held Momma's hands. "Welcome home, Ann Katherine." His eyes looked deeply into hers. "I still see tragedy in your face, but those whose lives you touched will be forever blessed." He paused, thinking. His face was again serious. "Time will mend the pain."

"God decided," Mr. Raymond observed that evening, after hearing some of the story about Momma's expedition north. "These things are out of our hands. Perhaps this won't always be true. Natural science and doctors' knowledge may do amazing things in the future. I hope I'm here to see them."

He turned toward Papa. "James, remember that delightful breakfast-table series by Oliver Holmes of Boston a few years back? His words were refreshing—like sunshine. You and I have spoken about them."

"He's an intelligent man, Robert. A man of prose and poetry. His words are vivid and wise. They probe us humans like little darts. He knows our weaknesses, and he points them out. I laughed, but I also felt a little sad when I recognized some of these as my own shortcomings." Papa chuckled softly. "I guess we all have them."

"We all do, James," Mr. Raymond said smiling. He now turned toward Momma. "Ann, he's also a physician. He has good ideas. A doctor friend wrote me about his studies on contagion. Holmes reported years ago how fever was carried to women in childbirth by doctors themselves. Many fine women died from that." Robert wrinkled his forehead and looked intense. "Not new thoughts. Others have written about the fever. Holmes reviewed this and made the right conclusions. It's pretty well confirmed by many doctors now."

"How terrible," said Momma, sighing and shaking her head sadly. "Especially when doctors cause the illness themselves. They're supposed to cure, not hurt others."

"Even more terrible," continued Robert, "is that the ways of preventing it were known but not used—for years. Simple things like washing hands in limewater. I suppose some very prominent and proud doctors didn't agree with Holmes. You'd think they'd have tried it anyway. I wonder why this hasn't been used by surgeons who treat our soldiers. Bad fevers are seen constantly. Why does it take so long for new ideas to be put into use?"

"Robert, the old doctor I spoke of, Doctor Stevens, washed often."

"Who?"

"In Gettysburg. He was the first doctor I met there—and as old as the hills. He also poured a blue liquid on scissors and instruments before he used them. Maybe some astute men see into the future. They're ahead of their time." Momma's face was bright as she spoke. "He was so right about many other things." Suddenly her face was sad again and her eyes moist. She was thinking about Henry.

Robert Raymond and Ann Lynn were correct. Brilliant new methods were not far off. They were too late, though, to help the wounded during the War Between the States.

Momma healed gradually; life went on as usual—cooking, washing, and fixing. She found solace in hard work. She slept but little. Their home was scrubbed till the paint and varnish "groaned."

Aunt Suellen was a tower of strength, filled with compassion and hope. "Ann, we'll help with that. Cook and I scrubbed that last week. You rest awhile. We'll take over. The girls are capable, too. I certainly found that out while you and Jim were away. They helped with the yard and also indoors. They can cook too. Now you just stop and sit awhile. Tell us more about Gettysburg. It helps to talk. There's pride in our family with what you did. Your daughters especially should hear."

"They couldn't have survived without you, Suellen. I'll just do a little more. Thanks, though. There's healing here as I work. I need to do it," said Ann.

Their delightful neighbor, Mary, Mr. Raymond's new wife and companion, came often. She stood amid the disarrayed household of Momma's labors and spoke encouragement. "I'm so impressed with what you were able to do in the North. It took courage. I wish I'd been there with you. Maryland's my home—over the Potomac. I could have helped, I think. You spoke highly of the Sanitary Commission. They've done so much. They've mobilized a nation. You were helping with their work. It helped our men and theirs. I'm proud of you, Ann Katherine. But may I call you Ann, though? It's less formal."

"Certainly. And thank you, Mary. Your husband's a lucky man. He's found a wonderful woman."

Two days later, Momma suddenly stood quietly among her furniture and work. She started to cry and held Mary and Aunt Suellen close. "Again I thank you both," she blurted. She then sat down, exhausted.

"Come with us, Ann. We'll help you upstairs and into your bed clothes. We need you, but we also need a mother who is well. Your children depend on you too, so don't disappoint them. Come with us." Aunt Suellen and Mary led her up the stairs to that inviting four-poster bed; except for a little broth and crackers, she slept for two whole days. All the women worked while Momma slept and dreamed and became whole again.

Aunt Suellen and Mary displayed their ingenuity as they directed the revival of the family to a more normal life. The children weren't left out. "Kath, go help in the kitchen. You can shell the peas and cut those carrots. Annie, it's your turn to help Uncle Wen in the garden. Jim needs your help too."

Annie glared back. She decided Aunt Sue meant business and hurried outdoors.

"Mary, you work with Dee on your McGuffey Reader. I'll go over it with both of you this evening; Emmie will help Mrs. Raymond and me with the furniture. Everything's clean—your Momma did that, but it needs arranging. Now all of you git." Aunt Suellen could be firm, and as Kath had said often about their mother, feathers flew. She also noticed the cure bottle of brandy was hardly ever touched these days.

When Momma descended the stairs, her shoulders were back; a wan smile pervaded those delicate lines. Her chin was held high. "God put us here; we can be happy," she said.

"Welcome back, Ann," said Uncle Wen, seriously, as she descended the stairs. His face brightened. "I heard about all your dreams. Sue told me you talked constantly while you slept. Much happened there in Gettysburg, I'm sure. So much to think about. And we want to hear all about it. The troubles as well as the good things. You can fill in the details later. No hurry. It'll take time, I'm sure, but we're patient."

It was weeks before the family knew much of the story of Ann Lynn's travels. Few of her letters were received. Most were lost. Many details finally came from the notes she had recorded while on the road and at Henry's bedside. She had written on a rough wooden shingle that was kept in her old carpetbag. The colors of the patchwork had revived with washing. A candle and a minimum of neatly folded changes of clothing had filled the corners of the bag. Stubs of pencils were organized in a small sewn purse tucked within. A rough comb and other toilet articles completed the traveling kit.

Sheets of paper and a myriad of notes in her firm hand had cascaded from the bag as she opened it when she arrived home. Her family then listened for hours while sitting around the stone hearth in the parlor as Momma expanded on these notes with many memories.

Papa made a record of what his wife, Ann Katherine, related. Long after the sun set, he sat at his desk and wrote. He told his children:

> Some day our family's story should become part of the history of this war. It has now invaded much of our land. It's been like a plague. It will go away, finally. Perhaps we'll even forget what we common people have thought and felt. It should be remembered, though. War isn't just armies and faceless soldiers. It's the people and the common fighting man who face the terror. The history books usually tell about only the generals, the politicians, and the government officers. We should remember the people too. Momma has told us about the people. In the end, it's these folks who should

make the decisions. Unless they hear about the suffering, how can they decide what's right?

"I love your family, James," said Sarah. "And Emmie and I have become special friends. She's my age, and we have so much in common. She loves a home and cooking and a family. We had a wonderful day while you were in town with Annie and your parents. Tell me what you all decided about the wedding."

"We men waited outside the church, while Annie and Momma made plans with the minister. He's a nice person, Reverend Barkan. I enjoyed his sermon last Sunday. I noticed you were all smiles when Annie and John held hands. Kath behind me kept squirming and moving. She seemed to be watching you and me too. Does she know we're engaged now? Maybe she was listening when we talked outside the night before last—Saturday night. When the moon came out, I thought I saw someone in the shadows by the back gate."

"Kath's a nice young woman, James. And the moon was lovely. And you kiss very nicely." She gazed into his eyes. "I won't forget that night. You had just introduced me to your mother and father. Your father looked me over like he was examining a textbook. Then he smiled and said, 'Don't let her go, James.' He didn't explain what he meant."

"He told me that again later on. And he was serious. He also said, 'She's a wonderful lady.'" James smiled. "He likes you. Don't worry."

"Tell him thanks. And we should tell your parents about our engagement, before we tell all the others. What I wonder is do they need another daughter? They have quite a family of girls already." She laughed shyly, but there was a note of worry in her voice. "What my family needs is a son. You should hear them talk about you when you're not there," said Sarah.

"Some of it's good, I hope?" She looked pleasant, but didn't answer. He thought he'd better not ask again. He then changed the subject. "I'm still sad about your cousin, Will. What a tragedy."

"My family misses him," she replied. James nodded his head slowly, and his lips tightened as he looked at her lovely face and thought about their great loss.

Suddenly he smiled. "Enough about bad things. We're here for a wedding. It's a happy time." He looked quizzically into her eyes. "Some of what your family says about me is good, I hope."

"Most of it. But you're not perfect, you know." She tried to look stern, then laughed. "You thought I meant it, didn't you?"

"At first. But you said 'yes' last week anyway." He smiled. "We'll tell Momma and Papa tonight." He kissed her gently—then again and again. Off in the distance, he saw his sister, Katherine. She was smiling as she watched them.

James suddenly realized Sarah was talking again. "Harold Gills and George Collins will be here tomorrow for the wedding. We'll have to meet them at the train station. I'm glad some of your friends are coming from Richmond."

"I believe Emmie may know Harold Gills. He told me they met here in Staunton just after the fighting in the mountains to the west. She was looking for someone who had lost braid from his uniform or something. Harold wasn't the one, but they became friends. He's often told me he wants to see her again. This'll surprise her, I'm sure," said James.

"You'd better tell her in advance. It's embarrassing not to know someone when they remember you so well."

"You tell her, Sarah. It'll be better coming from another woman." He hesitated as he rubbed his eyes. "I'm sure glad they're on leave. As to meeting them, it won't be a problem. I can borrow a shay from the Mentrons down the road. We'll salute Annie and John at the church. Bridged swords and things. We'll be very military. It'll be fun. And the flowers. You and Emmie—you'll be gathering those. The church'll be beautiful. But don't forget, I need a brother too. John and I have become friends. He'll be my new brother. He seemed a little shy when he told me he was taking Annie away. I just smiled. Finally I said, 'She'll be in good hands, John.'"

"I lost someone close too. My cousin. We'll never quite get over it. He and Henry both gone! It doesn't seem real. But life goes on. Thankfully." Her eyes sparkled in the sunlight.

Annie married John Ingram, that fine young man with the broad shoulders and flaxen hair. "Finally," said Papa happily. "It's about time, I might say. You worried us, Annie." His daughter's face beamed. Annie was usually very articulate, but for now she just smiled as life whirled around her.

It was a small wedding—a few close friends. James and Sarah were there for several days, then they returned to Richmond. He, Lieutenants Gills and Collins, and a captain friend of Emmie's, Bill Reagin, bridged swords above the heads of the bride and groom as they left the church among shouts and well-wishing. They all saluted Annie, then stole a kiss or two, and shook hands with the Lynns' new son and brother.

They were all in their best bib-and-tucker, threadbare in places and patched here and there. The gold braid and the blades of the swords, however, shone brightly.

"Sorry to leave my first best love," Annie finally said to James, who glowed with happiness. People had just gone through the receiving line outside the church, and he and Annie were talking.

"You aren't leaving us," he replied. "I've always wanted John for a brother. I didn't tell him that before, because I thought you might change your mind. Ladies are inconstant, you know."

"You mean fickle," she chided. "We are not."

Annie stood close to him and pursed her lips. She then patted his cheek and smiled broadly. "Now hush that talk, James. I'm a married woman now. I can get angry at men if I want to." Her eyes were bright. "I guess you know me, though. Maybe better than I do myself." She laughed while looking hard into his eyes. "You're a ladies' man. You know about ladies, I suppose. Don't you?" She tried to look stern.

"I'm not sure I agree with you, Annie," said James. "I've enjoyed some of the fairer sex, though. You know that." His cheeks became red as he saw Sarah watching him from a distance. He looked away for a moment. "You embarrass me, Annie. Sarah doesn't know about all my . . ." He took a deep breath, trying to think of something gallant to say. "All my, uhh. All those pleasant experiences I foolishly told my sisters about before I met her."

"She probably knows more than you realize," said Annie, giggling.

"You're making me blush, my little sister. But you do look lovely."

"I'm trying to make you blush," she said gleefully.

"I don't understand all there is to know about ladies," he continued. "But I do know you, Annie. You're lighthearted and laughing, so often, I might even say you sparkle, but I don't want to speak too many nice things. John's lucky, though. You have depth and caring inside." He saw John turn toward them. He was only two paces away. "And you're sensible too. I think he knows that."

"I've known that since we first met," John answered. "It took time, but I think she's mine now." He squeezed her hand. "I'll share her a little, though."

Later that day, they had lemonade and little cakes on the lawn behind their home. With Uncle Jim's care, the gardens were bright with flowers. All their neighbors came. Annie glowed with pride. She hardly left John's side. Kath had never seen her so happy; her arm entwined his like the branches of a willow tree. She also saw men inside their pantry sipping fairly large amounts of Uncle Elmer's brandy. Aunt Sue talked with them for a while, but she didn't drink with them. Later, Kath saw her take several glasses of lemonade. James had brought the lemons from Richmond.

Evening came. Kath was upstairs to get a little gift and poem she had written. She heard Annie's happy laughter on the stairs near her room. The door to Kath's room was slightly ajar, and she peeked cautiously out. "I love you, my sweet," said John softly.

Annie fell into his arms like a rag doll, her head bent gently back and her shoulders arched over his arm. His right hand lifted her head so their lips touched. He kissed her ever so gently, then drew her toward him, hard, so that their bodies seemed crushed together.

Kath heard Annie mumble, "We were meant to be together, John—for ever and ever. I hope Momma doesn't see us like this, though." Annie, for all her coquettishness, was more shy than Kath had realized. "I guess we'll be sensible with time, my love, but may this feeling last forever. It's such a good feeling, John!"

"It will!" said John firmly. "Also, Momma would understand." He smiled at his bride. "She told me she wanted a son like me. You have a fine family, Annie. Maybe I should say, we have a fine family. My mother and father passed away when I was young, as you know. My sister, Mary, and I lived with them here in the Shenandoah. Mary then went to live with an aunt and uncle in Ohio after that. She's all I have left now, and she still lives in Ohio. We're on opposite sides in this war. It's wonderful to have a family again. I never knew folks could be so nice."

"Thank you, my husband. They are nice. And I treasure them. Some day I'll meet your sister. I'll write to her while we're on our honeymoon," Annie said.

"I hope the letter gets through. Now quiet, you lovely thing," he said with a sparkle in his eyes. "You talk too much." He swept her up in his arms, kissed her again, and carried her into the bedroom.

Kath heard a soft giggle, then Annie's voice said, "Now, John!"

Suddenly, there was silence.

John and Annie left for their honeymoon the next morning. They were to stay in a small cottage along a narrow stream just east of Staunton. Annie enjoyed being called "Mrs. Ingram" as her family kissed them good-bye. They hurried off. John was due back for duty in three days.

Sarah, James, Emmie, and Lieutenants Gills and Collins sat in the

Lynns' shaded yard and talked. Dee was reading on the covered walkway at the back of the house. Mary and Kath had been playing and laughing in the woods beyond. Mary had then gone for a walk, while Kath crept back into the yard and sat in the background and listened. They were discussing fascinating things. Kath wanted to travel. Now she heard about other places. When older, she, too, would go to Richmond and other places she hoped.

"Davis has lost touch with the people," said Gills. "For loyalty and support, you need to cultivate what some folks call the 'little people.' The president and Mrs. Davis see mainly their social equals, the wealthy, self-important folks and officers in the government. They forget the crowds in the streets."

"And many families who were well fixed before the war now look like vagabonds—thin and hungry," said Sarah.

"But the speculators and thieving quartermasters look well fed and comfortable," observed Collins.

"Also, the new rich," said James. "Including private blockade-runners, swindlers selling arms, dishonest merchants, as well as those who trade private cotton and tobacco to the North for things we need here but don't have. Then they sell it at inflated prices to us in Richmond and elsewhere."

"People need assurance from Davis," continued Sarah. "The government's 'strong hand' has seized food, used martial law, conscription, price fixes, and for a while it took away habeas corpus." She shook her head sadly. "To get support, our president will have to spend more time with the little people who supported him in the past. And I understand that armed bands in North Carolina and Tennessee are resisting the conscription. They were once very loyal to the South. Now they want to take over resources like our salt mines in Saltville, Virginia. We need that salt. Davis should think more about this sort of problem rather than just moving armies every time Stuart makes a foray, or that bumbler Burnside, the Union's best excuse for a general, gets bogged down in the mud."

"That happened to Burnside last January, Sarah," said Gills. "And he might have been successful then if it hadn't rained so hard and long." He hesitated. "I agree that he shouldn't lead armies, but he is a proven corps commander."

"He's now the Yankee commander of the Army of the Ohio," observed Collins. "Maybe that's good for the South. He's at Knoxville and blocking our main railroad link with Bragg in Chattanooga. As a result, all our troops have to go through Atlanta to reach Bragg."

"That's right," said Lieutenant Lynn. He thought for a moment as he arched his finger in front of his lips. "He may be a bumbler, but Burnside's certainly in a strategic position. The Virginia and Tennessee Railroad goes to Knoxville. And, Sarah, that's a region where many citizens have been cheering for the Union since the beginning of the war. Is that right, George?"

George Collins thought about how he should answer that question. He had worked for Judah Benjamin in the State Department. Benjamin still kept the president aware of matters throughout the Confederacy, including the waning enthusiasm of its citizens, as well as the numbers in various regions that supported the administration. "There are still many loyal people near Knoxville, James. That'll give Burnside problems, thankfully. Also, his supply lines are long. Everything comes to him from far to the north. He's very vulnerable, I believe. But we need to get an army up there and hit him—hard and soon."

"Perhaps Bragg can use Longstreet for that, unless he weakens his own lines excessively," added Harold Gills. "Sour-faced Bragg is our bumbler when it comes to fighting, though. Davis was just out there to consult with him. He and Davis are close friends. Instead of dismissing Bragg, he relieved D. H. Hill from his command. Hill was Stonewall Jackson's friend and a fine soldier. People in Richmond are angry. Bragg has a unique way of making people dislike him. He works hard and has a fine knowledge of tactics and strategy, but he just can't fight. What we need is another Lee out there."

"Well, we can't take Lee from Virginia. We'd lose Richmond," answered James with a wry smile. He then became serious. "That would be a final disaster. I'm not sure who else we can use, unless Davis decides to put Joe Johnston back in command in the West."

"If Lincoln's other problem, General Rosencrans, breaks out of Chattanooga, the Yankees'll move into Georgia. What would we do then?" asked Collins.

"I guess we'd continue to fight," said Gills. "What else could we do?" No one answered that question. The alternatives were too painful.

Lieutenant Gills looked discouraged. He smiled compassionately at Emmie. "You ladies are probably bored to tears. But these are things we have to face, I'm afraid. And General Grant's not doing much in the West right now. At least that's what I understand. Maybe they'll bring him to Chattanooga. That would be our undoing."

"Or Sherman," replied Emmie. "Those two are some of Lincoln's best."

"Lincoln finds it hard to find generals, too," answered Gills. "At least in the East. He's got some good soldiers out there in the West, though. Grant and Sherman are impossible for us. McPherson too. We're holding here in the East, but we've been cut in half there at the Mississippi." He looked over at Sarah. "The problems of a commanding general are overwhelming at times. Poor intelligence. His troops scattered to protect supply lines. Vague information. All kinds of conflicting reports. And armies get bogged down in the mud, Sarah. Unfortunately." Gills then glanced at the faces around him. "I just hope Lincoln's less capable generals make some mistakes at Knoxville and Chattanooga like Burnside did at Fredericksburg."

"I hope they do too," answered Sarah. Then she laughed. "And I'm learning something about generals today. Thank goodness we have Lee here in Virginia. He's wonderful to look at. But that scowling man Bragg. He's grim."

Gills continued talking. "What you said about North Carolina and Tennessee is certainly true. Armed bands of patriots are resisting conscription. Also, people in Georgia and Alabama are despairing of the war. Some are forming peace societies or petitioning their representatives in Congress. These four states plus Virginia represent much of the Confederacy now that we've lost the Mississippi."

"One of our problems in Richmond is our head of commissary, General Northrop," observed Collins. "Davis supports him and all his inefficiencies. He rejects most new ideas. He sells meat to officers at regular prices, but lets other people starve. And morale diminishes. That doesn't create support. Also, he's terribly poor at bringing food into the cities, as well as getting it to our soldiers."

"George, you're right," said James. "I've been able to get some meat that way for Sarah's family. I'm not sure it's fair to others, though. Some folks are desperate. They sell furniture, silver, china—family treasures—for what they can get. Then they enjoy a brief day or two of pleasure with the good food from the undercover markets. You can buy almost anything you want there."

"Main Street auctions are like a carnival, James. You know that. We've walked by them many times. Family treasures in the streets. Then they hire out slaves to the government to build trenches, and buildings, and many, many forts. They get a little money that way, I guess."

Sarah smiled coyly, then continued. "Common people struggle while high officers visit 'Locust Alley.'" She saw James looking slightly embarrassed. "Yes, I know about it, James. Those bawdy places are known all over the city. Even Benjamin was almost caught in one of the fine lavender parlors not long ago, while others couldn't get enough food to feed their children. And the champagne, whisky, brandy, gambling, Faro tables—they're notorious. Even Mary's father—you've met him often, James—says that the government could support the war with what those tables take in. On every third door on Main, in some areas, there are gold numbers on painted glass. Some folks call these places the 'gates to hell.' "

"There are many, many soldiers on leave, Sarah. And there aren't many homes they can go to. Some of those places are certainly comfortable and fun after they have been in a battle. They deserve entertainment," said James.

"Not that kind of fun." There was a crafty smile on her face. She saw Emmie smiling too. "There are reading rooms and other nice places like our new theater, the Richmond. It's on the site of the old Marshall that burned. As to who goes to that alley, it isn't only poor soldiers on leave.

"Vagabonds, speculators, deserters, and all kinds of men spend time there, I'm told." She emphasized the last two words. "Also, others say that many of the military titles you hear in those houses are from the overpainted women who own them." She looked pleasantly at the men around her.

"Well, we all need culture," said Lieutenant Gills. "When Emmie visits me in Richmond, we'll go to the theater. And I'll stay away from those other places."

Emmie shook her head. She had listened carefully. "You may be hungrier there in Richmond than we are, Mr. Gills, but I'd sure like all that excitement. Thank you for inviting me. I do accept. Maybe I can get a job there. I hear that many women are now working in war factories in Richmond. They're taking over men's jobs."

"You'd better visit me first," Lieutenant Gills said, smiling. "I have folks that would love to have a pretty girl stay with them." He saw Emmie smile warmly. "And working is not always safe. Earlier this year we had a big explosion in an ordnance building on Brown's Island. That's in the James River. The women were removing bullets from the powder in condemned cartridges. Dishonest speculators had bought substitutes. Thirty women were killed. Some were never found. It was ghastly. Those who survived looked like casualties after a battle—burned and torn."

He saw Emmie cringe.

"I wish I knew all these things," blurted Kath. She had been listening intently.

Sarah smiled. "What men talk about isn't always nice, Katherine. It sounds like we have lots of problems, too. Our talking won't solve them. Fighting may. Thus these men'll go back to the war very soon. Unfortunately too soon! The war's all around us now—East and West."

"Enough about bad things," Emmie insisted. "I've made all kinds of gingerbread, and we still have that lemonade." She turned and looked at her younger sister. "Kath, you look hungry, too. How about bringing out that platter from the kitchen? You helped prepare it this morning, and now we all can enjoy it. And that poem you wrote for Annie. Let's hear that, too."

Kath smiled and nodded yes to her older sister. As she walked away, she heard Lieutenant Gills speak. "'Starvation parties' are the new thing in Richmond now. There's no food. Just music."

Kath walked very slowly and continued to listen. "It's starvation without music for the poor," said Sarah. "That's what caused the bread riots in April when women and children marched on Capitol Square."

"I saw them go past the War Office," said James. "Thousands of them."

"Then they went down the hill to the produce stores. They carried off baskets and aprons full of goods. The rougher ones later went on to the auction shops on Main Street. Finally the city battalion arrived and threatened to shoot," said Sarah.

"Old Mayor Mayo led that battalion," said James. "I know him fairly well. He probably would have shot them if they hadn't stopped the looting. Later that day, Davis spoke to the people out there. I hope he knows what his words meant to them. If he did it more often, riots wouldn't start in the first place . . . "

Kath was out of hearing now. "Someday I'll be grown. I wish I were a man. All those things they can do. And see. Our armies are getting battered. That's no fun if you're fighting. But at least all the soldiers have been marching and seeing the countryside, while little girls like me stay home." She thought for a moment. "I'm not so little anymore, though." A look of pride crept over her face. She smiled. "Someday I'll be out there with the soldiers and see the country."

As Kath carried the platter outdoors, she heard Lieutenant Collins say something about Libby Prison. "Those are Yankee mouths we have to feed. Also, we need rations for the soldiers on Belle Isle in the James. That's the prison for Yankee privates. Thousands and thousands of men are housed out there. It was a beautiful island before the war. It isn't now."

"Why?" Kath blurted. "Why don't they send them to some other place?"

"Because we don't have enough prisons yet. Also, President Davis believes they should be kept close to Richmond. That may change." Collins looked down at his hands, then again at Katherine. "There's not much you can do with prisoners, Kath. I wish we could put more of them to work. Backgammon, checkers, reading—all of these help. But the men get bored with sitting around. I'm sure they all make plans to escape. We thus need more and more men to guard them. And because they're near Richmond, the Yankees make cavalry raids to try to free them. The prisoners and guards, plus troops defending the city, and thousands of civilians, already hurting for lack of food, create a real problem."

"It is a problem," said James. "And people in the North believe we're mistreating our prisoners—even starving them. There are violent feelings up north about that. But their men eat as well as most of our people do. However, Confederate fare in wartime is not what it used to be."

"Or what it is today—in 'Locust Alley'!" Sarah teased.

James, Sarah, and their friends returned to Richmond. Kath and her sisters again experienced the monotony of long days. Annie came home, and her husband went back to the war.

Other battles would be fought, but the great offensive by the South was over. The Mississippi River was lost with the fall of Vicksburg, as well as the whole southwest. Later, Chattanooga fell as Yankee troops rushed up mountains and conquered seemingly "impregnable" positions. The doorway to the heartland of the South was open, and vast hordes of Union soldiers were pouring through into Georgia.

Atlanta would struggle, but a tight "cord" of Yankees would throttle her efforts. The many battles and the tragedy of thousands of deaths would wrench the hearts of almost every family in the land. Incredible numbers of men would face each other and fight. Henry's trials were multiplied a hundred thousand–fold as soldiers from the North and South suffered but carried on or were consumed. As Henry had said, " . . . it was wild and uncanny . . . , as if ghosts and goblins circled about!" Kath's imagination spread and deepened as she began to believe that even great mountains and valleys cowered beneath the thunder of guns and the anger and shouts of brave men.

Mr. Grant did replace Rosencrans at Chattanooga. After defeating Bragg, he was ordered east. By a special act of Congress, the rank of Lieutenant General was reactivated. It was a position once held by Gen. George Washington. Grant was to be appointed to this position and command all Union armies. Richmond would again be threatened. Two soldiers, Grant and Lee, would continue the struggle for control of Virginia. Only one would win.

CHAPTER XXXIV
The Far Side of the River

"There's a pretty young lady downstairs asking for you, Captain Lynn."

James looked up at Private Rollins who was hovering over his desk with a lecherous smile covering his face. It was near dusk, and Lynn had been deep in thought about railroads and repairs. The rolling stock was limited because of breakdowns from normal wear as well as cavalry raids and accidents. This equipment was vital for troop movements. "I'm busy, Mr. Rollins," James said curtly. He'd been constantly interrupted all day.

"Well, your sister, Mrs. Ingram, will just have to wait, sir."

"Mrs. Ingram? Annie? She's here? Why didn't you say so, Private?"

Rollins smiled. "I did, Captain. And I'd get down there in a hurry if I were you. Sergeant Johnson is entertaining her right now. And he seems very interested, and he's asking all kinds of questions. Her husband's been hurt in the fighting east of Richmond, and she wants you to help find him, I believe."

Lynn and Rollins hurried to the stairs. James had been promoted to captain since he'd last seen Annie. He had seen her husband, Lieutenant Ingram, some weeks before when John was directing trench and fortification construction north of the city. They were surrounded by trenches and redoubts now. James thought to himself, *There's no imminent danger, but cavalry raids are certainly occurring often.*

James could hear Annie's bright voice; she was bantering with the sergeant just inside the building entrance. He was no match for her enthusiasm, and her flashing eyes had subdued him into the role of listening and answering meekly as she asked him about his family and wife and children. When she saw James, she ran to him, threw her arms about his waist, and kissed him hard. Then she stood back and looked. "You're a little thinner, James. But you're still handsome." She kissed him again.

James heard the sergeant speaking quietly to Private Rollins. They were behind Annie. "Son, next time you be an officer. Then you can be kissed by pretty women."

James grasped his sister's arm and directed her to a small alcove across the entrance hall. There was a wooden bench in a corner tucked below a hissing gas jet. The flame cast gray shadows on the floor and walls. "What happened to John, Annie? You must have some idea where he is?"

She pulled out a letter and showed it to her brother. "He's at the Chimborazo Hospital here in Richmond, James. He was hurt in the fighting at a place called Bottom's Bridge."

"That's east of here on the Richmond Road along the peninsula. About six thousand cavalry were sent there by Gen. Benjamin Butler. He's the 'Beast' who held New Orleans. He's now the Yankee commander at the mouth of the James." He ridged his brows, then looked kindly at his sister. "That fight was in early February—a month ago. The Yankees were trying to free prisoners from our Libby Prison here in Richmond. I didn't know John was in that battle," said James.

"He was directing road repairs there when word came that the Yankee cavalry was close. He wrote that he was talking to an elderly woman about her burned farm at the time. Stragglers had apparently destroyed the woman's farm a few days before, and she was in tears. John was drawing a plan for rebuilding the home. See. Here's a copy of the sketch. He sent it with his letter," said Annie.

"He's an architect as well as an engineer," James observed as he looked carefully over the sketch. He then looked up at Annie's face and saw pride in his sister's eyes once she had understood the meaning of his words.

"I married a fine man, James, and we have to find him. His ankle was broken when a shell exploded near him, knocking down a heavy pole that fell on top of him. Several others close by were killed. I'm just happy he's getting better."

"We'll go to Chimborazo right now, Annie. But tell me, how did you get here?"

"By train. With Emmie. Lieutenant Gills met us at the station. She's with his parents. His father brought me here to the War Office in their wagon, and Sergeant Johnson was kind enough to help me find you." She smiled at the sergeant. "Thank you, Mr. Johnson," she said loudly. She could see the sentry post beyond the door, and she remembered her apprehension about getting by them when she arrived. The sergeant had been understanding and kind.

"Is Emmie well?" asked James.

"She certainly is. Mrs. Gills, Harold's mother, has several injured soldiers staying with them. Emmie went right in and started to help. When I left, she was making gingerbread with the sorgo syrup we'd brought. It was already in the oven. And you're invited for dinner tomorrow, James. Also Sarah. But we'd better find John first."

James suddenly saw that Annie's eyes were moist. He held her hand. It was trembling. "We'll find him," he said softly.

"You can use the carriage behind the building, Captain," said Sergeant Johnson. "Ezmeralda's not much to look at, and the army doesn't want her, but she'll get you there. And, Captain, one more thing. Office workers and city people are being sent to the trenches north and west of the city. There's a large Yankee cavalry group approaching. We'll have to stop them. You may be needed. We don't think they'll reach us till the morning, so you have time to visit the hospital. But be back later. The colonel is counting on you."

Annie and James walked out to the carriage. A scowling, high-ranking officer walked by them. "Good evening, sir," James said to the man. He didn't answer. As they reached the carriage, he continued. "That's General Bragg himself. He's adviser to Davis now. In a way, however, he directs all our armies, even though he lost that big fight at Chattanooga. He's Davis's friend. I guess that's why he was chosen."

Annie laughed. "He does look unpleasant, doesn't he? Just like folks have told me."

"We're almost there, Captain," said Sergeant Johnson. They could hear the sporadic firing of guns close by. A motley group of ambulatory soldiers from the hospital, stragglers from the city, shop workers, and teenage boys were behind James.

"This way, Captain," a voice shouted. The man was a wild-eyed major from the State Department. "Hurry! They're about to charge."

James's men were led into a series of muddy trenches filled with untidy, nonprofessional soldiers who probably had been dragged from bed or off the streets. A number of distinguished citizens also were standing with these troops.

Captain Lynn walked behind his troop of unkempt men—cautioning,

305

threatening, and encouraging them. "Hold your fire, men. Let them get close. Patience. A little longer. Now fire!" The guns then seemed to explode in one great crash. "Reload and fire again! Keep firing! That's the way! Good job. I'm proud of you." He saw many horsemen fall and lie motionless before the ramparts.

Just then a bullet struck a log in the embankment in front of James, and a man fell beside him with blood gurgling from his mouth and throat. As Lynn raised his head to see the battlefield better, a shell exploded nearby and pieces of metal whirred about him like angry bees.

There was a burning above his right ear. He rubbed it with his left hand, while he continued to fire his pistol with his right. Suddenly he saw blood on his fingers, and Sergeant Johnson was looking at the wound.

"It's not bad, sir. Just a scratch. And look at those Yankees. They're running like scared hounds." He looked James in the eye. "We beat 'em, sir. We put up a good fight. Look at 'em. Your sister'll be proud. Here, we'll bandage that head of yours."

"Miss Emmie, I shouldn't have brought you. My brother Harold'll probably kill me. That bullet came too close. It could've killed you."

Emmie Lynn looked kindly at Harold Gills's young, pink-faced brother. She smiled. "Charlie, I'll take the blame. Don't you worry none. I insisted. You know that. And we're fine." She looked out at the street. "But some of those boys aren't so fine. Just look at them!" They saw groups of soldiers from the trenches nearby walking slowly back into the city. Some were limping, a few were bleeding and being helped by others, and some were talking and laughing, their eyes filled with pride. They had won the battle.

Suddenly Emmie looked with a start. "That man looks like James, my brother." She pointed across the street at an officer ambling close by. It was her brother, and his head was swathed in bandages. "It is James. And he's hurt. Please, I hope it's not serious," she continued. "Please!"

"But he's walking and smiling," answered Charlie. "He can't be hurt bad." Emmie didn't hear this. She was hurrying across the road toward Captain Lynn. She grasped his arm, then kissed him on the cheek, which was smeared with blood.

"Well," said Private Rollins. "I guess I'd better become an officer if I can. That's the second time in two days he's been kissed by a strange woman."

Just then James grabbed Emmie and kissed her hard, smearing her

306

dress with blood from his shirt. His shoulders were wet from the bleeding.

"I'm fine," said the captain, smiling. "It's just a scratch." He looked at her serious face. "But Emmie, you shouldn't be here. You could have been hurt."

"You are the one who has been hurt," she said wryly. "I've already lost one brother." She didn't continue.

The sergeant was pleased with this display of affection. He wished she'd talk about him that way. Emmie saw that James wasn't seriously wounded. She then looked at the man beside him. "Thank you for helping him, Sergeant." She saw that the sergeant, too, was injured. There was a long scratch on his face and blood over his cheek. "We'd better clean that, sir. Here, I have some perfume in my purse." With this and a clean handkerchief, she scrubbed the sergeant's wound carefully and expertly, while Rollins stood by with a longing look in his eyes. Emmie saw this. She smiled warmly at him. "I'm happy you weren't hurt, Private."

"Private Rollins," he said. His voice cracked as he continued to speak. "I do have a little scratch here on my arm, ma'am. It ain't much, ma'am."

"Well, we'll clean that, too." She did, and Rollins nearly fell to the ground when he felt her gentle fingers touch his skin. His face reddened and he stammered softly, "Thank you, ma'am." James suddenly realized that she had conquered both his friends with caring and kindness.

"Captain Lynn will need some stitching, ma'am. Not much though," said the sergeant.

"You're coming with me, James. To Sarah's. We'll patch you up there. I'd take you to Lieutenant Gills's home, but his mother already has three soldiers to care for. She doesn't need another one. Besides, Sarah wouldn't forgive me if I didn't bring her fiancé home."

Charlie Gills and Emmie led James off through the streets. There were ambulances and doctors moving toward the battlefield to help the more seriously injured—Confederate and Union soldiers alike. Work details would soon be needed to bury those who had not survived the fighting. The sergeant just stood and smiled. "Well, I'll be danged," he finally said. "I'll have to get me a wench or two pretty soon. That sure was pleasant. What a fine lady."

Emmie was reprimanding her brother as they walked along. "James, you just stay out of the fighting. As I said, I've already lost one brother. We need you. Now let's get that head fixed."

They walked up the low steps into Sarah's home. She was waiting there patiently, wondering if James had been in the fighting. The Confederate soldiers in the trenches north of the city hadn't been involved in a battle. General Kilpatrick, the Union commander, had scouted the area and decided it was too strongly defended. He retreated north, then east toward the Peninsula.

Colonel Dalghren with five hundred hand-picked men was ordered to cross the James River and approach Richmond from the south. A crossing was not available, and he stayed north of the river and attempted to breach the Richmond fortifications from the west. He was driven back with heavy losses. The colonel, too, would finally be killed as he retreated to the Union lines. His father, Admiral Dalghren, would inquire about him in Washington, but word of his defeat would not be received until days later. Another fine officer died in the war with his men. On his body papers were found directing an assassination attempt against President Davis. It was never confirmed whether these papers were authentic or not.

"Oh, God! He's hurt!" said Sarah as they entered. "Is it bad? James, are you all right? James?" She soon realized he wasn't badly injured. "I just knew you couldn't stay away from the fighting. When you were hurt before, we both suffered for weeks." Sarah turned to Emmie, while Captain Lynn tried to think of something humorous to say. "It isn't serious, is it, Emmie?"

"Not really, I believe. We'll have to look at that wound, though. He was talking much of the way home until I scolded him for the fighting." She winked at Sarah.

"Men!" Sarah said. "They worry us to death."

Both women worked at unwrapping the bandages that were tied in several places. Sarah went to get scissors from the sewing room. The bandage strips were soaked with blood, and the wound continued to ooze after the bandages were removed. Sarah now brought a bowl of water and several towels, and Emmie gently scrubbed the skin while James winced and twisted a little. "Hey, that hurts," he said, smirking. "Stop it."

"There's dirt in here," said Emmie firmly. "We have to get it out. This'll teach you about being out and fighting. It does hurt. It's supposed to. And it will be stitched. But I suppose every doctor in town is out there on the battlefield now. Momma's taught me to sew wounds, James. We'll just give it a good try."

"Oh, no you won't, Emmie," said James.

"Oh, yes she will," said Sarah. James lost. Emmie expertly closed the wound with well-placed sutures from the Robertson's sewing room. Sarah marveled as she watched Emmie's fingers push the needle through the flesh, then, holding the thread with one hand, tie a firm knot with the other. Her fingers seemed to fly over the wound.

".Those are square knots," mumbled Emmie. "There. That'll hold it. You're almost as good as new, James." She looked quizzically at her handiwork and pointed. "There's some tension here, though. I'll put in one more stitch—a relaxing stitch, James." She used a thick thread and a long needle. The latter was pushed from back of the wound under the skin to well beyond the opposite wound edge. The needle was withdrawn then pushed back in the opposite direction and tied firmly—a mattress suture.

Her brother writhed and turned. "My God, that hurts. What are you doing there?" he shouted.

"That's got it. We're done. That'll hold it, I'm sure," said Emmie.

"It looks lovely," said Sarah. "At least the work looks lovely. Not the wound."

"Let me see," said James. Emmie handed him a mirror, and Sarah held a small oil lamp, while Captain Lynn turned his eyes so he could see Emmie's work. "It is beautiful, my sister. Thanks! Where did you ever learn that?"

"The war's gone on for a long time, James. We've seen a lot of injured soldiers. Your mother taught me to do this. And I've helped in the hospitals for years."

Both the captain and Sarah looked with pride at Emmie. Sarah said to herself, "We women are learning. We aren't weak sticks, unable to do our part. And we'd stop the war, if we were in charge." She suddenly heard her mother coming in the rear door. "We're in here, Mom. I want you to meet James's sister. Emmie, this is my mother, Mrs. Robertson."

Mrs. Robertson and Emmie shook hands, then hugged each other. "Don't forget me," said James, smiling.

"We won't," said Mrs. Robertson. "And I see you're well patched up now. I met Sergeant Johnson on the street. He told me about the injury. You men are lucky you have someone around to patch you up. And Emmie and Sarah, I'm proud of you. Now let's have something to eat. I was able to buy some beef. We'll eat well tonight. It's not much, but enough."

Emmie suddenly saw that no servants were helping them. "Where is Lawrence?" she asked. "James has told me how much he admires him."

"He's been taken to work with the burial parties, I'm afraid. He also helps dig trenches and forts. That's what helped us save the city today, Emmie." Mrs. Robertson smiled wanly. "And our cook is working at the hospital. We're all doing our part. Like you, she learned to help the soldiers right here in this home. Probably Sarah and I will have several more injured men in rooms upstairs soon. There have been small battles along the Rapidan north of here."

"Small?" said Sarah.

"Well, they're not another Gettysburg," said her mother. "Thankfully!" She looked again at Emmie. "And we had four soldiers with us for several weeks after that Mine Run affair near New Hope Church a while back. Meade was looking for Lee's weak spot. That's what Sarah's Pa told us. The men were finally transferred to the hospital. Then two more soldiers were with us after the Bottom's Bridge fight."

"That's where Annie's husband was hurt, James," Sarah said.

"That's right," said the captain. "He's nearly well now, though. And those skirmishes near the Rapidan come often, but Lee's ready for them. He's kept the Yankees back."

"I hope that Bobby Lee will continue to protect us," continued Mrs. Robertson. "Mead's massing a big army along that river. And Grant has come East, I understand. He may be directing the fight right close to Richmond soon—when the spring comes. And it's not far off now. I hope Grant goes back to the West before the fighting starts again. He's a tough soldier, I understand, and he doesn't give up. May the Lord help us!"

She hesitated for a moment. "The killing's not over. And what we saw today was only a small, small fight."

General Ulysses S. Grant reached Washington, D.C., on March 8, 1864. The next day, President Lincoln presented him with the commission, constituting him lieutenant general in the Army of the United States. He became the supreme commander of all Union armies. On March 10, Grant traveled by train to the headquarters of the Army of the Potomac at Brandy Station, Virginia. There he met with George G. Meade, whom he retained as commander of that army.

Days later, in Nashville, Grant talked with William T. Sherman, whom he had placed in command of all Western armies. They discussed strategy. The plan was simple, as Sherman said: ". . . (Grant) was to go for Lee, and I was to go for Joe Johnston."

Grant remained in the East with General Meade's army, the army that had fought Lee for so long and had so often been defeated. This army was at the Rapidan River looking south.

"I'm back." It was Papa. Kath met him at the door, and they traded big hugs. "Hello, dear. My, you're pretty," he said. "Ah, my children again. I love you all." Dee and Mary had squeezed under his arms so that he would hug them, too. Momma came quickly when she heard his voice. Aunt Suellen and Uncle Wen were in town. "I suppose Emmie and Annie are still in Richmond," he continued. "The Federals attacked that city, but they were pushed back, the papers said. Not much was accomplished, but the city's safe."

"How's Amherst, James? Is everyone well?" asked Mrs. Lynn.

"Most everyone. I saw Georgie, Annie's friend. He looks bad without his left arm, but he's working with his father and assisting with the training of the militia." Papa thought a moment, wondering if he should say more. "Doria was hit by stragglers, Ann. Our horses were run off, and one cow was taken."

"Oh, no!" said Mrs. Lynn.

"Yes! Unfortunately. Also, the tool shed and one barn were burned, and they started a fire at the back porch, but Elmer managed to put that out. The house itself wasn't damaged, thank the Lord. And the silver's safe. Elmer had buried that. But your lovely settee was damaged, and those little silver spoons on the wall in the dining room were taken." Ann Lynn's face was pale.

"And they slashed two paintings, the landscapes. And tore down some of the drapes, but they can be fixed. Mary was scared to death. Finally she fed them well, and they left. Elmer, also, lost one of his barns. He wasn't there to protect it. He was trying to save our home. That was another group of soldiers, I believe. Your sister was frightened, but she wasn't hurt, thank the Lord!"

Momma looked devastated. "At least our house is safe. We have so many memories. I guess destruction's the way of the future now, and we've been fortunate big armies haven't marched through Amherst—or Lynchburg. Who were they, James?"

"Probably stragglers from General Custer's brigades—that Yankee! They attacked Charlottesville last week and a few other places in the county. Albermarle County, that is. That's thirty miles from our home."

"How's Elmer? He's been put under a lot of strain," asked Mrs. Lynn.

"He didn't look well. He tires so easily now, and that trouble with stragglers hit him pretty hard. Too hard. If I can get my school situation taken care of, I'll go back there and help. I have those lectures I promised to do at the Augusta Seminary. It has been on hard times with the war, but it's still open. Maybe Wen can get back there before I can. Somehow we'll work things out."

James was at his desk in Richmond. It was filled with letters and requisitions. He's felt very tired all day. He was trying to remember the name of the new commander of the Department of Richmond. The commander and Davis had made a series of sorties to review the defenses of the city. *The trenches and forts are well planned, I've been told,* James thought. *But with a big army at the Rapidan, and Grant the overall commander, things don't look auspicious.* He tried to remember the man's name. "Maj. Gen. Robert Ransom," he finally said with a wry smile.

"Also, P. G. T. Beauregard was appointed the commander of Southern Virginia and North Carolina. I guess he replaces Pickett in that position. I hope the Yankees don't get that far. That department includes the defenses at Petersburg just south of here. Perhaps Meade'll knock himself out on the ramparts around Richmond, and he may not even get this far. None of their other generals have—except McClellan, and he was stopped cold."

Captain Lynn kept rubbing his eyes, then squeezing them tight. There was sunshine outdoors, and it wasn't cold, but he'd felt chilly all day, and his muscles ached from head to foot. "Perhaps it was that spicy meat I ate at the tavern yesterday. It tasted good, but my stomach rumbled all night." He then thought how much he missed Sarah. "She's away with her folks. And I need her. She always makes me feel better. But they're in Goochland County now with friends, I believe. Her Pa was distraught after that cavalry raid last month, and now he's worried about all the Yankees up to the north of us.

"And Emmie and Annie are probably home by now. I hope they're safe. But with Custer making those raids near Charlottesville, it's a worry." He thought a moment. "I really appreciated Emmie sewing me up that day. The doctor said it was a beautiful job. It's healed, but my head sure aches right now. God, I feel terrible."

James staggered to his feet. As he went through the War Department entrance, he mentioned to Sergeant Johnson that he felt very ill.

"You look as white as a sheet, Captain. You'd better go and rest. I'll explain to the colonel."

James wandered aimlessly for a while. He couldn't go to Sarah's. Also, Mary was away, sensibly. Where should he go? Then he remembered there was a haven where he'd be taken care of. Lil's door was always open. He hadn't been there for a long time.

He walked unsteadily down the alley to the rear of Lil Rawling's place. He knocked on the back door. He soon saw an eye through the peephole above the knocker. The door opened. "Come right in, Captain Lynn. We haven't seen you for quite a while. Welcome."

James tripped on the door sill as he entered, and he almost fell. Lil was in her office across the hall. She came out quickly, grasped James's hand, and helped him to stand. "You haven't been drinking, I hope." She looked at his flushed cheeks and felt his forehead. "Your skin's hot as sin, Captain. That's a fever you have." She looked kindly at the soldier. "Rose, get Melanie. She's a good nurse. The two of you can help the captain upstairs. He'll need to rest for a time."

James was semiconscious in the upstairs room. He felt the two women undressing him while they giggled as he struggled. The cool bed-sheets were a blessing though. He tried to thank them, but he realized Melanie was climbing in beside him. "You're having a chill, Mr. Lynn. We'll just have to warm you up a mite. Rose, I'll keep the captain warm, but we'll need more blankets." As Rose left the room, she said something about a chamber pot below the bed. Her voice seemed very far away.

It was a long time before James awoke. The place beside him in the bed was empty, but Rose was sitting close by. "I see you're waking up, James. You had a good sleep." She came over, turned him so he was face down, and massaged his back expertly. "We have some broth downstairs. And crackers. A little food will help, but we'll take it slow." She left the room.

James sighed as she went away, but he kept thinking, *That sure felt good with her beside me. I feel a lot better already. Maybe it was just the sleeping. Or maybe it was that wonderful massage. It did feel good. And she's nice.*

As he lay there, half-asleep, he heard voices in the room across the hall. His door was slightly ajar. "Just one more time," a man said. "That felt wonderful!"

"You're a real tiger!" the woman answered. "But we can try it once more. Just relax and enjoy it." Just then Rose came in through the door and closed it tight. She helped James to sit, then fed him the broth and crackers. It tasted good—the first food he'd had for almost twenty-four hours. You'll stay here tonight, Mr. Lynn. Lil said she owes you a lot for those legal services. I'll come back a little later. And there are more blankets if you need them. Now get some more sleep." She smiled broadly, winked, and left the room.

The door was carefully closed. The captain tried to stay awake and even thought about opening the door a bit, but sleep quickly overcame him. He awoke to a beautiful dawn. "I'll have to get back to work soon, but maybe I can stay a little longer. This bed feels so good!" He wanted to wake Rose who was in a chair nearby, but he soon drifted off to sleep again.

As he left Lil's later that day, she asked him several questions about her deed to the property. He felt there was no problem, and he thanked her profusely for her help. "President Davis just had a personal tragedy," she told him. "His son, Joe, fell from the railing on their upstairs veranda. The city's in mourning. It's so sad. It wasn't the war directly, but it must have had something to do with it. It's brought tragedy to most of our people. Now a little tike has died, and it hurts us all."

Meade's army moved around Lee's flank and crossed the Rapidan River unopposed. They were headed for Richmond. It was a bright spring day, and the dogwood was blooming. Meade's officers had had a rousing celebration some days before their long columns began to march. They were expecting victory. Few of these men, though, would survive the battles ahead.

The army now entered a tangled forest of trees and low shrubs known as the Wilderness. The region was crisscrossed by narrow roads walled by vegetation, and there were few open areas in which an army could maneuver. General Lee lacked cannons and manpower. His troops would be effective here, however, because the Yankees would be less mobile, and the South's forces could fortify their positions with earthworks and felled trees. Lee waited.

It was here where Lee had trapped Gen. Joe Hooker a year before, and it was a region that the Confederates knew well. There was intense fighting for two days, and thousands died, some horribly, as fires raged through the pines and oaks and shrubs. When the Battle of the Wilderness ended, there were 17,000 Union and 7,000 Confederate casualties.

Meade's army moved back to disengage from the enemy. His men expected to be ordered north in retreat. This they had done many times before. They did not retreat. They continued south and east toward Spottsylvania, a crossroad that would place them on Lee's flank and rear. A Union veteran said, "Our spirits rose . . . We marched free. The men began to sing."

As the Army of the Potomac crossed the Rapidan, other Union armies went on the offensive. Federal expeditions operated against the

Virginia and Tennessee Railroad in southwestern Virginia. Sherman advanced into Georgia. Averell moved into West Virginia, and Butler started his corps up the James River. Sigel's regiments marched south in the Shenadoah Valley amid the echoes of other legions that had fought there and died. His men headed toward Staunton, while Meade marched toward the capital of the Confederacy. Southerners braced themselves for the coming battles.

When Grant was stopped at one line, he sidestepped and attacked at another. He didn't retreat as had other generals from the North. Lee's lithe army followed closely and won great victories, but the Army of the Potomac could not be stopped.

"Grant's soldiers are paying dearly for each step forward," said Mr. Raymond, the Lynns' neighbor. "They're advancing against strongly fortified positions. Lee's fine at defense as well as attack. He's a great soldier. As the Yankees try to go around him, he's there to stop them. Grant's army's still led by General Meade, that sour-looking soldier. He fights hard, but maybe we're better. Meade fought Lee at Gettysburg. He stopped us there. Sad. These are old-time regulars now. They know their business. They've gotten very efficient at killing."

Sigel's effort was a diversionary valley offensive bent on the destruction of lush farms and orchards in the Shenandoah, which had been providing food for Lee's army. There were few soldiers in the valley to resist Sigel's advance. Most had been transferred to Lee east of the Blue Ridge Mountains.

"Our problem in Staunton is that we have no one left to fight for us," continued Robert Raymond to the Lynn family. "We're mainly old men and boys, clerks and convalescing soldiers. Our town will be destroyed."

It was early May, 1864.

Gen. Benjamin F. Butler's army was directed to move up the James River. His objective was Richmond. If he, the "Beast" of New Orleans, moved quickly, he would probably achieve the glory he sought. The capital's defenses to the south were manned by only a few soldiers.

Butler was a shrewd and powerful politician. Even Lincoln found it impossible to prevent his appointment to an important command. General Grant's first impression on meeting him was favorable. Butler was a good administrator, and his energy was great. His tactical ability in the field was unknown. In the South, his name was anathema. He had scorned the sacredness of Southern women, and men had been hanged in Louisiana without proper trial. He was an easy person to hate.

On May 5, 1864, thirty thousand of Butler's troops landed at City Point and the Bermuda Hundred, just south of the James River. In the distance, to the southwest, the steeples of Petersburg were seen by his men. Fifteen miles to the north was Richmond, the goal for which armies had fought and thousands had died. Butler's Army of the James was on the far side of the river from the capital, but in a fifty-mile region, there were fewer than ten thousand Confederate soldiers to oppose him, and it would take time to move these men between Butler and the city.

The general proposed a night march to Fort Darling (Drewry's Bluff) on the road north. His officers opposed this, so Butler did not order it. Drewry's Bluff was the site where the Union fleet had been turned back down-river in 1862. The Lincoln administration considered it the key to the southern defenses of the city.

Instead of moving quickly, Butler moved cautiously. On May 6, there was minor skirmishing as the Federals attempted to cut the Richmond and Petersburg Railroad. President Davis in Richmond heard the sounds of the guns, and his War Department received dispatch after dispatch urgently requesting help. The people of the city were desperate. They knew that if Petersburg fell, an important railroad junction would also be lost. This point connected the capital to much of the South. It was a vital supply line.

The guard at Camp Lee near Richmond was gone. They had been ordered to join Lee's army. General Ransom, in command of the Department of Richmond, had a small force north of the city. He hurried his men south. These forces were augmented by hastily mobilized government clerks and civilian workers. Defenses north of Richmond were thus stripped of soldiers. If the city were attacked from that direction, there would be few troops to defend it.

Midshipmen under eighteen years of age with instructors as officers were acting as skirmishers. Beauregard had not yet arrived, and General Pickett was still in command at Petersburg. He gathered the few units available there. General D. H. Hill, who had been dismissed at Chattanooga by Davis, was bringing remnants of troops from North Carolina— on slow, rickety trains. The guns at Drewry's Bluff were now manned by gunners from the tiny Confederate fleet.

Butler fought a series of skirmishes and minor battles. His scattered units managed to tear up a few miles of track, but little damage was done. Finally, on May 12, a week after his arrival south of Richmond, his entire corps was on the road marching north. By then, Beauregard was in command, and he was ready. His forces nearby Drewry's Bluff would fight Butler on nearly equal terms.

But other events were occurring. To the north of the capital, Gen. Phil Sheridan was approaching Richmond with ten thousand horsemen. He was a tried and capable Western cavalry officer brought east by Grant. Jeb Stuart was at his flanks and rear, but he couldn't prevent the destruction of miles of railroad and much equipment. It was a wild and intense battle. The Union force could not be stopped. Finally, in the rolling countryside around Yellow Tavern, not far from the capital, these forces collided. In the fight that ensued, this fabled cavalier of the Confederacy, J. E. B. Stuart, the "eyes" of Lee in so many battles, was critically wounded. He was carried from the field and soon died.

Stuart's troops were defeated, but they had given Richmond time to mobilize some semblance of a defense. Civilians, wounded veterans, and office clerks had reached the trenches north of the city. This region had previously been stripped of troops, but now a few men stood ready to defend it. The future of Richmond was still in doubt.

CHAPTER XXXV
Maybe We Won't Have to Die—Today!

"Mr. Robertson, you shouldn't have come."

"I had to, James. We have few others left. I heard the guns to the north. If we lose this one, we've lost the war. We have to try. And I have to help. You have several other businessmen behind you. If they can fight, so can I!"

"But, Sarah. Your family. You're needed."

"They need you too, son. We'll fight them together." They walked on silently with the other ragtag volunteers. James heard the hushed murmur of voices behind him, and an occasional laugh and words of bravado. They wanted to get at the enemy and destroy him. They all heard the guns just over the rise to their front.

"Major, where do you want us?" shouted James to one of General Ransom's officers who had hurried back from Fort Darling where he'd faced General Butler. The Yankees eight miles to the south were still working laboriously getting their troops into position.

"That way, Captain. And hurry!" said the major. He pointed north along an irregular path that led to the earthworks and trenches.

James started toward the crest of the low rise in front of them and shouted as he ran, "Sergeant Johnson, move the men quickly! Up the path." As he reached the top, he continued, "Sheridan's men are out there. You can see them." He was pointing north across the field.

"Double quick, men!" ordered the sergeant. His voice boomed like a horn.

"Our people are retreating from the outer defenses," shouted the major. "Hurry!" The captain and the sergeant led their ragtag troop along the path down into the earthworks. A disorganized group of men in the field beyond these works was retreating back to them—to the safety of the inner defenses.

"They're our troops," shouted James. "Don't shoot. Let them get back here. We need them. That's Sheridan across the field. He's the one we want to get. They're professionals. And tough."

"So those are the Yankees," said Robertson, smiling. "I wondered what they'd look like. They don't seem so tough, do they?" Sheridan's troopers were partially dismounted far in the distance. Officers seemed to be among them, conferring and planning and pointing toward the city's defenses.

"They aren't attacking, if that's what you mean," said a man with white hair beyond James's small group. "We're stronger now. They may be stopped."

"Mr. Mayor," said Robertson. "You shouldn't be here." Old Mayor Mayo looked like a wrinkled apparition, his hair blowing in the breeze, his face toward the enemy. He stood there with pistols in both hands.

"If Davis can come with pistols at his side, so can I!" said the mayor. "You're right that their people don't look like much from here, but they're good fighters. You men keep down. They're unlimbering out there." Several cannons were being moved into position. James then saw puffs of smoke in the Yankee lines and several shells struck just beyond the Confederate trenches close to where the major had given them directions. The Southern batteries began returning the fire.

"Where's Davis?" asked Robertson.

"Somewhere that way," answered Mayo. He pointed to the east along the earthworks. "He's still with General Ransom, I believe." He hesitated a moment. "I was at our outer defenses when Sheridan's men came at us. I was mounted, and I made a glorious retreat to these works. My face is still red, I'm afraid."

"Where's your horse?" asked James.

"Somewhere behind us now, if it didn't run off. I hope it wasn't killed by that shell," replied the Mayor.

Robertson and Mayo then shook hands as James's troops moved farther on. Sheridan's men seemed to be forming for an attack, but no forward movement was seen.

"Glad to have you with us, sir," said a voice near James. The captain looked at the man's grizzled face and mustache. He had a German accent, and James had seen him before.

"I know you," said the captain.

"We've met several times, Mr. Lynn. Joe Houck's the name. I'm part of the Tredegar Battalion. We've talked down at the Works. You were after axles and wheels for the rolling stock. Remember? Several months ago."

"But you and your men do the work," said James. "And we need you. And many more of you. You men should be behind the lines. You're too valuable. We still need what you make. And you can't be replaced."

Houck laughed. "If we lose our city, you won't need us anymore. We have to do our part, too." James didn't pursue this further. They shook hands, and both turned toward the enemy. The captain's men were lined up along the trench with rifles resting on the rampart.

Suddenly there was a shout: "They're mounting up, Captain." It was Houck. "I think they're getting ready to ride off. Maybe we won't have to die—today! I think we've won this one, Captain." There were shouts up and down their lines, and several salvos were fired at the Yankee cavalry as they started east.

"We won this one," James replied. He nodded his head to emphasize what he'd said. "But how many more can we win? There are lots more Yankees out there somewhere. God knows how many. And they'll be back." They both laughed sardonically.

There was gunfire out beyond the Yankee position. "That may be Stuart's men coming up," said Houck. "They've reformed their lines. There coming in on Sheridan's rear. Thank God." Unbeknownst to these men, Stuart would soon die from wounds received in battle, but his troopers were still fighting. They were attacking Sheridan like injured bulls. The Federals continued to head east.

The Union cavalry would not reach their lines for days. Sheridan would later brag that he could have entered Richmond, but that it would not have been possible to hold it. Others explained why he didn't: "It would have been difficult or impossible to get back out." We will never know which story might have become true. Sheridan retreated.

The Yankee cavalry now moved southeast, using captured locals to show them the roads. A few of these guides were shot when they gave false information. The Federals were now attempting to reach Butler on the south side of the James River. They were unsuccessful, but they did burn a farmer's mill and fight a series of small battles and skirmishes. Then they recuperated at Haxall's Landing along the James River. Finally they rejoined Grant on May 24. Meade's (Grant's) army was then close to the North Anna River. He would soon reach a site called Cold Harbor farther south. This place would be anything but cold, and it would become the place where more Yankees would die in several hours' time than on any other field during the war. Later, the name, when spoken, would cause much anguish.

Lee was to the northeast of Richmond, anticipating Grant's movements. General Bragg and Mr. Davis now shifted their attention toward Drewry's Bluff and Fort Darling eight miles to the south. Butler was completing the disposition of his troops.

"Charlie, where's your brother?"

"He's with Beauregard near Drewry's Bluff, Captain Lynn. I'm not sure what unit. He just said they'd have to stop him. Butler, that is."

"They do have to! And they'd better!" said Lynn. "We're still outnumbered."

"Well, Harold wouldn't take me. Your sister took me to that fight west of Richmond two months ago. We weren't afraid. And I'm even bigger now. I'd have shown those Yankees." James looked at Charlie Gills. He was nearly six feet tall, a gangling teenage boy with curly hair and flushed cheeks.

"How old are you, Charlie?"

"Thirteen. Does it matter?"

"Well, my sister Emmie said how fine you are. And I believe she told Harold to keep you out of the war. We need a few young men left." He saw Charlie scowling at him, but he thought this was much-needed advice to a fearless young man.

"They're fighting now," said Charlie. "Hear that rumbling?"

"And that growling and coughing sound is the cannon," said James, smiling wryly. "We'll head for the Capital. It's high up there. Maybe we can see what's happening." They started walking quickly toward Capitol Square. People around them were heading in the same direction, and James heard worried voices as they walked.

"If they push Beauregard back, they'll be in the city," said one man.

"Well, I'm leaving with my family," said the other.

"Why aren't you out there fighting?" said the first.

"I make harnesses for Lee. He needs me, I'm told. And that's a young man's fight out there. The Yankees are getting close to Staunton now, too. We get food from there. God help us if the valley's lost. Sigel's burning homes and farms right now in the valley. It's become a total war. Yankees everywhere. If Petersburg falls, and we also lose the Shenandoah, we'll really starve. And we don't have much to eat right now."

James was suddenly aware that his family was being threatened in Staunton. "God, can we take any more?" he asked himself. "It's been one battle after another."

"There's smoke out there," shouted Charlie. "I wonder what's happening."

It was starting to rain. The morning fog had cleared, and for a while, the smoke from the battle to the south could be seen. Clouds then rolled in, and James couldn't help but imagine that the soil on the battlefield near Drewry's Bluff was being washed clean of blood by the raindrops. He wondered if this were also happening at Spottsylvania to the northeast, where a horrendous battle was still being fought.

Large numbers of battle casualties were reaching the city, and the walking wounded were everywhere. James had been told that thousands of men had been admitted to Chimborazo Hospital and that rail cars were arriving one after another, filled with sick, bleeding men. The Federals had had even more casualties. "What is it like for Grant's soldiers?" he wondered. "Probably much like it is for ours—they just hurt."

James passed the corner of the War Department building. He was deep in thought and almost knocked down a senior officer who was hurrying toward a carriage. It was General Bragg, advisor to Davis. He was smiling, and for the moment, his grim visage was gone. "Captain, I've seen you here before. It's Lynn, isn't it? Railroads and rolling equipment?"

"Yes, sir. It is," James replied.

"Beauregard's winning at Fort Darling, and Meade's army's moving away from Spottsylvania. We're winning, Captain." James could see the light in the general's eyes as he continued. "And Sigel's been stopped at New Market on the Valley Pike. He's retreating north. It was General Breckenridge who stopped him. A good man. And a veteran. He was the vice president before Lincoln took over in the North. He received help from some two hundred VMI cadets. Brave boys. A number of them were injured, and about ten died in the fight. We'll have to remember that. They fell among some good soldiers." He hesitated a moment, rubbing his brow, deep in thought. "Unfortunately, Grant'll replace Sigel, I suppose. We can probably beat him again if he's left in command."

"Thank God we won, sir," said James. He was thinking about his family. They were safe for the moment. "My family lives in Staunton, General. They probably saw those cadets go through town. Earlier in the war, these boys went west from Staunton with Stonewall Jackson. It was back in '62. Now they've been back fighting again."

"And a number have died!" said the general. "But they've helped our cause. And after that fight south of here today, the open door there to Richmond is now locked. I hope." He was pointing south. "I believe Butler'll be back in the Bermuda Hundred soon, and maybe Beauregard can keep him there. I'll bet that vain politician isn't smiling now."

Both Butler and Beauregard had lost many men. The Confederates had attacked, and the Federals were finally driven back into the Bermuda Hundred. This is a spit of land bordered by a loop of the James River to the north and the Appomattox River to the south near where it flows into the James. Beauregard's entrenched troops to the west of the Federals were like a "cork in a bottle." It was an ignominious defeat for Butler's men.

"Sergeant, did I hear you were in that fight at New Market? We're proud of you!" said Annie Lynn smiling. She was in town with her mother. The sergeant was a big man with broad shoulders. Annie saw that his blackened face was pale, and his arm was in a sling with a large red spot covering the torn sleeve. But his smile was radiant as he saw a pretty woman addressing him.

"We won it, ma'am. It was a tough one, but Sigel's been stopped for a time, I'm sure. Our people were jeering as he started north, I was told."

"And who's this fine young man, Sergeant?" Annie saw that he was having trouble standing, and she helped him sit on the carriage step.

"This is Billie McClain. He's not feeling so well right now. He and I were both hit in that fight. It was a shell that came close. Perhaps you can help us, ma'am. There aren't many doctors left in town, I'm told. They've gone north now to New Market. We came back to town on that wagon over there." He nodded toward a rickety old wagon across the street.

"You can both come to our home, Sergeant," said a voice behind Annie. "If we can't care for those who fight for us, what can we do?" Ann Katherine Lynn had suddenly appeared from around the corner of the store. She was smiling until she looked more carefully at Billie. "He's pale as a sheet, Annie. You'd better help him into the carriage. Why, he's just a youngster!"

"But there's a man inside!" said the sergeant firmly. "He saved my life when that shell exploded."

Annie and Momma helped them both into the carriage. Billie blushed as Annie assisted him up, then climbed in beside him and held his hand. "You're beautiful, ma'am," he said softly. "And thank you very much for helping us." He looked up at her eyes. "Thank you!"

"You're fine, too," she said. "And we're proud of you. Both of you!"

"We'll go back to town later, Sergeant," said Momma. "We'll notify your units then. We'd better get this young one home first. I have several daughters who are fine nurses. We'll find a doctor later." Momma cracked the whip, and Nellie started for home. She knew the way well.

"This sure beats a wagon, ma'am!" said the sergeant, smiling.

Billie McClain awoke in the early morning hours. The pain in his arm and at the side of his head was intense. He knew he had been groaning, and he thought he was dreaming as he remembered how the Lynns had worked over him the night before under an oil lamp in the small cottage behind their home. He could remember the soft eyes of the woman who had worked with him, scrubbed him clean, and gently bandaged his wounds. She had then sat with him and talked in a low, droning voice, comforting and encouraging until he fell into a restless sleep.

What did she say? he thought. He couldn't remember completely. *It was partly about books and things. Also, she talked about her family.* He suddenly opened his eyes. She was still there. And she was beautiful. He could hear the leaves rustling outside, and moonlight was coming in through the window. "What time is it?" he asked.

"About 1:00 A.M., Billie. You go back to sleep," said Emmie. He could see her warm smile in the dim light. She had put her hand on his uninjured arm. She could feel him tremble. Billie knew, though, that this was not from pain, but from the overwhelming sensation of the touch of a handsome woman. Her voice was soft and caring.

Emmie kept her hand on his arm. He could hear the sergeant snoring across the room. He thought about the battle and the incessant noise of the guns when they had charged. He could see others fall. Then the explosion. It was to their right and very close. He suddenly knew he'd also been hit. There was numbness in his arm and face. It didn't hurt yet, but he was bleeding. He helped a man nearby who was kneeling, holding his arm. It was the sergeant. They had staggered a few steps from the spot, when a second shell struck very close to where they had stood a moment before. The force of this shell threw them off their feet.

The sergeant rose slowly, helped Billie to his feet, and supported him as they slowly returned to their own lines. The sergeant kept saying, "Thank you, son. Thank you. You saved my life. That last shell would've killed me sure." Billie then thought about the wagon ride and the pain.

Emmie heard him groan and murmur several times. "Too many memories," she said to herself. Then her patient fell into a troubled sleep. "He'll get well," she decided. "His body will. I'm not sure about his mind and the memories." She took several deep breaths and stared at his pleasant face. Then she thought about her own family. "We've been through so much," she continued softly. "So has this young man beside me. And he's barely fifteen now."

At New Market there were 830 Federal and 575 Confederate casualties. Forty-seven VMI cadets were wounded, and ten were killed. These were relatively small numbers compared to the total losses by the South, but the courage of these young men, not fully grown, created a legend. To this day, each spring at the Virginia Military Institute, there is a solemn review to honor the cadets who fell at New Market. In other regions of the South, many Union and Confederate men were similarly lost. Perhaps these solemn reviews, also, honor these soldiers, as well as many others, North and South, who died during this tragic conflict.

The Battle of New Market was a minor event as far as the numbers of men involved in the fighting. But the effect was great. It allowed a vital wheat crop to be harvested and the western end of the Virginia Central Railroad, the supply line east, to be protected. If the battle had been lost, Lee would have been forced to weaken his army at Spottsylvania to protect his line of supply, and Grant in May 1864, might have prevailed.

The Southern ranks in the Shenandoah had not only been lithe but very deficient, yet General Sigel had been defeated at New Market just west of the Massanutten ridge. General Breckenridge was in command there. He was now ordered to join Lee's army. He arrived at New Cold Harbor on June 2 and was deployed near Turkey Hill, a half-mile south of the road to Old Cold Harbor. He was a veteran corps commander. The buildings of the capital could almost be seen to the west, and church bells were heard when the guns were quiet.

Breckenridge went forward with the support of two of General Wilcox's brigades, and the hill before him was cleared of Yankees. This was the right flank of Lee's line. His artillery now controlled the bottom land south to the Chickahominy River. Only cavalry was beyond that stream.

In the evening that day, Lee received a telegram from General Imboden in the Shenandoah. General Hunter, who had replaced Sigel, had driven the depleted Confederate forces from Harrisonburg. It might now be necessary to send Breckenridge back to the valley and further weaken Lee's thin line defending Richmond. Staunton was again in jeopardy of being taken and destroyed. Yet, the capital had to be saved.

"The Yankees are coming again," Kath's father told his family.

"They're just a few miles to the north."

Uncle Wen wrinkled his brow and breathed deeply. There was a look of pain on his face. "We have no one left to fight for us!"

"We have some cavalry forces close," said their friend, Robert Raymond.

"Can they stop twenty thousand Union veterans?" asked James Lynn. No one answered. The family sat there looking stunned. Kath saw that even her mother, who usually could see light beyond a wall of hopelessness, looked defeated.

CHAPTER XXXVI
Those Ragged Men

Captain Lynn was startled by a tremendous thunderlike rolling sound. It came from east of Richmond. Since a general attack by the Federal army was expected at any moment, he had remained at the War Office throughout the night, sleeping in his chair. It was terribly uncomfortable. He had finally moved to the floor, using a small cushion for his head.

Sleep was difficult, at best, but, in the early morning hours, he had drifted off among troubled dreams. The heat was intense, and it had been raining. He and the rest of the city were now suddenly awakened by the loudest firing of guns ever heard in Virginia. He shook his head, trying to think clearly. For a moment he didn't know where he was.

The evening before, he had spent an hour with Sarah Robertson and her family. He and his fiancée had briefly tried to plan a date for their wedding. "We can't be married now," she had said. "How can we with Richmond about to fall? Lee's outnumbered almost two to one." She shook her head sadly. "We may be retreating tomorrow—if our line is broken. Oh, James, why do we live at such a terrible time? Annie, your sister, has hardly seen her husband. Where is he now?"

"I don't know, Sarah. I hope he's not on the front line with Lee. He may be. And Harold Gills. He and Emmie are engaged. He's still with the State Department, but I think he's up there with the army. Possibly he's with Hoke's men. I understand he led them just west of Gaines' Mill near New Cold Harbor. Hoke was with Beauregard until two days ago. A peremptory order was sent to Beauregard to hurry him north to Lee. He came here to Richmond by train—the Richmond and Petersburg line— then marched east. Cavalry had been holding the region near Cold Harbor until Hoke's troops arrived. That was the firing we heard yesterday." Sarah nodded her head knowingly.

"Gaines' Mill was where Lee won that big fight in the Seven Days' battles back in '62. Back then, the seven days of fighting were only an introduction to what we're seeing this year. Lee's and Grant's armies have been in combat daily for almost a month now. Huge battles. And thousands killed," said James.

"It may be ending soon, if Grant breaks our line. You stay out of this, James! Please!" She had a pleading look in her beautiful, soulful eyes. "Please! Please!" she begged.

James suddenly held her in his arms and gently kissed her cheek. "I'm sorry, Sarah. I'm only a soldier. I go where I'm told. For the time being, I'll be at the War Office. After that, who knows? We'd better go in now and see your family. The rain's soaking everything. If it continues, maybe there won't be a battle at Cold Harbor in the morning."

Sarah looked at his face and saw lines of sadness. "And God help my family in Staunton," he continued. "The Yankees are marching toward the town. They'll be fighting there in a day or two. Or sooner. General Imboden's been pushed out of Harrisonburg by Hunter. That Yankee's the man who hates all Southerners. And he's not far from my family's home right now. Only fifteen or twenty miles north."

"He does hate us!" Sarah had retorted. "And he was born of a Virginia family."

The guns to the east of Richmond continued. It was a frightening sound. The entire Union army had attacked. The rain had stopped, but the watershed to the west of Old Cold Harbor had created bogs and small lakes. Everything was wet. As the shadows of night had begun to fade, Lee's ragged men had stood ready in the mud. They formed a sprawling thin line between Grant and the capital. After the first cheers and shooting of muskets, the crash of firing intensified over the whole line of battle. It swelled and lessened, crescendoed and diminished, as Grant tried to break through anywhere and everywhere.

In the afternoon the day before, James had taken a dispatch to General Lee's headquarters. He had then visited with friends in Brigadier Evander Law's Division, and finally returned to the city. These men had been ready and were positioned just north of the road to Old Cold Harbor. They were now at the center of the battle. He wondered how they were faring. "They're entrenched, but if they're overrun, they may all be dead soon. Or now!"

James shook his head. "I probably should be there with them. It's sad. We fight for what we think. But are we right? It doesn't matter, though. We can't stop fighting. That's up to powers above the average poor soldier." He suddenly was thinking about Sarah. "She hears the firing, too. I wonder what she's thinking now. Like me, though, it probably doesn't really matter."

The firing seemed to be fading a little. Sergeant Johnson rushed into the office. "I have orders for you, sir. You're to accompany Reagan, our postmaster general, to Lee's headquarters. You know the way. You'd better hurry, sir."

They rode toward New Cold Harbor and Lee's headquarters. Lines of ambulances were hurrying back to the city along muddy roads trodden by many feet and deeply rutted by the movement of heavy military equipment and other vehicles. The cast-off flotsam of war covered their path—hats, buckles, pans, forks, all kinds of things.

Along the way, flooded cooking fires, spits, and parts of tents stood as lonely sentinels where an army had rested perhaps the day before. Lee's men had spent last night in deep, wet trenches, standing ready to repel the Yankees. Now sodden, dirty, defeated soldiers caked with mud, the walking wounded, passed by in small groups. Some hobbled, others were helped along, many were in wagons from which a red fluid oozed like blood from the scuppers of a wooden ship in battle. Some of the men were bandaged, others bleeding from open wounds. Arms were in dirty slings, and many heads were wrapped with stained cloths streaked with red.

Unbeknownst to Reagan's small group, the Southern casualties were relatively light even though the two armies were very close together during much of the battle. In the Confederate trenches, the Union officers could be heard commanding their men to continue forward. The soldiers themselves realized it was futile. Lee's defensive position was strong and held by veterans who could not be broken. Over seven thousand Federals perished in about an hour. In a somber way, it would be a victory for the South.

It was only a few miles to the headquarters of the Army of Northern Virginia. Judge Meredith and Judge Lyons, prominent citizens of Richmond, accompanied Postmaster-General Reagan. James, being a lawyer, talked briefly with these men, then moved ahead of them, leading the way. James could hear them commenting on the dishevelled hordes along the highways. He knew that these soldiers were the disorganized casualties of any battle. The fighting troops were forward, desperately holding the battle line.

James and the others finally arrived at their destination and found Lee alone except for a single orderly. The thundering went on as repeated volleys were exchanged, and furious artillery action continued.

Reagan questioned Lee about the great activity of the artillery. "Yes, more than usual on both sides," said Lee. "This does not do much harm." He pointed to the infantry lines where Reagan had thought musketry was like the tearing of a sheet. "That's what kills men," continued the general.

"General," said Reagan, the Texan, "if he breaks your line, what reserves do you have?"

"Not a regiment," was the answer. "And that has been my condition ever since the fighting commenced on the Rappanannock." Lee's eyes were firm as he explained. "If I shorten my lines to provide a reserve, he will turn me; if I weaken my lines to provide a reserve, he will break them."

The general looked tired as he thought about the condition of his army. "Some of my soldiers have got scurvy," he said. "And my men need food—meat and vegetables. Some of them are even eating the roots of the sassafras and the wild grape. They're desperate. And they're exhausted from constant fighting and marching." James saw Reagan and the judges squinch up their faces. They mumbled some reply about seeing the commissary general on their return to the capital.

Reagan also queried Lee about his exposure to the shelling and even musket fire. "Your headquarters are so close. Why? The army'd be lost without you!"

"My generals are as good as any commander ever had . . . but still it is well for me to know the position of our lines . . . "

Lee had nodded to James on his arrival, then the senior men had stood off and talked. Finally, Lee had gone in and written a note. It was handed to Captain Lynn and directed to General Bragg. The orderly told him to go back immediately. James turned his horse to go. "Thank you, son," Reagan shouted as he rode off.

"They're coming into the city," said Papa to Wen and Aunt Suellen. Momma had made bread from the recent wheat harvest, and while the house smelled wonderful, the news was devastating. They had heard the sounds of the guns the day before to the north. They had prayed that somehow the Yankees would be delayed.

It was June 6, 1864. The Confederate cavalry had been defeated at Piedmont, eight miles north of Staunton, and their commander, Gen. W. E. "Grumble" Jones, killed. Now, a day later, Gen. David Hunter's men were entering the town. He had set up headquarters at the Virginia Hotel in

Staunton and had met with the mayor and members of the town council. They had been told that the people and the educational institutions would not be harmed, but all manufacturing facilities, warehouses, army goods, and things vital to the Confederate war effort would be destroyed. His name from that time on would be an anathema to the citizens.

Ann Lynn was in the backyard, tending the wounded soldiers. Billie McClain was feeling much better and eating huge amounts of food. The sergeant, though, two days before, had taken a turn for the worse with a bad fever. Momma felt his head. *He's finally improving,* she thought. *And Billie's well, thankfully. I hope his family received my letter that he's recovering. But those guns yesterday. I hope these men are safe if the Yankees come. I wonder if they even take boys as prisoners when they've been fighting.* "Billie, we may have to hide you." She was now mumbling in a low voice. He didn't hear her.

The letter about Billie recovering had been signed by all the Lynn family in Staunton. "Youth!" Papa had commented. "He'll be back at VMI in no time." He and Billie had spent much time talking about marching and tactics. And Papa had praised the cadets many times for what they had done at the beginning of the war. They had helped train an army for the field. Now with Hunter approaching, he, too, wondered if these soldiers would be safe at their home.

He also worried about his own children. "Where are Kath and Annie?" asked Papa.

"They're in town. They're trying to buy shoes for Dee, using an outline they drew of her foot," answered Sue. "She had big holes in both of her shoes."

"I'd better go look for them," said Papa. "Wen, you stay here with the women."

"I will," he answered as he nodded his head. Then he turned to his wife. "Suellen, why did they go just now? They knew the Yankees were close."

"It was quiet this morning when you and James were in the fields. I'm sorry. I thought it was safe." Her face was ashen. "The wheat was harvested, and I thought you weren't worried. I should have known. And I shouldn't have let them go. I'll never forgive myself. Oh, God, let them not be harmed!"

The heat seared Katherine's cheeks as she ran. Annie's hand squeezed hers like a vise. The nails dug deep into the flesh. She pulled her sister along the narrow alley dwarfed by high brick walls, which rose toward the sky like cliffs. They were between a store and a warehouse. Kath's eyes burned from the acrid fumes, and her chest heaved as she inhaled the smoke and hot gases. "We've got to reach the street, Kath. Run! Run!" shouted Annie. "Don't you dare stop, my little sister! Or I'll grab you by the hair and pull you out."

Kath had no intention of stopping. "We're almost there," she struggled to say. Her hand was twisted and sore from Annie's grasp. Suddenly, like a crash of thunder, an explosion pushed out the walls behind them. Bricks, parts of the roof, and moldings from the wall were crashing down close by them. It was like a mountainside falling.

They finally emerged, blackened and sore. Kath's face was bleeding, and Annie was limping. She had twisted her ankle. Dishevelled and angry, they ran headlong into a Union officer. He had heard their screams. "Why were you there? Damn you!" he shouted. He suddenly realized it was two young women. "We destroy buildings. Not people," he said quickly. "Why were you there?"

"We were just trying to get home," answered Annie. She was breathing hard, and her eyes were tearing from the smoke. She hadn't realized this was a Federal soldier. She opened her eyes and stared. Her face was suddenly twisted and angry when she saw him, but there was beauty in her dark eyes and the outline of her face, which he noticed immediately. "You're a Yankee! I hate you! I hate you!" she shouted. He saw that her clothing was singed and covered with soot. "You're burning our town. I hate you!" she continued. She had walked up to him and was pounding his chest with her fists. "I hate you!"

The officer put his hands to her shoulders and shook her gently. "I'm sorry, ma'am. We have orders. We don't like it either. And we're only destroying military equipment and army things. I am truly sorry, ma'am."

Annie looked up at his eyes. He told the truth, she was sure. "Why must it happen? These are good people." There were tears on her cheeks.

"We have to! Now I have to get you to safety." His voice had become a little more harsh. He turned to the private close by. "Take these women up the street a ways. Keep them safe. They're under arrest until I come for them."

"Yes sir, Captain. This way, ladies," said the private. He was smiling.

Kath saw the captain wink at the private as he marched them off. Annie was ahead of them and didn't see this or realize that the captain was smiling again. He whispered to the private, "I'll see them home safely when this is finished."

As they walked, smoke was swirling around them. Kath imagined this was like what one would find in the angled corridors of Hell. The sky was now darkening, and flames lighted the street with an eerie glow. Other buildings were burning. She saw that the newspaper office was gutted, and the printing equipment was in the street being broken up by soldiers.

Annie was still sobbing. Her town was being destroyed. She was a prisoner. Also, she had received word that her husband, John, may have been captured. He had accompanied a General Ransom to Drewry's Bluff to fight a politician named Butler. James was trying to get details. "Oh, God!" she said. "Please keep him safe. And keep my brother safe, too."

Papa had headed for the town. He quickly saw that the streets were filled with Union soldiers. He returned toward his home, then went northwest to the valley where he and Wen had planted crops. The wheat had been harvested, but corn was growing. He planned to reach the town via the north side. Mounted men suddenly rushed out of the woods nearby the narrow path that he was following. "Halt!" came the command. "Halt or we'll fire!"

He stopped and turned. He held his arms well up in the air to show submission. A horseman was coming fast toward him. The man held a sword in his hand. It was raised high as if to strike. James Lynn tried to protect himself. The blade struck hard across his arms, and the horse's hoof hit his leg. He fell to the ground. He was aware that several men had dismounted and returned to where he lay. "He's not dead," said the man. The soldier had a black hat and blue uniform. "He's just a civilian. Probably owns that field over there. Well, we've destroyed that. It was only corn. Should we take him in, sir?"

"No. Just leave him here. We have enough prisoners. We don't need a civilian. And he probably lives hereabouts. They'll find him."

James heard the troops ride off. He reached down and felt his foot. There was a tender swelling over the top near the ankle. He suddenly realized both arms were bleeding. The left arm had taken the main force of the blow. "It's cut to the bone!" he mumbled. "If he'd had a heavy sword or a saber, I might have lost the whole lower arm. It would have come right off. Oh, God, maybe I am lucky!"

As he twisted his foot, there was a sharp pain near the ankle. "It hurts terribly! But I'm alive." He struggled to tie his handkerchief over the deeper wound on the left. "That's certainly hard to do," he said. "And just minutes ago it would have been easy." The bleeding seemed to have slowed a little. He felt exhausted. "I'll just rest awhile." He fell back, then everything went blank.

It was a warm night. The glow of fires in town cast shadows over the landscape. Ann Lynn stood on the porch of her home, her eyes searching for her husband's return. Hopefully, her daughters would be with him. Dee was clinging to her side and sobbing. "They'll be safe, won't they, Momma?"

"We pray they will, dear." Momma's voice trembled a little. "Someone's coming, Dee. It's a carriage. Run tell Aunt Suellen and Uncle Wen." Dee rushed inside. "It is a carriage," Ann Lynn continued. "James wouldn't have come that way. And there are soldiers behind. Maybe he's been arrested. There's probably martial law in town."

Suellen arrived running. "Who is it, Ann?" she asked. "I see a man and two women in the carriage."

"It's me, Momma," shouted a voice. "Me, Annie. Kath's here, too. Are you all right?"

Momma didn't answer. An officer in blue was stepping down from the carriage. "Good evening, ma'am. I'm bringing your daughters home. I'm Captain Merritt with General Hunter. You'd better keep these ladies inside. They were nearly killed in the fire, and my men almost shot them when they ran out of an alley."

In spite of the report, Annie was smiling. "We're fine, Momma. Just fine." Kath had run over to her mother and hugged her. She then felt Momma's comforting arm on her shoulder.

"Captain Merritt knows all about you, Momma." Their mother looked at her daughter with surprise. "His uncle is Doctor Stevens," continued Annie, "whom you met at Gettysburg. He's heard all about your cooking and what you did for the soldiers there. He wants to thank you."

"I do want to thank you, Mrs. Lynn. My uncle sent glowing letters to my family about you. Perhaps we can talk later."

"May I invite you in, Captain? Your men may not want to wait, though."

"We're ordered to make a short reconnaissance west of here, ma'am. We should be back in an hour or so. Perhaps I can visit then? It's very nice to meet you," said Captain Merritt.

Ann Lynn took a deep breath. "I met many fine people in Gettysburg, Captain. Your uncle was a special friend. A kind, wonderful man. Please visit us later. We have a little tea. But there's no coffee. I did make bread today, though. My children like it."

"I'm sure I will, too," he said, smiling. "And I have a little coffee. I'll bring that. And I must tell you what my uncle wrote me: 'Time passes too slowly when friends are apart.' He really wanted me to visit here. I can see why. I'm sorry it's at such a trying time."

"Your bread is wonderful, Momma." The captain smiled as he heard Mary say this. She had at first stood in awe of the Yankee soldiers. As they rode off, she continued, "They don't seem so terrible. They're just people."

"In town they seemed terrible," murmured Annie. She had been standing in the background. Momma had noticed how the captain's eyes had kept straying in Annie's direction. Though soot-covered and with hair uncombed, she looked lovely. "We were lucky to find someone who knew the Lynns," her daughter continued.

"But he was kind to us before he knew that our name was Lynn," said Kath. "He is nice, Annie."

"He does seem nice," Aunt Suellen said. "But Ann, where is James? I'm worried, too. I hope he hasn't been taken by the soldiers."

"I certainly hope not, Sue. And we don't dare search for him. Someone else could be lost." She tried to smile, but her face became shaded with worry. "There are many thousands of soldiers here now. And they aren't our men. Most are nice, but some are not. I hope Papa's safe. I pray he's safe!"

Several hours had passed. James raised his head and looked around. The moon above was bright. There was smoke and the glow of the fires to the east. It was a while until he remembered what had happened. A sturdy rough branch was close by. He used it as he struggled to stand.

"Well, I'm up," he grunted. "Now to try to get home." He staggered for what seemed miles. It was actually only a part of a mile. He reached a road close to his home. In the distance he saw a familiar figure. It was Mr. Mentron, Mark's father, his daughter's good friend. "Mentron, help me. Please help!" Papa was desperate, but his voice was shaky. The man didn't hear him. He shouted again. This time Mr. Mentron heard.

"My God, James, what happened? You're hurt. And bleeding." He rushed toward James Lynn and helped him stand. "What are you doing out here? There's martial law now, I've heard. You could be shot. Were you?" He looked more carefully at Papa. "Who hurt you?"

"I was looking for Annie and Kath—trying to get to the north side of town. It was in our fields down there." He pointed. "A troop of cavalry. I'm not sure whose they were. I know there are troops other than Hunter's coming this way from the west. They've been destroying miles of the Virginia Central tracks." He groaned as he tried to stand on his left foot. "You'd better get me home, John. I do feel weak."

"Good that it's only a short distance, James. I can see that your ankle's terribly sore. You'd better lean on me. That's the way. Let's go home," said John Mentron.

"My husband, James, was hurt, Captain. Not real bad, but bad enough. But I think he can come down a little later with Emmie's and Annie's help," said Mrs. Lynn.

"Emmie stitched the wound, Ann," said Suellen. "She did nice work. They're holding cold packs of well water on the foot right now. They'll also put a tight bandage around it and over the ankle. That's what Annie told me. James'll almost look like new."

"He's lucky to have such good care," observed the captain.

"He had cuts on both arms, Mr. Merritt. They'll heal though. I'm sure you've worked with many wounded men."

"We have, Mrs. Lynn. Too many. It never seems to stop. I'm sorry it was one of our cavalry patrols that did it. There are sharpshooters around, and a few of our soldiers have been hurt that way. Also, you have some organized units close by. It's still a war. Unfortunately."

There was silence for a moment. Momma thought it better not to pursue this further. Both sides were to blame. And sometimes civilians got in the way. "We have some good bread here." Kath was coming into the parlor carrying a platter. "Please try it, Captain Merritt. And thank you so much for the coffee. We haven't had real coffee for a long time. Thanks ever so much."

"Tell us more of Dr. Stevens, Captain," said Suellen. "Ann has spoken so often about him. He was unusual. He's way ahead of his time, I'd say. With all the fighting, we need good doctors. Unfortunately, as you said."

"He is unusual. He's been caring for the wounded for many, many years. He's now with Grant. Where, I'm not sure. I suppose he'll retire after the war. He's older now, you know," said Captain Merritt.

"Old in years," said Momma. "Not in ideas or knowledge. When you write, send him my best wishes. His life means much to me. We were good, good friends there in Gettysburg."

Hunter's army was joined by Generals Crook and Averell. They had come from farther west and destroyed long sections of the Virginia Central tracks and the rolling equipment in that region. These combined forces marched toward Lexington.

"They're gone," said Uncle Wen. "Thank God! But, James, you should see the destruction. The smoke's still rising and fires keep smoldering. Stores are destroyed or looted. And our factories, mills, foundries, railroad station, all gone. Just rubble. The *Vindicator* fared better than the *Spectator.* They'd hid their presses. You heard about the *Spectator* from Annie and Kath. The other's presses are now printing news again. About those 'Yankee fiends.'"

"And the fields have been trampled or burned," said Emmie. "Crops just destroyed. Including ours. Maybe we can replant, though. We'll help, Papa."

"At least the schools and charity buildings are standing. Hunter kept that promise," said Suellen. "And the Stars and Stripes are gone. I watched them put up the Confederate flag earlier over the town hall."

"We're in the Confederacy again," said Papa smiling. "But I feel sorry for Lexington. They're about to be invaded."

"Perhaps it won't be worse than what we've had," said Momma. "And they didn't find our soldiers back there." She pointed toward the little cottage behind the house. "Some of our walking wounded in town were made prisoners, I understand. And they weren't armed."

"That's sad," said Suellen. "But Breckenridge is back in the Valley. Maybe he can stop those monsters."

"Hunter has nearly eighteen thousand soldiers now, Suellen," said Wen. "I don't think Breckenridge can stop him. He has only about three thousand men. They can skirmish and slow him down. But he'll take Lexington."

"I hope not," continued Momma. "One bit of good news, though. Mr. Green, the schoolmaster, is returning, James. Now you can do more teaching at the Augusta Female Seminary. Adult students. You'll like that."

"Green's been hurt, I've heard. Then he was a prisoner. It may take him some time to get started here again," replied James.

"He lost a leg," said Robert Raymond. "He's alive, though."

"And anxious to get back," said Momma.

"And Mary Baldwin's worked her fingers to the bone to make a fine school, James," said Robert.

"It is a fine school. She's done a wonderful job. She was a student there once."

"I'd like to teach," said Dee.

"You will," said Emmie, laughing. "After you grow a little."

"I'm getting bigger." Dee was a little angry. "See!" She stood up.

"You have grown," said Momma.

"I know Mary Baldwin," said Suellen. "She was sensible and went to the Reverend Doctor McGuffey at the University of Virginia for advice. He's helped with the curriculum."

"She's building an excellent institution," their father added. "We in Staunton can be proud—if we survive the war."

Lexington was taken. The Virginia Military Institute, the pride of the South, was burned. Charred, roofless walls remained. The home of Gov. John Letcher of Virginia was in Lexington. He had encouraged guerilla warfare, and sudden raids by Confederate irregulars to harass Hunter's wagon trains had angered Union soldiers. In retaliation, the governor's home was destroyed by fire.

Lee now detached his Second Corps under the command of Gen. Jubal Early. It was ordered west to the Valley. Hunter, though, made plans to move east, and his troops scouted the region to Lynchburg. In mid-June 1864, his main army crossed the Blue Ridge Mountains and lay siege to that city.

Breckenridge delayed Hunter's advance, but he could not stop him. Early, though, had moved quickly. His troops joined Breckenridge to defend Lynchburg. Hunter made "light attacks," but he decided the city could not be conquered. This was a humiliating defeat for the North. Hunter finally withdrew and moved west. He was deep in the enemy's land, with a long supply line. Also, he was facing first-rate troops. His army now headed for the Kanawha Valley in West Virginia. The upper Shenandoah Valley was soon free of major Federal forces.

Hunter's retreat gave much satisfaction to the towns he had passed through and destroyed. " 'Old Jube' is a fighter," Robert Raymond said proudly. "Now that Hunter's gone, maybe Early will be a second Jackson and go north." He did.

But there was other fighting in mid-June that worried the Confederate high command and President Davis. Grant's Second Corps under General Hancock had reached the James River and his troops were crossing a wide part of that stream by pontoon bridge. This joined Wilcox's Landing to Windmill Point on the south shore. Also, W. F. Smith's Eighteenth Corps had gone by water up the James River. These troops reported to Butler at the Bermuda Hundred. Lee anticipated that Grant would finally cross the river, but he could not be sure how many troops would remain north on the Peninsula.

Lee's main force was still entrenched to the north. His lines extended from Malvern Hill to White Oak Swamp. He reasoned that the Federals would possibly attack Richmond from near Long Bridge on the Chickahominy. They didn't, in fact. They were headed from a back door to the capital through its twin city, Petersburg. Beauregard was there. But he had only three thousand men to resist the Federal's sixteen thousand.

Lack of rations, inadequate maps, delays by various commands, mixed-up orders, and overly cautious generals saved Petersburg. Also, the courageous men in the trenches there would give Lee time. It was June 15. The next day, Beauregard stripped the Confederate defenses at the Bermuda Hundred and brought these troops south to the city of Petersburg, increasing the number of defenders to fourteen thousand.

But two more Union corps were coming up—Warren's and Burnside's. The battle was still in doubt. The Union army had an astounding opportunity. Petersburg, a vital railroad junction and manufacturing city, was within its grasp. An attack in force would have collapsed Southern defenses. The attack was fragmented, though, and only a few Federal divisions near the battlefield were used. Still, the outnumbered Confederate troops were pushed hard. They were hurt, but they held. There were losses of ground in the outer perimeter, but Petersburg did not fall.

Finally, on June 17, Lee was convinced of the danger. A. P. Hill and R. H. Anderson were ordered to the beleaguered city. The fall of Petersburg, and the capture of the Confederate capital, which seemed so likely and had been possible, was not accomplished. The war would now continue for almost another year.

CHAPTER XXXVII
The Twilight Begins

The Shenandoah Valley had been roughly treated. In many communities, there was much to burn and take. This was true at Staunton.

Prior to the war, the town had been a transportation center with five stagecoach lines. A major railroad, the Virginia Central, connected it with eastern communities, including Richmond. There were saw and grist mills, factories that made wheeled vehicles, shoes, blankets, boots, and clothing. With the war, it became an army freight station, food storage depot, training center, and a source of fresh horses. Workshops and storehouses were built. Ammunitions and weapons were stored there.

In June of 1864, usable supplies were seized, and the manufacturing and storage facilities were destroyed. The Yankees departed from there on June 10. Even though Staunton had been despoiled, other communities had suffered more.

Lee was "pinned" at Petersburg. He could not maneuver in the open and destroy armies as he had done so often in the past. However, he could send lieutenants to trouble Lincoln and the people in the North.

Gen. David Hunter, the man "vindictive . . . toward all Southerners," had been defeated. He had moved beyond the Valley to West Virginia. Confederate troops commanded by Gen. Jubal Early were back in the Shenandoah in strength. He was a shrewd and hard-fighting soldier. Early may not have had the fire of a Stonewall Jackson, but he was dependable, and he was ready.

The Valley was strategically unique for the South. Confederate troops moving north were placed in the heartland of the Union. In contrast, Federal soldiers going south moved away from the sensitive area of Richmond, the capital, the center of government, and the prime manufacturing region of the South.

"Tough 'Old Jube' will be with us soon," said Uncle Wen. "We're done with Hunter. I hope."

"He's retreated to West Virginia," said Suellen. "In town, they say he's gone for good. And Early's close, I'm told. Maybe we'll see some of his men soon. They're veterans. They've been fighting the war for us for years."

"Some of the original corps commanders for Lee have been injured," said Papa. "We're lucky we have good men like Early who can take over. Ewell and Longstreet are both recovering from injury or illness now. I'm not sure which. Maybe if God's good to them, they'll be back with our troops later on."

Wen thought a moment. "Early commands Lee's Second Corps. R. H. Andersen and A. P. Hill command his First and Third. Those two are both in front of Petersburg, trying to keep Grant out of the city. And more important, they're trying to keep him away from Richmond. Also, each army has probably dug deep trenches by now. If they have, frontal attacks will be suicide. Both sides knew that."

"We have a letter from James," said Momma, smiling. "He's Major Lynn now. It's a recent appointment, he says. And he's still with the War Department, thankfully."

"I hope he stays there!" said Suellen. Her face looked intense, and she closed her eyes as if thinking. "I believe he's relatively safe in Richmond for the time being, and our armies still need supplies. A major, though. He's too young. But we must send him our congratulations. I'll write tonight."

"We'll both write," said Ann Lynn smiling. "And I, too, hope he stays there." She held up the letter. "They're under siege now, he says. And City Point on the James just south of Richmond is becoming a huge supply depot for the Yankees. James mentions that you can almost see that depot from Capitol Hill in the city. At least on clear days."

"Read part of the letter, Ann," said Wen.

Momma read:

The Yanks are heavily entrenched here. Their lines run from north of the James near Richmond to east and south of Petersburg, a distance of over twenty-five miles. Technically, it's not really a siege since Petersburg isn't surrounded, but it's a type of war that professional soldiers tell me we probably can't win. With Sherman wreaking havoc in Georgia, it's become a fight of attrition—and starvation.

Sherman's troops, by the way, were badly hurt when they attacked our men at Kenesaw Mountain north of Atlanta. When he's stopped, though, he's sidestepping like Grant did here in Virginia. One of these days, he'll besiege Atlanta, I suppose, as Grant has been able to do at Richmond and Petersburg.

We've already been cut in half at the Mississippi. Now we're being cut in quarters. You people in the Shenandoah Valley play a vital role for food. Keep planting and replanting. We need what you grow. And the area near Petersburg is becoming a wasteland. Trees are being cut for fuel, for roads, forts, and many other things. Grant has captured the railroads coming from the east into the city.

Lee's still in Petersburg. He receives supplies via the Richmond & Petersburg, the Weldon, and the Southside railroads. But they're vulnerable now, too. Grant has tried to move west and capture the Weldon tracks, but he has been driven off with big losses. Fortunately, our losses have been relatively light. I'm sure that doesn't give much satisfaction to those who are hurt, and we still have thousands hospitalized close by. Will keep writing. Your loving son, James.

"That's a nice letter," said Suellen. "He sure seems to know what's happening. And he sounds in good health."

"I just hope he stays out of the fighting," said Papa. "With miles of railroad track gone, he's still vital for the war effort. The railroads have been his main job at the War Office. It's the Tredegar Works in Richmond that provides much of the steel, as well as the finished rails. He's worked with the Tredegar people for years. He knows their problems. And food and other supplies for an army would be difficult to transport without the railroads. I believe James is making a real contribution. I hope he's not needed in the front lines."

"Those are our men," Annie shouted to Kath and Mary. "Thank goodness they're back." She turned to her aunt. "But, Suellen, they certainly look worn out."

"They are. They've marched many miles. I would be worn out, too. But they're a proud group, I'd say." They all continued to watch as General Early's divisions marched through Staunton.

People were cheering; ladies were throwing kisses and waving handkerchieves and small flags. Summer flowers decorated guns and blanket rolls. Canteens clinked against bayonets, and men occasionally left their ranks to steel kisses from pretty girls. One kissed Katherine. She stood embarrassed for a moment and blushed. Finally she laughed and said, "That was fun."

Convalescing soldiers stood with the crowds along the way and shouted wishes. "Go get 'em, boys," a man beside Kath called at the top of his lungs. It was so loud that it frightened her. Then she, too, started cheering.

Uniforms, what there were of them, were patched and soiled. Felt hats of all shapes, some decorated with blossoms, covered heads. Arms and parts of legs of many were wrapped with bandages or stained cloth. Suddenly a band began to play: "We are a band of brothers, and native to the soil, fighting for the property we gained by honest toil . . ." Whole regiments joined in the singing, and the people in the crowd sang too. For a moment they all forgot the dirt and the burned buildings and the thousands who would never come home.

Regimental battle flags were unfurled. They rippled in the wind. Many were dingy and torn. "Look how dirty they are," said Mary.

"They're the pride of a regiment, though," said Annie, smiling. "They lead men into battle. Many have died for those flags. It's what they mean, not what they look like, Mary. It's like that old blanket you used to treasure. It wasn't what it looked like. And may I say, it didn't look like much!" Annie smiled compassionately. "It was what it meant to you." Kath saw Mary's eyes sparkle. Her little sister understood.

"There's a man here to see you, Papa," said Emmie. "He has lots of gold braid. It's General Early. He told Momma and me that Tom Jackson always talked about your work at Lexington and Washington College. He wants to meet you." The sounds in the distance, the shouts, the cheers, and the music were easily heard.

"Come in, General. Please come in," said Papa, smiling. Emmie knew her father was delighted.

James and Jubal shook hands. "It's nice to meet you, Professor. And those are our troops marching through Staunton. Not the Yankees that you saw so recently."

"Thank goodness it isn't those beasts," said Papa. "And it's a pleasure for me to meet you, too, General. I'm sorry you find me in bed. My ankle still hurts from my injury, especially when I walk. But my arms have healed." He held them up and pointed with pride. "Emmie did the stitching."

"Good job, Emmie!" said the general.

"Thank you, sir," she replied. There was a delicate blush to her cheeks. "We women are learning."

"You have learned," he said. Early then turned to James Lynn. "I'm

343

sorry you were injured, but with this fine care, it looks like you're healing. Thousands of soldiers as well as civilians have been mauled by this war these past few years. And I'm always visiting friends at hospitals. Many haven't made it through, though."

Jubal looked at Papa's arms. "Your good wife told me you were cut down in a field close by—unarmed and all. That is sad. Perhaps in the dark, they thought you were holding a gun. One never knows. And at night, it's hard to tell friend from foe. That's how Stonewall was killed. And Longstreet injured: by their own men."

The general hesitated, then continued. "We're heading north. It'll be forced marches for some days. Maybe we can worry Lincoln a little. If we had the men, we could do more than just worry him. Perhaps, though, we can take a little of the pressure off Lee."

"I hope so," said James Lynn. "And, General, when Grant moved south from Cold Harbor and crossed the James toward Petersburg, why didn't Lee hit him then? He was a long thin animal for a while. And vulnerable. Was Lee fooled and in the dark? He's getting older, you know. Like me!"

"Our government and the people of Richmond have been asking about that, too. It's not true, though, that he was fooled. He knew that Grant would have to cross the James. His problem was balance. How many of his divisions should be moved to defend Petersburg. What he did represents the consummate defense. If you check numbers of troops north and south of the river, Lee's balance was just about right.

"Since the beginning of May, we've been outnumbered. And with my corps ordered to the Valley, Meade's and Butler's Federals have had a better than two-to-one advantage. Yet Lee still controls both Richmond and Petersburg. And even more recently, he set that trap for the Yankee cavalry—their Third Division commanded by Gen. James Wilson. It was brilliant. They were tearing up miles of the Weldon, the Richmond & Danville, and the Southside tracks both south and west of Petersburg. Wade Hampton's cavalry with Rooney Lee's help pressed them from the rear, while "Little Billy" Mahone's infantry hit them in the front. Then Fitz Lee's horse came in on their flank. It was a rout. I've received a note telling me I should have been there to see them run.

"Now we have miles of tracks to repair, but wagons have taken over at those points for a while. It takes more time, but it's possible."

"Can we win?" asked Emmie.

"We have to keep trying," answered the general. "Well, I have to go.

We have to find Sigel somewhere that way." He pointed north. "We'll beat him. Then we can worry Lincoln. Also, we need money and supplies. Now that I've seen what they've done here in Staunton and Lexington, maybe we can do the same in the north."

Momma entered the room with a tray. "We have some good tea here, General," she said, smiling. "And bread. Please stay a while longer." She set the tray down on a round table covered with a flowered cloth. The sun sparkled off the silver teapot.

"Thank you, Mrs. Lynn," said Early. Emmie poured the tea while Momma insisted the general sit in a deep, upholstered chair. "This feels wonderful," he said, smiling. "But I can't stay long. I'm just here to pay respects. But thanks." He then got up and seemed ready to go. He was sipping a cup of tea, with a buttered slice of Momma's cornbread in his other hand.

"Try these cakes, too, General," said Emmie. "They were made from our own sorgo."

"Thank you, Emmie. I will." He looked into her eyes. "I knew you were the young woman who does that stitching of cuts and wounds. We thank you for what you've done." He looked around the room and smiled. "And we thank you all for what you're still doing."

"Momma taught me to close wounds, General. We've had lots of practice with three years of war. Someday it'll be over. Perhaps we can win, if Europe supports us."

"That's been an unknown since the beginning, Emmie. May some of our dreams come true, though," said the general.

Momma saw that his dark beard was coarse and scraggly, but there was an intensity of feeling in his deep eyes. "May God go with you," she said. She had thought when she first saw him that he was only a hard-fighting man, determined to destroy the enemy. Now she knew differently. He also had a mind and heart to complement his appearance.

"Thank you ma'am," said the general. "It's nice to be in a home with a family. May God be with you, too!"

Macy Windover, Annie's friend, sat with Emmie and Annie in the dining room. The oil lamp flickered occasionally. Oil was precious, and the flame was kept low.

"John's been captured, Macy. It's official now. I have a letter, in a woman's hand. Not his. He's been very ill. Maybe pneumonia. He seems to be getting better, though. Thank the good Lord. I want to go to him, but

Papa won't let me even try. God, please make him well. Please!"

"At least he's alive, Annie. My brother died in that Wilderness battle in early May. He's buried there somewhere. We heard of his death, but we don't know where his grave is," said Macy.

"Isn't it terrible," said Emmie. "Family and friends, just gone. Give our sincere sympathies to your family." She patted Macy's hand gently, then squeezed her arm. "And, Annie, John will get well. I know it in my heart. He's strong. And good. We all need him, and we love him. He'll be back, I'm sure." She touched her sister's shoulder and smiled. "You'll see."

"I hope that makes a difference," said Annie. "There are thousands of prisoners North and South. And many haven't lived. It's frightening." Her eyes were distant. "I do pray you're right, Emmie."

Kath sat in the background and listened. She didn't speak. Later that night, she said a silent prayer for both families. The war seemed so near. *It's all around me*, she thought. *We win one battle, then there's always another. And more soldiers die. And Papa and Annie and I were almost killed, too. What more can happen?"*

James sat with Sarah in the garden beneath a large magnolia tree. He noticed that her family's once-beautiful home had a seedy look. The grass was untended, the bushes in the yard were untrimmed, and moldings and iron work had not been painted for a long time. They were holding hands. There was a rumble of cannons in the distance, a sound so frequent that neither noticed it. A pale moon was struggling to shine, but fluffy clouds kept getting in the way.

"My father's nearly well," said James. "And I've told you about Annie and Kath. They were almost killed in the fires. And I still worry about John. He's evidently been terribly ill. I think he may be jailed at Point Lookout near Washington. I'm not sure. Old Jube Early is headed that way. Maybe he'll free all our prisoners. Lord, I hope so."

"Do you know for sure if John's there?" asked Sarah.

"No. But I think he may be."

"James, that's why I worry about you. They'd love to capture a major from the War Department. You stay out of that fighting."

"I go where I'm told."

"Yes. I know. You've said that. But you didn't have to go to Burkeville when that column of Yankee cavalry was about to attack it."

"Maybe Lee knew it, but I didn't. That's an important railroad crossing. The Southside and Richmond & Danville railroads cross there. We can move supplies either to Petersburg or Richmond from that point. We have a lot of hungry men—and horses. The Danville line brings food and fodder from the huge growing areas of the Piedmont in North Carolina. It's vital," said James.

"Well, you almost got killed again. Just look at your face. Another scar. That wood splinter almost hit your eye."

"I think it did. At least it stuck in below my eye. It went right up under the skin for about an inch. A shell hit a pile of railroad ties. The splinters flew all over. One of the men beside me got it right in the chest. Then he died—poor man."

"What about poor James? And poor Sarah? And it's too bad Emmie couldn't put in the stitches like she did several months ago when you were gallivanting around during the Dalghren raid—in the trenches to the west of here. At least it didn't drain pus when she did the sewing."

"Well, it's stopped now," he said, smiling. "And I'm nearly well. It sure was sore for a while until that pus drained. But in that fight at Burkeville, it was boys and old men with clerks and a few railroad people who held off the whole division of Wilson's cavalry. A good defense. Finally, Rooney Lee helped us, and those Yankees were driven off. They did a lot of damage, though. We're still repairing the tracks. And it's a vital region."

"I'm not interested in the fighting. We have plenty of that to watch. I'm thinking about you. Perhaps you've forgotten that fever. Your whole face looked like an overgrown tomato. The doctor here said you might even die. Maybe you've forgotten that little interesting part of the story," said Sarah.

"But I'm well. Let's forget about it. Your mom was nice enough to keep me here with you. And it's been wonderful. Now I have to get back to the war. I'm still a soldier." She looked at him longingly, wondering what to say—how to change his mind. "You'd better tell me about Lee."

"He's certainly been a fine leader. When he sees a hole in Meade's line, he hits it hard. Other than that, he's on the defensive. And he's kept the Yankees mainly east of Petersburg. They keep trying to extend their lines south and west." James looked very serious. "Nasty little battles go on constantly. And the trenches are close over much of the perimeter. In places, you can almost throw a stone from our lines into theirs. Thankfully, the roads to the south and west are still open."

"I guess a lot depends on Old Jube to take the pressure off," said Sarah. Her voice was soft. "He fought that battle at the Monocacy River in

Maryland, and won. His men have 'legs and grit' the papers say. They go up to thirty miles in one day. He collected $20,000 cash at Hagerstown, and $200,000 from Frederick City in Maryland. Evidently he threatened to lay the towns in ashes."

"He's wrecked and burned mills and workshops and torn up miles of the Baltimore & Ohio. That does my heart good, after what I've seen the Yankees do to our railroads. Also, Early burned the home of Governor Bradford of Maryland and has turned toward Washington. I can imagine the panic," said James.

"I suppose they won't have time for our men in prison there," said Sarah. "Early's probably being followed by a swarm of Yankees right now. I hope he can free some of our soldiers, though. Including Annie's husband." She thought a moment. "At least Lincoln's city will face some of the problems we've seen here—raw troops and convalescents in the trenches. And the people in the city will be frightened—like we've been many times. It'll serve them right. Those Northerners have been safe for the whole war."

"So have I been safe," said James.

"Not really," she answered. There was a growl to her voice. She looked at the jagged scar on his cheek.

On July 11, Early neared the defenses of Washington. His men marched up the Seventh Street Road toward the arsenals, the Treasury's stores of gold, and the U.S. government offices. Men, boys, and soldiers just released from hospitals stood in the trenches to repel them.

As Early looked at Fort Stevens ahead of him, he was hoping he would see the Confederate flag run up over the Capitol dome very soon. Only a few troops now stood in his way. The defenses seemed weakly manned, but Union skirmishers were before him, and a thin line of blue soldiers was observed entering the works. He thought they were first-rate troops.

On the parapet, a tall gaunt man, hollow eyes filled with sadness, large ears and a prominent straight nose, stood watching as the first shots were exchanged. The attack, though, was suddenly stopped. Further reconnaissance was needed. Early sent his cavalry to find another window or door into the city.

The morning sun cast golden light over the Capitol dome on July 12. Lincoln was back at Fort Stevens that afternoon. Haze, dust, and the wilting heat of summer obscured the Confederate skirmish lines coming forward. They seemed to sway and undulate across the parched fields. They were struck by a withering fire, but the Union pickets were pushed back. Men were fighting before President Lincoln's eyes, and lead and fragments of shells wrenched bodies and tore arms and legs. Lincoln had seen men go off to war. He had seen them in pain where they were cared for in hospitals. Not until this moment had he witnessed men falling and dying in battle.

While he watched, an officer close by was struck down, and Surgeon Crawford of the 102th Pennsylvania was hit in the ankle. Another young officer near Lincoln was said to have shouted, "Get down, you fool."

The fortifications were too strongly held, and that evening, Early retreated toward Leesburg on the Potomac. His wagons were laden with booty and money. Nobody stopped him. The chain of command for the troops in Washington was indefinite. Four separate subdivisions of the army had taken part in the defense of the capital, and Grant was too far away to make decisions.

The organization and command of troops to deal with the threat from the Shenandoah now received careful attention, but Lincoln delayed the appointments of the several officers proposed by Grant. This indecision gave Early another opportunity. He defeated Crook at Kernstown and destroyed the railroad facilities at Martinsburg. He went north to Chambersburg in Pennsylvania and burned the town, then threatened Moorefield and Cumberland in Maryland.

Finally, Gen. Philip Sheridan was sent to the Shenandoah. Thus began the highly successful Valley campaign by a Union army. Meade (Grant) was at Petersburg, Sherman in Georgia, and Sheridan now in the Shenandoah Valley. These were capable, professional officers. Their leadership foreshadowed Southern defeat. The days of the Confederacy were now numbered. The twilight of the Confederate States of America had begun.

In almost every doorway of the South, there was darkness. For most, gaiety and enthusiasm were long gone. The household inside had learned to do without many of the things that had been thought essential before the war, such as coffee, sugar, wool, medicines, and meat. Even writing paper was in short supply. Numerous letters were written on paper stripped from walls, using inks made from berries. Railroads were shattered, and steel, too, was in limited supply. Salt, so vital for the preservation of food, was now rationed, and the government took over saltworks and guarded them with armed troops. Desperate citizens scraped old barrels clean for the salt.

General Lee was well aware of these problems. He limited his use of such items whenever possible. Meat for his own table was eaten only twice weekly. His usual fare was cornbread with cabbage, boiled in water. The South was growing weary, but the "bitter year" of 1864 would last three more months.

There was still devotion to the cause, especially by women. They had agonized as family members were led off to war, never to return. And they had denied themselves many, many things, while they struggled to keep hope alive, and clothing on those they loved. Atlanta had fallen in early September, and when the population was ordered away before the city was burned, a "beautiful girl," according to one witness, "was seen to step among her companions, and . . . (kneel) . . . to kiss passionately the soil she was about to foresake."

Not only were economic resources disappearing in the South, but manpower was desperately limited. Men were needed not only for fighting and farming, but also for manufacturing the products needed for war. In contrast, Union cities were "bathed" in luxuries, and replacements for losses were readily available. Both regions, though, were distraught with sadness over the death and injury of so many fine men, young men.

Westward toward the West Coast moved a steady stream of hardy people, immigrants and natives alike. Council Bluffs, Iowa, in April, May, and half of June 1864, had 75,000 men, 75,000 cattle, and 30,000 horses pass through. The Midwest and Northwest had become vast growing areas. Advanced technologies were being used for growing and harvesting crops. These helped supply food to the huge Federal armies in Virginia and Georgia. The migrations west portended the future development of America, but large segments of the people to the east were still trying to survive a terrible war.

Though Petersburg was now the target of the main Federal effort, the capital was not free from Yankee threat. Fort Harrison, eight miles south and a little east of Richmond, was attacked by a determined Union enemy. The effort was contained, and many wounded were transported to the city.

"That's a lovely dress, Emmie."

"Thank you, Macy. Momma and I made it. It's from drape fabric we brought from Amherst."

"Well, it's pretty. But where is Annie?"

"She'll be down," said Kath. "She just received word that John has died. It was a terrible blow. Evidently it was from his sickness."

"I think she knew it was going to happen," said Emmie. "She's stronger than we realize. She cried. But then she put her shoulders back and said, 'He wouldn't want me to do a lot of grieving.' Momma then hugged her gently, and they both went upstairs. I heard them rereading the letter."

"She's writing her sister-in-law now," said Macy. "Annie told me that she wants to meet her soon. I'm sure she will do it somehow."

"She is strong," said Mary Jane Revels, smiling. It was a wan smile, and her gray eyes were deep and sad. "We all get news, and so much of it causes pain. I'd like to be with Annie, but I don't think I should force myself upon her just now. Give her my love."

"I will," said Emmie.

Aunt Suellen looked at the women around her. The young ones, Mary and Kath, had grown so much over these past years. They were almost a foot taller now, and much more mature. Suellen had at first been overwhelmed by the news of John's death and had cried for some time. Her cheeks were still moist, but she now returned to the parlor and listened. This was her family, and these were her friends.

She and Wen had wanted children, but they had not been so blessed, and their lives had been lived as part of another family. *It's been a good life—mostly,* she thought. *Perhaps, though, from the beginning, it was ordained that this life should be lived for others. And we're to be supportive and encouraging, and give of ourselves.* She looked again around the room at the serious faces. *So young. So lovely,* she thought. There was a moment of silence.

Suellen smiled. "I'm proud of all you young women. Perhaps we ladies have a deeper sense of what the South means than men have. And we all have suffered so much. Our men have given much, but so have we. Somehow, though, we'll get through this terrible time. And the Lord has a way of mending things if we're patient. We may have to find new ways. It will be hard, and it will be different, but what isn't?" She saw that they were all listening.

"Macy, you lost a brother, yet you can give love and help to others. Mary Jane, you lost a father. He died gloriously, Wen has told me. But it hurts just as much. Kath and Mary and Emmie, your brother, Henry, died at Gettysburg, but you still continue giving of yourselves. Also, your

351

brother, James, has been injured three times, and your father was struck down in that field close by. He still hurts from the injury.

"And, Kath, you and Annie were almost killed in the fires here. You've all suffered. Yet look at you. Daily you work at the hospitals, help in town, and do some of the work in the fields. I'm proud of all of you. You're an honor to this land." Suellen was on her feet, and there were tears in her eyes. She was patting the girls' shoulders, hugging the younger girls, and looking carefully into the eyes of all these young women. They were friends. "We're all proud of you," she continued.

"Thank you, Aunt Suellen," said a soft voice. It sounded caring and distant. The women stood up. It was Annie, standing behind Suellen. Annie's eyes were hollow, and her face was pale. She was dressed in black.

CHAPTER XXXVIII
A Crumbling Dream

Not all households in Richmond were poor. Some folks lived in luxury, even during troubled times. The Yankee spirit of entrepreneurism was very much alive, and some of those who accepted the risks became wealthy. It was a bright fall day in late September 1864. The sky was mostly blue. Bleakness for a few seemed to have blown away like clouds before the wind.

"Will you have some more lamb, Captain?"

"That's an excellent roast, Mrs. Avery. Yes, I will." The table was laden with delicacies. "The wedding was beautiful, ma'am. Your daughter, Lavonne, was a lovely bride."

"But your eyes were on Marie, weren't they, Captain Lauren? She's the apple of my eye, too." Mrs. Ellen Avery smiled warmly and looked softly into the captain's eyes. Her bright blond hair was plaited into a loose chignon at the side of her neck. "Mr. Avery has been fortunate during this war. Those oysters were from the blockade fleet that made it past Mr. Lincoln's boats and into port at Wilmington. And we have some fine port and Havanas for you men after dinner."

"Marie and I enjoyed the play at the Richmond Theater two nights ago, Mrs. Avery. That was an enthusiastic crowd singing 'Dixie.'"

"Did you enjoy the ice water from the silver water cooler there? The papers say it was especially installed in the Dress Circle for the comfort of patrons. It's meant to be enjoyed."

"We did. But I worry about laughing and playing at a time like this. Our muddy trenches are a stark contrast."

"Well, many people high in government are enjoying the relative quiet around Petersburg now," said Mrs. Avery.

"And my men find the weakest excuse to laugh," he continued. "They do it even when snipers' bullets fly over their heads. Horse racing, cards . . . ," he looked across the table at Marie, "pretty women they've known. They talk about all of these."

Captain Lauren sat back and sipped the steaming coffee from the cup that had just been placed beside him. He looked pleasantly at Mrs. Avery. "I saw Judah Benjamin strolling down Main Street. Our secretary of state didn't seem to have a care in the world. He twirled his gold-headed cane and chewed on his big cigar. He didn't forget the ladies, though. He smiled at all of them as they strode past. Then he met Reagan, our postmaster. They smiled and laughed and walked on together."

"Benjamin and our navy secretary went on a little outing downriver the other day. Good Madeira, and all kinds of fine things," continued Mrs. Avery. "They used a borrowed army ambulance for the trip. Even Reagan, since his wife died, has been socializing more. And he and George Trecholm have become good friends. All these men eat well. Memminger was our previous secretary of the treasury, a thankless job. Happily, Trecholm gets along with Congress better. But he's no more successful than Memminger was."

"Lee says they're all 'busy eating peanuts and chewing tobacco.' Maybe he's right," said the captain, smiling.

Jefferson Davis was the political leader of the South. He was a lonely man in the truest sense. He now struggled to find answers for a crumbling dream. The rumble of guns was never far off, and windows rattled with the sounds. Thin men manned his battle lines. They could not be beaten in an open fight, but they were being slowly whittled away nevertheless.

These men fought not for Davis or a political cause, but for themselves and for Lee. Outside Davis's office, people would stroll by and talk. He could hear their voices beyond the windows. Many were shabbily clad with rags and makeshift clothes. As the sky grayed and colder winds came, teeth chattered because overcoats and warm clothing were gone. Hands were thrust deep into pockets, and torn strips of cloth covered shoulders for a little warmth. Some would laugh and say it was draped around them as a shroud. But business went on, and folks would meet and discuss and gossip—an eternal human trait.

"Sarah's been transcribing a brief for me, James. It's upstairs. I'll get it. I need your thoughts." Mr. Robertson left the study. The gas jet over the chair flickered and hissed.

James heard the ladies talking beyond the door. He could just see the edge of the glass chandelier, sparkling in the dim light. Mary, Sarah's companion for many years, was on the far side of the table, and several of their friends sat with them. He could hear Mrs. Robertson's musical voice. He sipped the sherry from a crystal wine glass, and relaxed and listened. Not all was war.

"Why would she marry that man? He has no formal schooling." James didn't recognize the voice.

"He reads much, and is intelligent enough to become an officer. He's capable, I'd say," said Sarah.

"His manners are poor. And he licks his fingers, I understand," said another voice. "And he's hoping to be a professional soldier. If he does, she'll never see him."

"And that leg. He lost it at Gettysburg," said Mary.

"He's a hero, I'm sure," observed Mrs. Robertson. "I don't know about his manners at the table, but he's gentle and kind with women, and he has a wonderful smile."

"But he has no fortune, no money. She'll scrub her fingers to the bone if she marries him," said the first voice. James felt like peeking through the door to find out who was talking.

"Oh, shoo," said Mary. Her voice was shaded with a touch of sarcasm. "It's not his leg or his fortune. It's the man. And I agree that he's gentle and intelligent. As for being a soldier, there have been good military men down through the ages. It isn't their looks. Bonaparte wasn't handsome. A little man, but he became an emperor. He wasn't lucky. But he was a superb leader, and the consummate soldier. Some of his officers rose from the ranks and now have descendants who rule as royalty. Bernadette was one of them. His family sits on the throne in Sweden."

"And just look at Andrew Jackson," said Sarah. "A good Southerner. He came from the back country, I'd say—primitive and unrefined. But he became president. It isn't only money and appearance. It is the man inside."

"Maybe she's thinking about me, when she says that," said James, smiling.

A firm voice came from the dining room. James thought it was Mary's mother. "God's nightshirts, ladies, a man with four fascinating maidens talking about him is fortunate indeed. Now you just pay attention to your own men. Stop talking about others."

"We will, Momma." Mary sounded sincere. "But it's fun. Delores, tell us about your beau. He wears stays, didn't you tell me? Like we do?"

"Now, Mary, that's personal. He is kind, considerate, and capable. I worry about him at times, though. A painted young thing approached him at the dance last week. She looked like a ghost, but he seemed interested. I had to push her away."

"She had better stay away from your man," said Mary, smiling. "You have claws like a tiger. I remember that girl you fought when we were children. Her face looked like it had been scratched by a cat afterwards."

James heard the ladies giggle. *It's nice to be fought over,* he thought. He then smiled and dreamed, and sat back as they continued to talk.

Suddenly Mr. Robertson returned. He shut the door. "I have it, James. It was hidden below some of my papers upstairs. This is about the Tredegar Works that have done a lot for our people. But you know that only too well." He picked up his glass of sherry and sipped slowly, enjoying the taste. "Recently they've done even more. Now they're wondering about some of the legal implications."

"I know they've sent missions to unfought regions in Virginia. And in those areas, they've increased production of corn, bacon, and many, many things. But I guess they compete with our government's impressment of food. Seddon and Davis aren't very happy about that," said James.

"That's right. And Tredegar's been more effective than the government. Those who raise food, also profit. We have to protect what Tredegar's done," said Mr. Robertson.

"What do you find is the problem?" asked James.

"Bartering. Money is so devalued. People have boxes of it, and it's almost worthless. Tredegar trades nails and spikes for food—and even minerals. Then they've fitted out blockade runners to bring in clothing and cloth for civilians. They ship out cotton for trade. Some question whether their ships meet the required fifty percent of cargo as arms. Then there are their leather tanneries. And leather is vital. But the quality of government-made shoes is very poor. They certainly haven't pleased the men who wear them. And Tredegar complains about the quality. They wonder what they can do about it."

"I know. Our men trade them to captured Yankees as soon as they can." James hesitated for a moment. "Mr. Robertson, what should we do with all these prisoners? Grant won't trade our men for his now. And our people are starving. These captured Federals are a real burden. How do we feed them?" James wondered.

"Poorly, I guess. But they eat as well as most of our people do. And the Union doesn't do much better for our men in their prisons. Camp Douglas, near Chicago, is one of the worst in the North. Recently, they lost one of every ten of our men in the space of one month."

"I know about those prisons. My sister, Annie, lost her husband that way. Pneumonia, I guess."

"That's sad. At least we share what we have with the Yankee prisoners. But we have our problems with our own people who are hungry. The women in the arsenal by the James River finally struck. They were so cold and hungry that I don't blame them. They couldn't work."

"I know. I was there to give a speech. Those women were so pale and starved that we had to do something. We finally distributed potatoes, bacon, and wheat flour. We also gave them lumber from the barges. And now there's a store just for the ordnance people—with reasonable prices," said James.

"The pillars are falling, James. But none of us can stop trying. You and I at least have food on our tables."

"I appreciate that. But we are being slowly stifled. It's insidious. Grant's taken the Petersburg & Weldon Railroad now. The Southside's still open. If it falls, so will Petersburg. And another problem, the governments in Mississippi and Alabama are both resisting conscription," James added.

"So do our foundries and factories like the Tredegar Works."

"They have to. The Tredegar battalion did fight with Lee when Meade's army moved toward Richmond last May, but the men decided they were needed more in the factories. They deserted and returned to work. Meade was stopped, but the production of steel and other products was cut significantly. We need those men where they are—at the Tredegar Works. Lee has pleaded with Davis to keep them there. He also has told this to Josiah Gorgas, our ordnance chief."

"That man, Gorgas, is a wonder. We'd have lost the war by now without him," said Mr. Robertson.

"Even when our mercury supplies in Texas and Mexico were lost, he found alternative methods," said James. "He uses chloride of potash and sulphuretted antimony to replace it. I'm not sure of the process, but these chemicals come from around Richmond. The mercury is needed to make rifle caps. You can't shoot a rifle without the cap. And he gets the copper, which is needed from old turpentine and applejack stills. He is remarkable."

"But we're being cut down piece by piece. Being stifled, you said. Old Jube Early's starving men hit Sheridan hard at Cedar Creek in the Valley. They ripped the Yankees apart at first. Then they were so hungry that they stopped when they reached the wagon trains and gorged themselves," said Mr. Robertson.

"I know. It gave Sheridan time to reach his troops and start them forward again. They attacked us and captured thousands. And we lost the battle. I guess a few are reforming near Staunton, but too few to do much good."

"James, we have a report that Sheridan's burned over two thousand barns filled with wheat, hay, and farming equipment. And thousands of cattle and sheep have been taken, as well as horses."

Mr. Robertson looked very serious. He had been smiling a little, trying to deny the problems they faced. He took a deep breath, then continued: "Near Harrisonburg, not far from Staunton, a Yankee engineer was murdered. I'm not sure if it was actually a murder, but all houses in the area were burned. Oh, the terror that kind of thing causes!"

"And the hate."

"James, this is enough. We'll work tomorrow. Let's join the ladies." He picked up a cut-glass decanter from the side table. The red liquid seemed to glow in the light. "We'll pour some more sherry first. All this talk is too depressing."

It was late afternoon in autumn. A fine rain was falling. Papa rushed home from business in town. "Uncle Elmer's sick," he said breathlessly. Uncle Wen was sharpening tools on the covered walkway beyond the kitchen. Momma was assisting with the cooking. She saw that James was waving a letter that he had evidently just received.

"What happened, James?" Momma asked plaintively but with a hint of strain. "I'm almost afraid to ask. Poor Joan. My sister'll need us."

"Elmer collapsed. He's very ill."

"Oh, Lord! That's terrible!" said Wen, shaking his head. "We'll have to go and help with the farm. I'm so sorry for Joan." He thought a moment. "But she's strong. We all know that." His words trailed off to a whisper. "Is that a letter, James? You'd better read it. Elmer's getting old, and I suppose we should expect this."

"So are we getting old," said Papa, smiling wryly. He looked knowingly at Wen. "But you're right, we should expect it. And sickness comes more often now. Still, we're healthy for the moment, except for Elmer." He hesitated. "Yes, we have a letter. Your sister wrote it, Ann. There are a few words here from Elmer—scrawled and irregular. That tells the story. His arm and leg are paralyzed, and it doesn't look good. We'll have to go back.

Joan is worried. She should be. You have a fine sister, Ann Katherine. She's taking good care of Elmer, I'm sure."

"It'll take time to close our house," Momma cautioned.

"It will, but we should leave right away. We'll miss Staunton."

"I love this home. We have so many friends here now. It's become part of me," said Momma. "And, except for Henry and John, we're still alive. We've all been hurt and sick, but we have a home. Thankfully!" She gave a perceptible sigh. "With all the great battles that have gone on around us that's a blessing."

"Yes," said Aunt Suellen. She and Emmie had just come in from the back yard. Her voice was firm. "We've met so many fine people. And, perhaps, we've suffered less than many of them. They and this city will always be part of us."

"Suellen and I will pack, James. You go on ahead. Emmie will go with you. She's a gem—both with a home and with healing. I mean that, Emmie," Mrs. Lynn said.

Emmie and Papa left for Doria early the next morning. It wasn't easy during wartime. Several times they were directed to give up seats, then to wait at the stop for the next train. Also, they stood much of the way, or sat on the hard, dirty floors.

Soldiers had first choice for seats. They were nice, though. They let Emmie sit in their place. She experienced a thrill at being with all these men. It was fun. Some of them were handsome, and she realized that they all found much to laugh about. This surprised her, when she considered all the tragedy around them—burned barns, fields laid waste, chimneys standing as sentinels among the ruins of houses.

Several even approached her about being their girl. This pleased her, but she quickly let them know she was engaged and she was going to Amherst to care for her uncle. She saw her father smiling as he watched and listened to the bantering going on about her. A few scheduled trains never came, and often there was no explanation.

They even walked some of the way along the Orange & Alexandria tracks toward the next town when they heard a train was stopped there for repairs. And they hid from Yankee cavalry once. The horsemen passed so close that Emmie felt she could almost reach out and touch them. When it was all over, her face brightened. "That was frightening, but wonderful," she exclaimed. "Exciting. It was like being in a stampede. Papa, I wanted to leap up and ride with them. Men are so lucky. I'd like to be a soldier, too."

"I'm glad you resisted that impulse," he said, laughing. "We both probably would've been killed—or captured."

"Why not?" she said sharply. "At least, why shouldn't women be soldiers? We're as good as men—at least with a gun. Henry taught me. You didn't know that, did you, Papa? We may not be as strong, but we are just as determined. And we have the heart to do it. You'd be surprised."

"I am surprised, Emmie. Maybe I'm afraid to find out. And don't forget, it hurts you just as much to die. Besides, it's bad enough to have men wanting to fight. Women, too? God forbid. We need you to stabilize our angry world. You take your anger out on us men. We need it."

"Momma says you need it, too," she said smiling. Papa saw the glow of achievement in her eyes. She had gotten a rise out of him, and she was enjoying it.

"Your mother would agree, I'm sure," said Papa, grinning. With the delays, their trip took three days.

Most of the rest of the family returned to east of the Blue Ridge a week later. Annie was with them. Their trip with Momma was uneventful. Uncle Wen and Aunt Suellen stayed in Staunton to finish closing the home and attend to other details. Uncle Elmer, that pink-faced, fiery old man, who called the daughters "sweet unworldly women," had suffered a stroke. Many people call this apoplexy. He would improve, finally, but it would take months.

"It's so frustrating," he said a few days later to Papa. "Most of me is still strong as a bull, and my mind's good, but I just can't get around. I hope I'll be back in the fields soon."

There was a lisp to his voice, and James Lynn could see that food and fluids had run down over his cheek. *It's sad,* he thought. *A good man being cut down when he's needed so much. At least we can help him. And we should. He's done so much for us.*

There was great sadness at leaving so many friends at Staunton. Some of these folks, however, would remain close to the Lynns for the rest of their lives. When Kath returned to the farm, she was excited. Their dear, old house remained comfortably nestled in the rolling green countryside among copses of trees and a red patchwork of cultivated fields. Its stone walls were crested with great hand-hewn beams, which just peeked out beyond the stones. Mounted above was the weathered siding of the upper floor, topped with a steep split-shingled roof. She was at first surprised that it was still there, then realized it looked different. It seemed smaller than before.

The roof harbored the same five dormered windows, like the eyes of a big, friendly animal. Hewn posts and sills framed the familiar doors. Great hardwoods stood beyond, with angled, gnarled arms black against the blue sky. They stretched upward, the branches still clinging to the colored autumn leaves. Each gust of wind, though, blew some free, and they twisted and twirled in the air.

The flowers of spring were gone. There were no daffodils or glorious wisteria bushes in bloom. Kath thought about the lancet-shaped bunches of purple flowers that had decked the yard not long before they had left for Staunton. The bushes were still there, but it was long past their blooming.

She could see the charred walls of the house and the burned timbers of their old barn, both of which the Yankees had set afire. Fortunately, little damage was done to their home. When she entered, the rooms seemed to have shrunk. It was as if some mighty hand had compressed the stones. "What's wrong?" she asked her mother. "It's smaller."

Momma laughed. "You grew!"

Emmie ran to them as they entered. She hugged them all. "Welcome back to Doria," she said. "And, Momma, you're still fresh and wonderful like a bride. It's nice to have you here again. This is truly our home, now that you're back." She stood away and looked into Momma's eyes. "Papa and I have missed you." She looked at the others. "All of you."

"It certainly looks clean and comfortable," said Momma, smiling. "Thank you for getting it this way."

"Momma, you're to sit now while your daughters do the work." Emmie looked serious. "Kath, you take her bag up to her room. And Mary, you take those covers off the furniture and fold them neatly." She now smiled warmly. "Dee, you can read to Momma for a while, then she can rest."

"What can I do, Emmie?" asked Annie. Her face solemn.

Emmie thought a moment, while smiling at her sister. "Annie, you take care of those plants of Momma's on the back porch. They need tending and water. I'll be polishing the silver. Luckily it was hidden when the soldiers came. And the young ones"— she looked at Kath, Mary, and Dee—"can help with the silver, as well as with all the laundry that's piled up from the trip. We'll all help with that."

Emmie forgot one thing. Momma didn't know much about rest. She did sit for a short time. She always saw something to do, however, and did it. She too had changed. She looked a little thinner and older. "Now you girls are just being too nice. I'm not that old. Let me say hello to Mary. I've

missed her wonderful cooking. Uncle Jim's here somewhere. I still treasure him. I always will. Where are you, Jim? And you say that Old Will is
in the back? I'll find him." Her vigor amazed them; they knew she was
pleased to be home.

Kath's sisters had also changed. They were not only older, but they
had also matured mentally and physically. Annie had been married. Her
husband was dead. She still wore black in his memory. She tried to hide
her excitement at being home, but it poked through her "veil of grief" and
gave some of that "old" light to her eyes that Kath remembered so well.

Mary and Kath ran down to the rope swing over the little creek. It
was still there, but it, too, had become smaller in their eyes. One thing
hadn't changed. The rolling countryside, backed by the ever-present Blue
Ridge Mountains, was as vast as they had remembered. *Possibly,* thought
Kath, *it's even greater than before. Perhaps that's because I love nature so
much. It's so wonderful to have it be the same or better, and to know it will
always be there.*

Kath read more now from the large library that Papa had built over
the years. And she sat for long hours with her elders in the evening and
talked about the war and politics. She wondered if politicians thought
more about the next election rather than the next generation. She hoped
that someday she would become a statesman. She thought about that for a
while. "Or a stateswoman!" she decided.

She didn't think about the banalities of the job. Some years later she
was employed as secretary to a representative of the state legislature. She
would learn then that she didn't have the desire for politics. The job would
teach her much, but the process of trying to pass legislation was so slow
and tedious.

Through the winter, the family heard with sorrow about the terrible
decimation of the Valley. Thousands of homes and farms were destroyed.
James, her brother, still wrote long letters home: "I'm sure you know that
Lincoln has won the election. His popularity was helped by Sherman's
taking of Atlanta, and Sheridan's burning of the Shenandoah. Now 'Billy
Sherman's bummers' are marching toward the East Coast and the sea, cutting a swath of destruction many miles wide. There is rightful wrath in
Georgia toward this American Attila. It will be a long time before it can be
forgotten. Sherman, as a child, was gentle and bashful. How war changes
men!"

Robert Raymond wrote also: "James, Mr. Green is back in Staunton,
and he's taken over at the school. He likes teaching, and he's doing a good

job. A brave man, I'd say, with that one leg gone. His hair has grayed, and his skin has become leathery. He was wounded in 1863 near Chancellorsville and spent months in Union hospitals near Washington. He was later placed in a prison camp and finally exchanged. He won't fight again. He has an artificial leg, and it's very hard for him to walk. The children like him, but they miss you . . . I'll write more details later . . . "

George Morgan visited once. His missing arm caused Kath much anguish. It seemed so unnatural. She knew it caused him embarrassment, and he kept trying to turn away so that his injured side would not be seen. She remembered the night so long ago when he had proposed to Annie. "That was a happy time," she murmured. "So much has happened. And now he looks so much older."

George and Annie talked for several hours. They wandered along the paths they had walked when they were courting. He would smile wanly, then she would smile. They weren't in love, but they had both suffered much pain in the war, and they were friends. He did bring some important news. Alvin Ripon had died in the fighting near Charleston, South Carolina. His grave was probably deep in the sand on one of the offshore islands near the city.

On the farm, the Lynns were removed from most of the terrors. Many shortages existed, but all were overcome, dispensed with, or substitutes created. Aunt Suellen waxed dramatic on several evenings about their good fortune. They were spared hunger, their home was still standing, and their fields weren't destroyed.

Momma brightened the conversation further. "I have a letter from Doctor Stevens whom I met at Gettysburg. You all remember the fine young officer, his nephew, who visited us when Hunter was in Staunton? He saved Annie and Kath, and brought them home to us. Even if he was a Yankee, his words gave me hope that we can be friends again. Well, Doctor Stevens gives me even more hope. I'll read the letter. 'Dear Ann, I think about you and your family often. I was happy to hear that my nephew, Robert Merritt, was able to visit, even if it was under difficult circumstances. He was most impressed with your fine family.'"

She looked around the room. All were listening, especially Annie. Ann Lynn continued: "'I have his letter before me now. He was especially impressed with your daughter, Annie. She was strong and caring at a time when she and Kath were nearly killed. He has been working to find details about Annie's husband, John. As you probably already know, John died of infection. My nephew sends his sincere sympathies. We would both like to visit you one of these days when this great war is over. It has been hard for all of us . . . '"

Annie's eyes had been lusterless much of the time since John's death. This spark of interest in her life, by another person whom she had met so briefly, gave her hope that the future was not entirely dark. She remembered his firm hands on her shoulders. She could still see his deep concern as he looked at her frightened face. He was handsome. The whole family suddenly saw a smile crease her lips and her eyes brighten. She blinked them several times, as if pushing back tears, then looked at the family about her. Finally her face turned toward her mother. "Momma, I remember your saying that if someone is remembered with love, he never dies. I feel that way about John. I'll always love him, but I'll still go on living and meet new people. Thank you for reading that letter."

"You should meet new people, Annie," said Momma. "John would know that. We can't dwell on death. Our lives are with the living." She looked caringly at her daughter. "And we'll soon have a nation to rebuild. We need you!"

Life went on quietly at Amherst. After all the bustle of the city, Kath thought it was almost too peaceful. There was always worry about the course of the war. Fortunately, Sheridan stopped short of Staunton with his depredation, and Richmond and Petersburg still stood. This gave the Lynns some satisfaction. Also, there were rumors about peace negotiations, but Papa believed that Davis's demands for a separate South would not be negotiable with Lincoln. Some folks thought the war could still be won. The fighting continued, and men died.

Soon the conversation at Doria was directed differently. It was about marriage. James and Sarah were planning a date. And it would be a double wedding. Emmie and Harold would be married at the same time. James suggested it should take place away from Richmond. He mentioned several towns along the Richmond & Danville and Southside rail lines. "Where should it be?" Ann Lynn asked her family.

"I'm not sure," said Emmie.

"Neither am I," said Annie, smiling. "But it's wonderful. I'm so happy for you, Emmie!"

"Why not at Farmville?" said Momma. She had a dreamy look in her eyes. "I grew up there, you know. I have no family there now. They're all gone. My mother's sister lived in Tennessee, but since before the war, she hasn't answered my letters. She was ill from a fever, the last I heard. My pa died when I was young. Ma raised me and got me some schooling, but she passed on years ago from a stomach sickness with bleeding."

"That was just after we were married, Ann," said Papa.

"Yes, but I'd love to go home again. My sister can't leave Elmer prob-ably." Momma smiled. "Maybe we can entice her, though. But why not Farmville?"

CHAPTER XXXIX
The Pain of Fire

Sherman moved into South Carolina. It was there that the people had proclaimed: "The Union is dissolved." The citizens of that state now felt the full fury of an invading army. No significant Southern troops were available to resist the devastation. The Yankee line of march was outlined by smoke from a thousand fires. Cotton gins and barns became infernos. Fields were trampled, fence rails were used for corduroy roads and cooking fires, cattle and corn were confiscated, and nine of ten houses were destroyed. Columbia, the capital, would soon burn and smolder.

Charleston, also, would fall. The Eastern army's approach from the sea had failed, and the struggle had gone on for years. Now a Western army cut the lines of supply, and the city soon surrendered. Lee's defense plan for the southeast coast, which he had developed in 1862, had been successful. Defeat by water had not been possible, but Sherman's men plowing north cut off the roads to the city. This was the fatal blow.

Near Petersburg, increasing numbers of deserters were received into the Union camps. With fewer and fewer troops, Lee had to defend a longer and longer battleline. Many in the Confederacy demanded discussions with the North about peace. Lincoln considered peace only for a united country. He asked his generals to let them down lightly, and, if possible, limit the loss of life. He hoped that the South would not be destroyed, and that it would soon become productive and whole. Lincoln was generous, but unyielding. An undivided nation free of slavery was paramount.

The sun was bright. A crisp wind buffeted the train. Snow partially covered the ground, and the steel rails were rickety and rough. Momma was excited. She was going home to Farmville for the first time since the war had begun. This was where she had grown to adulthood. This was the region she had known for a lifetime. It was farming land.

The abundance of rich soil stretched to the horizon. A mist was rising from the moist ground as the heat of day beat down. Along the Appomattox River close by, black willows and mottled sycamores abounded. It was a harsh winter for the South, but this region was relatively untouched. The rail tracks throughout Virginia, though, were irregular and worn. The train bounced along like a marble on a washboard. The years had been hard, and resources were dwindling. These were difficult problems to correct.

"That's where I grew up," said Momma, pointing out toward the rolling countryside. Her voice was excited. "It's still beautiful. See that hill? My home was just beyond."

"Oh, Momma, it's wonderful," said Annie. She was beaming. "I can't believe you were a little girl once."

"Well, I was! And it doesn't seem so long ago, Annie. It was a lovely home. At least it used to be. I hope it's still there."

Annie squeezed Momma's hand. "Maybe we can visit it after the wedding."

"We will," said Papa. "And Ann, Mr. Gills, Harold's father, went to school near here, I believe. That's what his letter said. He, too, is excited about coming back. Just as you are."

"Hampden-Sydney College, James. It's a beautiful school. Patrick Henry and James Madison were founders or at least supported its incorporation toward the end of the last century. And President Harrison was a graduate years ago. It's one of the oldest schools in Virginia; it's just a few miles south of here," said Ann.

"I've heard people talk about taking the waters in Farmville," said Aunt Suellen. "There are medicinal springs here, I believe."

"I remember Pickett Springs." Momma squinched up her face, thinking. "I believe there's another one, too, but I don't know the name."

"Well, that might feel good while we're here," said Papa smiling.

"I'd like that, too," said Mary. "Let's do it while we're here. And, Momma, do I look a little like you did when you were young? I've seen your picture on Papa's dresser."

"Very much like me, darling."

The train suddenly came to a lurching halt. There were people outside milling about. "There's James," said Annie. "And Emmie, there's Harold. My, he looks handsome with that gold braid."

Emmie ran to the window across the aisle. She started to wave. "Here we are, Harold. Here we are." The window was closed because of the wind and smoke and cold. Now she opened it a little. "Here we are!" Emmie shouted.

"George Collins is with them, Emmie," exclaimed Kath. "See? He's waving too. He looks nice. I sure wish he were my beau."

"He's twice your age, Katherine," said Annie, laughing. "I'm sure he wants a more mature woman."

"Like you, I suppose." Katherine had a smirk on her face for a moment. "Well, at least he enjoyed talking to me when he and Harold visited in Staunton." She looked into Annie's eyes. "And you're still in mourning. Momma said so. You're to stay away from handsome men friends like that."

Annie made a face. "Quiet, little girl." She suddenly had a naughty glint in her eyes. Katherine knew that look.

Aunt Suellen and Uncle Wen were up in the aisle taking baggage and coats. Now the others did the same. They all headed toward the exit.

Kath pondered the difficulty of bringing goods and weapons from overseas into the ports of the Confederacy. "Our little blockade-runner ships are almost stopped," she mumbled. "That's what my brother, James, told me at the wedding." Her hand was poised over her diary. She had started it in Staunton and kept it locked from her family. The striped wallpaper in Papa's study became etched in her eyes as she stared blankly at the walls and thought.

"James said it was because most of our Southern ports are closed by the Yankee navy. Harold suggested that, too, when he spoke about the naval battle we lost at Mobile Bay. I saw that in the papers. It was a major port. Now it's gone. 'Damn the torpedoes, full speed ahead,' were the words he quoted the Union admiral as saying. Was that from the newspapers or from special information Harold has from our State Department? He still works there. I guess he should know.

"Well, does it matter? Sarah and Emmie both had those fine pieces of imported silk to cover their shoulders at the wedding. Lovely pieces, and hand-embroidered. Emmie said they had done the embroidery themselves, In private, I suppose. Not even Momma knew about them before the wedding. And Sarah had covered her shoes with what was left of the fabric."

Kath closed her eyes and visualized how handsome both brides were at the wedding. She thought about how Sarah's slippers had peeked daintily out below the escalloped hem of her dress, and how Emmie had used some of the silk to create a wonderful corsage. She slowly nodded her head as she murmured, "Old married folks now, but both are so beautiful!"

Emmie and Harold had gone to a little hotel at the outskirts of Lynchburg for their honeymoon—a place that Papa had suggested. It was quiet and far removed from the war.

Kath saw the lace curtains at the window move in the afternoon breeze. The window was open only a crack. Dee and Mary were in the L-shaped room across the hall, preparing lines from Shakespeare. She could hear their giggles as one emoted and then the other. *They may not be a Junius Brutus Booth,* she thought, *but they're learning the words.*

Kath smiled, then her face changed. "Why did James and Sarah go to Petersburg? It's a lovely city. Or it was. I'm not sure now. But it's literally almost right at the cannon's mouth. Like taking a trip to Dante's Inferno." She hesitated. "Well, everyone to their own way." She would have preferred the quietness of Lynchburg—or a remote place like Doria. The beauty of the countryside, of all the animals and flowers, were what she preferred. She recorded these thoughts in her diary.

"But what about Annie? Is she happy?" Kath had watched her sister spend a long time with George Collins at the wedding. "What a handsome man," Kath said softly. "And he, too, has lost a brother in the war. It seems that every family we know has lost someone." She put her elbows on the table and squeezed her hands together. "And they seemed so solemn at dinner. Both George and Annie just picked at their food. What will come next?"

George had returned to Richmond with Sarah and James the next day. The Lynn family members who remained had then spent the day at Farmville. There they enjoyed the waters and met the folks that lived in Momma's old home. The house was neat, but the demands of war had been harsh. The father had been injured at Petersburg, but he was still alive. A son was with troops in Tennessee.

Kath closed her eyes and thought about Annie again. Her sister had sat silently in a deep chair when they returned to the farm. It was a kind of nervous exhaustion with her limbs slackened and her shoulders bent forward. "George is a fine man," she had finally said to Momma. "But he's still determined to win the war. And I don't think he needs me. It's like there's a wall between us. We could never be happy—unless this terror ends. There must be happiness somewhere."

"There is, Annie!" Momma had answered. "Maybe it's a state of mind, but you'll find it. You have great love in your heart. And love is patient. It endures all things." She then had gently stroked Annie's hair. "Be patient, darling. Love will come."

Momma's usually right, thought Kath. *But what of Sarah and my brother? I hope love doesn't end for them when they visit Captain Lauren's home in Petersburg. What a funny place to go for a honeymoon. Right into the lions' den. And big cannonballs fall there every day. "Man-made earthquakes," Papa said!*

The quietness in the once commercial city, Petersburg, was now constantly interrupted by the crashing of guns and the marching of soldiers. There were mellow brick churches, stone bridges, stately Hustings Court House, listing gravestones behind rustic fences, elegant homes, and a memorial to the men who had died in the War of 1812.

At the beginning of the Civil War, Petersburg was Virginia's second largest city. Steel rails connected it with Lynchburg, Norfolk, Richmond, the Carolinas, Georgia, and Tennessee. It was nearly as important a hub as Richmond. Cotton mills and tobacco plants abounded. Merchants had bid for "baccer" at the auction house on old Sycamore Street, and farmers had displayed their produce from the fields. Now, steepled churches set among tall trees dotted the skyline, and wrought-iron and wooden fences still set off the previously well-ordered homes of the residents.

Covered bridges stretched across the Appomattox River to the north, and bells summoned workers to their long days of toil in the mills producing tent cloth and sheeting for the armies. The rocky, angled stretch of the river to the west provided water power.

It was here that the newly married Lynns had come. Major Lynn had been ordered to the city by his senior officer, Colonel Wright.

Sarah looked tired. "James, I'll never come here again. There were shells falling all night. One almost every two or three minutes. It was dreadful. The colonel knew we were just married. Why did he order you here? It was like that shooting gallery at the farmers' market we went to last year. One crash after another. At least those were small crashes."

"You'll eventually get used to it, I'm told. And none of the shells even came close."

"That's true. But they hit something. I heard the fire brigades all night," replied Sarah.

"Well, we'll leave tomorrow for your family's summer home. It'll be safer there, I'm sure. You're right, though. I shouldn't have brought you. There is danger, but the colonel said the city was quite safe. He was wrong, wasn't he?" James laughed, but Sarah's face was long. "I guess he hasn't come here often with the war and all. Also, I only had the two days off for the wedding. I didn't want to leave you in Richmond. Now I have several more days of leave starting tomorrow."

"I do love you, James. Even more than before the wedding. You've always been kind and thoughtful," said Sarah.

He smiled at her, then chuckled. "Even when I bring you to places where we both can be killed?" He didn't wait for her answer. "It's our being together that we both cherish, my darling. And this little cottage that Dick Lauren's family has let us use is just charming." He hugged her again. "Dick will meet us here about noon. We'll get a brief glimpse of Lee's lines out there." He pointed southeast.

"I'm not sure I want to go. But I guess I will. I promised him I would. He said it's safe." She hesitated. "His family has a lovely house—big and rambling with a fine yard." She pointed through the window.

"Except for the shell holes," James laughed. His voice was strained, but he was trying to lessen her apprehension. He looked into her eyes. They gleamed like emeralds. Then he held her gently. "Now you just stop worrying. We'll be all right." She snuggled her head against his shoulder, and he patted her back, then squeezed her tightly.

"You're right," she said. "The trees are budding and spring is almost here. We should be happy." She looked through the window. "That was a lovely sunrise today. And it's nice of Dick's family to lend us this little cottage. We're like old married people now. And for these few hours, it's felt like our own home—comfortable and warm." She smiled at him. Just then a shell exploded in the street before the house. Sarah flung herself into his arms again and hugged him hard. He saw tears in her eyes; the house across the street was in flames.

Sarah Lynn walked hesitatingly up the wooden steps. A rough railing was on one side. At the top, she could see where large pieces of the wood had been torn away by bullets and shell fragments. Mud was everywhere, and the parapet was decked with sharpened stakes that jutted forward like the jagged teeth of some great animal. Smiling faces were in the trenches to her right and left. Dirty men, covered in mud and some with clothing stained with blood, were watching.

"That's why we want you back with us, Johnnie Reb!"

"Well, you can't have her. She's ours, Yank!"

The two voices sang out loudly over the quiet battlefield. The lines suddenly exploded with calls and shouts. Sarah waved her arm, then her fingers touched her lips and moved gently away, blowing slightly and smiling as if she were sending a kiss over the lines. She saw men in the distance in blue uniforms stand and wave. A thousand faces seemed to be watching her, and telescopes and glasses glinted in the sun, observing and admiring this lovely woman.

She drew her treasured silk kerchief from her shoulders and waved it to her own men, then toward the Yankees. She tried to shout, "I love you all!" but the sound was drowned by a thousand voices.

It was almost spring. In Petersburg, trees were budding, but on the battlefield, everything was dirt and mud. James was below watching. He worried: "Will some fool now try to shoot at my lovely bride?" No one did. This was a moment of peace, and two vast armies stood watching. Soon, fighting and death in the trenches would begin again. Perhaps this peace was an omen of the future. There was deep caring within the hearts of men on each side. There was a oneness and a desire for reunification that underlay the dirt and hate and desire to destroy. Fighting and death, however, marked most moments of each long, tedious day.

It was not unusual for Southern women at Petersburg to mount the parapets and view the soldiers from both the North and South. For a moment, the viciousness and fighting stopped, and minds went to other things like love and family and home—a brief interlude in the interminable war.

Emmie stood at the railing just outside her second-floor room in the small hotel in Richmond. This was to be her temporary home until she and Harold found suitable quarters. Sarah was with her family to the west of the city. James had stayed in the capital and helped with the moving of government documents.

Rumors were rampant. Some were true. Lee was retreating. Richmond would be lost. The army was broken. All kinds of things. "Why am I here?" she mumbled. "People are praying in churches for deliverance. Next I'll probably see the Yankees marching up the hill. And where is Harold? He said he'd be back soon."

Emmie looked to the east across the Shockoe Valley, expecting to see the enemy approaching. Where Broad Street descended to the Virginia Central Depot, the lush foliage of spring was dotted with yellow flowers. Beyond, on Church Hill, the steeple of old Saint John's Church stood pristine against the sky. Smoke was curling up from the river and beginning to blot out the beauty and freshness of early April.

Wilmington had fallen. It was the last open port of the Confederacy.

Sleek ships with arms had been turned back to Nassau. Early's little army in the Shenandoah Valley had disintegrated under the pounding by Sheridan, and a new Union army under Schofield had marched inland from the east coast to meet Sherman in North Carolina.

The evening before, after hurried packing, Davis and most of his cabinet had rushed to the Richmond & Danville Depot near Fourteenth and Canal Streets. They had delayed leaving the city, hoping for word from the army. But Lee's thin line was turned. Finally, a whistle blew, and the train lurched forward, passing over the bridge and out of sight to the west.

Shutters were closed in the more prestigious parts of Richmond. With an explosion at the ordnance works, groups of unkempt men spilled out of the dives and bars. They headed for the warehouses to salvage what they could. Whisky barrels were torn open, and some were poured into the streets where furious citizens knelt to drink and save what they could. The troops from the defenses east of the city were retreating west. The townspeople jeered and threw garbage at them. Anger and frustration fed upon itself. The army had protected the people for four long years. Now this protection was expected. Mobs started fires, which spread from building to building.

Emmie watched with horror. There were few troops left to give much semblance of order. "Why am I still here?" she asked again in a loud voice. "And Harold said not to leave the room. He'd be back. Oh, God, where is he?" She thought for a long moment. "My brother said something about marching west with one of the regiments. I pray he's safe! Davis got away, though. I saw him leave on the train last night. And they've taken all the gold bullion, James told me."

Emmie looked down Main Street. There was smoke rising from the warehouse district and other parts of the city. People were shouting and milling about below. She saw a group of men in a carriage heading east out of town toward the Yankee lines. She recognized one as Old Mayor Mayo, to whom she had been introduced several weeks before. A woman in the hotel had told her he was going to surrender the city. "Surrender Richmond?" she wondered. "We've lost. This is the end. Without Lee, we can't hold out." There was a burst of flames from down near the river. Then an explosion rocked the capital. The sound echoed back and forth across the city.

Below her, a regiment of Southern soldiers was marching westward. She called desperately to them, asking what was happening. She waved a large handkerchief like a flag, but no one looked up.

Suddenly there was a loud knock on her door. It was Harold's voice. "Emmie, get ready. The Yankee columns aren't far off. They're coming. I'll get you to my family's place. They're going west to Goochland County, my grandfather's home. My family has a wagon. We must get you out of here. And hurry. We have to leave right now! There'll be more mobs in the streets after the home guard leaves. And there aren't many soldiers left. That regiment below is probably one of the last." He looked into her eyes and saw the terror. "Come, my sweet. We'll make it." He held her for a moment, then they went down the stairs.

Emmie had only a very small carpetbag for the few things she was taking. One was her wedding dress and another, her lovely embroidered silk shawl. A building across the street was burning fiercely. All kinds of vehicles were moving west. A man lay dead on the sidewalk. His face was frozen in a grim smile. She had heard shots. "He's a looter, Emmie. The few patrols here didn't wait long for justice."

"I see the head of their column off there," a tall thin man said to Old Mayor Mayo. He saw that His Honor's hair was scraggly and disarrayed. The slight breeze whipped over them like a warm blanket.

"Do we have a flag?" the mayor asked.

"I don't even have a handkerchief," said a third man. "What will we use? We don't want to be shot when we try to surrender."

"Gentlemen, may I suggest we retire to those bushes, and, perhaps, remove some of our clothing. It may not be dignified, but it's better than having this wind pass right through a big hole in the center of us. And may I say, I don't bleed well in my old age."

The men looked carefully at him. His face was worn from long years in office. He had been a good mayor, though, they thought. And this was a humbling moment in his life. Perhaps it was the most difficult time in his long and dedicated career.

One of the men removed a piece of his shirt. Another took laces from his shoes. The mayor broke off a long branch from a small tree. "Well, we're ready, gentlemen," said Mayo. "Let's get this over with before the whole city goes up in smoke. I'm afraid we need martial law now. If we're injured as we approach the Yankees, please tell my family I love them. God be with you, and bless you all for being with me."

Thus perished Richmond, the symbol of the Confederacy. Stark walls and grim ruins would be its epitaph. But it would rise again from the ashes. It would have a heart and soul once again. This would take years.

At Five Forks, southwest of Petersburg, Lee's right flank had been broken. The major supply line to the city, the Southside Railroad, had been taken. Lee had notified President Davis that he could no longer hold the city. The proud Army of Northern Virginia, a mere shadow of its former self, retreated. Richmond, too, was lost. It was being devastated by fire. The capital was surrendered to Federal troops by Old Mayor Mayo. Armed Union soldiers now established martial law. A semblance of order would soon return.

The Confederate divisions marched west toward Lynchburg. Grant's soldiers followed closely, nipping at their heels, and racing to intercept the retreating troops. Continuous skirmishes precipitated several desperate battles. Exhausted men fell or surrendered. Lee's objective was to reach General Joseph E. Johnston in North Carolina and fight on.

James Lynn opened his eyes carefully. All kinds of fearsome noises surrounded him. Men were moaning close by. Screams came from just beyond the wood-framed door. Shouts sent shivers of fear through his body: "We'll take that one next. The other one beside him won't make it. He has more than a surface wound. It's inside the chest. Bring that first one over. That's the way. And he won't even feel it. He's still unconscious." A moan came from outside the door. "It'll have to come off. The bones shattered. See. It's in pieces."

Major Lynn closed his eyes again. "At least it's not me," he mumbled. "But all those around me. They're still hurting, too." He had seen several men with their clothing partially cut off. One had a stump of a leg, which was wrapped with a dirty cloth. The other man was swathed with bandages over his arm and upper chest. His face was raw, and his head was oozing blood from one side. There were others nearby, but they were just dim apparitions, like ants partially crushed but still moving about. Suddenly he heard a terrible cry from outside.

"Stay still, Sergeant. We'll have to finish. We thought you were unconscious. You couldn't have walked on that leg again anyway."

"Not my leg, Doctor. Oh, God, not my leg!"

"Son, I'm sorry. It had to be done." James heard this. He had a sudden feeling of dimness. He tried to open his eyes again, and for a moment he saw vague shadows, then everything disappeared.

He awoke again. There was an old man sitting beside him. "Stay quiet, Major. You've been hurt." James could see a tent flap whipping above him, partly sheltering his body from the sun. It was fixed on several poles that seemed to have been quickly erected, and if the wind picked up, they would probably blow away. He had been moved out of the small home. It was still close by him. Paint was peeling off the clapboard siding. "This is the James Hillsman house, son. Hillsman's still a prisoner in the North. His family was here, though. They evidently ran off soon after the Yankees arrived. There were twenty cannons right around this spot just yesterday."

"Is this at Sayler's Creek? That's all I remember. Except I felt that terrible shock to my leg. Then I guess I fell. I had been with 'Old Bald Head' Ewell ever since we left Richmond." James looked across the shallow valley. He could see a small creek flowing below, flooded from the recent spring rains, and a low ridge beyond it. The ridge looked familiar, and he thought he saw the spot where he had stood with Ewell's men. He remembered the Union battery firing at them, and he could still visualize men falling around him. "Was it a dream?" he asked the older man.

"No, son. It was real. You can still see the dead about the field. Both ridges. But you didn't lose that leg, I'm happy to say. It's a pretty big cut, though. And you lost a chunk of muscle, too. It'll be a little stiff, but it'll heal." He looked at the soldier beside him. His eyes were kind. "I'm Doctor Harrison from near Rice. The Yankees let me through their lines to help the wounded." He put his hand on James's shoulder and squeezed gently. "Stay quiet, Major. You'd better not try to walk for a time. It'll be weeks, I'm afraid. You were talking about your new bride."

"I don't remember that, sir," replied James.

"Well, you were still half-asleep and mumbling. At least she'll be happy to know you weren't more seriously hit. Now sleep again for a while. You'll probably be transported to one of the hospitals, but I'm not sure what the Yankee doctors have planned. There are many wounded Federals here, too."

"Did we win, Doctor?" asked James.

"No! We lost. Somehow Ewell and Anderson became separated from the other divisions."

"That's what our men were saying. I was so hungry and tired that I didn't know where we were. So were many others. We didn't have rations at Amelia Court House, and we were starving."

"Well, Lee lost thousands of men in this battle. Mostly captured. I talked to Commodore Tucker, who was with Ewell. He was taken, too. Grant's men also destroyed that unarmed wagon train that was just ahead of you," said Doctor Harrison.

James shook his head. "I guess the war's nearly over. What do you think, Doctor?"

"You're right, Major. Lee can't have many men left. And Grant's right at his heels. I think he's with one of the Yankee corps near Farmville now. I'm not sure. And he still has a vast army, with Phil Sheridan riding hard just to Lee's south."

Major Lynn shook his head, then closed his eyes. He remembered his wedding at Farmville, his mother's home. He thought about his bride. "How will I get word to Sarah?" he mumbled. The doctor was with another patient now. "Well, for the moment I'll just have to wait." He felt his injured leg. It was terribly painful. "At least it's still there." He fell back. He was asleep again. The laudanum had given blessed relief from the pain and worry.

At the Battle of Sayler's Creek, Lee lost 7,700 men, almost one-fourth of his remaining army. He also lost many general officers: Ewell, Barton, Simms, Kershaw, Dubose, Custis Lee, Corse, and Hunton. On the western ridge overlooking Big Sayler's Creek, Lee had watched the disintegration of R. H. Anderson's corps—soldiers without rifles, mule drivers without wagons, and thousands of thin, wasted faithful men. "My God!" he was quoted as saying. "Has the army been dissolved?"

On the evening of April 7, Grant was in Farmville with the Union's Sixth Corps. That night, cheers and shouts arose, and a regiment sang "John Brown's Body" as they marched and carried pine knots for torches. Fires of straw were lighted at the roadside. It became a grand review, and whole divisions sang the chorus. Grant's headquarters were at the Prince Edward Hotel at the corner of Main and Second Street. Several months before, Major Lynn's family had stayed there during the wedding. It was from that hotel that Grant would first communicate with General Lee about the surrender of the Army of Northern Virginia.

The Lynns received news via Lynchburg and Amherst that Lee was retreating. They thought that possibly James and their new son-in-law, Harold, might be with that army's ragged divisions. There was no way to get news of them. They all prayed that they and Emmie and Sarah were safe. The Confederacy was shattered. Richmond was still smoldering.

"I hope we don't face further tragedy," said Sue.

"I guess we have to be ready for it, though," replied Wen.

"Let's talk about pleasant things," said Momma. "We'll trust God with the lives of our family."

Papa listened to their fears. "Ann, you're right. There's nothing we can do." He looked around at the others. "Lee will probably move west, then south to join General Johnston. Remember him? He's 'Retreat'n Joe,' of Peninsula fame. He fought hard battles in Georgia, though. And he's a much better soldier than I believed earlier. I suppose if Lee reaches Johnston, they'll fight on and lose more men. Perhaps it is better that the war end now."

The Army of Northern Virginia was desperately trying to survive. We now know that Lee's commissary had failed. Amelia Courthouse, on the road west, was bare of rations. Foraging was necessary. The delay was disastrous, and only small amounts of food were available. The hungry men had marched on. Grant followed at their heels.

"Friends tell me in town that provisions are being sent to Appomattox Station," said Uncle Wen. "It's not far from here. It's really just on the other side of the James River. You can almost walk there. I hope troops don't fight here at Doria. They'll be close, though."

"They're probably headed toward Lynchburg," said Papa. "That's at least thirty miles away. Then, if they survive, they'll move south." Kath was listening with great interest. Momma would later remember the intense look in her eyes. At the time, it didn't seem important.

Katherine Lynn would later write in her diary:

> As Lee's army raced to escape, I made a decision. I would be up at dawn. I told my family that I really looked forward to a long walk in the woods. This was something I had done for years.
>
> "We know, Kath," Momma answered, "but be home early. You have chores. Don't forget and stay out all day."
>
> "I won't, Momma," I answered.
>
> I slept well and awoke just before the sun rose. It was a nice spring day. I felt warm all over, but a little scared with my plans. I had grown, though. I felt mature and fairly sensible, and I had great pride in our soldiers. We had been told about the terrors of enemy troops, but I had earlier decided that they were much like our men and would be kind to women. And I felt like a woman. I couldn't, though, suppress the overwhelming desire to be with men in battle. These are thoughts forbidden to us females.
>
> Also, I have for years walked and delighted in the fields and forests. My parents know about these habits. They are no longer surprised by my long absences. That day, though, I would go to the mountain, as my brothers

had before me. I would see the army. Why should I be different from them? I knew the country all the way to Appomattox like the back of my hand. I would go there. As my uncle had said, "You can almost walk . . ." Well, I decided to walk.

Early in the morning of April 9 of the year 1865, Katherine started southeast. It was about three miles to the James River. She knew where to cross. She had done so before. The sky was clear, and the low hills were brightened by the moon and the just rising sun. The morning air was crisp, and a heavy dew lay upon the green foliage in the woods and fields.

The glow of pink above the rolling hills to the east was beautiful. The twitter of little birds seemed to guide her way along a path over streams and other nooks hidden in fond memories of her childhood. The Blue Ridge to her west just captured the light of the sun. With a small sack holding a jar of water and crusts of bread, she trekked on.

CHAPTER XL

An Appointment at Appomattox

Katherine Lynn approached the hamlet of Appomattox. She was very apprehensive. Should she have come? She wasn't sure, but there was a strong desire to go on. It was Sunday morning of early April of 1865. There was a low rumbling and crashing as if huge boulders were falling. It was deafening. "The gods must be angry," she murmured. "It sounds like they're hurling big stones. One right after the other."

It was a bright day with clouds climbing up to cover the sun. The foliage glowed in the pleasant spring air. Among the crashes and rumbling, she heard a sputtering noise, which she later knew was the sound of thousands of muskets. This crescendoed to a deep, ominous roar.

Over hills and through valleys, she had wandered. Bluebells grew in the moist earth of the bottomlands; delicate pink spring beauties were bunched over the creek banks and flood plains. Lemon yellow, bell-shaped merrybells nodded casually from the floor of dense woods. Her shoes were wet and crunched on the rocks and dark soil as she walked.

Kath was excited. She hurried up the last rise, then walked down a gentle slope in woods along a gurgling brook. This stream drained, she later learned, into the north branch of the Appomattox River. As she reached the edge of a copse of large trees, Kath realized she was at a place overlooking a giant "bowl." The ground below was broken by little streams and low hills. These wandered lazily over the valley floor.

This was a vast amphitheater. Dusky masses of men in multi-ranked formations were seen as large rectangles and other geometric forms. Blocks of cannons stood in lines, and clouds of dust filtered above men on horseback who were riding singly or in slowly moving columns. They dotted the sides of the rolling surface of the "bowl." Some men were on horses that stood restlessly, heads moving and hooves pawing the ground. Other animals reared up high, as their riders shouted commands. She could not hear the voices above the noise, but their sabers were pointed upward and shaking like the tongues of adders.

Bugles sounded. A shrill echo rushed across the valley. Cavalry in blue turned and metal flashed in the sunlight as pistols and rifles were unsheathed. Long rectangles of blue were massed around ragged men in gray and butternut. These blue columns formed a vast cordon that nearly surrounded the remnants of the once great Army of Northern Virginia.

Shells from cannons burst overhead, forming clouds of fire and smoke; others seemed to plow along the ground, sending fragments of stone and bits of earth whirring in the air.

Katherine had arrived at the mountain. She was amongst men in battle. It was an exhilarating moment. She was hidden in the branches of a fallen oak. She watched with fascination. The tree was large. Only her uncombed curls showed between the foliage.

Suddenly the noise of pounding hooves came rushing toward her. It was frightening. Would she be discovered? She couldn't see the rider, but she sank down like a drowning swimmer. Then a dark form rose above her like a dike. It blotted out her view.

"What the hell? I'll be damned! A little girl. What in God's name are you doing here?"

"I am not little. I'm nearly full grown. Why aren't you down there with your men? I'm ashamed of you. Besides, your swearing is terrible. My folks taught me not to swear," replied Kath.

"Hmmm," he murmured, chuckling. "I like your spunk, young lady. I'm a courier—from Grant's staff. You've heard of Grant, I hope. Sorry for the swearing. You surprised me, though."

"General Grant," she squeaked with surprise. "The, ahh, real General Grant. I'm very honored, Mister, uh, Mister?" She hesitated.

"Lieutenant River," he said, smiling. "I'm bigger than you. I should be asking the questions. Perhaps I should bring you in as a spy. God knows, though, you don't look like what I've imagined a spy should look like. Maybe I'll just spank you instead."

"Don't you touch me," Kath threatened. Then she laughed. "I'm sorry. I like to walk. I live near the river—up that away." She pointed northwest. "I heard all the noise. I had to come see what was happening. And I can't hurt anyone. And besides, I'm not a spy. I'm just looking. You make so much noise, it's heard miles away. And I hope your soldiers don't feel threatened by a girl. I've heard about Yankees, though. Uncle Elmer says they eat children. I'm too big for eating, I hope." She swallowed with difficulty. Her face became squinched, and she glared hard into his eyes.

"I guess you've told me," he said. "I'm sorry your Uncle Elmer feels that way. And I truly don't want to hurt you." He was dark and bearded with deep blue eyes. "I have a sister about your age. Her hair is blond like yours. What did you say your name is?"

"Katherine. But you can call me 'Kath.' You sure looked mean at first, but you smile nice." She hadn't met many Yankees before. She then remembered Doctor Stevens's nephew in Staunton. "I'm happy to say, the Yankees I have met have been very nice." Suddenly she knew they were caring people like her men. She looked at him again. "You are handsome," she offered.

"Thank you, Katherine. You're very pretty, like my sister. But you get yourself out of here, or you'll get that pretty head of yours shot off." He was right. Her cheeks tingled, but she wondered if he wasn't in just as much danger.

"What about your head?" she said with a laugh. "If you were my brother, I'd prefer you with your head on, too."

"Git," he said. "Go, or I'll use the flat of my sword on your backside. Now I mean it. Git." She ducked low and started northward, as he rode off. Then she turned around and headed back to that shaded place in the branches of the oak. The story still unfolded.

The two armies faced one another like angry monsters. Tongues of red struck out toward the masses of men, and splinters from fences and bits of rock flew up among them. This was Lee's last great effort to break through the wall of Union soldiers. He fought to open the old, rutted stage-coach highway that led to Lynchburg. It wound like a serpent past the Appomattox Court House, a spot that would now be long remembered.

Yankee cavalry stood firmly astride the highway and blocked the road. The great Stonewall Brigade, pushing for this one escape, tore back the cavalry screen. Beyond the horsemen stood a solid line of Union infantry. Shells were fired among the charging regiments. The men in gray drew back.

Suddenly, lone horsemen, from several points along the Confederate lines, rode forward toward the Union formations. In their hands, they carried flags made from white cloth. This was the end of an era. It was also a beginning. A country was reunited. Katherine watched with fascination as these horsemen reached the Yankee lines.

The men in gray saluted. A few more cannons fired, then all was still. Finally, a burst of cheers arose. This echoed back and forth around the valley. Kath saw hats fly in the air; some men seemed to be weeping. Lee, the Confederate commander, had surrendered.

Later that day, Grant and Lee sat together in Appomattox Village. After they met, more cheers were heard, and regimental bands began to play. Also, cannons fired a salute, but Grant ordered that they be stopped. "They are our brothers . . . ," he said. Fluffy clouds floated in the near clear sky. It was Palm Sunday of the year 1865, an important day in history.

Katherine returned home at dusk. Momma and Papa had been worried, but not overly distressed. "You've been wandering in the fields again, I suppose," said Papa. He knew his daughter well. The overwhelming news of the surrender had reached them.

"This has been a bad day for the South. Lee has surrendered." Papa sounded sad. He couldn't speak for a moment, then his words were like a soft echo, which Kath could not understand. Finally, he was able to continue. "Katherine, I know it's for the best. I've often prayed it would end— so many have died. I never thought I would be sad when it was over, but I am. I'm also thankful. However, we've lost a great struggle. We human beings need pride. At this moment, ours is being severely tested."

"Papa, I'm sorry. The war's been going on as long as I can remember. It almost seems like the way things should be. I've dreamed about how strong our soldiers are. I never thought they would lose. They did. I know it's for the best, and now James can come home." She tried to look appropriately surprised. "I saw them today," she blurted, forgetting her family was not aware of the place she had visited. "Ahhh, umm," she stuttered, then she closed her jaw firmly.

"Saw whom today, Kath?" Momma questioned. "Where did you go?"

"Those little yellow birds," she answered quickly. "While I was walking." She thought it best not to tell the real story for a while. Perhaps she would—later on. For the moment, her family might not be too receptive to surprises.

Momma and Papa talked about the problems they would face in the years to come, but Kath's mind still lingered on that field at Appomattox. She was immersed in what she had seen and felt. She was still living in the past; it was not yet possible for her to think about the future.

It was a week before she dared tell her family about her escapade that day. She thought it better to try it out on Papa first. She would always remember his surprised voice. It was almost a shriek. "You what? My God, you might have been . . . !" He stopped in the middle of " . . . you might have been . . . " as Momma came to listen. "Well, Kath, it's done," he said softly. "We'd better write it all down." It was many hours before they finished writing.

"Papa, don't get mad. I went back to see our soldiers surrender. It was so sad. Suddenly it was all over, and we started home." She then told her father about her wanderings on another day, when she had trekked back to Appomattox.

"You can't go to bed yet, Kath. I've a feeling we're just getting started." They talked at length about what was done and how it should be phrased and written. With great patience, he drew out what she had seen and thought.

Katherine Lynn had been watching when the fighting stopped. Now she came back to the place of that last battle. She returned to Appomattox Court House, just east of the Blue Ridge Mountains of Virginia. It was a dark day, and a fine rain was falling. There was a sense of deep sadness in the air. As she waited, the silence was occasionally interrupted by the chirping of birds, soft coughing, and the murmur of voices. Faces were moist, mostly from the rain, but some from tears. She continued to watch . . . and listen. Her clothing was wet, and water from the rain dripped over her face and into her eyes.

"There they are," said a woman nearby. "Their last march. Oh, God! It's so sad!"

"They fought so hard," another woman answered.

A man farther off spoke hesitatingly. His voice was soft and strained. "God, it shouldn't end this way. We need something to remember. Not silence! They fought the war for us, and so many are dead. Where are the shouts and the cheers?"

Katherine saw the marching column of gray soldiers. There was no band or even a drum to lead the way and give a proper cadence to this last march. Tired feet scuffed the ground, and weapons and canteens made a soft clinking sound. Beyond the marching soldiers, through the mist, she could see the blue-gray hills of Virginia.

She looked again at the approaching regiments. Rifles and other weapons were to be stacked in front of Federal divisions standing at rigid attention. This was the formal surrender of the Confederate army, the Army of Northern Virginia. Many of the troops had been injured. Arms were in slings, and hands and other parts of the body were wrapped with torn strips of cloth and bandages.

The whole long column was decked with the red and blue of stained and ragged battle flags packed very close together now because few men were left. Thousands and thousands had been cut down. The flags were the symbols that had led troops into battle. They were the essence of pride.

They, also, would be surrendered. Brigades had been reduced to regiments, and regiments to companies, but these ragged pieces of cloth remained the embodiment of manhood.

Katherine thought about the words the man behind her had spoken. "There should be something more for us to remember," she said. "Not just silence!"

As she stood and watched, she began to think of the time when the first shadows of the storm had become real to her. She thought about the happiness and the sunshine and the fields and streams around her home.

She suddenly remembered that she was but a little child of eleven when the mysterious word, war, had become a frequent topic of conversation with her family. "Such a long time ago," she said to herself. "We all sat near the hearth. That was the center of life for me then.

"And war didn't worry us in those days. Maybe it was because Henry played with soldiers. We were used to the lines of toy soldiers and guns. 'Bang, bang!' we would hear." She shook her head as she thought about her brother and her oldest sister, Emmie, who played with him. Katherine smiled wanly, and a soft laugh crossed her lips. "Emmie was a great nurse, but a bad general. 'No, no!' Henry would shout. 'You do it this way, dummy.' Those soldiers would fall and die, but they were always well and ready for battle again a few hours later.

"Maybe that's why we children didn't think war would be really bad. It would be different and kind of fun. We wanted to get away from the dullness of ordinary days. Then we did. Too far away. And now it's over. But the memory is there!"

It was April the twelfth, the day Lee's troops formally surrendered. She heard a whispered prayer by an ancient gentleman beside her, "Lord, please honor all these brave men!"

"Many around us certainly share that wish," mumbled Kath. They all continued to watch quietly, though. Deep inside, they wanted to shout. They wanted to do something to show their pride and love and thanks.

She gazed up at the wrinkled old man. His cheeks were pale—that ghastly blue-gray color that comes with age and illness. He looked somewhat embarrassed at having shown a weakness. *Perhaps*, thought Kath, *we should be strong and not feel the pain of all this. But it's hard not to cry. Papa would have cried. And I don't believe it would have been from weakness—just hurting inside. They fought so hard—and bravely. And so many are now gone. How do you show the others how we feel?*

The Confederate troops marched forward. They stumbled over the rutted road toward the ranks of Federal soldiers standing at attention. Kath saw sadness in the eyes of the men. There was no joking or laughing. And their faces were washed with the rain, giving them a misty look, as if their thoughts possibly were far away, dwelling on memories of better times. There were no shouts or cheers. A ghastly quiet reigned.

Kath squinted her eyes, trying to see the soldiers better. She wanted to shout—to do something. She swallowed hard and clamped her jaw tightly closed. What could she say that would turn back the gloom that surrounded them? "There should be something more," she said again. "Not just silence!"

Suddenly, like a crash of thunder, a bugle call sounded across the valley. She turned her head. It seemed to come from the ranks of Union soldiers. It echoed back and forth over the valley. "But why? What was that for?" she said. For a moment, she had no answer. The demise of this once great Confederate Army was imminent. "Is there anything else to do or say?" she mumbled.

But the bugle call heralded not demise, only great respect. As the echo faded, the silent ranks of Federal soldiers brought rifles up, then out before them. The movement of arms and the slap of hands on metal filled the stillness. It's surprising how sounds have an instantaneous meaning to those who hear them. There was a sudden change in the ambiance of the moment. In an instant, the gloom and darkness had dissipated—somewhat. It was like clouds parting, letting the rays of the sun shine through.

Kath's sisters and friends in Staunton during the war had learned the marching commands from seeing real soldiers and from books in their father's library. They knew well the "Carry Arms" salute. They had saluted when Lee passed through Staunton years before. They had done so for the militia and for regiments of Southern troops. Now Kath saw it done with great feeling by real heroes for a respected foe.

"They saluted. They saluted. It's the marching salute!" she shouted. "Oh, God, thanks! It is a salute. The Yankees care. They do care!" She supposed that all those around her knew this, and she was a little ashamed that she had blurted these words out so intemperately to the folks nearby. She had heard several gasp but not speak. She looked at the face of the ancient man beside her. A tinge of pink now etched his cheeks; tears ran unashamedly down his face.

The man grasped her arm, then squeezed it gently. "Thanks. Thanks for what you said. You've spoken for all of us." He was looking deeply into her eyes. It was a gentle, caring look she would not forget. He spoke again. "Thanks!"

The troops of the once great Army of Northern Virginia had truly been cast down. You could see it in their faces and their walk. However, through this action by Union soldiers, they were saved the complete despair of such a fateful day. Over the years, they would help rebuild a nation. It had now become their nation, too. It would not be spoken of as, "The United States are . . . ," but "The United States is . . . !"

General Gordon, the commander of the Confederate Second Corps, quickly braced his shoulders back. His spurs touched his horses's flanks as he pulled on the reins. The horse reared up.

Kath saw Gordon's lips move, but she couldn't understand his words. He drew his sword and saluted. Then a glint of light flashed from the blade as the sword point touched the toe of his boot.

Gordon wheeled back toward the ranks of Southern soldiers and shouted the command, "Carry arms!" With machinelike precision, muskets were brought to the salute position to honor a gallant opponent. The men from North and South thus paid solemn respect to one another, as one foe breathed its last and faded into memory.

The people around Kath had been watching cheerlessly. Now they felt deep gratitude for what they had seen. This was a day they and Katherine Lynn would remember for a lifetime. It was a sad day, but it was lighted by being with men of great courage. Possibly, their spirit is still with us today; perhaps, it makes our country a little finer. These men fought and died for what they believed. Can any act show greater caring?

The Union officer who saw the Confederate soldiers as ". . . the embodiment of manhood . . . ," and who had ordered this salute was Gen. Joshua Chamberlain, winner of the Congressional Medal of Honor and later elected the governor of Maine. There was strength within that man.

Often, cataclysmic events seem to be needed to bring out the fine, selfless qualities of dedication, bravery, and service. The American Civil War was such an event. Unfortunately, war brought out the worst in some persons—they profited while others died.

When the war ended, the armies, those GREAT ARMIES, were dissolved. The dedicated men of both the North and South went home. They had been missed, and their families, too, had suffered.

Now fields would be replanted and shops reopened. The stage was dark, but a glimmer of light was there on the far horizon. Somehow, somewhere, what these men had done would be remembered, God willing.

Kath went home. When she was much older, she would remember with pride that these men of the North and South had helped rebuild an injured land. Also, she would know that she had worked with them. She would tell her children and grandchildren, "They were heroes. And I knew them. May God bless them all!"

During the years following the war, though, life in the South was not easy. James Lynn, Katherine's father, gave a prayer one evening. His family listened. Kath would remember it as speaking accurately to the feelings of many friends in Amherst. "Lighten our hearts, Lord. Lessen the pain. Blot out the anger within us. Life needs to be sanctified. When what men do conflicts with your will, only you, God, can bring renewal. Lord, renew our lives! Show us your reasons and your purpose. Give us guidance. And help us to face the hurting that continues after such a great and devastating loss!"

Epilogue

Southern veterans went home through an impoverished land to exhausted families and wasted countryside. They returned alone or in small groups. There were no marching columns, no fife or drums, no jubilation such as Yankee veterans found. It was not the physical loss that hurt the most. It was the crushing of will. The Southern secretary of war once observed, "No people ever poured out their blood more freely. . . . " Still, this was not enough. Beyond all the destruction and death came a loss of spirit—the animating quality that gives vigor and direction to the lives of a people.

Most farms and homes in the South were remote from towns. Many men retired to isolation. They were hidden, as in darkness, where bitterness could grow. Soon they would be goaded by new armies of men sent south—the carpetbaggers and the soldiers of occupation. These Northerners would rule by martial law.

The war arose through the will of men, but the violence transcended all expectation, and went far beyond all reason. "The Almighty has His own purposes," said Abraham Lincoln. Now both sides prayed for guidance. Even the victors felt discouragement and emptiness.

But this feeling of loss was sensed most keenly by Southerners. For many it would never go away, and for a few, it would never be forgiven. Yet, they had a great love for America. Also, they perceived that what had happened could never be turned back. They worked now to make life whole for the country that had again become theirs. But financial hardships and the lack of tools impeded many efforts.

Thousands thus moved away. Some traveled West. Others left the country, and still others went north, out of financial necessity. A few, however, wanted to feel Yankee soil beneath their feet, to stand below the dome of the United States Capitol, and to gaze at the White House where Mister Lincoln had lived. This was where he had sat, troubled. This was where he had sought answers. Perhaps they would find within the essence of the man who had spoken words that gave meaning to that terrible time.

Lincoln's plan for bringing the seceded states back into the Union, though, was incomplete. It was like a cone flattened at the top. With his death, the point was missing. His humanitarianism and shrewd skill for quieting opposition were gone. The U.S. Legislature quickly wrested the authority for directing Reconstruction from the executive branch of the government. Reacting to the "black codes" voted by reconstituted Southern legislatures, the men of moderate persuasion who dominated the U.S. Congress became more radical and vindictive. They now refused to seat representatives and senators from the reorganized Southern states.

These states had been in a condition of temporary probation under the presidential plan. Lincoln had said, "We must extinguish . . . resentment if we expect harmony. . . . " This was the feeling of many citizens throughout the North. Events, though, change lives. Lincoln's assassination at a time of rejoicing was thought by many to mean that the divine intention was caution. This was a religious age. Also, the repressive "black codes" that had passed in the South gave rise to doubt. Thousands and thousands had died. Would what they fought for be lost? The better impulses of the victors were stifled. Had Lincoln lived, would things have been different? We will never know.

Reconstruction thus became a bitter time, but the world did not end. It was a new beginning. A great country would rise. The Lynn family had suffered. So had most other families North and South. In regions where armies had marched and battles had been fought, lands and homes had been destroyed. Men and women from these regions had retreated to "safety" in long, disheveled lines. They had been dispossessed. Many found or would find only impatience and a lack of caring for their plight.

After the war, these homeless suffered the most. For years, they stood within the shadows, tormented by military occupation, and subject to continued hostility and uncertainty. If they returned to their land, burned homes and Yankee hucksters, the carpetbaggers, awaited them.

Many thousands of former slaves, also, hunted desperately for a place to begin again. They were free, but hunger and fear stalked them, and violence often erupted. They sought peace, as they struggled to find a way to provide a living for those they loved. They had seen the destructiveness of the war. Now they felt the persistence of its pain. The Thirteenth and Fourteenth Amendments to the Constitution gave them some protection.

The Lynns' son, Henry, a fine man, had died at Gettysburg. He was missed terribly. A cousin of the Lynn children also had been killed—at Fredericksburg, behind a stone wall. This was a tragedy they learned about long after the war. Another cousin, the son of Uncle James whom they had met at the dance in Staunton, had also been taken. He wasn't killed by bullets, but by measles. Illness destroyed many thousands.

Annie's husband, John Ingram, had died in a prison camp of pneumonia. She would never forget him. "He was so kind and gentle," she always said. "And there was beauty in his soul." Kath would know this. Annie had shown her his many drawings of buildings—lovely creations that never would be built. Annie wrote long letters to John's sister in the North. Finally, joyfully, they met!

Also, Sarah's cousin, Will, had been killed in Gettysburg. He had fought with Kemper's brigade in Pickett's division in 1863.

Others close to them had been lost or injured. Both the Ripon boys were dead. Annie's early beau, George Green, had lost an arm. They continued to be friends. Also, Emmie's special, Marc, had died. She had met him at Lynchburg early in the war. He had written her often. Suddenly the letters had stopped. After the war his family sent a note. He, too, had fallen at Gettysburg.

Another of Emmie's beaus was also taken. Jesse Chandler had lived a few houses away from the Lynns in Staunton. As Kath's father said, "His cheerful smile is now gone . . . I wanted him as a son . . . "

Kath's close companion, Mark Mentron, finally served as a private in the militia near Staunton. He was never injured, and he was not in battle. For this she was happy. He remained a lifetime friend. The family would always remember the sugar he had provided them in the winter of '62–'63.

Many friends had lost husbands and sons and fathers. The Lynns anguished over the life of each. Others survived to help rebuild the country. James returned to them after he recovered from wounds at Sayler's Creek. He spent weeks in a Union hospital at Burkville, then was transferred to the larger hospital facility at City Point on the James River. This had been Grant's post of command during the Petersburg seige. Sarah, his bride, had been desperate. So had all the Lynn family. Finally, a long letter arrived. Sarah would always treasure it. She had gone to his side, arriving about the same time as James and Ann Katherine Lynn, his parents.

Harold, Emmie's husband, had retreated with Lee toward Appomattox. He had been injured in a rearguard action and left for dead. A farmer found him close to Amelia Courthouse and nursed him back to health. The farmer's son went to Richmond to find Emmie. She was not there. She was helping with the wounded north of the little town of Jettersville. Finally, through Harold's parents, word came that he was injured but alive.

Both returned to Richmond months later where they saw the ruins of Harold's family's home. It had been burned.

After his recovery, James practiced law. Harold worked in Washington, finally being accepted at the U.S. State Department. He was conscientious, but there were others in government who resented his presence. He finally returned to Richmond and practiced law with his brother-in-law, James Lynn. He and Emmie had five children. James and Sarah had three.

Kath later became engaged to the man she worked for in the Virginia legislature. They were married several years later and lived happily. She worked in business. This caused some distress within the family in that day and age. The difficulties, though, were finally overcome. Kath's husband also practiced law for years. He and James and Harold became good friends.

Professor and Ann Lynn, Uncle Wen and Aunt Suellen continued farming. Gradually, all the children left home.

Doctor Stevens's nephew, Capt. Robert Merritt, visited Annie at Amherst. They became good friends. He returned again in the fall. They were in love. She traveled north to meet his family. Doctor Stevens was there. He held her firmly, then looked into her eyes, Finally, he turned to his nephew and said, "Don't let her get away, son!"

The history of Kath's other sisters is a story for another day. Kath always believed they all contributed much to their newfound country. Somehow, finally, they landed on their feet and carried on for good as teachers and business people and mothers. Thus the Lynns headed courageously toward the twentieth century. They saw homes, dreams, and businesses rise from the ashes. As their father sagely observed, "Usefulness and caring beget a strong nation!"